KAYNDO

Book 3: Ring of Defense

By: Terri Luckey

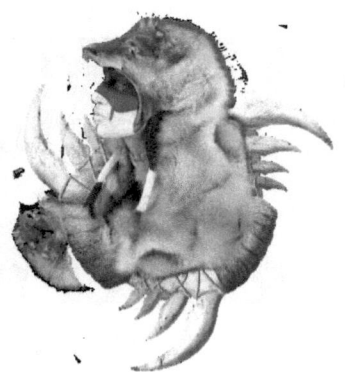

Logo by Art 4 Artists
(http://www.art4artists.com.au/)

Kayndo 'Ring of Defense'
By Terri Luckey
© 2016 Terri Luckey Books

ISBN-13: 978-0692630822
ISBN-10: 0692630821

This is a work of fiction. Names, characters, places, and incidents are either the product of the author's imagination or, if real, are used fictitiously.

Cover by Art 4 Artists (http://www.art4artists.com.au/)

******

For more information about my books contact:
www.terriluckey.com

******

I dedicate this book to my husband, Brian. His support and encouragement made it possible.

TABLE OF CONTENTS

Map

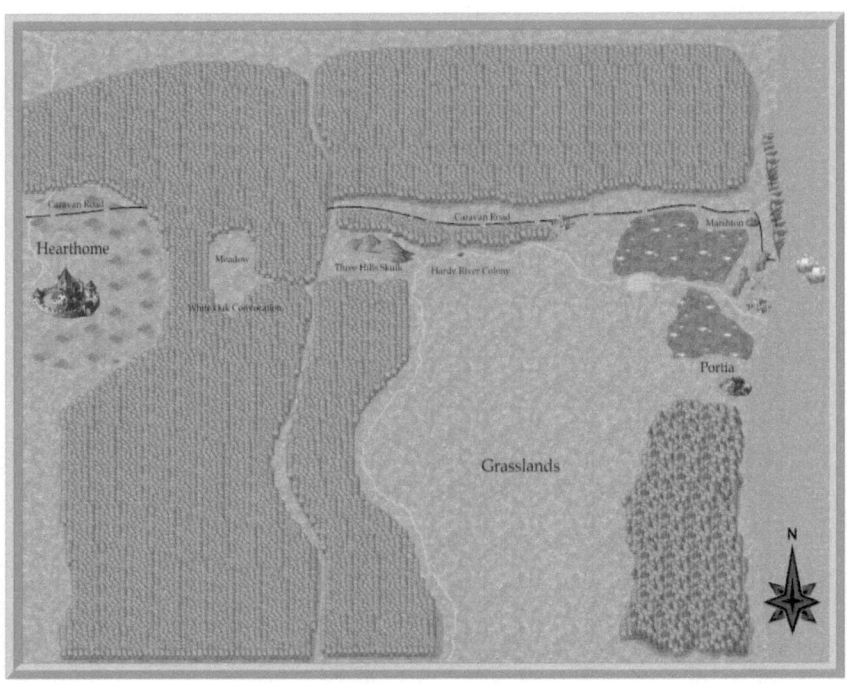

1

Graydee's chosen

"If you let fear freeze your actions, your foes will have won without even striking." ~ Leeto

Steven

The door slammed, and Steven's fear—like a cold icicle that lived in the pit of his belly—sent chills cascading through his body. Could the door shutting mean he was alone? Another escape opportunity like this might not come. His lone candle barely lit the dark cellar as he darted around the stacks of barrels. Dust tickled his nose as he rushed up the cellar's dank steps.

A thump above froze his feet. Had someone come in instead of leaving? The tavern wasn't open yet, but that didn't mean much. Mort had a reputation for not refusing thirsty customers, even the most disreputable. He just employed two muscle-bound guards and inflated his prices.

If the guard was upstairs and learned Steven wasn't in the cellar making room for the new barrels, it could get ugly. Should he go back down the steps? It would be safer. But for how long? He needed to help himself and the other adrifts before he ended up dead like Caspian.

With the cook at the market, and Mort fetching the new barrels of ale, that left only one guard. If he was upstairs, Steven would just have to get past him. It might be easier if the guard wasn't so large. He sucked in some courage and continued but much stealthier.

His hair fell in his eyes, so he pushed the black locks gummed with cobwebs behind his ears. When he reached the top stair, he opened the door to the hall and the nub of a candle he held flickered and went out. Figured. He set it down on the step and moved down the hall. At the main room of the tavern, the lingering scent of stale ale and yesterday's thin cabbage soup sent his stomach rumbling as he tiptoed across the floor. The light from the few lamps and the smoky fire in the hearth revealed only an assortment of scratched tables and chairs, some that stood crooked after experiencing one too many brawls.

Just a little farther to the door. Steven reached for the latch and pulled it open so hard the door thunked. He darted through with his heart in his throat.

The guard stood maybe ten feet away speaking to another man. He pivoted around to face Steven and held out his hand. "Stop."

Without pausing, Steven raced in the other direction through the alley. The sound of clomping boots on cobblestones pursued him. Blood pounded in his ears. Don't look back. Go faster.

His feet ached as he drove them harder against the cobblestones in the narrow alleyways, weaving around the few people. Decrepit buildings and homes lined the alley and choked out most of the sunlight, leaving plenty of shadows, so he sought them out. His breath came hard and his side stabbed him with pain. A few more blocks and he'd be out of the bottoms, the seediest area in Harthome. After that, people would crowd the streets of the capital city of Taluma, and it should be easy to get lost among them. Then he could find the clanspeople and somehow convince them to help. He had to make it.

He glanced back. No guard. Had he lost him?

A beefy hand snaked around Steven's arm, and he careened into a huge mass—Mort. His boss's mouth parted, revealing his missing front tooth as he leered at Steven. "Going somewhere?"

Steven's heart sank. He jerked back, but Mort's grip tightened. No way could he break free. Mort wouldn't be persuaded with reason, but maybe he could distract him long enough to free himself.

"I'm sixteen today. That makes me an adult, so I choose to leave."

The guard caught up to them. "Sorry, boss. I was busy telling Chandler what you wanted, and the kid ran off."

Mort's other hand curled into a fist. He drove it into Steven's gut. Steven's breath whooshed out, and pain exploded as if his mid-section had split in two. Mort let go of him.

Steven bent over, holding his stomach, and retched. Tears stung his eyes, but he refused to let them fall. He must get away. Sidling back, he turned to run, but Mort caught his arm again in that vice-like grip. If Steven fought, Mort's guards would jump in. Steven flung his other arm up to protect his head.

Mort's fist knocked his arm away and crashed into his temple. Flashing streaks of light filled his vision. Mort released him as Steven crumpled on the alley's paving stones and curled into a ball. The apple he'd had in his pocket rolled away.

Mort's eyes lit on the apple. "I thought I taught you better than to steal from me."

Mort kicked him over and over. Sharp spikes of pain tore into him. He didn't let as much as a moan pass his lips. Not when Mort would receive satisfaction from his pain. Mort stopped kicking but left his foot against Steven's side, pinning him to the ground.

Steven removed his arms from his face. The only people in the alley were a stumbling drunk and a toothless old hag, who wouldn't meet his eyes. But others were lurking. A ripple in a ragged curtain in the nearest home gave some watchers away. Desperate, he called out, "Someone fetch the Kagards!"

Mort's cruel eyes roamed the alley. "He's an adrift, who needs to be taught better than to steal. Anyone care?"

Mort's other guard dropped the handles of the cart and joined him. No one else appeared. Not much chance of Kagards helping Steven anyway. He needed to free himself now while Mort's gaze was fixed on the drunk shuffling away. He rolled out from under Mort's boot and pushed off with his hands.

Mort kicked him again, flipping him onto his back, then brought his boot down on Steven's neck. Steven coughed and gasped, trying to draw breath. Oily hair hung limply in Mort's sweaty face as he peered down at Steven. Would Mort crush his throat?

Mort's hazel eyes narrowed. "Remember what Bigham said I could do to you if you ran again?"

Steven's mouth dried. Would Mort really kill him? Probably. Steven must get away, but how? His strength was gone, and everything seemed to swirl. Oblivion beckoned. He repeated to himself Caspian's words. "Adrifts can't stop the storms, but we don't let them sink us, we bob back up and float." He fought to keep the encroaching darkness at bay, to stay conscious.

A gray streak bounded toward them, growling. A wolf. Steven's vision spun. Was there really a wolf? In the capital city? Maybe he was just imagining it after Mort's blows. Mort and his guards drew back, so he wasn't the only one seeing it. The huge wolf flashed its enormous teeth. It came to where Steven lay on the hard cobblestones. What would it do to him? Did it matter? Not if Mort was going to kill him. Steven couldn't draw the strength to fear it, anyway.

The wolf locked eyes with Steven. Those soft golden orbs pulled him into an emotional whirlwind. Acceptance. Worthiness. Belonging. Love. The sentiments swept into him and filled those places in his soul that had been vacant for so long.

Nothing had changed. His life was still in danger. His injuries hurt. He had no strength. But somehow everything was different. His burdens were shared. He wasn't alone.

A voice filled his mind. *I'm called Graydee, and I've chosen you. As long as I live, you'll never be alone again."*

Chosen? His father had told him the stories about the clanspeople and their companion animals, but Steven wasn't in any clan.

Then the wolf took a step toward Mort and his guards, growling and displaying its teeth.

The guards drew swords. Oh no. Steven made it to his feet, clutching his ribs. His instincts screamed at him to use the distraction to run. He didn't even have a weapon, but there was no way he could leave the wolf to be butchered when it was protecting him. He took a step forward to stand by the wolf. They'd die together.

2

Survival

"Fight for every breath, even if you'd prefer not to draw it." ~ Caspian

Steven

No, we're not going to die.

The wolf's voice reverberated in Steven's mind. Graydee—he said his name was Graydee. How did Graydee speak in his mind? And how did he seem to know his thoughts?

When I chose you we bonded, so I share your thoughts, feelings, and memories now.

Shouldn't it bother Steven what this wolf knew about him? A strange sense of relief surged up. He'd been hiding a lot for a long time. The wolf still accepted him, even though he knew his secrets.

Mort waved his sword menacingly, bringing Steven's focus back to the three armed men they faced in the alley. Mort pointed the sword at Graydee. "Make him leave, Steven, or he'll die too."

Steven didn't want the wolf killed. *You should go.*

No. Companions can't be made to do anything. We choose, and I told you, we're not going to die.

Why Graydee didn't think they'd die was beyond him.

I called to the pack for help. They're here.

Steven whipped his head around. Five more large gray wolves raced into the alley and joined them. Maybe Graydee was right, and they would survive this.

Mort didn't waver. "Free drinks and food tonight for anyone that helps us kill these wolves!"

Bands of scruffy men carrying knives or swords came pouring out of the ramshackle houses that closely lined the alley. Steven should have expected it. People in the bottoms either couldn't or wouldn't pay much to the king in land leases. They packed tightly together in shacks on the smallest of plots, so they'd barely pay anything. Free drinks and food might allow them to forget it.

Around thirty men now faced the wolves. Yup, they were going to die.

No, we have more help, Graydee sent.

Hooves struck cobblestones. Steven glanced back. Ten people on horses rode toward them, some in buckskin. Clanspeople. Maybe Kwin. Steven had wanted to find the clanspeople. Would they help him? The others wore black padded clothing and helmets. Those were Pericards and one face, in particular, stood out. Blake, the Pericard captain. Oh no. Blake wouldn't help Steven. He never had.

Mort seemed content to wait for the riders, leaving things at a standstill.

Those aren't Kwin, they're Calupi, Graydee's thought resounded in Steven's mind. *The tall blonde riding in the center is Dayvee. He's the Kayndo, and he'll help us.*

So there really was a Kayndo. He looked Steven's age. Could he talk to all the animals like the Kayndos in the stories?

He and his friends are your age. And yes, he can talk to us. Haven't you heard about the battle we fought and won at the castle?

He'd heard some things about it. But if Graydee really shared Steven's memories, shouldn't he know that answer?

I can access your memories. I just haven't looked at many. They're painful.

Yes, they were.

Dayvee called to Mort, "If you harm those wolves, we'll kill you."

"Those wolves are threatening us." Mort sneered. "We're in the right here, and you're outnumbered."

Steven's hope shrunk. The odds *were* with Mort.

Blake barked out, "I can go for more Pericards if we need them. Mort, lower those weapons."

"You can't go anywhere if you're dead, and I'm not about to lower my weapon until they call off those wolves and return what's mine."

"What's yours?" Dayvee asked.

Mort pointed at Steven. "Him."

"You can't own a person. It's against the Vita," said a guy with deep blue eyes and brown hair.

That's Brando. He's Dayvee's second in charge.

"Steven's my apprentice," Mort claimed. "He ran away this morning with things that weren't his. We were taking the thief back when your wolf interfered.

Steven's stomach churned. Blake would probably just hand him over.

If you go, I will too, Graydee sent.

That couldn't happen. He turned to Blake. "I'm sixteen today, an adult. I don't want to apprentice with Mort any longer." That's all he could reveal. If he said what he wanted to, he might gain their aid, but it would make Mort mad enough to kill them, as well as him.

"You don't have a choice," Mort retorted.

Dayvee shifted on the white horse. "Steven's chosen, so that makes him Calupi. I'm against any Calupi being held against their will."

Was being chosen by Graydee supposed to make him a Calupi?

Yes.

"I'm not about to condone him being held against his will either," said a sandy-haired Calupi with wide hazel eyes.

That's Tayro, Taluma's new king, Graydee informed Steven.

"Why should I care what either of you think?" Mort snapped.

"Watch it," Blake barked. "Your king and the Kayndo deserve respect."

Mort snorted. "Here in the bottoms, most aren't too worried about kings, Pericards, or clanspeople." He pointed. "You're surrounded." Steven looked back. More ruffians stood at the mouth of the alley behind the Calupi. "The adriftage said Steven was fourteen, so he's lying. According to his contract, he has to apprentice with me for two more years."

"Steven wasn't lying." The sweet voice came from a stunning golden-haired Calupi girl.

That's Elayni, Graydee's mind voice rang out in Steven's head.

"Calupi don't lie," said a tiny girl with auburn hair.

She's Chayla, Brando's life-mate. Companions can tell deceit and will reveal it, so Calupi don't lie.

He'd heard. That's why he'd hoped to find clanspeople. They would believe him. And in return for his information, they might help the adrifts.

Blake took a step forward. "Mort, I took Steven to the adriftage when he was ten. I had just become Captain. That would have been six years ago."

"It doesn't matter if he's an adult, he needs to fulfill his contract."

Blake's steel gray eyes pierced him. "Did you sign it, Steven?"

As if he had any choice. "Yes." He looked at the Kayndo. "If you send me back, don't let Graydee go with me. They'll kill him."

"I'll reimburse you what you paid," offered a Calupi with long brown hair pulled back into a single braid. He was older than the others, maybe in his late thirties, early forties.

That's Codee, Dayvee's uncle and second in charge of Wolf Mountain Pack.

Would this Codee really buy out Steven's contract? Mort liked money. And Steven's death wouldn't gain him any. Hope sprang up in Steven.

Mort glared at him. "His contract isn't for sale."

Steven's spirits plunged. "I should think you'd be glad to sell it and get something."

"Shut up," Mort snarled.

Blake turned his steely eyes on Mort. "Every adrift contract states if an adrift is adopted, the money will be returned, and the contract will be void."

"Hah." Mort sneered at Steven. "No one wants adrifts. And I doubt Bigham would return the money."

"I'll adopt him, and I'll repay you." Codee looked at Steven. "If you're willing?"

The old longing surfaced in Steven that every adrift seemed to share. To have a family. One that accepted and loved him. But that had led to nothing but disappointment in the past. Hadn't he said he wouldn't give into that urge again? He'd rely on himself so he wasn't crushed when others rejected him. They always did. And hadn't he had enough of letting others rule his life?

You should let Codee adopt you, Graydee sent. *He's a good Calupi. Even at your age, it will help you to claim a high-status father.*

But an adoption would mean leaving the adriftage and all the other adrifts. They had known Steven wouldn't be around forever. He'd prepared them. But what if Steven was trading one horrific situation for another? He couldn't stop a shudder.

To escape Mort, Steven would have to do it. "Graydee's vouched for you, Codee, so I'll agree to the adoption. But if you treat me badly, I'll run."

A sparkle lit Codee's light blue eyes, and he smiled. "Fair enough. What was the price of the contract?"

"Twenty silver," Steven answered. "I'll pay you back as soon as I can."

Codee dug the coins out of his pouch. "I'm not worried about you paying me back."

Steven was. No one should think they owned him again for a handful of silvers. He'd pull more jobs before he let that happen.

Blake dismounted and held out his hand. "I'll take it."

When Codee gave the coins to him, Blake took them to Mort. "Steven is being adopted, and you've been paid. Now unless you want to visit the dungeons, you and your men should leave."

Mort closed his fist around the coins. "We'll take this and anything else you have, including Steven." His guard swung his sword at Blake. The captain jumped back, pulling his own sword. The others with Mort charged toward them swinging weapons.

Steven's heart pounded against the wall of his chest. Figured. Mort wouldn't let him go, knowing what he knew. He and Graydee were at risk of dying again, and he still didn't have a weapon.

You should get out of the way of the horses and the Calupi's nails. Follow me. Graydee darted over to one of the ramshackle houses lining the alley.

The chakram weapons that the Calupi called nails were already flying. Crouching low, Steven raced after the wolf.

Put your back against the stone, Graydee sent.

Steven pressed his back against the bricks while Graydee stood in front of him, snarling.

Mort's other guard came running toward them. Now, what?

You get a weapon. Graydee sprung at the guard knocking him to the ground. The wolf clamped his teeth over the guard's wrist, shaking it. The guard let go of the sword, and it clattered to the ground.

Pick it up, Steven.

Graydee needed him. Steven scrambled forward and grabbed the sword. Graydee released the guard's hand to lunge toward his throat. The wolf's teeth sank in and ripped it open.

Steven's stomach churned. Graydee didn't need his help. The guard was dead.

No, but the other Calupi could use the help. And if we don't kill our enemies, they'll kill us.

Graydee was right. Steven forced down the bile gagging him.

I'm almost always right. Remember that, and you'll do fine.

Was Graydee trying to be funny now?

Why not? Ready to prove it won't be so easy to kill us?

Steven already ached, but he wasn't going to let that stop him. And he had a sword now. *Yes.*

He surveyed the others fighting. Half the Calupi and Pericards had turned their horses and were flinging their weapons at those behind them while the other half fought those in front. Several bodies lay around them. The petite Calupi girl, Chayla, was being dragged from her horse by a couple of ruffians.

Steven ran toward them. "Leave her alone!"

Two men turned toward him. Graydee attacked the bigger of the two. The smaller guy swung his sword at Steven. The training from Steven's father came back to him. Steven rose on the balls of his feet, and with a flick of his own sword, met the strike, and deflected it to the side. The guy grabbed for him. Steven yanked his sword up, hitting him in the shoulder. Blood spurted, soaking the guy's sleeve, but his sword swung toward Steven's neck. Steven ducked and raked his own sword across the guy's knees. When he toppled to the ground, Steven kicked his sword away from him. He was unarmed now. No need to kill him.

Steven turned to check on Graydee. The wolf had killed the bigger man. He heard a whoosh, something sailed by, and then a splat. Steven spun around. A chakram lay buried in the neck of the guy he'd just toppled, but the guy's fingers were curled around a knife. Steven gulped and looked for who saved him. Brando rode over. He yanked on a line, and his chakram came free.

"Thanks for saving me," Steven stammered out.

Brando smiled. "I owed you for helping Chayla. But next time, don't leave an enemy at your back. Kill them."

Steven sucked in a breath. Easier said than done.

Brando reined his horse around. "Chayla, are you okay?"

"Yes." She smiled at Steven. "Thanks to you."

"We need to get back to Dayvee," Brando said to her. "Stick close." As Brando and Chayla rode toward Dayvee, he exclaimed, "Cackles, a bunch are already running off. Fun's almost over unless Dayvee lets us go after them."

Steven shook his head. These Calupi must be crazy. *Watch out,* Graydee sent to Steven.

Two more men ran at them brandishing a club and knife. Graydee met the one with the knife and sank his teeth in his leg. The man stabbed his knife into Graydee's shoulder. Pain shot through Steven's own. Steven leaped toward them and plunged his sword into the man. Their enemy crashed to the ground, dead. Steven's bile rose again. He forced it down. He had to kill him to save Graydee. *How bad are you hurt?*

It's not deep, Graydee replied. Relief flooded Steven. He caught a blur in the corner of his eye as a club smacked into the back of his head. Pain flared, and his teeth rattled. The alley spun, but he mustn't fall. Adrifts couldn't sink. He locked his knees. The sword's weight dragged on Steven's arm, but he gritted his teeth and pulled the sword up to slash it across his new foe's chest. Graydee jumped on the man, knocking him over. When Graydee drew back, their enemy lay in a pool of blood.

The Kayndo shouted, "That's enough. The rest are fleeing. Let them go."

I told you we'd live, Graydee's voice was in his mind. So why did it sound as if it came from so far away?

The alley, the Pericards, the Calupi, all swayed in Steven's vision. His knees buckled, and the ground rose up and met him as his body plummeted into the hard cobblestones. Spots swam in front of his eyes.

Hoofbeats clattered closer. Chayla cried out, "Oh no. Is he dying?"

Probably, but it wasn't like Steven hadn't expected it. Would he see Caspian again? He had tried his best to keep his promise. Graydee's thought floated in, *No, you can't die. Please. I can't lose you too.*

3

Shared Pain

"The hardest thing to bear is shame." ~ Dayvee

Dayvee

Dayvee reined Ghostee to stop next to Steven's crumpled body. He looked so small lying there on the dirty broken cobblestones that paved the alley. His chest rose and fell, so he must be alive. His clothing and dark hair were matted with grime, so Dayvee couldn't tell if he was bleeding. Graydee's legs quivered as he dropped at Steven's feet. He must have been feeling the effects of Steven's injuries.

A quick glance at his sub-pack revealed their worry. Chayla's hand fluttered over her mouth. Elayni chewed her bottom lip, and Brando's deep blue eyes stayed locked on Steven. They didn't really know Steven, but they all loved Graydee. After Geno died, his wolf companion was consumed with grief. Maybe Graydee hadn't been thinking clearly. What else would explain him choosing someone from the city?

The voice of Dayvee's own wolf companion, Jaycee, filled his mind. *Steven's worthy.*

If Jaycee said it, Steven was. Dayvee would do whatever he could to help him. He signaled to Tayro with a tilt of his head toward Steven.

Tayro dismounted and knelt beside Steven to press fingers to his wrist. "His pulse is steady. Maybe the blow to his head just knocked him out. But I'm not sure it's safe to stay here and examine him better."

"It's not," Blake snapped. "People in the bottoms are like rats. You might only see a few, but there's plenty more. If they think we're weakened, they'll come. Their lack of scruples is why Varian recruited from here."

Dayvee sorted through all the animal whispers in his mind for one. The eagle flying a pattern above them. *What do you see, Spiro?*

There are shadows moving toward you. I don't know how many since they're staying hidden under the cover of buildings.

"The exam will have to wait," Dayvee ordered.

"We need a travois," Tayro said.

"Just lift him up to me." Brando held out his arms. "I'll keep him on."

Dayvee gave them a nod, and Tayro and Codee hefted Steven up to Brando on his horse. Graydee stood shakily. *Do you need aid?* Dayvee asked.

I'm dizzy, but I'll keep up.

We'll help him, Jaycee sent, as their wolf companions pressed close to Graydee to support him.

Dayvee clucked Ghostee into a trot. After a few city blocks, the streets widened, the conditions of the buildings and homes improved, and the smell of sewer and trash no longer choked him. They had to slow since more people crowded the streets. But in this section of Harthome, the people dressed better, and they strolled rather than scurried. Dayvee and his sub-pack finally reached the castle gates. Their horses clattered through to the courtyard beyond.

The huge castle of bleak gray stone loomed in front of them with towers at each corner. A chill raced through Dayvee. Geno died here, and Dayvee's feet were smashed within those walls. Last night, Brando and Codee destroyed the instruments that tortured Dayvee, but they couldn't erase his memory.

Ouch. Pain stabbed Dayvee's feet when he slid off his horse and onto his crutches, but he kept himself from expressing it out loud. The Pericards surrounded them as Dayvee hobbled alongside his friends. Brando and Codee carried Steven inside.

The staff ogled King Tayro and the other Calupi walking through the castle halls, but they moved aside to let them pass. Their curious whispers followed them, bouncing off the stone corridors. The sub-pack came to the rooms the late king had set aside for their use.

A colorful rug softened the stone floor, and there were some pillows scattered about. A low table perched in one corner, and lamps hung on the wall. Otherwise, it was empty except for the fireplace and a few shelves, just like their dens back home. Tayro had received richly appointed rooms fit for a king, but he preferred staying with the sub-pack. Few Calupi could sleep alone.

While Brando and Cocee carefully lowered Steven down on the rug, Dayvee plopped himself on a nearby pillow, and their wolf companions sprawled around him.

Tayro bent over Steven to examine him.

Once Tayro got him better, should Dayvee let the new Calupi join his sub-pack? That would be dangerous for Steven. The Kayndo was a target. And he had bigger problems to worry about than a new trainee. The invaders were coming. They didn't really believe in Kun or following the Vita. So if they weren't stopped, they'd slaughter the companions here, just like on their own continent. Defeating them wouldn't be easy. His focus had to lie on that.

Jaycee nudged him. *Graydee wants to stay with us. He's pack. I don't want to lose him.*

Neither did Dayvee. He owed it to Geno to help the companion Geno left behind, but he didn't want to get Graydee's new chosen killed too. And Steven was from the city. He lacked their skills.

You could give him a try, Jaycee sent.

Tayro gasped when he unclasped Steven's shirt and pulled it open.

Steven's ribs stood out prominently among a vast array of puckered scars and bruises in a myriad of colors. Dayvee gasped too. Red and purple hues differentiated newer bruises in the shape of a boot from older shades of brown, yellow, and black. On top of everything else, several cuts and abrasions painted angry lines.

Dayvee had earned bruises in training, and he'd gained scars when Nero and Varian tortured him, but Steven's were layered. Dayvee's weren't pretty, but they paled in comparison. Steven had been hurt for some time, and starved too. Compassion swelled in him for Steven.

Codee shot a glare at Blake. "Did you know he was being treated like this?"

"Of course not."

Tayro pulled bandages from his rucksack. "I'll tape his ribs, but first I need to get him clean so those cuts don't get infected. And he needs other clothing. The rags he's wearing are filthy."

"Give him Geno's things." Dayvee hadn't meant to speak sharply. He softened his tone. "Geno would want the Calupi who gave Graydee a reason to live to have them but put Geno's weapons aside for his family. Codee and Brando, help Tayro carry Steven to the bathing room."

Shilo, the companion of his Kwin friend, Reko, whispered in Dayvee's mind, *Reko and Gaylo are coming.*

Dayvee sighed inwardly. He wasn't looking forward to the meeting. Gaylo was both a spiritual leader and healer—a clan keeper— so Dayvee could use his help and support, especially since he needed to get everyone to the coast to battle the invaders. Only, Gaylo seemed awfully critical of his decisions lately. Probably because Dayvee had ignored his advice. How could it help to pray when Kun wasn't answering him? Kun hadn't healed his feet or kept Geno safe.

Brando glanced at Elayni. "You and Chayla stay with Dayvee." Brando crossed his index and middle finger before he picked up Steven—the signal to keep Dayvee shielded. As if he was incapable of defending himself. Dayvee groaned.

Chayla giggled. "Sounds as if you don't like girls."

"I like them." Dayvee loved one. His gaze flew to Elayni like a bee seeking nectar. She tucked a golden lock that had escaped her braid back in. His heart hitched. She was stunning. Her light blue eyes met his, and his breath caught. He tore his gaze away. He didn't deserve a life-mate, not as a cripple.

#

Steven

Steven's head hurt. Voices droned nearby, but they sounded like mosquitoes buzzing around him. Muted and barely audible. Where was he? *You're with me and safe.*

That voice in his mind. The wolf. Graydee. It all flooded back.

He cracked his eyes open to slits. He lay on a bed of blankets in an unfamiliar room with Graydee at his side. At the sharp draw of his breath, pain stabbed his chest. Bandages swaddled his ribs under a buckskin shirt that stood open. Someone had cleaned him up, dressed him in clan clothing, and bandaged him. Warmth infused his cheeks. It was embarrassing enough that someone else dressed him, but they'd seen his shame. The buzzing faded, and his dizziness. The voices became clear, and their faces.

"I still think you should stay here at the castle, Tayro." The Kayndo sat on a pillow, speaking softly. "There's no reason to risk our king yet. You and the Kagards can mount a second line of defense here."

The sub-pack sat around the Kayndo, packing parcels into rucksacks. The scent of smoked meat wafted. Tayro paused and looked up at Dayvee. "We have a better chance if we combine our forces. And how long do you think the invaders will let me remain as king if they win?" He stuffed his bundle inside the rucksack. "I'm going."

The Kayndo sighed, then turned his gaze to the two clansmen sitting across from his sub-pack. "So how many horses, mules, and donkeys will we have, Reko?"

"Two hundred horses, one hundred mules and donkeys," answered a tall Kwin with wavy brown hair. "More are coming, but they won't be here by noon."

"Are the clans culling the herds, Gaylo?" Dayvee picked up the last parcel and stowed it in his rucksack.

"Yes," replied a Calupi with black hair that was flecked with gray and a pecan tone face. "They'll bring meat to us, and the Botanees will send us grain. With the other supplies, we should be fine."

Dayvee glanced over his shoulder at Blake, who stood behind him. "What about the garrisons?"

"They'll bring all but fifty Kagards to join us." Blake's lips dipped into a small frown. "We don't have enough horses for everyone."

"They'll have to walk until more come in." Dayvee accepted a flask Tayro handed him and tucked that into his bag.

"If you'd give us more time—"

Dayvee closed the flap of his rucksack. "The bird who warned me about the invaders said the sea clans would do what they could to stop them. I'm not close enough to mind speak to the animals there, so they'll be fighting alone. Delaying will surely mean clanspeople's deaths." His face turned hard. "We leave today at noon."

Steven's headache made it hard to focus, but these weren't the only plans he'd heard about dealing with the invaders. Maybe he should tell these Calupi what he knew. They were done packing, but they still appeared busy. Brando whittled on a chunk of wood. Chayla wrote on a piece of paper. Elayni was sewing a pouch.

You should tell them, Graydee sent.

If Mort and Bigham learned Steven told, they'd offer a reward for Steven's death. He wouldn't survive long. But he would tell the Calupi if they agreed to help the adrifts.

"What about the new Calupi?" the older man, Gaylo asked. "Will you leave him here to heal?"

"No." Dayvee sounded firm. "We can always put him in a litter until he's on his feet."

The lines in Gaylo's face deepened. "What about after that?"

"If my sub-pack agrees, I'm going to ask him to join us. Will our pack approve that, Codee?"

"You can take anyone as a temporary sub-pack member without a vote." Codee was honing his knife. "It's been done with trainees before." His hands stilled. "But if he decides he wants to permanently join Wolf Mountain, your father and the pack would have to agree."

Dayvee crossed his arms. "Graydee would be happiest with his packmates."

Would you be? Steven asked Graydee.

Yes, but you don't trust anyone but me. If that means you're my only pack, I'll accept it.

Sorrow rose up inside Steven to almost overwhelm him. He was feeling Graydee's emotions again. The loss of his pack would devastate Graydee, but he was willing to sacrifice his happiness for Steven's.

"Steven's not Geno, he's a thief." Blake's accusation rang out. "He shouldn't be allowed too close to the Kayndo, and certainly not in the ring of defense."

How ironic that the one who took him to the adriftage would condemn him. But hadn't he known any acceptance would be short lived? He refused to shed the tears that stung his eyes. Would they take Graydee from him?

No one can take me from you. Graydee's nose nudged him.

Codee's eyes flashed. "Graydee wouldn't have chosen him if he wasn't worthy."

The other wolves in the room glided over to Steven. Their powerful bodies, the grace in which they moved, and the intelligence shining from their eyes awed him. As their noses touched him, some deep longing inside of Steven welled up. Why that reaction when he'd never known a wolf before today?

Your heart wants a pack, Graydee sent.

Steven couldn't resist reaching his fingers toward them. As he touched their soft fur, warmth filled his heart.

"The other wolves agree Steven's worthy," Dayvee said.

No, he wasn't. Steven needed to inform them. He sat up, and the stone walls swam but eventually his vision steadied. "Blake is right. I'm not a good person. And I need to tell you something important."

King Tayro came over to him with a flask. "Drink this first."

"What's in it?"

"Broth. You need nourishment."

Steven drank it, but his belly churned. The image of the guy he killed kept popping into his mind. He kept forcing it out, only to have it return, and the image brought bile rising in his throat.

Tayro handed him a bowl with some meat. "See if you can eat this."

Adrifts learned fast to take food when they could get it, but Steven knew if he ate much more he'd get sick. "Will you give it to Graydee? He's famished."

"I can't give Graydee something he already owns. He and the other wolves helped provide this meat, but it will take more than that to fill him." Tayro heaped a bowl full of meat and set it down for Graydee. Then he handed one of the rucksacks they'd been packing to Steven. "This was Geno's, and now it's yours. There's food inside, so eat as much as your stomach can take every two hours."

They were giving him more food? "Thanks." The guilt hit Steven as he slid the rucksack on. The other adrifts were hungry and could be in danger. "There are more adrifts who need help." Steven met the Kayndo's gaze. "If you'll help them, I'll tell you everything I know about people who plan to attack you."

Their faces had all hardened. Blake harrumphed. "After the Kayndo helped you, you'd hold back information that could put him at risk? Is your loyalty always subject to getting what you want?"

Heat crept up Steven's cheeks. Maybe he shouldn't have done that.

Elayni finished sewing and her hands went to her hips. "The invaders don't like clanspeople. If they win, they'll hunt us down and kill our companions like they did on their own continent. Do you want Graydee dead?"

Steven's heart hitched. "No."

Brando's eyes pierced him. "Then you better figure out which side you're on."

If these invaders wanted to kill Graydee, Steven would do anything he could to defeat them. But that didn't mean he had to do it with these Calupi. "I'm on Graydee's."

Graydee nudged him. *And I'm on yours.*

Codee's face softened. "He's only been conscious a couple minutes. Shouldn't we give Steven a little time to trust us before condemning him?"

"Steven, I understand why you set that condition." Dayvee pulled off his shirt to reveal scars similar to his own. "I've been beaten, and my feet were crushed. I know the shame of not being able to prevent it, and causing my companion pain. If my sub-pack was suffering like that, I'd do anything to stop it."

The Kayndo *did* understand, and the compassion in his voice broke through the walls Steven sealed his pain behind. Tears welled in his eyes. He ducked his head.

"Look at me, Steven."

Steven lifted his gaze to see the Kayndo's bright green eyes mist. "It makes me sick to learn it's happening to others. I promise I'll help the other adrifts, regardless of what you share with us." Dayvee's demeanor didn't carry a trace of disdain, only shared pain.

At that moment, Steven would do anything for the Kayndo. He glanced at the other Calupi, expecting to see more condemnation. Their eyes had softened too. The Kayndo was important, not like an adrift. Who would do such things to Dayvee?

Varian and Nero, Graydee sent. *But they're dead now.*

Good. Steven drew a breath. He rushed to get the words out. "Varian was recruiting people, like Mort and Bigham, who don't like the clanspeople. He said we couldn't win against the invaders."

Blake shrugged. "We already knew Varian was doing that."

"So you're aware that Varian contacted the invaders and negotiated with them?"

"No." Blake blew out a heavy breath and his gaze sharpened. "How do you know that?"

"Varian met with Mort at the tavern. He said the invaders agreed to let him rule here if he collected a tax for them. If Mort would help him take control, Varian promised to reward him and never interfere in the bottoms. He even demonstrated one of the ancient's weapons. Mort wouldn't do it without Bigham's approval, so he had me witness and relay the messages." A chill ran up Steven's spine. "Adrifts know to cross Bigham is to die a terrible death."

Graydee nudged him, and Steven ran his hands over the wolf's head, taking comfort from him. He drew a breath. "Bigham agreed to help Varian, and they recruited men. A few of the recruits went to the castle, but most of them were sent to Midway. Only Varian didn't deliver on his promises of wagons of guns or troops from the garrisons, so Bigham didn't have them flank you like Varian wanted."

"I was warned to look for an attack from our rear." Dayvee's brow furrowed. "I'm glad it didn't happen. Do you know what they'll do now?"

"No," Steven answered. "But the recruits haven't returned, except for the few who are hiding at the adriftage that escaped your attack on the castle."

"Maybe we can capture one and learn more." Codee stopped rubbing the sharpening stone over his knife. "How many would we face at the adriftage?"

"I don't know. I'm sure Mort warned Bigham I'm with you. He'll take precautions. He could have more help come, or they could be fleeing and taking the adrifts with them."

Shavings quit flying as Brando stopped whittling. "This day keeps getting better and better. One fight this morning, now two."

"We don't have time for more fights if we're leaving at noon for the coast," Gaylo said. "We need to concentrate on the invaders."

Brando's eyes sparkled as he slid his knife into a pouch on his belt. "There's time if we split up. Dayvee, will you let me go while you finish the planning?"

"Even though I'm certain you'll keep my promise to Steven, *he* might not be," Dayvee answered. "Are you okay with me assigning Brando, Steven?"

The Kayndo was asking him? "I just want the adrifts helped. I don't care who does it."

"Who else wants to go?" Dayvee asked. When all his sub-pack stood, Dayvee smiled. "I'm not sending all of you."

"Let me go, Dayvee," Elayni pleaded. "I'm tired of meetings."

"All right, Elayni, but at Brando's back." Dayvee crossed his index and middle finger.

Brando gave Dayvee a nod. Dayvee turned to the Pericard

Captain. "Blake, assign some of the Pericards and Kagards to go with them."

Blake saluted by thumping a fist against his chest and left to follow Dayvee's order.

Codee tested his knife against some hair on his arm. Fuzz drifted down. "Since I'm adopting Steven, it's my place to seek judgment." He clenched a fist, then opened his fingers to form a circle.

What did that mean?

Brando lifted his pinky. Chaya, Tayro, and Elayni lifted theirs.

Dayvee hesitated, then lifted his. "We agree. You'll go, Codee."

Steven rose, fighting the dizziness. "I need to go."

Codee sheathed his knife. "You should stay here and recover."

The room had quit swaying, and Steven's head didn't even hurt anymore. He could do it. "I feel fine now. And the adrifts won't trust you unless I'm with you."

"I can give them horses to ride so he won't have to walk," Reko said. "Have you ever ridden, Steven?"

"No, but I'll manage."

Brando hefted his rucksack onto his back. "You rode, but you didn't know it."

"Must not be too difficult then," Steven quipped.

"Brando, are you okay with Steven going with you?" Dayvee asked.

"That depends. Steven, I'm in charge when Dayvee's not with us. Can you respect that and trust me enough to follow my orders?"

Steven wanted to say yes so he'd let him go, but he needed to be honest. "I've known plenty of idiots in charge, so you have to earn my trust. But I'll follow your orders until you show me I shouldn't."

Dayvee laughed long and loud. So did the others. "That sounds like what you'd say, Brando."

"It does." Brando grinned. "So I'll accept it and let him come."

"Thanks." Steven let his gaze roam around the room. "Did you bring back the sword I was using?"

Codee picked the sword up off a shelf and held it out. "We had a hard time prying it from your hand."

"I don't like losing weapons."

Brando moved toward the door. "Let's go fight." The wolves sprang up and howled. They fell in behind Brando. The Calupi released howls too. They must love to fight, but that seemed crazy.

Howl with us, Graydee sent.

Steven did his best to howl. It didn't sound as good as theirs. Codee clapped him on the shoulder as they moved out the door.

4

Regret

"Don't dwell on the bad stuff. Find joy today." ~ Caspian

Elayni

Before Elayni left the room to go to the adriftage, she glanced back at Dayvee. The white-streaked cowlick over his forehead was sticking out again from his otherwise yellow head of hair. His shirt strained at his muscular chest, biceps, and shoulders. His green eyes caught her gaze, and her heart fluttered and legs weakened.

"Be careful, and stay behind Brando," he said softly.

Her temper rose. She lost her heart to the boy who protected her, but she didn't need it now. "I passed the same tests. I'm just as capable as you are."

His head fell. "You're more."

Sorrow wrapped itself around Elayni's heart choking it. When Varian crushed Dayvee's feet, he not only stole years of hard work, he stole his sense of worth. Now Dayvee claimed he wouldn't life-mate. Dayvee owned her heart, but he no longer wanted it.

Tayro winked at her. "I think everyone in the sub-pack is capable. Each of us is responsible for the death of several of our enemies."

She'd known for a while that Tayro was interested in her. With his sandy-brown hair that lay in a natural wave, his toned body, and his easy-going attitude, most of the single Calupi women tried hard to attract his attention. He was brilliant too. She could be a queen if she chose Tayro. Except no one but Dayvee could turn her legs weak with one look. She wanted only him. Her heart sank. Too bad he didn't return her love.

She hurried out of the room to catch up with the others. Horses waited for them in the castle's courtyard. They mounted and left the grounds but kept the horses at a walk through the crowded streets.

Blake had sent fifty Pericards. The residents of Harthome drew back from their intimidating presence.

She glanced over at the new Calupi riding beside them. He wasn't as tall as most clansmen, and he was far thinner. Nor did his shirt strain with muscles.

You can't grow when you're starved, Evee sent. *Steven's appearance will change now.*

He had already changed some. With his hair detangled and free of grime, it was as dark and shiny as a mink's, and those thick locks fell just past his shoulders. He wasn't as good looking as Dayvee. What Calupi was? But Steven was handsome in a rakish way. And there was something about him that grabbed one's attention like Dayvee always could.

Maybe it was Steven's eyes. She'd never met a person with amber eyes before, only wolves. And they were so expressive. When they were excited, like now, they gleamed. But when Dayvee had spoken of their shared abuse, they had been pools of sorrow.

Chase, one of the Pericards, pointed to a street, and Brando turned down it. Elayni reined her horse to follow. With just a shift of his weight, Steven had his horse turning. He rode like Reko, as if he and the horse were one. Even after riding for a few weeks, she wasn't that good. "Steven, were you just kidding about never riding? You sure look like you've been doing it forever."

"I wasn't kidding. We don't have many horses in Harthome, and I've only been out of the city once when I ran away from the adriftage." Steven glared at Chase. "He caught me."

Hopefully, he'd learn the other skills he'd need as a Calupi as quickly. The people around them thinned as they entered the bottoms, then stopped altogether, but they glimpsed shadows scurrying away as they rode deeper into this section of the city. They turned onto another street, and at the very end, came to a place that was different than all the others.

The rest of the buildings sat on small lots, but this one had huge grounds, with a brick wall surrounding it about five feet tall. Beyond the towering trees sprawled a building, more like a warehouse than a home, tucked back from the street. The wall stopped at a wooden gate with a bar across it.

"Is it locked on the other side too?" Codee asked Steven.

"Usually, but I'll check." Steven jumped down from the horse with one hand on his sword. He removed the bar, then tested the door. A gap appeared. "It's not barred on that side." Steven stuck his face up to the gap. "I don't see anyone." He pushed harder on the door, and it swung all the way open.

The gate was too narrow to ride in more than one at a time. "I'll go first," Brando ordered.

One by one they followed Brando in. The grounds appeared deserted. When Steven came through, a change came over him. His posture straightened, his head and shoulders lifted. Gone was the lost look, and it was replaced by the confident poise of a leader. "If the adrifts could get away, they'll be hiding. I'll signal." He whistled sharply.

A kid's face poked out from a tree. "It's Steven," he squealed. "Bigham's still gone."

Steven dismounted as several kids with grimy faces and ragged clothing ran toward him as if they were drowning and he could give them air. Their love and admiration for Steven bore similarities to how the clanspeople looked at Dayvee.

"How long ago did they leave?" Brando asked the adrifts.

No one answered. The adrifts looked at Steven. His mouth was moving. She could barely make out his whisper as he counted. He tapped his thumb and forefinger together a couple of times in some type of signal.

"They left about ten minutes ago," one of the kids answered.

Evee sent, *Dayvee says not to chase after them.*

Whoever hurt Steven had escaped the Calupi ring of pain. But the judgment might still be served. Calupi had long memories.

Steven's voice rose. "Sixty-one. Two missing." His eyes darted over the adrifts. "I don't see Misty. Where are you Misty?"

"I'm here, Steven," a small higher-pitched voice answered as a little girl came out from some bushes. She appeared to be around six or seven years old. "It's all my fault."

"What's your fault?" Steven asked.

"I took some crackers, but Bigham caught me."

Steven's lips pursed. "Tanner shouldn't have put you on the team."

"He didn't." She rubbed her wrist. "I'm sorry."

"What did Bigham do to you?"

"He twisted my hand." She hiccuped. "He said he'd break it."

"Let me see."

She gave him her hand, and Steven looked at it. "I don't think it's broken."

"Tanner kicked Bigham, so he let go of me to grab Tanner and took him upstairs. Then a Biggie came and screamed that Pericards entered the bottoms, and they needed to leave. Tanner whistled, so we scattered and hid, but he didn't come. He must be in the box."

Steven's shoulders sagged, then straightened. "I can't be lead anymore. I'm being adopted. Tanner will be your lead now, and it's the second's job to get him out. Who's going to do it?"

The adrifts' eyes widened in fright. Misty said, "I will."

A red-headed boy pushed forward. "No. She's too young. I'll get him." The boy didn't look much older than the girl. Maybe a couple years separated them.

Steven clapped his shoulder. "I'm proud of you, Derrick."

"Will you go with me?" Derrick asked.

"I'll walk you to the room, but you need to go into it alone because I won't be here next time." Steven moved toward the building with Graydee and Derrick at his side.

"Wait." Brando swung down off his horse. "Where are you going?"

Steven glanced back. "In the adriftage to help Tanner."

"There could be someone else in there. Calupi take on danger with a pack, so we'll go with you."

Elayni wasn't the only one who noticed the change in Steven. Brando worded his order nicely and gave his reason like he would to another clan leader.

Steven frowned. "I'd rather just me and Derrick go, but I can't stop you."

"Elayni and Codee, come with us," Brando ordered. "The rest of you Pericards, stay out here with the other adrifts but don't relax your guard. They could come back. And Steven, I go first."

#

Steven

Steven waited as the three Calupi joined them. This would be hard enough without watchers. His guilt already crushed his heart. After today, Derrick wouldn't be the same. His only crime was showing he had compassion, and now he'd be punished for it.

Brando, Elayni, and Codee pulled their nails, then opened the door of the adriftage and lunged in with their companions. He and Graydee followed with Derrick. Heavy drapes blocked the windows, but there was enough light to discern the table with ten chairs around it, the hearth, and shelves that lined the walls. Most were empty. Bigham left only a few jars of food and some pans.

"Bigham, please let me out." Tanner's shouted plea from upstairs choked Steven's heart.

"Bigham's gone, but Derrick's coming," Steven yelled out to Tanner.

"Is that you, Steven?"

Surprisingly, Tanner's voice was strong. Steven always had a hard time drawing breath when he was in the box. "Yes."

"Which way, Steven?" Brando asked. Steven pointed to the hall with several doors. "We go past the rooms for the Biggies to the stairs."

"Who are Biggies?" Codee asked.

"It's what we call the people Bigham hires to help him. We don't worry about their names since they're always changing."

Brando opened the first door and led them in. The room held a large bed, a dresser, a rug, a chair, and a hearth with wood stacked nearby but no people.

"Steven, hurry," Tanner cried out.

The distress in his voice tore at Steven. Tanner had been in there long enough for the cramps to hit. "No matter how many storms batter an adrift ..."

"We don't sink, we bob back up," Tanner finished.

"Keep saying it," Steven shouted.

"Adrifts don't sink, we float."

He whispered to Brando. "Can't we go faster?"

Brando pointed to one of the doors. "I don't want any surprises, so we need to check every room."

Steven groaned. "How about you check them while Derrick and I go on?"

"No, but if you open the doors, Bruno says the wolves can check them quicker than we can."

Steven rushed down the hall opening doors. The wolves bounded in, sniffed a couple times, and bounded out again. He had to wait only a minute at the end of the hall where the stairwell was before the others joined him. The wolves bounded up the steps, and they ran after them.

The wolves raced into the girls' dorm room with its rows of empty cots. Next, Steven opened the door to the boys' dorm that looked identical to the girls, then the work room with the tables piled with fabric and clothing the adrifts sewed for others.

When the wolves came out, Steven pointed to the last room and glanced at the Calupi. "Tanner's in there. Derrick's adrift, so he needs to go alone." Steven opened the door a little, and Derrick slid in. The Calupi couldn't have gotten more than a glimpse of the cot with ropes on top, the stool with more ropes, the whip on the floor beside it, and the box with the ropes around it before Steven slammed the door. Derrick's voice filtered through.

"Tanner, it's Derrick. I'll get you out as soon as I can get the ropes untied."

A ragged voice pierced the air. "Is Steven with you?"

"He's in the hall with some Calupi. He's being adopted, so you're our lead now. I'm opening it." Derrick gasped. "Oh no."

"Get them off me." Tanner sounded desperate.

Steven didn't want to think about what was on Tanner.

"I'm trying. I got them off. I'll untie your hands."

"Thanks." A thump sounded.

"Let me help you up," Derrick offered.

"Not yet." Tanner panted. "Oww."

That part was excruciating. When feeling came back. Steven hollered through the door, "I'm really proud of you, Tanner. Did Bigham rough you up much?"

Tanner's voice was still ragged. "Not that much. He got interrupted."

"Are you okay?"

"I am now." His answer filtered through the door. "But I don't know how you could do the box all those times."

"I did it to keep you from it. You need a second."

"I know." The regret in Tanner's tone clear. "Come on, Derrick."

Derrick's voice trembled. "Now?"

"I'm sorry, Derrick, but now."

Steven didn't want the Calupi to believe them cruel. He needed to get them out of here. He glanced at Brando. "We need to go back outside."

"What's going to happen to him?" Elayni asked.

"It's adrift stuff. You wouldn't understand."

Brando gave him a pointed look. "You should think hard about doing things you already regret."

"He's right, Steven." Codee put a hand on his shoulder.

Steven wasn't a good person, and one less regret wouldn't change that. He shrugged off the hand. "It needs to be done, and we should leave."

Brando crossed his arms. "Not until they come out."

Steven sighed and leaned back against the door. Tanner's voice came through the thin walls easily. "Fold and tuck yourself so you'll fit."

It probably wasn't easy for Derrick even though he was younger. Just two feet tall and deep, the box didn't give you much space. But if you didn't make yourself fit, Bigham would, and he didn't care if he broke your bones to do it.

Derrick sobbed. "Don't close it."

Tanner must have done what Steven did to him all those years ago because pounding sounded next. "Let me out," Derrick cried. "Please, Tanner, let me out."

The memories flooded Steven. Pitch black, his sweat dripping from how hot it always seemed, not being able to move much or draw a full breath. The cramps setting in. His body begging him to get relief. Bigham telling him it was his coffin, and he would die there. He gulped for air.

Brando ordered, "Move, Steven."

Steven forced his memories away and shook his head, no.

Elayni's face flushed red. "If you won't move, we'll go through you."

Their companions told them it's a test, Graydee sent. *But they'll still stop it unless Derrick agrees to it.*

"Derrick," Steven called. "Tanner needs a second, but it doesn't have to be you. Do you want me to go ask Misty to take your place?"

The pounding stopped. "No," Derrick sobbed. "I can do it."

"We're coming in." Steven opened the door and walked in with the Calupi on his heels.

Tanner sat on top of the sturdy wood box. His nose was swollen. He had bruises on his face and a split lip. Tanner turned anguished eyes on Steven as Derrick's sobs filled the room.

Steven needed to stop the crying. "Derrick, there will always be someone like Bigham who will hurt adrifts because they enjoy seeing our pain. Are you going to give them that satisfaction?"

"No. I'm sorry I cried." Derrick's voice was muffled as he choked back his sobs. "I'll float."

Elayni glared at him. "I've seen *you* cry, Steven."

"I didn't break the rule. When can't leads cry, Derrick?"

"In front of adrifts 'cause they need our strength, or when someone enjoys hearing our pain. I'm sorry I sank."

"You didn't. You went under for a minute, but you came up."

"Is Tanner going to do to me what Bigham did to him?" Derrick asked in a shaky voice.

"No."

"Good, but I'm still not sure I can last."

"You already have. Time's up." Steven motioned to Tanner.

Tanner jumped up and opened the box. "Come out now." Tanner gave Derrick his hand and helped him out, then clapped his back. "I'm proud of you."

"I won't forget you if you're in there." Derrick wiped his tear-streaked face with his sleeve. "I'll sneak in as soon as I can."

"I know you will," Tanner said.

Steven went over and slapped Derrick's shoulder. "We're both proud of you. Now go find some joy. Show the other adrifts you survived, and tell the team to get those jars of food Bigham left. Make sure they're portioned out equally."

Derrick ran to the door, then stopped and glanced back. "They're older. You think they'll listen?"

Tanner gave him a smile. "They'll listen. You're second now." Derrick smiled back, then went out into the hall.

Elayni's eyes flashed as she shrieked, "How could you be so mean to a little kid?"

Derrick stuck his head back in. "I'm not little. I'm ten, and it wasn't that bad."

"Derrick—"

"I know, Steven. It's important that everyone eats something today." Derrick closed the door.

Elayni's hands went to her hip. "Doing that to him was wrong."

Tanner's teeth clenched. "I'm glad Steven did it to me, or I might not have brought him water, and he'd be dead. And without that experience, it would have been worse today. Derrick had to know a little before he became second."

"Why don't you have an older kid be second?" Codee asked.

Steven took his rucksack off. "The older are gone a lot apprenticing so someone younger has to help the little kids." He rummaged through the rucksack for the flask. "Can you leave us alone now?"

"No." Elayni snarled. "We're not letting you hurt Tanner too."

"Steven doesn't hurt us. He's tried everything to stop Bigham," Tanner argued. "We even attacked the Biggies together."

Steven finally found the flask and took it out. "That was a mistake that got adrifts killed. So now we do what my lead, Caspian, did. A few protect the many. And Tanner, I did hurt you because I picked you, and I'm sorry." He didn't really want to discuss Bigham's cruelty more, but it could help Tanner. "Do you want to talk about today or lock it away?"

"I'm trying not to think about it." Tanner shuddered. "But don't be sorry. I'm proud you chose me, and you have way more scars than me."

"Our scars aren't a contest, and I'd rather you didn't catch up." Steven held up the flask. "King Tayro gave me this for my injuries. It helps. Is it just your back and lip?"

"Yes."

"Take off your shirt and sit on the cot."

The red slash marks from the whip pierced Steven with guilt as he swabbed the liquid over Tanner's back. Tanner didn't even flinch. When he finished, Tanner put on his shirt and asked, "What's going to happen to us now?"

Tayro and Dayvee are discussing it with Blake, Graydee sent. *The Pericards will tell the adrifts the plan.*

"Steven will take you to join the other adrifts," Brando answered Tanner. "Elayni, go with them. Codee and I have something else to do."

Codee's eyes sparkled. "I'm beginning to think you like me."

"Just your muscles," Brando shot back.

Tanner's eyebrows arched as he glanced at Steven.

You should listen to Brando. Graydee nudged Steven with his cold nose. *He's in charge.*

Graydee was right. Steven had been acting like a lead, and he wasn't now. Only Tanner didn't trust Brando. Neither did he, but he would listen as long as Brando's orders didn't hurt them. "Let's go."

5

Changes

"New challenges are what make life interesting."~ Leeto

Logan

The spray dampened Logan's face, and the wind tossed a lock of his own hair into his eyes. The tang of salt, the boat swaying beneath his feet, and the heady view of miles of ocean invigorated him. He turned to view the approaching coastline. He should be happy to see the shore, yet he wasn't. These last several days, he had the illusion of freedom. But with land filling the horizon, and the dinghy rowing between ships, his illusion burst.

As the small boat drew alongside Logan's ship, he took in the changes in his estranged brother. He'd seen little of Garth these past three years, and it was usually at a distance. Garth's body had matured, but his red shock of hair and green eyes hadn't changed. Quite the opposite of Logan's black hair and brown eyes, and Garth's chin and nose jutted out sharper than his.

Garth smirked, then hollered, "Permission to come aboard," as if it were funny, not a request at all. Garth's arrogant air was the real change.

How Logan would love to deny his request, like Garth denied all of Mother's. Logan was still the heir to the throne since at seventeen he was a year older, but their father, King Nolan, had revealed Garth was his favorite. An unwelcome heir often lived a short life. These soldiers might throw him overboard if he refused Garth.

"Permission to come aboard granted," Logan called out to his brother.

First came two of his brother's henchmen, with guns slung over their shoulders. Then the dinghy rocked, as Garth stood carelessly. The other men in the boat grabbed the sides to keep it steady. Garth climbed up the lowered rope over the ship's railing. The dinghy returned to the second ship in the armada of twenty that trailed them. Each held a hundred soldiers, a small crew, and supplies.

"It will be a while before they get here." Garth pointed at the canoe rowing out from shore. "Aren't you going to offer me a drink?"

The canoe was a long distance off, but Logan wasn't going to face his brother and two armed men alone. "We can have drinks in my quarters, but the invite is only for you."

Garth's eyes widened. Fear crossed his face.

The urge to erase the fear from his little brother's face rose in Logan as he had countless times before. Garth wouldn't believe his reassurances now. But unless he was forced to, Logan wouldn't kill him. He gave him a cheeky smile. "There's nothing to be afraid of unless you plan to attack me."

His brother's laugh was hollow. "If harm comes to me, they'll kill you." He waved his arm dramatically at his men. "Wait here."

When they entered his quarters, Logan wondered how much nicer his brother's were. As a prince's quarters, this wasn't much. A desk, two chairs, a few trunks, some maps, and a small bed filled the room. They weren't supposed to be on a pleasure trip but going to war.

Logan didn't really have any choice but to come. He'd been ordered to win Taluma for Father. A refusal would have brought his and his Mother's loyalties into question again. Logan couldn't risk what might happen to her. And there was no point. If not him, another would gladly take his place. All Logan could do was try to keep the slaughter to a minimum.

"Have a seat, Garth." Logan waved at one of the chairs. When Garth sat, Logan went to his decanter, poured a glass of wine, and handed it to him.

Garth shook his head. "After you."

"I don't drink. I can't dull my wits and deal with your assassins. But I'll take a sip so you know it's not poisoned." Logan lifted the bottle and took a swallow, not bothering with a cup. The last three years, he'd burned with the desire to get some answers. Now was his chance to ask. "So Garth, after three years of hurting Mother, do you ever intend to stop?"

Garth swirled his cup of wine. "I just told the truth, and you should have denounced her too."

"I didn't consider it wrong for her to teach us the history that included Kun and the clans." Logan sat behind the desk. "She isn't a religious zealot wanting to overthrow Father. You just wanted to hurt her."

"I returned the favor." Garth sipped his wine. "No one cared about me. I wasn't the first born."

Did he really believe that? "I expected her to hate you after the dungeons, but she cries when you refuse to see her. And I didn't let you follow me around because I didn't like you. What happened to you?"

Garth's hands trembled as he lifted the cup and swallowed another drink. "I grew up."

Was the shaking hands a sign Garth had a conscience? Could Logan reach it? "If you keep trying to do like Father, the same insatiable craving for power will consume you and everything around you, and you'll be as miserable as him."

Garth's face flushed. "You're just jealous because some people care about me now instead of you."

"And the second you lose favor, they'll discard you. But if ruling means so much to you, I'll step aside if you prove to me you'll help the kingdom."

"I have Father's support." Garth slammed down the cup. "You're the one who needs to prove himself. One more mistake and he'll denounce you for good."

"It wasn't a mistake to show mercy."

"You're too weak to get the job done, and Father knows it."

A knock came at the door, then a muffled voice called, "They're here, requesting permission to board."

Logan stood. "We're coming." When they reached the deck, Logan looked over the rail at the four men in the canoe. The face he expected wasn't there. "Who are you?"

A man in a strange accent stumbled out, "Varian sent us."

"Then one of you can come aboard and explain where he is," Logan ordered.

They lowered the rope, and the one who spoke shimmied up it. Logan took in his stained clothing, the scruffy beard, and beady eyes. His gut told him this man wasn't to be trusted. But then again, few traitors could be. Certainly not Varian. It hadn't really surprised him when one of their scout ships was contacted by Varian. He'd want to save his own neck. But Varian, of all people, should know King Nolan couldn't be trusted either.

The man climbed over the railing and straightened. "I'm William. We received a message that Varian's dead."

Logan tried not to reveal his shock. Varian had thwarted several attempts back home to kill him. "Do we still have an alliance?"

"Varian said we'd be rewarded richly, so we could still be persuaded to help you. But those rewards need to be up front."

Garth spoke sharply. "According to Varian, your people don't have guns, so not killing you should be reward enough."

"You shouldn't underestimate the Kayndo," William retorted. "Varian's dead, and he had guns. But if you want our help, you'll be paying for it."

Logan didn't trust any of his Father's bought allies. Loyalty switched too easily with a bigger purse.

"I'd rather kill you," Garth threatened.

William's mouth tightened. His Adam's apple bobbed up and down. Logan shot Garth a dark look. He might be hanging by a thread, but he was still in charge. "That's my decision, brother."

Garth spat out, "Then make it."

"What rewards do you want?" Logan asked.

William shuffled his feet. "Varian promised weapons, plenty of ammunition, and gold."

"And what will you deliver in exchange?"

A gleam lit William's eyes. "The Kayndo's army is coming, but it will take them several days. We can slow them and whittle down their numbers, plus give you updates on where they are."

Logan rubbed his eyes. His lack of sleep was catching up. "Do you have spies with them?"

"No. Anyone who joins them has to give a vow of support in front of an animal companion. They'd know a lie."

The reward he requested was already in chests on board, for Varian. "We'll give you your reward, but you better earn it, and we want maps too."

Garth crossed his arms. "If you double-cross us, you and your friends will beg me to kill you."

"We won't." William licked his lips. "Where do you want to go?"

"The capital, but we can't leave threats behind. How many cities are close?" Garth asked.

"Portia's a city to the south, but it's a few hours away, and Marshton's to the west on the way to the capital." William pointed to the shore. "That and everything north is clan territory. It's wilderness."

A huge thunk sounded. One side of the deck lifted a little and tilted. Logan almost went sprawling, and some people did. The ship righted. What hit them? Logan ran to the railing and looked down. Several black and white whales broke the surface of the water to swim side by side, then turned around and came to a stop. Were those people riding on them? They *were*. They even held some kind of forked spear. "Are they clanspeople?"

"Yes, Orcans." William's eyes were almost as wide as the crew's.

A piercing scream came from above. A sea eagle flew over them with a tube clutched in it talons. The bird dropped the tube, and it fell to the deck to roll down one side. A sailor grabbed it and brought it to Logan. He opened it to find a rolled piece of hide with writing. It was in one of the ancient languages—the language most of the stories about Kun were in. He and his brother could read it thanks to Mother, but they'd probably be the only ones who could.

"Turn around and go home. That was just a nudge. If you continue on your course to invade us, we'll wreck your ships, and you'll be shark bait."

He better warn the other ships. It took time to pass the signals with flags to one another.

"What's it say?" Garth demanded.

He handed the note to his brother. Of course, Garth read it aloud for all to hear. "We should just shoot them."

How could Logan convince these clanspeople they should surrender peacefully before they were slaughtered? "Quit trying to make my decisions."

"What do you want to do? Turn around? Father said anyone that retreated was to be shot, including you."

Logan wasn't told that. Did Father want to give Garth another excuse to kill him?

Garth barked, "Fire on that eagle and those whales." His henchmen and the soldiers raised their weapons.

"Don't shoot," Logan screamed, hoping they'd listen.

#

Steven

As Steven, Tanner, and Elayni emerged from the adriftage, a cheer broke out from the group of adrifts gathered on the grassy lawn. Steven forced himself to smile. "Derrick, come here."

Derrick ran over to Steven, and he put one arm around his shoulders and the other around Tanner's. "Adrifts, let's show your new lead and second how much we appreciate what they did." Tanner and Derrick displayed beaming smiles as the adrifts swarmed forward to praise them. Steven stepped back.

Elayni was speaking to the Pericard, Chase. Some of the Pericards went into the adriftage. What were they doing?

A few minutes later they came out with Brando and Codee, carrying bundles of broken stuff. They stacked it in a pile. Codee pulled a few pieces from the pile and slathered something on them from his pouch. He sat them in a bare spot, drew out some stones, and struck them together. A spark flew, and the wood caught fire.

Brando waved at the pile next to the fire. "This is everything that was in that room that hurt adrifts. All of you should pitch some of it into the fire. Steven, why don't you start?"

Steven went over, grabbed the ugly whip from the top, and threw it in. "Burn."

Misty clapped, and in her high-pitched voice, chanted, "Burn, burn, burn."

Then all the adrifts threw something in and chanted. The sparks flew as the flames grew to consume the things that harmed them.

Chase came over to Steven with the Calupi. Derrick and the other adrifts sidled away to put some space between them. They didn't trust the Calupi or Pericards. Tanner bravely stayed at Steven's side.

Brando waved at the fire. "Ash can't hurt any of you."

Maybe not, but Steven's memories refused to burn away. "I appreciate the thought, but there will always be something to hurt adrifts."

Elayni glowered at him. "Dayvee won't let adrifts be treated like that again. You should have trusted us and not put Derrick in that box."

"Trust you." Tanner snorted. "What do you know about adrifts? Why don't you look at all the bare spots where Kun won't let grass grow?" His eyes misted. "Those are the graves of our friends, and fewer have died with us in charge than ever before."

Steven whispered in Tanner's ear. "Adrifts are here who need your strength. Compose yourself."

Tanner sucked in a ragged breath as Steven raised his voice to include all the adrifts. "Tanner forgot it doesn't matter what others think. He needs reminded, and since the Biggies aren't here, make sure he hears you."

Misty laughed. "Do it, Steven."

"Tanner's your lead now." He pushed Tanner forward. "Go ahead."

"What do they say about adrifts?" Tanner asked.

"We're worthless," the adrifts shouted.

"Does it matter what they say?" Tanner asked.

"No!"

"Why?"

"They don't know us," they yelled.

"Who do they say cares about us?"

"No one."

"Does it matter what they say?"

"No."

"Why?"

"Because they're wrong," they screamed.

"Who cares about adrifts?" Tanner pointed skyward.

"Kun cares."

"Anyone else?"

"Adrifts care about adrifts."

"Convince me."

"We care about adrifts!" they roared.

"Okay, I'm convinced. Let's not let each other forget it. Remind each other you care."

Steven clapped Tanner's shoulder. "I care about you."

"Thanks. I care about you, too, and I'm really sorry you'll be with people who don't." Tanner left to join some of the other adrifts.

"He really has a low opinion of us," Elayni said.

Steven shook his head. "No, he wouldn't have gotten angry if he did."

"So you believe we don't care about you?" Elayni asked.

"You don't know me. You got a glimpse today, but you didn't like it. I know that I'm not good enough for you or Graydee, but I can't convince him. He cares about me, and adrifts do. That's it."

"You're wrong." Brando said. "We care. Chase, tell them what's going to happen."

Chase gave the adrifts an abashed grin. "We Pericards brought you here so you'd be provided for. We didn't know Bigham would abuse you. Now we feel terrible, so we want to help. My mother loves to nurture people, and she takes care of our injured. Blake sent a Pericard to ask if the adrifts could come there. She said she'd love it. We'll take you, and then rejoin the Kayndo."

Steven signed to Tanner. *Send in the team. Nothing of value*

*should remain. Bigham profited enough from us. The Pericards might
not agree, so bring it out in sacks.*

Tanner gave him a nod and signaled the team to go. Adrifts
sprinted toward the building while Chase kept talking.

"My mother's going to see if she can find the adrifts real homes.
And the Kagards we leave in Harthome will check on them. We won't
make the same mistake twice. They'll get fed, and they won't need to
steal."

Like Steven believed that. Just how many times had adrifts been
disappointed before? Several of the adrifts fingers were flashing. Misty
signed, *Can we trust him?* Tanner signed, *How do I watch over
everyone if they send us to different places?* Derrick's fingers were
saying something else. Too many were signing at the same time.

Brando chuckled. "I might not know what you're signaling, but I
can guess. Steven can't tell you what the future will hold. But if
someone hurts you again, find a clansperson and ask them to get a
message to the Kayndo's sub-pack. If we can't come, we'll send
someone. Now tell them goodbye, Steven. We need to return to
Dayvee."

Steven tried to memorize each face. "Goodbye, adrifts. If I get
back to Harthome, I'll visit."

"Goodbye, Steven." The adrifts voices blended together as he
mounted and followed the Calupi out the gate into the maze of narrow
streets that ran through the Bottoms.

The Calupi and Pericards bunched together, riding three abreast,
except for Steven who rode with only Graydee at his side. Curtains
rippled in the shacks around them as unseen bottom dwellers watched
their progress.

Unshed tears burned Steven's eyes. The adriftage was a terrible
place to live, Bigham was sadistic, and adrifts were treated terribly.
But for six years, adrifts were the only friends he had. Now he didn't
know if he'd see any of them again.

He had to make the best of it. Caspian always said to live for
today. Find joy in each one because adrifts had no guarantees about

tomorrow. He was supposed to be Calupi now, but he didn't feel as if he belonged to their world. Calupi must not live long lives either. If they did, wouldn't Graydee be trotting alongside Geno instead of him?

Most Calupi live longer than adrifts, Graydee sent. *You are good enough to be Calupi. And I'll keep reminding you until you believe it too.*

Codee trotted up to ride beside him. "I know the adrifts were like a family to you. I'd like to give you a new family, and we all want to help you. You just need to trust us."

"Trust has to be earned, and it can't be one-sided. You don't trust me, so why do you expect me to trust you?"

Elayni dropped back to ride on his other side. "What makes you think we don't trust you?"

"How you acted with Derrick. I bet when you misplace something, you'll be thinking I took it. But I don't blame you. You don't know me."

"We're trying to get to know you. Would you steal from us?" she asked.

"I've never stolen from an adrift, but I won't lie. If Graydee was hungry, I'd steal again to feed him because I love him."

"One of our Calupi tests is stealing meat from a predator, so we've stolen too." Codee wiped at some sweat that escaped his headband. "But we don't steal from other people, and once we teach you how to harvest Kun's bounty, you won't need to."

Running footsteps came from behind. Steven glanced over his shoulder to see Derrick sprinting toward them. He reined his horse to a stop.

Derrick rushed up panting. "The team found something of yours." He handed Steven a duffel sack.

Steven opened it to see weapons. Only two but better than none. "Thanks. I thought Bigham sold them all."

"They were in that locked chest in Bigham's room. The team broke the ancient's lock."

"Figures he'd put them in the one place I couldn't risk opening.

Thank them for me."

"Sure. Take care of yourself, Steven." Derrick ran off.

The Calupi looked at Steven with curious gazes, but he wasn't revealing what the bag held. He wouldn't give them up again.

"Cackles," Brando exclaimed.

"What's wrong?" Elayni asked.

"A petrel bird flew from the coast to tell Dayvee the ocean was stained red with blood. Only a few Orcan's and their whales survived the invader's slaughter. He wants to leave for the coast immediately, so we're to meet them outside the city's gates." Brando shouted, "Yah!" The horses jumped into a gallop.

6

Decisions

"Good decisions require thought." ~ Codee

Codee

The Kagards opened the wooden gates they'd repaired, and Codee galloped out of the city of Harthome with the others who had gone to the adriftage. Must've been three thousand people milling on the plain outside the city walls. Beyond them lay great herds of buffalo, deer, and elk, packs of wolves and coyotes, the flocks of birds, and tons of other animals. Including the animal companions, they must've numbered tens of thousands. The real strength of the Kayndo.

Dayvee was already there mounted on Ghostee with the rest of the sub-pack and Pericards around him. His blonde hair waved in the breeze, and a sparkle lit his bright green eyes. The crowd was shouting, "Kayndo! Kayndo! Kayndo."

As they joined him, Dayvee acknowledged their group's return with a chin lift, a sign he considered the task he gave them well met. Then he turned his gaze to the crowd and raised his hand. The crowd quieted.

"Thank you for your support. We didn't invite these invaders to come and slaughter our people and companions. We never asked for this fight, but we won't run from it. We'll run to it!" Dayvee lifted his fist in the air. "Who will give them a fight they will not forget!"

A sea of fists stabbed the air. "I will!"

"We'll make them regret the day they came. This is our continent. They will not take it!"

"They will not take it," they yelled back.

"We need to act as if we are all one clan. Stay close to your leader and companion assigned to you. I don't want anyone to face threats alone. May Kun go with us!"

"May Kun go with us!" they roared.

Pride in Dayvee infused Codee and brought a lump to his throat. If he could take even a little credit for who Dayvee had become, it justified staying all those years at Wolf Mountain.

At Dayvee's signal, the Kwin led them away since they knew the route. Everyone followed, but they were already dividing into smaller groups to make their way to the coast. Buffalo clan didn't travel as fast as wolf clan, and most city people weren't used to traveling long distances. Dayvee divided the provisions so wagons traveled with each group. The wild animals branched around them, taking their own paths. Deer, elk, bears, buffalo, mountains lions, and more wound through the fields and forest while birds flew above them. Uneasiness prickled the base of Codee's neck. A foe wouldn't have any problem finding them.

The Kwin led them onto the caravan road to the coast. The broad road that was built by the ancients still ruined the face of their land, even with the sand covering it. City people maintained the road because it brought fish and salt to them.

Clanspeople wouldn't normally risk contaminating their soul by using something of the ancients', but Gaylo said the sand over the top should protect them. To help the wagons with their tents and supplies move faster, Dayvee decided to take it. At a windswept area, a buckled black patch of the stuff the ancients formed their roads with poked through. Codee shuddered.

This close to Harthome, planted fields checkered the sides of the road and divided the wooded terrain. The forests here held more hardwoods with fewer pines than their mountain home. Codee glanced over at Steven riding beside him. It had been a quick decision to adopt the young man. Sixteen years ago, after the heavy price he'd paid, he'd promised himself never to make another decision rashly. But something about Steven pulled at Codee. And before he knew it, he was offering. Codee hadn't even consulted his life-mate, Jolay. It still felt right. He didn't regret it. And maybe, this time, it wouldn't turn out badly.

I like Steven, Wilee sent.

Me too. Steven's eyes were wide and his head kept turning. Much of this he probably had never seen. "If there's anything you have questions about, just ask."

"Why were you shocked when Brando assigned us to ride at Dayvee's back?"

Was Codee that easily read? "To protect a leader's back is a great honor to Calupi."

Steven's shoulders sagged. "So you didn't think I should be here?"

"Brando wouldn't let anyone ride this close to Dayvee's back unless he trusted them, and he doesn't trust quickly. But I was just as shocked he'd give me the honor since I'm on a list he keeps of people he believes harmed Dayvee."

Brando dropped back to ride beside them. He chuckled. "Worrying about my list again, Codee?"

"No. I'm guessing you must like me since you keep coming near."

Brando laughed. "Actually, I came back to speak to Steven." His deep blue eyes locked on Steven. "You're riding here because you risked yourself to protect one of us. But you didn't want to follow my orders at the adriftage. If that continues, people will assume you don't support the Kayndo. So do you?"

Steven's head tilted as if he wasn't sure how to answer. Codee should explain. "If you don't support Dayvee, when there are so many that do, clanspeople won't accept you being with him."

Steven's face scrunched. "I don't think Kun would have given Dayvee the gifts unless he's worthy, but I'm not positive. So I need to get to know Dayvee before I can fully support him. But there aren't any adrifts here I feel responsible for, so I shouldn't have problems following your orders."

"Then I'm ordering you to take out whatever you're hiding in that bag and show it to me."

Brando was testing him. Steven had made it a little too obvious he didn't want to share the contents. Dayvee, Elayni, Chayla, and Tayro kept glancing back. They were riding too close together not to hear the conversation.

"I'll show them to you, but I won't hand them over willingly." Steven crossed his reins over the horse's neck, reached into the bag, and drew out a rope with balls and a curved stick. The bola and cumback stick.

Elayni gasped. "If you stole those, we won't be able to protect you from the Kwin's judgment."

"I didn't steal them. They were my fathers, and the adriftage stole his weapons from me. These are the only two I was able to get back."

"Was your father a clansman?" Brando asked.

Steven snorted. "No." His head lifted. "He was the best warehouse guard in Harthome." Pride infused his voice. "No thieves got by him."

Elayni pushed a lock of hair that escaped her braid behind her ear. "Then how did he get clan weapons?"

"I don't know, but he wouldn't have stolen him. He liked a lot of weapons, and he was friends with a weapons craftsmen, so he probably bought them."

Codee knew that couldn't be right. "Clan weapons aren't for sale. And the craftsmen we use have agreed not to make them for others." He nudged his horse closer to Steven. "Can I see them?"

Steven shook his head. "I won't hand Father's weapons over again."

"I'll return them to you. I just want to see if they're imitations."

Steven hesitated but then handed them across to Codee.

Cackles. One ball on the bola had a horse's head engraved in it, and the other held a black curvy line, Black River's herd mark. The cumback stick had an R, and the curvy line again. Codee's spirits sagged. Steven wouldn't be able to keep these weapons. And that meant problems.

Codee handed them back. "Those aren't imitations. They belonged to someone from Black River Herd. Whoever owned them is probably dead since that's the only way a clansperson would give up their weapons, but I doubt the family will allow you to keep them."

Steven picked at a bur on his horse's mane. "They're all I have left of Father."

"I'm sorry. We don't keep many possessions, and when we die, they're distributed to those who need them," Codee explained. "If our weapons break, they're buried with us, but otherwise, they're the one thing the family keeps. And they'll want a family member to use them."

"Are people from Black River herd here?" Steven asked.

Dayvee twisted in the saddle to look back at him. "Yes. They brought a lot of the horses we're using."

"Will you tell them?"

Dayvee nodded. "They'd tell us."

"So I don't have a choice?"

"I won't force you," Dayvee answered. "But the Kwin will since clan weapons hold pieces of a family member's companion. Do you want to turn them over the hard way?"

"I have regretted not having a weapon a thousand times. I said if I ever got Father's back, I'd never give them up." Steven's anguished eyes were soft. "At least, this time, someone will cherish them." He looked at Codee, and his voice trembled. "Do you want me to give them to you now?"

Codee didn't want to be the one to take them from him. *Wilee, can you let Nolte's companion, Novu, know we have some weapons to return to his herd? Ask him when he can meet with us.*

Wilee sent, *Tonight.*

"Nolte will come for them later," Codee informed him. As Steven stowed the Kwin weapons in his rucksack, Codee took off the extra weapons on his own belt. Codee fingered the beads. "I know this can't make up for losing those but in the clan, fathers usually give their children their first weapons." He held out the pouches to Steven. "I always planned to give these to my son, so I'd like you to have them."

Steven shook his head. "Thank you, but I can't accept them. I have nothing of value to give you in return."

Did city people expect a return on gifts? Codee's reined his horse to where he was practically brushing Steven's leg. "All I want is for you to use them well. Please take them." He dropped the pouches in Steven's lap.

Steven caught them. He opened the first pouch and drew the chakram out, looked it over, and then drew the knife out and hefted it. He read the inscription out loud. "Zago."

"Wasn't that grandfather's companion?" Dayvee asked.

"Yes," Codee said. "Father gifted those to me before he died. I brought them in case I needed extra weapons. Now I'm glad I did."

Steven flipped the knife over. "I'll cherish them."

"You probably don't know how to use our weapons, but we'll teach you," Codee said.

"I'm good with a knife or tooth as you call it. I'm not as good with the nails." Steven's tone had turned defensive.

Had Codee's face revealed his disbelief? But what Steven considered good probably wasn't the same as clanspeople. "I'm surprised you know how to use our weapons at all."

"Father had a set of tooth and nails too," Steven slid the weapons back in their sheaths. "But when the adriftage took them, I couldn't keep practicing. I apprenticed awhile with the weapons maker who was friends with my father, and I was able to practice with his, but that was several months ago."

"These weapons you used, were they engraved with the faces of animals, and did they have symbols like rivers, plains, or mountains on them?" Codee asked.

Steven attached the pouches to his belt. "Yes."

Codee shot Dayvee a pointed look. "We need to talk to this weapons maker."

Steven glanced over his shoulder. "I saw him with some of the city people behind us."

"Why didn't you say anything to him?" Codee asked.

"He doesn't want anything to do with me." Steven blushed. "It's my fault since I stole from him."

"You and Codee should ride back to find him," Dayvee said. "We need to know if he's selling clan weapons."

"All right." Steven picked up his reins. "But if you want Codee to confront Clint, you should know that he's the best swordsman I've ever seen, outside of my father."

"He's right, Dayvee." Blake must have been listening. "Clint makes our weapons, so I know him. I can go with them if you'd like."

Brando's deep blue eyes glittered with excitement. He wanted to go.

"You can go, Blake," Dayvee said. "But not you, Brando. If he's that good, we need him, and you're too quick to maim." Dayvee glanced at Codee. "There's a huge meadow close to the Accipi convocation where we can camp. They say they'll have it ready with firewood and everything else we need, so if not before, meet us there."

Everything we need? "Cackles, Dayvee," Codee exclaimed. "When you accepted their hospitality, did you think what it would mean for a small group to host one of this size?"

"They invited me and the sub-pack to stay with them at their home. I didn't think they were offering hospitality for the entire group."

"Everything we need means they'll feed every one of us. But they're not going to admit it could mean their convocation will go hungry all winter. Not with the pride of their entire clan at stake."

"How can I fix it?"

"You can't. If you bring out our supplies and refuse theirs after you already agreed would be like a sucker punch. When we leave, you can make a gift of supplies. They might accept it, but it will still hurt their pride."

Dayvee ran a hand through his hair. "That was a stupid mistake."

"It wasn't stupid when you haven't visited many clans. I'm sure you'll receive more offers to host us, so just make it clear up front you appreciate their aid in finding suitable camping areas, but we won't accept hospitality since every clan already donated the provisions we're carrying, and we don't wish to burden anyone more."

"Okay. Thanks, Codee."

"Sure, we'll meet you after we find Clint."

#

Dayvee

When Codee, Steven, and Blake rode far enough down the road and they disappeared from sight, Dayvee turned to his sub-pack. "While they're gone, I want to discuss Steven with you. Since he's from the city, he might not be that capable, but I want him and Graydee with us. How do you feel about it?"

"After what we saw at the adriftage?" Elayni chewed her lip. "He reminded me of Leeto."

"Exactly. I'd be doing the same type of stuff if Leeto was my only influence. But I had you and Brando telling me Leeto was wrong."

"So you want us to teach him differently?" she asked.

"Yes. Any pack he joins will recognize his leader skills and have him doing it eventually."

"I agree." Brando swiped at a fly. "I even want him to join our family."

"What?" Tayro exclaimed. "You didn't let us join for years, and you'd invite Steven in a few hours?"

"He chose to make the adrifts his family and loved and protected them. Like we do for each other. He didn't make all the right decisions, but he tried. I want him to choose us for his next family, but he's not ready yet. He doesn't trust us."

Tayro frowned. "He wasn't even sure if he should support Dayvee."

"I was thrilled he wants to judge me for me," Dayvee said. "So I can be myself, not the Kayndo, and our sub-pack is the one place I can do that."

Tiny Chayla sat up straighter on her horse as if to make herself appear taller. "My heart says it's the right thing to do, so I vote yes."

Tayro lifted his pinky. "Graydee does need us, so I agree."

"Elayni?" Dayvee asked.

She was still chewing her lip. "I don't know."

So unusual. Elayni would normally mother anyone who had lost their family. "Is there another reason you don't want him in?"

"Yes, but she's not going to tell you." Brando gave her his crooked grin. "I noticed how you look at Steven."

Elayni put a hand on her hip. "Stop, Brando."

"No. It's okay for you to be attracted to someone, but it's not okay to keep him out just so you're not tempted to stop waiting for the guy you really love."

Dayvee's stomach felt as if it were punched. The air in his lungs came rushing out. Wasn't it the right thing for her to move on? But if it was right, why did it hurt so badly? He squeaked out, "Brando."

"What Dayvee? You love her, she loves you. It's no secret. I've known it since we were twelve, but you keep acting like a rabbit. You should learn you have competition."

"Don't you think I know Tayro, Frudo, and several others are interested in Elayni?" Tayro's face flushed, and he dropped his head.

Of course, there was interest. She was gorgeous. Dayvee's heart plummeted. "Did you really have to rub my face in it?"

"Yes. Because you gave me permission to tell you when you're acting like an idiot, and you are." Brando rubbed the back of his neck. "Your crushed feet aren't holding you back, just your stubborn refusal to do what you should."

"Enough," Dayvee snapped. "Elayni and I don't need you to figure out our relationship."

"I'm just tired of seeing my best friends unhappy. Do you enjoy being miserable?"

"No, but you can't fix it." Dayvee chopped the flat of his hand, ordering Brando to be silent. Elayni's cheeks were red. Was she embarrassed or angry?

Her chin jutted out. Ah, she was angry. "All right. I agree to Steven joining the sub-pack and family."

#

Steven

It seemed as if Steven had passed hundreds of groups of people trying to find Clint. Those on foot had spread out for some distance down the road behind Dayvee. They weren't following in a column but in small clumps. At least the groups of people stuck to the road, so they didn't have to search the woods or fields around it. Steven examined yet another one. No Clint. Steven shook his head at Codee and Blake who rode alongside him. They clucked their horses into another canter. Clint wasn't out of shape, so why would he be this far back?

Maybe he changed his mind about coming? He didn't think Clint had seen him with Dayvee, but maybe he had. Clint told Bigham he never wanted to see Steven again. Would that have made him turn back? If they kept going, they'd be back in Harthome soon. He didn't see any people coming up. Had that group been the last? Wait. What was that clanging sound? Like swords hitting each other. Raised voices too. Someone was fighting near here.

Graydee sent, *We'll check it out.* He and Codee's companion wolf, Wilee, raced into a field where it bordered some woods. The wolves topped a rise, and he lost sight of them.

It couldn't have been thirty seconds before Graydee sent, *There're a dozen men fighting against two. There's several already dead around a couple of wagons of supplies.*

He drew up the memory of Clint, a huge man with biceps as big as Steven's leg, his chestnut hair, broad face, and ready smile. He flashed the mind picture to Graydee. *Is he with them?*

Yes. He's one of the two men fighting off the others. The other guy was just run through, so it's just him now. They're circling him. He'll die soon.

No. Clint had been good to Steven before he stole from him. He couldn't let him die without trying to help. He clucked his horse to a gallop and raced to join him. Codee yelled something, but it was lost in the flurry of his horse's pounding hooves.

Steven put the reins in his teeth and drew his weapons.

7

Revelations

"Don't rush to judge before learning as much as you can." ~ Kwutee

Steven

As Steven topped the rise, his heart pummeled his chest. At the edge of the field, men from the bottoms with a few of the Biggies had Clint surrounded.

Clint's eyes grew wide when he saw Steven galloping toward them. "Get out of here, Steven."

Blood already marked a cut on his leg. Steven nudged the horse with his feet to guide it toward those crowding Clint. They dodged away from his horse's hooves.

"That's the kid Bigham and Mort want," one of the Biggies exclaimed. "The reward to capture him is forty golds, and twenty for him dead."

That was a huge reward. Steven let his tooth fly to bury in the Biggie's chest. Then he threw his nails at another man. The guy dodged, but the chakram still sliced his side. While Steven drew his sword, the injured man grabbed Steven's leg and yanked him off the horse. Steven's sword flew from his hand as he slammed into the ground. The collision knocked his breath from him. Graydee lunged at his attacker, biting his leg, but more of them swarmed Steven.

When he tried to get up, one kicked him. Steven tumbled while another kicked his sword farther away. Clint limped forward, swinging his sword to press the men back. Codee and Blake galloped up. Codee threw his nails while Blake stabbed one. Steven jumped to his feet.

Clint flicked his sword at another foe. "Steven, get the slingshot off my belt and the stone pouch."

Steven grabbed them. As fast as he could, he loaded the slingshot and flung a rock into a Biggie's forehead. The Biggie slumped to the ground as Steven sent another stone flying. Only four attackers left in front of them.

Pain burst in Steven's head, and blackness swallowed him.

#

Steven

When Steven came to, he was on his horse who was trotting back down the road. He recognized the strong ropy arms that encircled him as Clint's. Pain rocked his skull.

One of the enemies clobbered you from behind. He tried to escape with you, but I stopped him, Graydee sent.

Thanks. Steven was hit in the head again?

You should have someone fight at your back.

Steven doubted there'd be many volunteers for that. Oh no, he hadn't retrieved his weapons, and Codee had just gifted them to him.

Codee retrieved them for you. They're in your pouches.

Steven would have to thank him. Where were Codee and Blake?

They'll catch up. They were going to bring the wagons back, then track the attackers to learn more, but Clint and you needed to go to Tayro for treatment.

Clint's arms were too tight against Steven's bruised ribs. "You can let go, Clint. I'm awake."

His arms loosened but didn't drop completely. Steven's shirt hung open. He tugged it together and fumbled with the laces. One of them was torn, so he pulled it tight to shut it.

"Sorry about that," Clint said. "I was trying to check for a heartbeat."

Clint must have seen Steven's scars. "You were probably sorry to find it beating."

"No. I was thrilled. I regret the things I said to you."

Clint did appear to be feeling bad. Steven shrugged. "You were right. I was trouble. Who could blame you for not wanting me around?"

"I didn't want to risk my weapons being stolen." Clint sighed. "But if I had known how Bigham was treating you, I'd have confronted him."

You should tell him the truth, Graydee sent.

It won't change the past.

No, but you're still upset about how fast he condemned you.

It might be a stupid thing to take pride in but at the adriftage, Steven's skills were admired. He wanted Clint to know he wasn't a fumbling idiot. "I'm too good of a thief to drop a knife I'm stealing. I wanted to get caught."

Clint's arms tightened around him again. "But why?"

Steven wriggled, and Clint loosened his hold. "You threatened to go to the Kagards if Bigham wouldn't let you adopt me. He said if you did, you'd die."

"What about the second time?"

"You shouldn't have come there, and it would be dangerous for you to know the truth."

"I said I didn't want to see you, but I did, so I went. Now tell me."

"We don't survive the adriftage without getting good at stealing. If adrifts live long enough, they work for Mort, and Bigham gets a cut. Mort tests you at the tavern before sending you on jobs. When he told me to lift your purse, I had to drop it in front of your nose before you *caught* me. Mort guessed I did it on purpose. That's why I was punished for *stealing*."

"What was the punishment?"

Steven shuddered as the bitter memories flooded him. "You were there."

"That night is hazy," Clint said sheepishly.

How Steven wished he could forget the agony of that night. Without thought, Steven's hand had flown up to his chest where the old scars hid under his shirt. He dropped his hand and forced himself to say calmly. "Mort's guards held me down while he threw hot coals on me to teach the adrift better than to *steal*."

"I did nothing?" The shock and self-recrimination in Clint's tone appeared genuine.

"You were in a drunken stupor, and if you had tried to prevent it, you'd be dead, outnumbered like today. Why were you fighting those men anyway?"

"The driver of the supply wagon called for help when a couple of them stole the wagon. Me and a few others chased them. When we caught up, we found a lot more enemies and another wagon." Clint's tone was full of sorrow.

"Did you lose friends?"

"I just met them, but I didn't want to see them killed."

Steven's stomach flipped. He didn't like seeing people die either. Losing people and supplies already couldn't be good. *It's not,* Graydee sent. *Everyone isn't near a companion, so Dayvee wants you to warn those you see to keep the supply wagons in the center. And you need to ask Clint about the clan weapons.*

Okay. Hopefully, Clint didn't get mad. "Why did you let me use the clan's weapons?"

"Someone had to test them. Frankly, you're better with them than me. That's one reason I paid Bigham over the normal apprentice rate for you."

Steven rubbed his aching temple. "Did you make Father's?"

"No, I wouldn't do that. Ren didn't say how he came by them, except to claim they weren't stolen. I made him his sword and his bow, but those aren't clan."

He's speaking the truth, Graydee sent.

Clint slowed the horse to a walk. "I made a weapon for you too. The slingshot you used today." He crossed the reins and took the slingshot and pouch off his belt. "Here." He handed them to him.

The slingshot wasn't bone like Steven's father's but wood. It didn't have eagles carved on it, but it had the sun, several squiggly lines, a little boat, and then another sun etched into it. Why would Clint do that for him? Steven traced the carvings. "I don't understand."

"The sun on the bottom was you happy with Ren, the lines are the storm waves of his death, the boat is you adrift, the sun on top was you finding joy again with me. But after you stole from me, I figured I didn't really know you."

"You didn't."

"We could change that if you're willing to be friends again."

Steven's elation rose. Then he tamped it down. Hadn't he learned better? "It would be asking for trouble."

"I've learned some things are worth trouble, but either way, I want you to have them."

The slingshot was Steven's favorite weapon, but it wouldn't be right. He held it out to Clint. "I can't take it. Everything I have I need, so I have nothing of value to give in return."

"You already gave me the value. I sold a lot more weapons with you demonstrating them." Clint chuckled. "People thought if a kid could use them, they could."

Steven stroked the slingshot feeling the smooth finish. "Thank you." Steven put the slingshot and pouch on his belt. He was certain he'd need them.

#

Dayvee

Dayvee glanced at the sun. The days had grown warmer and longer. They still had a few hours left before sundown. Woods bordered both sides of the road. They'd left the fields around Harthome behind. He hated to stop, but they were almost to the Accipi's meadow. Would all those following make this camp tonight? Or camp wherever they were?

This slow pace was frustrating. He needed to go quicker to help the clanspeople battling the invaders. And now enemies were after their supplies.

When the woods opened up to the large meadow, the babble of a brook announced water nearby. A group of clansmen wearing tunics decorated with feathers came toward them. Padded leather circled their arms between their wrists and elbow.

"Greetings, Kayndo," the one in front said. "I'm Shuto, leader of White Oak convocation." An eagle cried out from above. Shuto lifted his right arm, and the eagle swooped down to land on the padded band encircling it. Shuto's arm sank under the force, but he straightened it. "And this is my companion, Skyto."

The bird gave Dayvee a piercing gaze. *My wings will soar where you guide us, Kayndo.*

"It's an honor, Shuto and Skyto. We thank you for your hospitality."

"Your need is our need. Your people can set up camp here. He pointed to the North. The creek is over there, and our convocation will bring food."

Codee had been right about the Accipi feeding them all. "Go ahead, everyone." Dayvee waved those behind him forward. "Set up camp."

They poured into the meadow, except for his sub-pack and a group of the Pericards.

Shuto lifted his arm, and Skyto launched himself in the air with a flurry of wings. "Our home isn't far, but we don't reveal our location to most. If you're ready, I can take you and your sub-pack there."

"The Pericards have to stay with the Kayndo and King Tayro to guard them," Chase proclaimed.

Shuto stiffened. "Our convocation wouldn't feel comfortable with that many outsiders, but the Kayndo and King won't come to harm while they visit us."

Chase was shaking his head, no. Dayvee shot Chase a glare, then turned to Shuto, "Sometimes those around me forget I make the decisions. We don't need more guards, but there are two more Calupi that stay with my sub-pack, Steven and Codee."

"That's fine, Kayndo."

"Chase, Wilee's passing my orders to Blake. You should set your tents up."

"Yes, Kayndo." Chase saluted with a fist over his heart, then rode into the meadow with the other Pericards.

Shuto pointed to Ghostee. "It's not easy going for horses. If you turn them loose, the Kwin will collect them."

His sub-pack swung down. Dayvee grabbed his crutches from the leather scabbard running down Ghostee's side.

Don't insult me, Ghostee sent. *I can get you to wherever you need to go.*

"My horse doesn't want easy." Dayvee waved. "Lead on."

Ghostee picked his way through the dense forest as Shuto led them off the road and back west. Their wolf companions flitted through the forest, moving silently all around them. Before long they came to an older stand of white oaks. The trunks were wide and the foliage was so dense light barely dappled through.

"We're here." Shuto pursed his lips and whistled a piercing cry similar to an eagle's.

A rope snaked down from a tree. There was some type of structure up there, but they blended in so well with the canopy it was hard to pick them out.

Shuto blushed as he glanced at Dayvee. "We normally just climb up the ropes, but we have a basket we take supplies up in. You and the wolves could ride in that."

We wolves would rather sleep down here tonight, Jaycee sent.

There was no way Dayvee would ride up in some basket like an invalid. "My feet don't work, but my hands do. I might not be very quick, but I can climb your rope."

Brando arched a brow. Dayvee sighed. "Don't even ask."

"I won't, but I'm going behind you in case you slip. Shall we let the others go first?"

"Fine, Brando."

While the others climbed, Dayvee dismounted on his crutches. He fed Jaycee and gave Ghostee some grain.

Ghostee finished eating and trotted off. *Call when you want to leave.*

Elayni had made it up the rope, so Dayvee hobbled over to the tree. "Give me your crutches," Brando said.

Dayvee rested his feet on the ground a second and handed them over, then grabbed the knotted rope. He *would* do this. He lifted himself with his arms to the next knot. Brando fastened his crutches to his rucksack and followed. Dayvee's shoulders ached when he reached a platform. Without having to ask, Tayro leaned over to grab Dayvee's arms and give him a boost up onto the platform. It gave beneath Dayvee a little, then snapped back.

Cackles. Would this thing hold them? Made of some type of cane or sticks lashed together with a rope frame, it didn't feel that sturdy. Brando swung over to land beside him and bounced too. He gave Dayvee a grin. "I wonder how high I can jump on this."

Elayni put her hands on her hips. "You'd probably end up jumping right over the side."

Brando grinned even bigger. "You want to bet?"

Elayni shook her head. The leafy canopy kept them shielded so the light of the descending sun only speckled through. From here, Dayvee could pick out more platforms in trees around them. He inspected the one beneath his feet.

It made a wide circle around the thick trunk. Near the trunk, large basket-like structures hung dangling from more ropes. Blankets and pillows lined the longer ones. Did the Accipi sleep in those?

Welcome, Kayndo. Skyto perched in a cylindrical nest of sticks tucked in between the trunk and the crook of a branch above them. Hmmm. Clans adopted many of the habits of the animals they lived with.

The aroma of roasting meat, onions, and garlic from a hanging clay pot sent Dayvee's mouth to watering. When Brando handed Dayvee his crutches, he picked his way to the more stable center.

"These are for sitting." Shuto pointed to a large basket suspended on its side from ropes. Shuto sat in it, and the basket swung some.

Dayvee would rather sit on the floor, but he didn't want to hurt Shuto's feeling. When he maneuvered himself into one, he tilted it forward to keep his feet on the platform so it wouldn't move.

"Where's the rest of your convocation?" Tayro and the others gingerly sat in baskets.

"Most of them are seeing to our guests needs, but the children begged to serve you. They wanted to meet the King and Kayndo. I'll allow some to help if you don't mind?"

"Of course not," Dayvee answered.

Shuto whistled again. Five children swung from a nearby platform on vine-like ropes to land bouncing on theirs. Dayvee would guess they were between ten and fifteen years old. Smiles wreathed their faces. An adult swung over next, the Calupi messenger, Drako.

"Thank you, Drako, for sharing your stories with them," Shuto said. "I'm sure it made their work go faster."

Drako ruffled the smallest kid's hair. "I'm glad they enjoyed them."

All the clans loved Drako to visit and share his stories, but wasn't he supposed to be watching their former prince? Dayvee didn't need more problems. "Where's Tibalt?"

"With the Ursans. Last I saw him, the bears were teaching him how to wrestle, but I better go see if he needs rescued."

Brando laughed. "Being flattened isn't going to help him get over his fear of animals."

Drako's eyes twinkled. "After the last two days, I think he's over his fears, but this will be a good test. I'll see you later." Drako slid down one of the ropes to the ground and trotted off.

The young Accipi studied the Calupi. Shuto pointed to Dayvee, then Tayro. "This is the Kayndo and King." He cleared his throat. "Our guests' needs haven't been met."

The Accipi children ran over to the clay pot to ladle food into bowls, and then carried it to them along with cups of tea. "Thank you " Guilt twinged Dayvee. Was he taking their meal? "Will you eat with us?"

"They've eaten and have more to do," Shuto replied. Clanspeople didn't lie, so they must have eaten something.

"Drako shared only one Kayndo story," an older boy said. "Can you tell us another after you eat?"

Dayvee pointed at Chayla. "She's the one who writes them."

Chayla's smile peeked out. "We have to work on getting ceremony clothes ready for Steven, but I'll share one with you."

"Yes!" They grabbed their vine ropes and ran off the platform.

The food melted in Dayvee's mouth. Delicious. "Shuto, how do you keep your homes warm in the winter?"

"We have hides that cover the platforms like a tent. The braziers and hot stones in our beds keep it warm."

Chayla finished her bowl and stood. "I'll join the children now."

Shuto pointed to the next platform. "Can you swing over to it?"

Chayla nodded. Brando got out of the basket chair. "Be careful, Chayla."

Petite Chayla reached up to pat his face. "Don't worry." She gave him a flirtatious wink. "If something happens to me, I'm sure you'll find another to life-mate."

Brando growled but didn't try to stop her when she grabbed a vine rope and swung away.

"Would anyone care for more stew or tea?" Shuto asked.

Elayni held out her cup. "I'd like water if you have any?"

"Sure." Shuto took her cup and poured water into it from a water bag. "We catch the rain so we don't have to haul it."

"I know one of your weapons is a slingshot." Brando pointed at a curved leather sheath hanging from Shuto's belt. "Is that another?"

"Yes." Shuto pulled out a weapon as long as half of his arm. "We call it our talon." The hilt took about one-third of its length, and the rest held a curved blade. "I plan for it to wear the invaders' blood. Most of our convocation will be joining the Kayndo in this fight."

"I'm honored." Dayvee shifted forward. The basket chair kept trying to suck him in. "I have an eagle friend, Spiro, who scouts for me. After the attacks on our supplies today, the Kwin are going to patrol, but I need more scouts covering a broader area to give us warning. I can assign your convocation the duty, but if you'd rather not, there are others willing."

"No," Shuto said sharply. "We should be the ones. Eagles are the fiercest birds and can see the furthest."

Many would dispute that statement, but Dayvee let it stand. "Then it shouldn't be difficult to keep me posted on where our enemies are."

"You can count on us, Kayndo."

8

Friends and Enemies

"Be content with the gifts Kun gave you. Jealousy turns friends into enemies." ~ Kwutee

Steven

After warning yet another group of the attack, the pounding in Steven's head had increased. How much longer before he and Clint reached the camp?

It's just ahead, Graydee sent. *Follow me.* As they trailed Graydee off the road into the woods, the sound of fast hoof beats came from behind him. Steven twisted to see Codee and Blake riding toward them.

"What did you find out?" Clint asked when they caught up.

"We tracked the four that escaped until their prints joined a couple of hundred more traveling east," Codee replied.

A chill ran through Steven. If Bigham's men were headed east, too, they'd probably continue to cause problems. A group of Kagards stepped out from the trees.

Blake swung down from his horse. "Chase, do you have sentries all around the camp?"

"Yes, Captain."

Codee glanced at Steven. "You and Clint are to meet Tayro at the tents of White River Pack while I join Dayvee."

As Codee turned his horse and trotted off, Graydee led Steven and Clint through the trees to a big meadow. Steven's jaw dropped at the sight of the tent city that crowded it and even spilled into the woods beyond. Large triangular shaped tents in vibrant colorful shades stood by small rounded earth-toned ones, large gray square ones, and several other types. Every shape and color seemed to be on display. Animals sauntered between them, and groups of people bustled around several campfires. Unfamiliar aromas and spices from the cookfires filled the air and set his mouth to salivating. The sights, sounds, and scents were wondrous, even if they were strange. So much different from the shacks that filled the bottoms and the people who lived there. But could Steven be more out of place? Like a fish trying to fly.

You'll get used to it. Graydee sent. *You belong with us now.*

Reko came up to Steven. "You can turn your horse loose."

Steven and Clint dismounted. The smoke tickled Steven's nose as he followed Graydee around some of the tents. A bear ambled close to them, and Steven jumped aside to give it more room. Graydee didn't even pause. While Steven was still watching the bear, a deer ran in front of him and pulled him up short. Finally, they got to where Gaylo and Tayro spoke with several other Calupi in front of some smaller earth-toned tents. They must be Calupi from White River Pack.

When Tayro and Gaylo saw them, Tayro broke off his conversation to greet Steven. "Are you dizzy?"

"No, I just have a headache."

Tayro poured a little liquid in a cup, then handed it to him. "Drink this."

It looked like muddy water. "What is it?"

"Willow tea."

At least there wasn't more than a swallow. Steven choked on the bitterness, but he managed to get it down.

Gaylo turned to Clint. "Let me see your wound."

Clint rolled up his pant leg revealing the deep cut across his shin.

"It needs stitches." Gaylo pulled out a needle.

Tayro took the cup from Steven. "Your other injuries need to be treated again. Take off your shirt."

Great. Some of the White River Calupi were already eyeing Steven. A group of them were around his age, and there were some pretty girls too. They'd see his scars, and his scrawny chest didn't compare to any of these clanspeople's muscular bodies. But he couldn't tell a king no. Steven pulled off his shirt. Gasps came from some of the watchers. A few were whispering to each other. Heat flooded Steven's cheeks.

Tayro poured a flask of something over Steven's cuts. "Gaylo and Dayvee plan to hold your ceremony within the hour."

Gaylo looked up from washing Clint's gash. "I need to know how to introduce you. Clan masculine names end in E or O, so if you're willing to go by Stevee, it won't scream outsider, but it's up to you."

Steven sucked in his breath as Tayro adjusted the bandages, drawing them tighter around his ribs. "My mother named me Steven, but Father always called me Stevee. I don't mind leaving Steven behind."

"Okay, from now on you're Stevee." Gaylo poked his needle through Clint's flesh.

Clint's teeth clicked as he gnashed them, and his breathing turned huffy, but he didn't cry out. Gaylo finished and knotted the sinew. "Stevee, do you know of a relative or friend of your parents who could speak for them at your adoption?"

Stevee didn't know of any relatives. Clint spoke through his clenched teeth as Gaylo wrapped a bandage around his stitches. "I'll speak for Stevee's father. He was my friend."

Relief filled Stevee. "Thanks."

Tayro pointed to Stevee's shirt. "You can put it back on."

While Stevee laced his shirt shut, Tayro ran his hand over Stevee's head, feeling the new lump. "Is this sore?"

"Not too much as long as no one's touching it."

Tayro snatched his hand back. "Sorry."

Stevee shouldn't be objecting. Adrifts didn't get treated by healers, much less kings. "It's okay. Thanks for treating me."

"You're welcome. Dayvee wants to talk to you about joining our sub-pack, so Graydee will take you to him."

Graydee nuzzled him. *Come on.* The wolf glided away, so Stevee hurried after him. He didn't get far before five young guys with wolves stepped out from behind a tent and blocked his path. Weren't they some of the Calupi that were just at White River's tents? The back of his neck prickled in warning at the looks they gave him. Like cats that spied a mouse.

They aren't supposed to fight outside of the ring, Graydee sent.

Did they always do what they were supposed to? "What do you want?"

One of them stalked closer to Stevee. He took a step back in reflex. A predatory gleam lit the guy's eyes. "Scared of a Calupi?"

"I just don't like people in my space, so I'd prefer if you stayed out of it."

The boy's arm raced toward Stevee. Stevee flinched, but the guy only poked his finger in his chest. "You have as much business guarding the Kayndo as a rabbit. Do you know who I am?"

Just one more person who hated adrifts on sight? Graydee nudged Stevee. *You're not an adrift now but Calupi.*

Didn't seem as if this guy knew that. "No, I don't know you."

"I'm Frudo, son of the alpha of White River, and I've been training all my life. I should be the one joining the Kayndo's sub-pack. You haven't even passed our Calupi tests."

I doubt he could pass the tests you went through, Graydee sent.

Frudo crossed his arms. "Just tell the Kayndo the truth, you don't want in."

"What if that's not the truth?" Stevee asked.

"Some people might feel sorry for you because of your injuries. But if a wolf sees a rabbit hopping around half dead, they devour it." Frudo uncrossed his arms. "You'd just get the Kayndo killed. Tell him, no, or you'll learn how Calupi can act like our wolves." Frudo took a step closer, almost closing the gap between them.

Stevee made himself stand still and not back up. Frudo took another step and rammed his shoulder into Stevee's. It was like a wall hit him. Stevee stumbled to the side.

"One other thing. You're not good enough to talk to Elayni, so don't." Frudo and his friends moved past Stevee and strolled off.

Stevee blew out his breath. Great. He could tell Dayvee no, but Graydee wanted to be with the Kayndo. And there was no way he could ignore someone as beautiful as Elayni. Oh well. If in six years he hadn't done the smart thing, why would he start now? He rubbed his sore shoulder. Next time someone wanted to gawk at his body, he'd have a fresh black bruise to go with the other shades there. He shoved his concern aside. No sense dwelling on it. It would just keep him from finding joy.

Graydee led him out of the camp and into the forest. The waning light of day barely penetrated, and everything lay in heavy shadow. Stevee picked his way carefully through the forest floor with its covering of old leaves. He drew in a deep breath. The pine, oak, and maple scents of the trees combined with a sweet mix of flowers and plants.

So much different from the scent of stale beer he had smelled this morning. Now he was surrounded by beauty, and many of these plants he'd never seen before. He didn't have to look for joy very hard. It bubbled up in him. There was nothing that Frudo could do to him that would make him regret seeing this or having Graydee as his companion. It wasn't anything new for him to be threatened. He'd already been in two fights today, but it still had been the best day of his life, and it wasn't over yet.

Graydee stopped *We're here.*

What? Just forest. Where were the people? And their homes?

Look up.

Stevee did, and a rope dropped from a tree almost on his head. Despite the blinding sun, he spotted something in the tree.

"Climb on up, Stevee," Brando's voice called down.

Apparently, the sub-pack knew about his name change. But Stevee wasn't sure about going up there. He hated small spaces. Would he feel confined? A deep breath helped his nerves. He grabbed the knotted rope to climb.

When Stevee arrived at the platform, he gaped at the strange home in the trees.

"Come on over," Codee called. "You need to eat before your ceremony."

Stevee tested the give in the floor, then bounced his way over to where the others swung in basket chairs near the trunk.

Shuto handed him a bowl of food they'd set aside and waved Stevee to one of the dangling chairs.

"Thank you." Stevee sat in the chair. "I think this place is amazing. I don't feel confined at all. It must be wonderful to live up in the sky with the stars."

Shuto beamed at his compliment. "It's always been my home, and I wouldn't want to live anywhere else."

Stevee took a bite of the food. Amazing. "This is the best thing I've ever eaten."

Shuto laughed. "You should have been chosen by an eagle."

No flying sack of feathers with a beak is better than a wolf with sharp teeth.

Stevee snorted. "I won't share what Graydee says about that."

Elayni giggled. "I can imagine, but you haven't seen our homes or eaten any dish of ours except for trail food."

"That's true, but this is going to be hard to beat." Stevee finished half the bowl before he was too full to eat anymore.

Chayla brought him some clothing. Beads adorned the shirt and pants, and a wolf was painted on the shirt.

"What's this?" he asked.

"It was Geno's spare outfit. Now it's your ceremony clothes." She pointed to the beads on the fringes. "There should be more. We all shared with you, and as soon as we get more, we'll add to it."

Stevee had never worn something so decorative. Gratitude swelled in him. "It's perfect. Thank you."

Shuto stood. "I know you needed to speak to Stevee alone. If you need me, just whistle." Shuto grabbed a rope vine and swung over to another platform in a nearby tree.

Dayvee ran a hand through his hair. "Stevee, you know Gaylo had concerns about you joining my sub-pack until we knew you better. He's talked to the other leaders. They can't order a Kayndo, but they can withdraw their support, which I need now."

Stevee had known his acceptance would be short lived. "I understand. I told you, you'd change your mind."

"But I haven't. We all want you and Graydee. And he'll be happiest with us. It's just that Gaylo wants you to swear a vow that you'll support me and take my orders. And I know you don't want to do that yet. But this is temporary, and if you change your mind or want to join another pack, I'll release you. So are you willing to do that?"

"Mort and Bigham are offering a reward for me, twenty golds for me dead, forty alive. To be near me would be dangerous, and the Kayndo shouldn't be risked."

Brando broke out in laughter. "Varian only offered thirty golds for Dayvee. How come they judged you a bigger threat than the Kayndo?"

"I don't know, but a lot of people in the bottoms will be trying to collect. That's going to put anyone near me at risk."

"I'm in charge of the Kayndo's defense." Brando rested his hand over his weapon pouch. "Those guys in the bottoms don't worry me. I didn't even break a sweat when we fought them."

"For that much gold, it might not just be them."

"I'm glad that you want to protect Dayvee. So if I'm wrong, and we find that you're putting the Kayndo at risk, then we'll ask him to release you. Agreed?"

#

Stevee's stomach churned as he sat in the meadow on hides next to his sub-pack waiting for Gaylo to call him. The crowd pressing so close to them felt confining and made his skin crawl. In front of them was a ring of stones, and it was free of people, except for Gaylo.

"Since there are strangers among us"—Gaylo's eyes pierced Stevee—"I'll explain a little of our history." Gaylo swept his arm up toward the sky. "When ash filled our sky, and our world was ravaged from the wars that had been waged, only a few people remained. Kun was sad they were destroying themselves and the world he gave them. He heard their pleas for help and sent our first Kayndo, JoKayndo. JoKayndo taught them a new way of life to live in harmony. They called this the Vita. And they all vowed to follow it."

The clanspeople chanted, "As our ancestors followed the Vita, so do we."

Gaylo gave them a nod. "Yes, we do. We don't take more than we need. We keep the quotas so there's a healthy balance. We don't own animals or land, only lease. We care for our neighbor by giving hospitality, and we don't manufacture things we don't need to contaminate our souls and world." He flipped his hand toward Stevee. "You can come forward now."

Stevee rose and went into the ring. His heart thudded, as he joined Gaylo, then turned to face the crowd.

"To help safeguard Kun's creation, some people were selected to have a special role, clanspeople. The Botanees were given the duty of caretakers for all plants. The Gollees care for the earth and the stones and gems within it. Those chosen by an animal companion care for their species. They formed the clans. Those who weren't chosen built towns and cities. A worthy king was selected by the companions to ensure they also kept the Vita. And if our world was in peril again, Kun would do one more thing. He'd send a Kayndo, one who had the ability to speak to all of the animals, to help us set our world to rights."

Gaylo put a hand on Stevee's shoulder. "Since Stevee was chosen by Graydee, he is now wolf clan and has the duty to care for our wild wolves, and defend the Vita. Do you vow, Stevee, with your companion's aid, to do this as long as you both live?"

"I do." Thankfully, Stevee's voice came out strong, even though his hands trembled from nerves.

"Since you've agreed to be in the Kayndo's sub-pack temporarily until you find a pack home, will you vow to support him, to obey his orders, to follow our pack law, and to protect those in the sub-pack until he releases you?"

"I will."

"Normally, we'd tattoo your pack mark on your hand now, but yours isn't decided yet. Dayvee wants you and everyone else to know you still belong, so I have agreed to give the Kayndo's sub-pack a mark of your own."

Dayvee rode Ghostee into the ring with the sub-pack around him. They formed a line beside Stevee.

"Hold out your hands." Gaylo went down the line of Calupi, etching a K on each of their hands, then sprinkling something into it that dyed the mark red. He placed it beside the tattoo of the mountain with a wolf paw. None of the Calupi flinched or reacted in any way.

Would Stevee be able to maintain such a nonchalant air when Gaylo did his? Gaylo came to him last. The needle scraped Stevee, and his flesh stung, but it wasn't unbearable. He admired the finished K. The sub-pack willingly inflicted pain on themselves for him. Gratitude filled him.

Dayvee leaned over to slap his back. "Well met." The rest of the sub-pack surrounded Stevee to slap his back, too, then filed out, leaving him in the ring. Their acceptance filled him with warmth, but it wouldn't last. They didn't know the things he'd done.

9

Unexpected Allies

"Different doesn't mean they can't make a good friend." ~ Drako

Logan

The sun was setting as they anchored off the shore. Good, maybe now Logan wouldn't have to see the blood that stained the water anymore. He'd been seeing it all day. Soldiers on the ships still sporadically shot in the water every time they saw so much as a fin. At least Logan didn't have to deal with Garth since he'd gone back to the second ship.

The shoreline looked wild and beautiful. Rugged cliffs with so many trees. Logan had never seen so many trees. He sighed. If Father had his way, this place would look like home all too soon. But what could Logan do to stop it? He hadn't been able to help those whales today. All he was going to do was get himself shot. Once Father set his sights on something, there was no changing it.

Two of the boats listed because Garth hadn't warned them first and they'd taken hits from the whales. But they should keep afloat until morning. If they tried to land now, it would take half the night, and Logan didn't want to face enemies in the dark. Exhaustion clung to him.

He should try to get a little rest, even if he could afford only a light doze. He had to be ready for Garth's next assassin. He stumbled into his cabin and closed the door, then stuck the thin sliver of wood into the notch he'd made for it. The door would open only a crack before hitting it. If anyone pushed beyond that, it would scrape and alert him.

Logan could have barred the door and made it a lot harder, but if an assassin couldn't get in, they'd change tactics and stab him in the back somewhere else. It was easier to defeat them if he knew where they'd attack. So he did his best to welcome them.

He put his loaded pistol under the thin blanket and waited. It didn't take long before he heard the creak. His heart pounded. With his eyes open only to slits, he studied the latest assassin by the light of the candle that flickered. As the man crept closer, Logan took in his dark hair, chiseled face, and the penetrating eyes that seemed as if they'd miss little. Recognition set in. He'd see him before in the ships rigging. He was the crewmember they called Roger.

Logan let him creep a little closer. Could the guy hear Logan's heart thundering? He shot up, displaying his gun. "You so much as blink hard, and I'll kill you. Garth won't care if another of his hired assassins who failed is dead."

Roger froze. "Garth didn't hire me."

"A crewmember's job isn't to sneak in my cabin at night, so if Garth didn't hire you to kill me, who did?"

"No one. This is for me. My real name is Rogee, and I'm Calupi."

Confusion slammed into Logan. "What did I do to deserve death from a clansman I don't even know?"

"Your orders killed everyone in my pack, including my companion. I'm here to serve justice, and if I accomplish that, I don't care if I join them."

Logan couldn't help it. He laughed.

"You would laugh at the death of my pack?"

"No. I'm laughing because it's ironic. You've got the wrong person. My father and a Sargent are responsible. I shot the Sargent that disobeyed me by massacring your people, and if I could get through his guards, I'd kill my father too."

"Like earlier, with the whales and Ursans?"

"Yes. Father wants us to be ruthless. My brother is, but I'm the disappointment. Our soldiers know it. And if I tried to shoot my brother, I'd be dead before I could fire."

"If you were king, what would you change?" Rogee asked.

"Pretty much everything. I certainly wouldn't be annihilating the few clanspeople left on our continent."

"Do you believe in Kun and the Vita?"

"I don't know. I'd like to believe in Kun, but I can't get past how many are suffering and nothing's changing."

"Then we will have to change it," Rogee declared.

"What do you mean?"

"You are not my enemy." Rogee crossed his arms. "We want the same thing."

"Well, I'm glad we got that cleared up, but I really need to sleep a little before the next assassin. If Garth didn't send you, there will probably be another."

"Why does he want you dead?"

"It's a long story. I'm too tired to get into it tonight, but I think both he *and* my father want me dead."

"If they want you dead, I want you alive. You can sleep now." Rogee slid to the floor next to the door. "I'll wait for the next assassin. They won't get beyond me. You have my word."

Was he going to trust him? Mother had said a clansperson's word was never broken, and they were loyal. If Logan was wrong, he wouldn't wake up. But he had to have sleep. He let his eyes close.

#

Codee

Codee would have a son again. Warmth filled his heart, and his gratitude swelled as he joined Stevee in the ring. *Thank you, Kun, for bringing Stevee into my life.*

Gaylo turned back to the crowd. "Codee has asked to adopt Stevee. His parents are dead, but a friend of Stevee's father, Clint, will speak for them." He flicked his hand at Clint.

Clint nodded. "I believe Stevee's father would be happy that Codee is adopting him."

"No, he wouldn't," a voice called out.

There were so many people, Codee couldn't be sure where it came from. Why would anyone say it? Some clanspeople might be jealous of Stevee being with the Kayndo, but would they sabotage his adoption just for spite?

"Whoever spoke, come forward," Gaylo ordered.

Some Kwin pushed their way through the crowd to the ring. When they got closer, Codee recognized the black sleek hair and hawk-like gaze of Nolte, the Black River's herd leader. Could this be about the weapons Stevee had?

"Why do you claim to know what Stevee's father wanted?" Gaylo asked.

Nolte stared at Stevee. "Because, before his death, Renolee sent me a letter telling me what he wanted for his son."

Exclamations and muttering broke out among the watchers.

Codee's jaw was agape. He shut it. "Is Renolee your father, Stevee?"

"Father went by Ren, but I heard Mother call him Renolee once when she was angry." Stevee's face scrunched. "But I don't understand why everyone seems to know him?"

"Renolee was Kwin, a legend among all the clans and my best friend," Nolte said.

Stevee shook his head. "Father never said anything about being Kwin."

"His companion's death ripped him apart, so he probably didn't want to revisit those memories," Nolte explained. "But one look was enough for me to know. Except for your eyes, you look exactly like him."

The memories flooded Codee of seeing Renolee compete at the clan meeting. When Stevee's cheeks filled out, his face would match Renolee's. Why hadn't he seen it?

Nolte took out a couple of hide scraps. He held one up and waved it. "This is his message to me." He held up the other. "This one's my reply that Drako couldn't deliver when Renolee died, and we couldn't locate you." He dropped his arms to his side. "The neighbor said you went to the clan meeting, but you never came, and we searched everywhere."

"Father told me to go to the clan meeting and ask to be adopted if no one came for me, but Blake wouldn't let me out the gate."

Nolte's piercing gaze locked onto Codee. "Stevee has a father. I adopted Stevee as soon as Renolee asked."

What? Codee's spirits plummeted. How could this happen to him again? Just like before, when he'd known the irreplaceable joy of having a son for a few minutes. Then lost him. Not again. No. This time, he'd fight for his son. Not with fists but with words. He'd always been good with words. *Please, Kun, let it be enough.*

"You know a Calupi father could help a Calupi more," Codee asserted.

Gaylo laid one arm on Codee's shoulder. "I think we should hold off on the adoption for now. We can discuss all of this privately."

Codee sucked in a breath. No sense arguing with a keeper. He had to convince Nolte. "Agreed."

Gaylo turned to the crowd. "The ceremony's over for tonight."

"Stevee," called out Folee, Red Butte's alpha. "Are you as good as Renolee with weapons?"

Stevee shook his head. "No, I'm not nearly as good."

"Don't be so modest." Clint smiled at him. "Even though Stevee was only ten when Ren died, he still taught him a lot. With more practice, Stevee will match his father's skill with several weapons. But there's one weapon Stevee would beat Ren with, and that's his slingshot."

More excited mumbling came from the crowd. "Would you be willing to show us?" Folee asked. "We could hold a little competition now."

Stevee backed a step. "It's too dark, and I haven't had any weapons to practice with for months. If you're expecting me to match Father, you'd just be disappointed."

"We can light up targets at night," Folee said. "I think everyone would like to see what Renolee taught you, regardless. We might be able to pick up some pointers."

"Show us," several clanspeople shouted.

Ghostee trumpeted from where Dayvee sat on him, watching. Dayvee raised his hand, and everyone quieted. "Practicing weapons before the battle is a good idea. If we leave early tomorrow, I'll camp before sunset, and we'll hold a competition. Stevee can join us if he wants."

Pride in Dayvee welled up in Codee. That was a good decision. It should make certain everyone did their best to keep up. No one would want to miss the competition.

"Will you compete, Stevee?" Folee asked.

Why did Folee keep pushing Stevee? Cackles. A Calupi who won weapons' competitions would raise a pack's rank. "I know what you want, Folee." Codee gave him an intimidating scowl. "If Stevee's good, you want to lure him away from Dayvee's sub-pack."

"I can't deny it. I need Calupi skilled with weapons, and Gaylo said Stevee's sub-pack assignment is temporary. Well, I'm offering a permanent home."

"I'll offer Stevee a pack home," Plevo called out. "Blue Marsh is higher ranked than Red Butte."

Then several more alpha leaders bellowed, "I'll offer."

Codee blew out a heavy breath. "You know Leeto will want him too. You're just trying to beat him to it."

"True." Folee gave Stevee a smile. "But I'm not as demanding as Leeto, and I'll be more forgiving to someone who needs to learn our ways. So what do you say, Stevee? Will you make Red Butte your home?"

"Stevee already has a home." Nolte shot Folee a glare. "Kwin aren't like other clans, so Stevee will have a home with us for as long as he wants. And he can still fulfill a Calupi's duty, just like our wives from other clans fulfill theirs. He can monitor the wolves in our territory."

Stevee's not ready to commit to anyone, Wilee sent. *He's asking how he can reject these offers without upsetting anyone?*

Relief surged up in Codee. *Tell him my advice is to say he needs to know them better before he makes a decision.*

"Thank you for your offers," Stevee declared. "But Graydee and I need time to get to know you before we decide on a home."

Codee, Clint, Graydee, and Stevee moved toward the ring opening where Dayvee waited on Ghostee with Nolte and a few other Kwin.

Stevee reached into his rucksack and pulled out the bola and cumback stick. He held them out to Nolte. He choked out, "Dayvee said I have to give these to you."

Nolte took them and turned them to see the weapons inscriptions. "These are Renolee's. Did he give them to you?"

Stevee nodded. "He told me to take all of his weapons and use them well. Bigham said they weren't allowed at the adriftage. I had to hand them over, but they'd be returned. They weren't. I think Bigham sold them. These two were all I recovered."

Nolte handed them back. "Then keep them like Renolee wanted and use them well."

Mist softened Stevee's amber eyes. "Thank you. I will." He wrapped the bola around his waist and slid the cumback stick in his belt.

Nolte held out two rolled scraps of hide to Codee. "These tell what Renolee wanted, and my response." He flicked his hand toward Dayvee and the sub-pack. "They've read them, but you and Stevee should."

Codee took them and unrolled the first to read the scrawled words.

Nolte,

I know I haven't been a friend to you in a long time, so I have no right to ask a favor, but my wife is dead, and I'll join her soon. There is no one I'd rather have finish raising my son, Stevee, than you. So if you can find it in your heart to adopt him, it would be a huge relief for me to know he'll be with you.

Renolee.

Codee handed it to Stevee to read.

"It's Father's handwriting," Stevee confirmed.

Codee hadn't doubted that. He unrolled the second scrap of hide.

My dearest friend, Renolee.

I had always hoped you'd come home before either of us saw Kun. To know differently brings me great sorrow. But the news you have a son has been a comfort. Of course, my answer is yes. Our home will be his, and he will not only be your son but mine. I wish we'd have known about Stevee earlier so he could have spent time with us, but I understand why you didn't bring him.

Our clan and herd agreed to my adoption of Stevee. It is done. The herd is as excited about having him come home as I am. I promise you my new son will be loved and cared for the same as my other children. I'm happy they will share the bonds of love we did. As soon as I return, I'll be heading to Harthome to collect him. I should be there within the week. I hope I'll be in time to see you.

Rest easy my friend. Once a Kwin, always a Kwin. So you should know, in this world and the next, my love and that of our herd will always go with you.

Nolte

Codee handed the note to Stevee, who read it over, then handed it back to Nolte.

Nolte put the hide scraps back in his rucksack. "I wish we'd known Renolee had shortened his name to Ren. We asked at the adriftage and around Harthome if anyone had seen Renolee's son, Stevee. They said they hadn't."

"Bigham wouldn't have admitted it, even if he knew." Stevee shuffled his feet. "He wouldn't have wanted me to leave and inform anyone what happened there."

"I want to know more about that. We have a lot of catching up to do, and you should meet your siblings." Nolte smiled. "Let's go home to our tent."

Dayvee cleared his throat. "Aren't you forgetting Stevee just swore vows, and he's in my sub-pack, Nolte?"

Nolte crossed his arms. "Gaylo said his assignment was temporary. Now that you know he's my son, won't you release him?"

"That will depend on Stevee. Do you want to make your home with the Kwin?" Dayvee asked.

"I don't know anyone well enough to decide on a home. Father trusted Nolte, but Graydee feels really sad at even the thought of separation from his pack, and I don't want him miserable."

"Then no, I won't release Stevee's vow. Renolee loved his

companion so much he couldn't bear to be with your herd after his death. Don't you think he'd agree Stevee's home should be where his companion is happy?"

"I think Renolee would want Stevee happy too. So I'd ask the Kayndo to at least allow Stevee and his wolf companion to spend time learning about Renolee and us before they make any more decisions.

"I'm willing to share him some." Dayvee yawned. "It's late and time to seek our bedrolls. But Stevee can ride with you in the mornings as long as Codee does, too, and they both return to us at noon."

Nolte nodded. "Agreed."

At least Codee would be going too. But could he convince Nolte to allow Stevee to embrace his Calupi life now?

10

Not Alone

"The loneliest place is surrounded by people that don't understand you." ~ Stevee

Stevee

Stevee wiped his sleeve across his eyes.

"Why are you crying, kid?" Caspian asked.

"I miss Father."

"I miss my parents and my brother too. I used to wish I was with them when our fishing boat capsized. But Father always said Kun has a purpose for each of us. Our purpose must be at the adriftage."

"I don't want to be here. I'm tired of being hungry and called names."

"What names?"

"They say no one wants adrifts. We're worthless."

"That's not true."

"It isn't?"

"No. If I didn't come back tomorrow, would you miss me?"

"Yes."

"I'd miss you, too. So see, adrifts care about adrifts. We can be proud of being adrift or ashamed. Which would you rather?"

"Proud. But what can we be proud of?"

"Surviving and helping other adrifts survive. We'll have more to be proud of too. We'll make our own sign language, our own rules, for adrifts only. Next time someone calls you worthless, just say to yourself I don't care what they think. They don't know us. They're not adrifts."

"Okay, I'll try to remember."

"I'll remind you if you forget. Now, the first rule we'll have is that adrifts can't cry in front of other adrifts or anyone like Bigham who'd enjoy seeing our pain."

Stevee choked back his tears. "All right, Caspian, I won't cry *anymore."*

"I have to go now."

Someone was shaking him. Must be Bigham. He needed to escape. Stevee jumped to his feet and ran. Somebody tackled him. He thrashed against them. He must get away.

"Stop. Stevee, wake up."

You're safe, Graydee sent.

Awareness flooded back. He had a wolf companion now. That conversation with Caspian happened years ago. So why did Codee have him pinned? Panic surged up inside him from being confined. "What are you doing?"

"I was trying to keep you from running off the platform." Codee got off him. "You were screaming, and when I tried to wake you, you ran."

"Oh." Stevee sat up. The sub-pack lay in bedrolls on the platform floor since they didn't want to sleep in the Accipi's baskets. They were staring at him. Heat erupted in his cheeks as if they were on fire. "I'm sorry for waking you."

"It's all right." Dayvee's head plopped back down. "Go back to sleep. We have an early morning."

Stevee laid on his bedroll. The top of it was soaked with tears. So were his cheeks. Some dream. His heart ached anew for Caspian as if he'd died yesterday. Even surrounded by Calupi, he felt so alone. He missed all the adrifts....

Stevee wheezed in the stuffy air. Complete darkness met his gaze. His throat felt dry as if he'd been chewing on bark, and his lips were chapped. So thirsty. A cramp traveled up his legs, but he couldn't feel his feet. Another evening stuffed into the box. He hated the box and the confinement of it. He squirmed, trying to get his circulation moving. Needles of pain pricked his feet as they woke up.

"Steven, I have something for you." Bigham's deep voice sent warning tingles surging up his spine. The slot in the top of the box slid back. Stevee gulped at the fresh air. Some slimy things fell on him, then slithered against his skin. His heart raced. He wanted them off, but his

hands were tied. Bigham closed the slot.

How long before Tanner would come? He thrashed as much as he could, trying to dislodge what burrowed into his skin.

"Steven, are you there?" Tanner whispered.

"Yes. Hurry," he whispered back. Tanner opened the door. "Get them off me."

"Stevee, wake up," Codee said sharply. It took only a fraction of a second this time before Stevee recognized his surroundings. His heart still raced. Sweat dampened his clothes. No way could he sleep now. Everyone in the sub-pack was staring at him again. Oh no. He rose. "I'm really sorry. Go back to sleep. I won't bother you anymore."

Stevee went to the edge of the platform and swung his legs over the side. The gaps in the canopy showed him the stars. A breathtaking view. He filled his lungs with the forest scents. The crisp night air felt good and dried his sweat. Frogs croaked somewhere nearby. Crickets chirped.

"Not going to jump are you?" Elayni whispered.

Stevee startled.

She sat next to him. "You were yelling Caspian's name. Want to talk about it?"

Stevee shrugged and whispered back, "If I'm awake I try not to think about it, but I can't keep them out of my dreams."

"You need to talk about the stuff that's bothering you."

Sheez. She wasn't going to take no for an answer. What if Stevee told her one thing? That might keep her from ever asking again. "I fell asleep and left Caspian in the box. When I opened it, he... he was wheezing. His stomach stuck out as if he were fat, but no adrift is fat. He made me promise some things. Then he just... stopped breathing. I should have forced air into him. But I heard Bigham stomping around, and all I could think about was not getting caught. I tied Caspian again and put him back in the box." Stevee choked out, "Caspian did a lot for me, and how did I repay him? I killed him."

"You didn't kill him, Bigham did. Why aren't you angry at him?"

"Adrifts don't get to be angry. Anger makes us do stupid things, and it steals our joy. I won't give Bigham that satisfaction. And there're lots of Bighams for adrifts. To survive, we have to be smarter than them."

"Another lesson from Caspian?"

"Yes. He was the wisest person I know. Bigham wouldn't even let us hold a funeral or mention Caspian's name after he died, so his story is forgotten, just like all the others that died."

"They're not forgotten if you remember them."

"But that's in my dreams mostly. You should go back to sleep. After tonight, I'll spread my bedroll away from everyone so no one loses rest over my nightmares."

"Then I'll move my bedroll by yours, and so will everyone else. You aren't the first one to have nightmares. We can't protect you from them, but we can be there for you when you have them."

"You don't understand. Mine are several times a night. No one would rest, and I can't be responsible for that."

"What about your rest?" she asked.

"I haven't needed much since I killed my best friend by sleeping."

"I told you…"

"I know what you said, but I was second. I'll never forgive myself for not doing what I was supposed to, so you can't."

"Calupi believe a burden is lighter if shared." Dayvee crawled over to him and put a hand on his shoulder. Then Brando and Chayla came over to rest a hand on his back.

Had they all heard?

Tayro came and squeezed his other shoulder. "Caspian must have been bleeding inside for his belly to be extended like that. There wasn't anything anyone could have done for him."

"I still should have been there for him."

"We might not be able to convince you to forgive yourself," Dayvee said. "But we'll share your burden."

Codee ruffled the hair on his head. "You're not alone."

No, you're not. Graydee sent.

"And you shouldn't worry about us sleeping." Dayvee shot Codee a smirk. "Leeto and Codee made sure we could function with or without it."

"Yeah, we're good at grabbing a nap if we need it." Brando chuckled. "I even took one in a rattlesnake nest once."

"But you need to get some sleep, Stevee." Elayni grabbed his hand and stood, giving it a tug. "Will you try?"

"Yes." Stevee rose and let her pull him back to their bedrolls where he laid down with the sub-pack around him.

...

Stevee wasn't able to sleep. And he didn't want to wake the others again, so he left.

The night sky had a touch of gray to announce the coming morning, so very little light peeked through the canopy of the forest. Heavy shadows of trees and brush lay all around him. Long ago he quit fearing the darkness of night and learned to welcome it as a thief's friend. Just how many times had he used its cover to steal food at the adriftage? Still, this uneven terrain made it difficult to avoid stumbling.

Stevee chose his way carefully, scanning for any sign of animals. Frudo claimed Stevee wasn't a capable Calupi since he hadn't passed their tests. He knew one of them was a hunting test. It couldn't be that difficult to hunt. He knew how to use weapons.

What would happen when Dayvee and his sub-pack woke and discovered Stevee gone? After the trouble Stevee caused them, they'd probably feel relieved. If he figured out how to hunt, he could provide for himself and Graydee too. . .if the wolf decided to come.

I will always come after you. You can't get rid of me. Graydee must've been within mind distance.

A crack of a stick alerted Stevee. He froze. Shadows picked their way through the trees. Could it be Bigham or some of his men coming to kill him? Maybe he'd been stupid to go off alone.

He grabbed his slingshot and readied a stone. Antlers. Several deer moved through the forest. He waited breathlessly until they drew closer. He chose his target. A young doe. Then let his rock fly. The other deer went crashing away as the doe fell, dazed from the stone.

Stevee ran to her and cut her throat with his tooth.

Thank you, Kun, for helping me succeed, and thanks, deer, for giving your life to sustain me.

Something crashed into Stevee's shoulders from behind, knocking him forward. Pain like fire stabbed them. He rolled and stared at the open jaws of a mountain lion.

#

Codee

Codee drifted from sleep to consciousness. He opened his eyes. Still dark, just a touch of gray in the sky. But the lamp hanging from the branch cast a little light. The bedroll next to his was empty. "Where's Stevee?"

All the sub-pack's eyes opened. Dayvee rubbed his temple. Must be several animals speaking to Dayvee at the same time and hurting his head again. "Graydee's below. He said Stevee wanted to figure out how to hunt."

Codee pulled on his clothes. "Alone?"

"Stevee asked Graydee to stay here since none of us took a companion when we did our hunting tests."

Codee stood. "To hunt alone is dangerous, especially if you haven't done it before." He grabbed his weapon pouches and put them on his belt. "Stevee knows we need to leave early. Is he trying to prove himself to Gaylo?"

Elayni shook her head. "Stevee's not concerned about Gaylo. There must be another reason."

"I think I understand it." Brando sat up.

Codee picked up his rucksack and turned back to Brando. If anyone could figure out Stevee's motivations, it would be Brando. He was really perceptive.

Brando slid his clothes on. "If people called us worthless for years, and then suddenly some people said they wanted us, would we believe it?"

"I don't think I'd trust it," Chayla answered.

Brando gave her a short nod. "Right. Stevee doesn't. And he

thinks we'll be concerned about losing sleep. He's giving us the opportunity to change our minds."

Dayvee ran a hand through his hair. "Like when you ran away, and I went in the Nowhere tunnel."

"Exactly," Brando said. "He's testing us."

"I'm going after him." Codee slid his rucksack on.

"Shouldn't we all go?" Chayla asked.

Codee walked to the edge of the platform. "You have other things to do. I'll bring him back."

Brando pulled his boots on. "I'll go. You don't know how it feels when people consider you worthless."

Hadn't he considered himself that? Codee grabbed one of the ropes hanging from the tree. "I can relate, and it's my place to go."

Dayvee gave him a nod. "Go ahead, but if you can't convince him, call, and we'll all come."

Codee jumped off the platform to slide down the rope to the ground below. Wilee nosed him, and the other companions came to press against him. Codee asked, *Will you help me track Stevee?*

A whimper came from Graydee, and he streaked into the woods. The other wolves raced after him.

Wilee sent, *A mountain lion jumped on Stevee.*

Codee's heart went to his throat as he ran after Wilee.

#

Stevee

The mountain lion's teeth lunged toward Stevee's neck. He threw his arms up to protect himself and by accident hit the lion in the nose. The cat shook its head and screamed. Then lunged again, breaking through his arms. The lion's teeth would rip open his jugular to kill him. He closed his eyes. Hot breath moistened his neck. Why didn't it bite already? He opened his eyes to see the cat's jaws withdrawing.

Graydee's voice filled his mind, *Dayvee asked the mountain lion to stop and told it to take the deer in exchange for your life.*

The lion grabbed the deer's leg in its mouth and dragged it away.

As Stevee sat up, he heard more crashing. Stevee jumped to his feet, reaching for his slingshot. *I'm here,* Graydee sent. Then Graydee leaped on him, sending him falling back down. Graydee's nose pressed through the tears in Stevee's shirt to sniff the scratches on his shoulders.

I'm glad to see you too. The other wolves came and joined Graydee in nosing him.

"Are you all right, Stevee?" That was Codee's voice.

"Yes," Stevee replied.

Codee ran out from the trees but stopped short before he reached them. Was he angry at Stevee? "Wilee says the lion scratched you?" His voice sounded strained.

"It's nothing." Stevee was just lucky Dayvee had intervened.

"You should get up and come over here," Codee ordered.

Codee didn't sound happy with Stevee. He was in no hurry to go closer. "Why?"

"I wish you trusted me enough to follow my orders. That patch of three-leafed plants all around you is poison ivy."

Stevee's gaze shot to the vines he laid in. "Yikes." He scrambled up and jumped clear of them.

Codee chuckled. "Now that's more like it. Take your water bag and soap and wash any skin that came into contact with them. Then change into your other outfit."

Stevee poured some water on his arms. "The wolves were in it too."

"Their fur usually protects them, but Wilee says they'll wash off when they're near the creek again. Remember that plant and what it looks like. This one too." Codee pointed to a plant with a hollow stem and pale green serrated leaves that were paired together.

Stevee soaped up, then rinsed. "Is that also poisonous?"

"No, that's Jewel Weed. It usually grows around poison ivy, and it's the remedy for it." Codee picked one. "These nodes between the leaves have oils that will calm a reaction." He handed it to him "You should apply some."

Stevee took the plant and broke the nodes open to rub the oil on himself. "I told Graydee I wouldn't make a good Calupi. I'm only skilled at stealing, and that's wrong." Codee might as well accept it. Stevee had. "I'm trouble you don't need."

"You're not trouble."

Stevee changed into his other outfit. "I didn't think you'd understand."

"I *do* understand. When my first life-mate died giving birth to my son, I was feeling worthless because I couldn't save her. I lost my son, too, so all the joy in my world had been extinguished." Codee let out a heavy breath. "I left and tried to make it easy for the predators to kill me, but Wilee wouldn't let them. After a few weeks, my life-mate came to me in a dream and told me to go back. So I did and focused on helping Leeto, Milay, and Dayvee. For years, I just existed." Codee smiled, and his eyes twinkled. "Then I met Jolay, and joy came back. And then you came, and I was given another chance at a son. You brought happiness, not trouble, and I don't want to lose it again."

Clint had also said he didn't want to lose Stevee. That lasted only until Stevee failed to live up to his expectations. "I don't think I can be what you need me to be."

"Just be yourself. All I want is to see you happy. That's enough. If you choose to be with Nolte or another pack, I'll accept that, but I won't accept you alone and miserable. I know what that's like. So if you go down that path, I'm going to come after you."

He's speaking the truth, Graydee sent.

Today's truth. Would it be tomorrow's?

Codee waved toward camp. "Nolte wants you to ride with him. So are you ready to go back?"

Hmmm. Did Stevee really want to? The longer he stayed, the more it was going to hurt if they rejected him. Maybe they wouldn't. Codee had come after him, Clint didn't. But Stevee had made Clint a lot angrier. Could Stevee keep the sub-pack from getting angry at him? Probably not. They weren't adrifts. But Graydee wanted a pack. Wasn't it worth trying?

11

Powerless

"Not being able to change what we believe is wrong is a difficult thing to accept." ~ Codee

Logan

The sun rose over the horizon and lit the ocean around Logan. He checked the other ships. They had come up to position themselves across the bay in one long unbroken line on both sides of him. Soldiers lined their decks. They were ready. He turned his spyglass to scan the shoreline. A movement up on the cliffs drew his attention. Clanspeople? If they attacked while they were landing, they'd have the high ground, and his soldiers would be terribly exposed on the shores. He could use the cannons first.

Logan swiveled so the spyglass scanned farther down the cliff line. What was that? Some kind of huts or something, and below them a dark jagged line pocked the cliff. A cave. A kid's face poked out from it. Oh no. Did they think a cave would keep their kids safe? He couldn't pummel those cliffs with kids inside.

An explosion rocked his feet. He stumbled, and the spyglass slipped from his hand. He caught it before it hit the deck. Smoke belched from one of the cannons. The soldiers on deck were loading the others. "What are you doing?" he screamed.

One of them pointed to the ship beside theirs. "The cannon flag."

His brother's ship was flying it. More explosions rocked the ocean and his ship as cannon bursts sounded from the ships all around them.

"Raise the flag to stop the cannons."

The soldiers looked at him like he was crazy. "It won't stop as long as Prince Garth flies his," the Sargent said.

"I'm in charge. Not my brother."

"We all know what King Nolan expects. We're not willing to lose our heads because you're too weak to do it."

"There're kids over there," Logan screeched.

The Sargent snorted. "We didn't win all the territory we have by stopping an invasion every time a kid was in the wrong place at the wrong time. You'll see a lot more of that, Prince Logan, so you should prepare yourself."

Logan pulled his gun. "What if I just shoot you?"

"Then the men will signal Prince Garth, and he'll probably shoot you. Now were going to do our job. If you can't take it, go below."

Rogee's anguished eyes beseeched him to stop them. But Logan was powerless. He couldn't do anything. No one would listen. The clanspeople here were going to be slaughtered just like Rogee's own clan had been.

Logan should go below, but he couldn't. Putting his spyglass up, he watched as cannonballs smashed into the cliffs. Rocks collapsed the mouth of the cave the kids had sheltered in. *Please, let there be another exit.* Broken bodies fell from the cliffs to the beach below. He didn't have the courage to focus on them to see if any were children.

The cannons finally fell silent. Garth changed the flag, and the dinghies were lowered over the side. Men slid down ropes to fill them. Logan would like to have at least one person with him he could trust. Could he trust Rogee after what just happened? He better not forget and call him by his clan name, or the soldiers would kill one more clansman. "Roger, come with me." The clansman followed Logan as he ducked under the rail and took hold of the rope.

"Prince Logan, you could stay with the ships," the Sargent said.

"I'm going." Logan slid down the rope to the waiting boat.

#

Stevee

"Nolte's two sons and his daughter are with him," Codee whispered to Stevee as they approached the Kwin. The first rays of the sunrise lit the horizon, and with the Kwin sitting behind the fire, Stevee could distinguish his new siblings easily. All three were tall and lean, with sculptured bodies, sleek black hair, and brown eyes that pierced like a hawks, just like Nolte's. Their faces held the high cheekbones so common among clanspeople, but the sons' features were rugged while the daughter's were more refined and gave her an exotic air.

Stevee guessed Nolte to be in his early forties like Father would be if he still lived. His commanding presence screamed leader. When Nolte moved to greet them, he reached for Stevee.

Stevee's reflexes took over. His arms moved up to block his face as he jerked back from Nolte.

Nolte's eyes widened. "Have you never been hugged?"

When adults at the adriftage grabbed you, it wasn't to hug. Stevee's cheeks heated. "Yes, but I wasn't expecting it."

"You thought I was going to hit you?"

Stevee lowered his gaze. "It's just a reflex."

"Look at me, Son," Nolte commanded. Stevee raised his head. Nolte's eyes were soft. "I will never hit you. Clanspeople often hug loved ones, but I won't do that until you're comfortable with it. Would our clan arm shake bother you?"

"I can manage that." Stevee reached out his arm and Nolte took it, clasping his forearm.

"These are your brothers." Nolte waved at the tallest. "This is Juvee. At twenty-three years of age, he's my oldest."

Juvee clasped Stevee's arm. "Welcome to the family, brother." Stevee squeezed his arm back.

Then Nolte pointed to his other son. "This is Denee, who is eighteen."

"Welcome, little brother." Denee chuckled and bumped shoulders with his sister. "Lulay is seventeen and happy to give up the title of baby of the family to you."

The beautiful Kwin girl gave him a smile. "Welcome, but I don't think we should call you baby. Maybe Little Kwin?"

Juvee's teeth flashed as he grinned. "I think Lil Kwin is a good name, much better than adrift. Wouldn't you say, Stevee?"

Not really. But they didn't know anything about adrifts. Nor did they need to name him little for him to realize all these Kwin were twice as broad as him, and much taller too. But he'd learned a long time ago the names people called him weren't worth worrying about. He just shrugged.

"Would you care for some breakfast?" Nolte asked.

"We have trail food," Codee said. "Don't we have to get going?"

"No. White Cliff herd is riding circuit around the first half of the line. We have the second, so we don't need to go yet." Nolte waved at a ground hide. "So sit with us and eat some cakes."

Stevee sat down with Codee, and Nolte handed them a flat bread in a round shape. Lulay brought them some tea.

Stevee took a bite of the cake. Sweet and nutty. "This is delicious."

Codee chortled. "You say that about everything."

After making a meal from someone else's discarded apple core, seeds and all, how could Stevee not appreciate this food? "To me it is."

Codee took a bite. "It is good. What's in it?"

"Raspberries, chinkapin nuts, and honey," Lulay answered.

"Mmm." Stevee finished his last bite.

"Have another." Nolte held a cake out. "You need to eat more."

Stevee shook his head, no. "I'd get sick." He brushed the crumbs from his clothes. "Tayro says I have to eat small meals often until my stomach grows."

Nolte's face clouded. "I need to know about the abuse you suffered. Does it bother you to talk about it?"

A shiver ran up his spine. Why did they need to discuss that? "Yes."

"Then we won't talk about it. Will you take off your shirt so we can see your injuries?"

Stevee didn't really want to display his shame. "Can I just show you and not everyone else?"

"No," Nolte said. "We all need to see so we can pass judgment. The Kwin teach those that hurt us what that hurt felt like so they can learn empathy and feel remorse. We don't bring more suffering to them than what they inflicted on us because then it is vengeance, not judgment."

"Nolte, we already passed judgment," Codee said.

"That doesn't change our right to." Nolte tugged at the neck of his own shirt and locked eyes with Stevee.

Stevee undid his shirt ties and drew it off. Nolte's eyes darkened as he stared at Stevee's chest. His siblings looked at him with expressions of pity. He didn't want that. "Have you seen enough, or do you need to gawk more?" Even to his own ears, that sounded harsh.

Nolte waved his hand. "You can put your shirt back on."

Codee handed his shirt to Stevee. "Nolte is not your enemy."

"Stevee has a right to be angry at me." Nolte frowned. "Renolee trusted me with his care, and I failed him."

Stevee slipped his shirt on and drew the ties tight. Codee was right, Nolte had been nothing but nice to him. "It wasn't your fault. I'm sorry about what I said."

"I should have sent Kwin as soon as I received Renolee's letter. Instead, I waited and came myself because I wanted to see my best friend before he died." Nolte put down the cup of tea. "I won't blame you if you choose not to forgive that error."

"Before he died, my best friend, Caspian, told me to look only forward since I can't change the past. There's nothing to forgive."

Reko came up with horses including the one Stevee rode yesterday, Shado. He was an older horse but steady.

"Reko, do you want to ride patrol with us since Grassy Knoll Herd isn't here yet?" Nolte asked.

Reko smiled. "Thanks. I'd like that."

Nolte crossed his arms. "Is that the horse you chose for Stevee?"

Reko's smile fell. "I assigned him Shado because he'd never ridden before."

"You couldn't tell he was Kwin?" Nolte asked.

Reko hung his head. "The signs were there, but since he was from Harthome, I ignored them."

"What signs?" Stevee finished his last drink of the sweet tea.

Nolte uncrossed his arms. "Most Kwin are born knowing how to ride a horse like a duck knows how to swim."

"We don't know if the gift is inherited or how it happens," Denee explained. "There are a few other people that riding comes naturally to but not many."

"Since you have the gift, you should be riding your horse." Nolte whistled, and a horse trumpeted. "All Kwin children receive a lease horse to care for and train, which is then theirs to use. When I adopted you, I selected the best for my son." A beautiful black stallion came through the meadow and pranced up to them. The sculptured head tossed, his hoof pawed the ground.

Nolte went over to the horse and stroked his neck. "Smokee has gone everywhere with me, but I have never allowed another to train or ride him. He has been a symbol of hope that you'd return to us. So come, greet your horse."

Stevee jumped up and went to them. Smokee nudged Stevee's chest with his muzzle. The horse's warm breath steamed through Stevee's shirt and moistened his skin.

"He knows his wait is over," Nolte said.

Stevee ran his hand over the warm neck, letting the long mane fall over his arm. "You are a beauty, Smokee." The stallion pressed into Stevee's touch as if he wanted it.

Graydee nudged Stevee. *Wolves are better than horses.*

Stevee touched Graydee's head with his other hand. *Does it bother you that I like Smokee?*

I don't mind if you appreciate all of Kun's creations. I do.

That didn't sound right. Graydee was a predator.

Yes, the weak need to die so the strong can survive. Wolves are strong, but I appreciate Kun's other creations. Only, He did create wolves best.

Stevee couldn't help the mirth that bubbled up in him.

Graydee's proud head lifted, and his throat rumbled with a small growl. *This is serious.*

I'm sorry, Stevee sent back. *So how are wolves best?*

For one thing, we have teeth.

Horses have teeth.

Not like us. They're flat. Not much good. If enemies are after them, they have to flee. If wolves and horses fight, wolves win. Now do you understand?

Yes, you are the best. I'd never want to replace you. Stevee touched the wolf's head again. *If the other wolves are as fierce and loyal as you, then I believe they are better too.*

Good, then I don't mind sharing you with Smokee.

"What do I do to train Smokee?" Stevee asked Nolte.

Nolte smiled. "You'll figure it out together."

Stevee wasn't sure about that. "What if I do something wrong?"

"The only thing wrong is to hurt him." Denee came over to them. "You should get on and start getting used to each other."

"You're rushing this," Codee said. "Just let him ride Shado."

Nolte shook his head, no. "The worst that could happen is he'll fall off or Smokee will go the wrong way. If that happens, he'll get back on or figure out how to turn Smokee and find his way back."

"But if he falls, he could be harmed more. His ribs are already cracked."

"I doubt he'll fall, he's Kwin. Stevee, do you want to ride Smokee?" Nolte asked.

Stevee really did. The horse was gorgeous, and he could imagine himself on it. "Yes."

Graydee sent, *That horse better not harm you, and I'm going with you.*

I'll be okay, Stevee sent, then he asked Nolte, "Should I put a hide on his back or reins on him?"

"That depends. Do you think you need them?" Denee asked.

None of the Kwin he'd seen yesterday used them.

"I think if Smokee hasn't had a hide on, he might not like it. So I should skip that, but I'll probably need reins to guide him."

"Okay." Denee held out a nose piece with reins. "See if you can get him to wear it."

Stevee took the nose piece and ran it down Smokee's neck. "What do you think, Smokee? Will you mind wearing this?" The stallion's legs trembled. He nudged the headpiece and snorted. Then stuck his nose into it. That was easy.

Denee put his hands together. "Okay, Lil Kwin, put your foot in my hands, and I'll give you a boost up."

Stevee did, and Denee hefted him onto Smokee's back. Smokee tossed his head and pawed the ground. Stevee clucked. Nothing happened. He leaned forward. "Come on, Smokee."

Smokee leapt into a canter. Graydee loped beside them with his tongue lolling.

Having trouble keeping up? Stevee sent.

No.

When Stevee straightened, Smokee transitioned to a trot. Riding Smokee was like soaring through the air. His feet barely seemed to touch the ground. His gait was so smooth that Stevee's seat didn't even rock. Smokee and Graydee maneuvered around the tents and people in the way without even breaking stride.

Stevee laughed at the thrill of it. He twisted to glance back, and with that, Smokee turned. With another twist, Smokee accommodated and turned again. When he shifted his weight back, Smokee walked. He didn't need reins. Smokee knew what he wanted. When they got back to Nolte, Stevee brought Smokee to a stop. He couldn't stop grinning. "Thank you, Nolte, for choosing him for me. It is a joy to ride him since he floats on air."

"I've been rewarded by seeing that same joy-filled smile of Renolee's. But I'm not Nolte to you, I'm Father."

It seemed disloyal, but hadn't his father chosen Nolte? "All right, Father."

"You can get down. Smokee won't leave."

Stevee jumped down.

"I have another gift for you that I've carried for a long time. Renolee gave me his headband when he left." He held up a band with symbols on it. "The horses mark you as Kwin. The black line means you belong to Black River Herd. It's the river that runs through our territory. I had the black colt painted in the center. It means you're my son. When you wear this, all Kwin will know who you are."

"We already gave Stevee a Calupi headband after he swore his vows." Codee crossed his arms. "Stevee's been chosen by a wolf, not a horse. You need to accept that. Let him go. Allow him to have a Calupi family and Calupi life now."

"I don't intend to lose Stevee again. He has a family, and he doesn't need another one. This headband will give Stevee status among not just the Kwin, but all those we deal with. So he can wear yours when he's with the Calupi, and ours when he's not." Nolte waved it. "Stevee, will you wear Renolee's headband?"

It had been his fathers. Stevee reached up and pulled off his Calupi headband. "Yes. I'd be proud to wear it."

"Then turn around." Stevee turned. Nolte placed the headband over him, tying it in the back.

"We'll go now." Nolte grabbed his companion's mane and vaulted on his back. "Stevee, I want you to stay close to us."

"Anywhere near me is going to be dangerous. Bigham and Mort are offering twenty golds for my death, forty for my capture." With the use of Smokee's mane, Stevee managed to jump on.

Denee extinguished the Kwin fire. "We won't make it easy to collect."

"No," Nolte said. "But the reward's a good idea. I'll double it and offer eighty gold for Bigham and Mort."

Wow. A person in the bottoms could live on that for a few years.

Codee mounted his horse. "Won't the council sanction you when they hear about that?"

"Why?" Stevee asked.

"Clans don't hoard money," Codee explained. "If we have excess, we share it with the clans that don't."

"This was never excess," Nolte said. "All Kwin children raised in the city receive money for their upkeep. For six years, Stevee's has been set aside and offered as a reward to the one who found him. Since I located Stevee, I'll offer it as a reward for those who hurt him."

Reko chuckled. "For that much, you won't have to wait long."

"Juvee will ride with Lulay," Nolte ordered. "Reko and Denee, I want you at Stevee's sides, and I don't want a fly between you if we encounter danger."

As Nolte led them off, Graydee loped in front of Smokee as Denee brought his horse next to Stevee. Reko closed in on his other side. When Reko's leg brushed against Stevee's, it felt too close. Confining. Now he knew why Dayvee complained about the ring of defense the sub-pack put around him.

Stevee whispered, "You don't need to stay that close."

Reko rolled his eyes and spoke softly too. "It's a compliment for Nolte to ask me to ride with him, but to be given the honor to protect his family is huge. Kwin women will take notice. Even your beautiful sister, Lulay, will talk to me. So like it or not, I'm your new shadow."

"I'm going to be riding at your back," Codee said.

Great. More confinement. Graydee sent, *Maybe now you won't get clobbered from behind.*

12

Your Worst Enemy

"The doubting voice from within yourself can be your worst enemy." ~
Codee

Codee

Codee wiped the sweat on his neck. The morning had grown warmer as he and Stevee patrolled with the Kwin around the different animal and people groups that comprised their army. The groups traveled at different speeds. There were spaces between them now, and the line stretched back for several miles down the road. Those gaps and the dense woods on both sides of the road made it easy for enemies to target them and steal their supplies without alerting everyone.

Stevee smiled as Denee explained some of the Kwin customs. If Stevee was so happy with his new Kwin family, shouldn't Codee accept that? Was he fighting to adopt Stevee because it was the right thing for Stevee or because he wanted to satisfy his own selfish desire to have another son?

They approached Elk Clan, and Nolte stopped to ask them if they'd had any problems. As Nolte introduced Stevee, one of them pushed forward to show Stevee a weapon.

Stevee beamed as he looked it over. "My father didn't have this one. What is it?"

As they gave a lengthy explanation, Codee repressed a yawn. Normally, clanspeople were more reserved with a person who they just met. Maybe it was Renolee's reputation? But city people, who didn't know anything about Renolee, were drawn to Stevee too.

Probably ninety-five percent of the people they'd met were enamored with him. The other five percent resented him. The same thing that happened to Dayvee. People either loved or hated him immediately. At least more people seemed to love Stevee than hate him. But he already learned with Dayvee it didn't take many enemies to do serious harm.

Codee would just have to be vigilant to keep anyone from hurting Stevee too.

#

Stevee

Stevee's stomach rumbled. He grabbed some jerky from the pouch on his belt and took a bite. They were half way through their third circuit riding around the lines. They passed yet another group, and the people waved.

This was sure different. Usually, adrifts received frowns or sneers. Some of the clanspeople had asked Stevee about Renolee. He hadn't shared much since the father he knew wasn't who these people knew. Father should have revealed that part of his life to him.

Nolte signaled, and they turned their horses. Now to ride back to the end of the line. Nolte glanced back. "Do you have any more questions?"

"Yes, how did Father get so many clan weapons if clans don't share them?" Stevee asked.

"Renolee was the exception." Nolte chuckled. "The first time we went to a clan meeting we were eight, and Renolee asked several clans about their weapons. I think they enjoyed his interest, and he ended up with several practice weapons.

"Our next clan meeting, we were thirteen, and he took those practice weapons back and challenged them to a competition. He said if he beat them, he wanted real ones. He broke all their records. I thought they'd be upset, but they seemed proud Renolee cared enough to master them. Maybe because he wasn't chosen yet. Then other clans gave him practice weapons, too, and he did it again. After he was chosen by a horse companion, the clan council voted to allow him to keep and use each weapon he won. He kept winning them, so I don't know the total. How many were stolen from you?"

"Twenty-two clan weapons, five city weapons."

"Some of Renolee's weapons are turning up. Last night I spoke to some leaders and asked them to return them to you. They think you should earn them by beating their best like Renolee did."

Well, at least Stevee had a chance of getting them back. "Has anyone else ever tried to win more clan weapons?"

"Sure, other kids tried to follow Renolee's path. It never worked. They have a hard enough time mastering their own clan's weapons, so the clans dissuade it now. Renolee had such amazing coordination it came easy to him, and it never took long for him to figure out how to get the most from each weapon. I'm looking forward to seeing you compete tonight."

Stevee didn't want to disappoint Nolte, but he was afraid he would. "I'd really like to practice."

Dayvee says two groups are headed toward us, Graydee sent. *It appears as if one is headed toward the center of our lines while the other is going to the end.*

They weren't far from the center. Stevee shifted to turn Smokee.

"No," Nolte ordered. "We're going to the end of the line. White Cliff Herd will protect the center."

Stevee guided Smokee back around. "Can we make it in time?"

Reko grinned. "If we ride the wind, you might get your wish to practice weapons."

"Yah!" Nolte shouted.

The horses jumped into a gallop. Smokee's long legs churned up the sand on the road, spraying it into the air. Stevee tucked himself behind Smokee's stretched neck like the Kwin did. Smokee's mane streamed behind him and stung Stevee's face. Graydee, running beside them, looked like a gray blur.

The wind pushed against Stevee until it seemed as if Smokee lifted into it and became one with it. This must've been why Reko called it riding the wind. The exhilaration filled Stevee, and a laugh burst forth from him. He couldn't hold it back, even though they raced toward danger. He was flying, and he felt so free.

When they reached the end of their line, city people were already fighting the intruders. The ruffians saw the Kwin coming and fled. Stevee let his cumback stick fly. It hit one of them in the back of the head then returned to him as the guy fell forward. Nolte threw his bola and the balls with the rope wrapped tight around another. The rest ran into the thick forest.

Dayvee says not to chase them, Graydee sent. *The eagles can't see under the trees, so we could ride into an ambush. He wants us to concentrate on protecting the supplies.*

Nolte, Denee, and Reko vaulted off their horses and ran to the men who fell. They grabbed them and tied their hands behind their backs. Then they slid ropes around their necks before standing them up.

Nolte retrieved their swords. "Good throw, Stevee. Do you recognize either of them?"

"I've never seen the one that Reko has. Denee's captive is a bottom feeder."

"What's that?" Denee asked.

"The lowest of the low in the bottoms. Stays drunk if he can beg enough to get it."

The man spit toward Stevee. "Adrifts are lower than bottom feeders."

"I'm not an adrift anymore." Claiming that felt wrong, like Stevee was lying.

"Those clan clothes and clan name can't change what's on the inside. You're a worthless adrift, who's going to wish you weren't born when Bigham gets a hold of you."

He was right about one thing. Inside, he felt adrift. Caspian said to be proud of it.

"Shut up." Denee tightened the noose on his neck, and the man gasped. Denee loosened it. "My brother was never an adrift. He's been Kwin from the day he was born."

Gratitude welled up in Stevee. It was nice to be defended, even if Denee got it wrong.

Nolte remounted. "Stevee, you and Codee should leave now so you can catch up to Dayvee by noon."

"Okay, Father." Stevee shifted to turn Smokee, and he and Codee rode back with their companions at their sides.

#

Codee

The Pericards swung their horses to the side to allow Codee and Stevee to get through to the sub-pack. Codee's unease quieted when he and Stevee fell in behind Dayvee. He had promised Leeto to keep Dayvee safe. He couldn't protect him if he wasn't with him, but Stevee needed him too. The sub-pack was short one Calupi. "Where's Tayro?"

Dayvee called over his shoulder. "He wanted to collect some plants. Blake and some Pericards went with him."

Tayro and the Perciards came out of the woods and cantered toward them. When they got closer, Chayla called out, "Did you find anything?"

Tayro grabbed a plant from his pouch and held it up. It had green leaves with red tips and flowers with purple petals.

Elayni smiled. "I hope you got enough to eat."

"I did." Tayro guided his horse behind her and joined their ring of defense.

"What is it?" Stevee asked.

"It's called *heals all* because it does a lot." Tayro put the plant back in his pouch. "You can eat it in a salad, but it's also good for a sore throat, fever, diarrhea, internal bleeding, and heart problems. A poultice of self-heal can be used to disinfect wounds too."

Stevee's eyes became pools of sorrow. "A lot of adrifts died of hunger and infections." His face scrunched. "I'd love to learn more about plants, but I'm kind of surprised a king wouldn't have someone go collect what you want."

"Not this king. Being a healer is part of who I am. I might not have as much time, but I won't completely give it up. And to trust the medicines, I need to see the plants for myself."

"We can help you learn plants, Stevee," Dayvee said. "We all know some, but Tayro knows the most."

"I'll start teaching him," Tayro offered. "Come on, Stevee. We'll go again."

As they rode away with Pericards around them, Stevee's voice drifted back. "I really appreciate you teaching me."

...

At least an hour passed. Shouldn't Tayro and Stevee be back by now? Codee kept scanning the woods for a sign. This was ridiculous. When he was with Stevee, he worried about Dayvee, and when he was with Dayvee, he worried about Stevee. Finally, Stevee and Tayro rode out of the woods. Stevee guided Smokee in beside Codee.

Codee's nerves calmed. "Did you learn much?"

"Yes, I wish I had known some of this before. Like pine cones. I didn't know they had nuts inside I could eat. I would have collected them."

Codee pointed up in the sky to show Stevee and spoke softly. "See that bird up there?"

Stevee craned his neck. "Yes."

"That's an ocean bird, an albatross. Dayvee must be getting news from the coast." Dayvee's face paled, and his posture slumped on Ghostee. It must not be good.

"What is it?" Brando demanded.

"The invaders aren't just killing the coastal clan warriors but their future. They're slaughtering the children." He flung his hand at those behind them. "We're moving too slow. I need to go on ahead with those that can keep up."

Codee's heart fell to his feet. The news was horrific. He had good friends among the coastal clans, but Dayvee couldn't let emotions dictate. "If you heard hyenas cackling, would you run out of your den to confront them without taking all of your weapons?" Codee flicked a hand at those behind them. "Every one of us is a weapon you might need."

His nephew turned anguished eyes on him. "So you're saying I have to let the children be slaughtered?"

"Send a message through the companions to warn all the clans to hide and not to engage the invaders until we do. If we're going to win, we have to fight them on our terms."

"I can't warn the towns and cities, and they're not as good as clanspeople at hiding."

He was right, but it didn't change anything. "If you let them goad you into acting rashly, we'll lose."

Dayvee ran a hand through his hair, tugging it. "I hate this. Kun should have chosen another to be Kayndo."

Codee didn't agree. "It's not something you can pass to another."

"I know." Dayvee straightened. "Fox clan has found us a suitable campground, but we'll be there three hours before dark. I think we should keep going."

Dayvee shouldn't do that. "You told everyone we'd stop early to hold the weapons competition."

"But that was before I received this news."

"The Calupi word isn't broken, and a few hours' travel isn't going to make that much difference. We can make it up tomorrow when everyone's in high spirits."

Hollering broke out behind them. Codee glanced back. Two clanspeople were arguing. Dayvee signaled Brando, and he rode back to break it up.

Dayvee sighed. "They're like dealing with little kids."

Codee's eyes twinkled, and he chuckled. "Leeto and I have said that often. But anytime you put several packs or clans together, this happens. They all believe their clan is the best, and fights are going to occur while they vie for respect and dominance."

Dayvee groaned. "Isn't anyone worried about battling the invaders but me?"

"Clanspeople face death everyday, and we can't stop living. But I think they are worried, even if they won't admit it. And the stress is causing the tension to be worse."

"I wish they'd focus their aggression on the invaders."

"A lot of them believe defeating the invaders will be easy with the Kayndo."

Dayvee snorted. "I don't."

"You shouldn't destroy their confidence. And holding

competitions will help relieve the tension. That's why we have so many at the clan meetings."

"I'll think about it."

Codee could only hope Dayvee would decide to stay, although with Fox Clan it could be far from restful.

13

Placing Bets

"Winners tend to know they'll win, so I determine whose confidence is false." ~ Brando

Stevee

As these new clanspeople walked toward them from the meadow, Stevee smiled to himself. They sure wouldn't make good thieves. They couldn't be missed. Their bright orangish-red capes stood out like the colorful foxes that capered around them. Their clothing, headbands, and jewelry were decorated with orange quills and beads in patterns. When Nolte had introduced him to the clanspeople they rode circuit around, there had been some from fox clan, but they hadn't dressed like that. These must be their ceremony clothes.

Dayvee beckoned with a wave of his hand to the one in front. The Pericards moved their horses out a few steps to allow him inside the ring.

The man's body was wiry. He wasn't as tall as the Calupi men Stevee had met, but what stood out most was his red hair. "I'm Hoke, the Vulape leader of Three Hills Skulk of Fox Clan. We welcome the Kayndo and those who support him to our territory."

Dayvee leaned down from his horse and clasped Hoke's arm. "Thank you. We appreciate your help with finding us a place to camp."

"I was told you wanted to hold a weapons competition. You and your sub-pack are welcome to come to our homes so we can show you hospitality."

"We've agreed not to burden anyone by accepting hospitality." Dayvee waved at the meadow. "We'll put up our tent here tonight."

"All right," Hoke said. "If there's anything you need, just ask." He and the other Valupe walked back to speak to those from other clans behind Dayvee.

"Good thing Dayvee didn't accept their hospitality," Brando whispered to Stevee as they dismounted. "Fox Clan loves pulling pranks even more than I do."

They hurried to set up their tent before the competition.

…

Stevee stood near the two targets the Kwin had set up. A tent pole and a square frame with a hide were anchored among the grass. The crowd of people staring at Stevee set his skin prickling in warning. When adrifts drew attention, it seldom was a good thing.

Graydee pressed against his leg. *You're Calupi now.*

Stevee's body didn't agree. It screamed at him to stay alert.

Dayvee raised his hand, and the crowd quieted. "Stevee has agreed to compete with the three clans which he has weapons for, Kwin, Calupi, and Accipi. Then he'll cross swords with the city people. We'll start with the Kwin."

Nolte and several other Kwin went to the first line Nolte had marked and cast their weapons. Then it was Stevee's turn. They expected to see the skill of Renolee, but that wasn't going to happen. If Stevee could give them a respectable showing, maybe they wouldn't be too disappointed.

His stomach clenched as he threw his bola at the pole. When it wrapped around it, like it was supposed to, Stevee let out the breath he hadn't realized he'd been holding. Then he flung his comeback stick at the hide target. It hit, bounced off, and he caught it when it returned. So he lined up behind the others at the second line.

By the fifth line, over half the Kwin had missed with both weapons and were out. At the seventh line, there were less than ten. Stevee's turn came again. The farther he got back, the more muscle the bola took, and his arm already ached. To try to loosen the strain, he flapped his arm. Then he launched the bola toward the target.

Oh no. It fell short. So much for the bola. Stevee threw his cumback. It hit the target and returned. He went to the eighth line to compete with just the cumback now.

By the ninth line, everyone had missed with the bola and only

Nolte, Reko, Denee, and Stevee still competed with the cumback. By the tenth line, there were only Nolte and him. Nolte made the throw and catch. Stevee's cumback hit the target but didn't make it back.

Nolte slapped his shoulder. "Renolee would be proud of you. When you gain strength, you'll be beating me."

"Good job, Lil Kwin," whooped his brothers, Denee, and Juvee. Other Kwin called out congratulations to Lil Kwin, and the crowd clapped and whistled. It hadn't taken long for most of the Kwin to use that nickname.

Dayvee rode closer on Ghostee and gave him a chin lift. "Now we'll hold the Calupi competition. I'll be on Ghostee. If anyone else wants to compete mounted, they may."

Since Stevee was more used to the angle from the ground, he opted to stay on foot. By the time they got to the seventh line, Only Wolf Mountain Calupi and Stevee remained.

They are rated the number one pack, Graydee sent.

At line eight, Stevee's nail throw fell short, but his tooth sank true. Dayvee, Brando, and Elayni hit with their nails but missed with their tooth. Codee's nails landed true from line nine. None of the others did, but Codee missed his tooth throw, and Stevee made his. Stevee had won the tooth competition, and Codee won the nails. The sub-pack slapped his shoulders and congratulated him. "Well met, Lil Wolf." Brando's words rang out over the din of the clapping crowd.

"What?"

Brando laughed. "You're Calupi, so I changed your nickname."

Sheesh. Would all the Calupi call him that now? And why would two clans and several packs want to claim Stevee anyway? Could they have heard about the reward and want to collect? He was certain his sub-pack and Nolte weren't after the reward, but they didn't know Stevee well. Wasn't he teetering on the edge of a roof, just waiting to fall?

When Dayvee raised his hand, the crowd quieted. "Now Stevee will compete against the Accipi using a slingshot."

The Accipi came to the line. Confidence soared in Stevee. This one he knew he'd win, and he did, beating Shuto at the tenth line.

"I told you, no one can beat Stevee with a slingshot," Clint boasted. "Keep walking backward, Stevee, and cast stones until you miss."

He glanced at Dayvee, who nodded. "Go ahead."

Stevee threw stone after stone, and each pinged against the pole. He finally missed, but it was at double the distance from where Shuto had missed. Shuto gave him a huge smile. "Congratulations. You beat Renolee's record with the slingshot."

The roar of the crowd as they cheered the announcement shocked Stevee. Graydee nudged him with his nose. *I chose well.* The pride coming through their bond sent Stevee's spirit soaring.

Brando slapped his back again. "You proved your ability to defend the Kayndo, but I wish I had known about your skills. I don't normally lose bets."

Was he serious? "You bet against me?"

Brando grinned. "You didn't show any confidence, but I won't bet against you again."

Stevee shrugged. "Maybe you should. I won't always win."

"The last competition will be the Pericards competing with swords," Dayvee announced.

Most of the crowd moved away. Maybe they weren't that interested in seeing city people compete.

Stevee was put against the Pericard, Jerrod, for his first sword match. The Pericards were bigger and had a longer arm reach than he did. He'd have to rely on his speed. His first few matches were easy to win, but they grew harder until they were down to four. Stevee and Chase would cross swords while Blake and Clint did. Stevee's arms already ached, and his ribs hurt.

"Ready?" Chase asked.

Stevee rose on the balls of his feet and nodded. Chase swung his sword. Stevee deflected it with his, but the strength behind the blow spun him. Blow after blow he met or dodged, but his arms felt like dead weight. He dodged Chase's next swing, and it left Chase overextended, leaving him an opening. Stevee darted closer to place his sword under Chase's neck but stopped his thrust an inch short. "Do you yield?"

Chase gave him a nod. "I yield."

Stevee lowered his sword. "I got lucky. Thanks for giving me this practice."

Clint had beaten Blake, and they were standing with the sub-pack watching. "I don't think that was luck." Blake handed a bow and a quiver of arrows to Brando. "If I'd have known how good you were before Graydee chose you, we'd have recruited you. And you're welcome to join any of our practices."

"Thanks." Stevee faced off against Clint for the last match. Stevee had never beaten him. He wiped the sweat from his face with his sleeve and tried to rise to the balls of his feet, but he stumbled, then fell. He staggered to his feet.

"Enough." Clint grabbed his arm to steady him. "You need to recover more, so we'll cross swords another day."

His sub-pack and Codee hurried over to him. Codee's forehead was furrowed. "Are you dizzy?"

Stevee's legs shook. "Just weak."

"When did you eat last?" Tayro demanded.

Warmth flushed Stevee's cheeks. "Not since lunch, but I don't feel hungry."

"Eat some of this." Tayro handed him a pouch. "Regardless of whether you feel hungry, you have to eat, or your stomach won't grow."

Stevee opened it and found some dried fruit and nuts. He put a handful in his mouth.

"You'll be needing your strength to use this bow." Brando held out the bow and the quiver of arrows Blake had given him. "I have no use for it."

Stevee swallowed the food. "Then why'd you bet for it?"

"It was to thank you since I made up my losses and then some."

"A bow would be great, but—"

"Think of it as a welcome to the sub-pack gift." Chayla gave him a shy smile. "All Brando's winnings go to us. It's one way he takes care of us. And none of the rest of us can use a bow, so you have to."

Brando grinned. "And Clint says you're good with it, so I'll win even more bets."

Stevee took the bow and quiver as Nolte descended on their group. "I'd like to invite you to the Kwin fires for food, drink, and dancing to celebrate Stevee's accomplishments."

Dayvee's sub-pack exchanged glances between each other. They lifted their pinkies. "Agreed," Dayvee said. "We will celebrate with the Kwin."

. . .

Stevee started as a log crashed in the bonfire and sparks flew. The sparks died before they reached where he sat on the hide between his new sub-pack and Kwin family. Every direction he looked fires fickered all around them. Lots of different clans were playing music and dancing. The music should have clashed terribly, but it didn't. Clanspeople wondered between the fires to visit each other, and share food and drinks. And everyone that approached them seemed to have a smile for him.

His sister Lulay held up what looked like crushed nuts in the shape of a small stick. "Try this, Stevee."

Stevee's stomach already ached with fullness after so many people brought him things to try. He shouldn't get used to people wanting to fawn over him. But for one night, he was going to let himself enjoy it. "Just one bite."

She smiled and broke off a piece for him. The sweetness of honey and raspberries, with the crunchiness of nuts. An explosion of goodness. "Mmmm. Delicious."

Hoke, the Vulape leader, came over with two other people from fox clan. One must be related to Hoke, he had the same lean build and red hair, but the other was stocky and had dark hair.

Hoke smiled. "I really enjoyed the competition today." He fingered a small wooden carving of a fox's head that dangled from his weapons pouch. "Brando, you've gained several admirers of your work in fox clan."

He must have been one of the people Brando lost to. "Why did you bet on me, Hoke?" Stevee asked.

Hoke chuckled. "Renolee won a bet against fox clan when he gained our throwing stars, so I knew not to bet against his son in any weapon's match." He held up a pouch and turned back to Brando. "I'll give you another chance to win this bag of beads if you want to bet again?"

"What kind of bet?" Brando asked.

"Simple." He took a beautiful blue bead with a starburst pattern out of the pouch. "I put this in a hand. You guess which it's in, I'll give you the pouch with 100 more beads just like it. But if you lose, my life-mate gets one of your carvings too."

Elayni shook her head. "I don't care if it's fifty, fifty odds. Don't bet against fox clan, Brando."

Stevee could probably win it. "I'll bet you, Hoke." The words left his mouth before he even thought about it. The sub-pack stared at him with wide eyes. Did they think him foolish? "But I don't have a carving, and I won't bet my weapons. Is there anything else you'd take?"

"Do you have another shirt?"

"Yes."

"Then I'll bet you that one." Hoke smiled. "We in Fox clan enjoy taking the shirt off someone's back."

Stevee's sub-pack had put a lot of work into this shirt, but he did have another one. "All right."

Hoke handed the bead pouch to his dark-haired friend. "Cover me so no one sees which hand I put this in." Both of his friends slid around to Hoke's back.

Hoke put both his hands behind his back, and his shoulders jiggled as he switched the bead around. He brought his hands back out, holding them out in front of him.

Everyone called out their guesses. Codee said right hand. Nolte said right. Brando said left hand. Hoke was holding his right hand closer to his body, giving the impression it was in that one, but Brando must not have trusted that ploy. Stevee never trusted the obvious.

"Which one of my hands, Stevee?" Hoke asked.

"It's not in any of yours." Stevee grinned. "It's in the left hand of your friend with the red hair."

Hoke's mouth dropped open as his friends came out from behind his back. The red-headed one gave Hoke a sheepish look and held open his left hand with the bead.

Elayni sputtered. "You were lying?"

"No." Hoke's dark-haired friend handed Stevee the pouch of beads. "Hoke never said he'd put it in his own hand."

Brando slapped Stevee's back. "How'd you know?"

The truth might make Stevee the chief suspect if anything came up missing, but he couldn't lie. "It's a thief's job to know where the valuables are hidden."

Nolte laughed. "Too bad I didn't have your help when I was searching for you." Was he saying Stevee was valuable?

That was the first time Stevee'd been called that.

#

Codee

Codee let his gaze wander to the other clanspeople gathered around the fire. Those that weren't dancing visited while their hands flew. They sharpened weapons, sewed beads, wove baskets, softened or sewed hides, and completed a number of other tasks. Clanspeople had to keep working. If they survived the battle, winter would come.

Pride filled Codee. The sub-pack he trained didn't only fulfill their duty as the Kayndo's guards. they worked on projects too while they scanned the area for threats. Brando whittled, Chayla wrote, Elayni strung beads, Tayro lined a waterskin with a bladder, the Kayndo honed his knife. Next to Codee sat Stevee, and even the new trainee stayed busy wrapping leather around arrowheads to attach them to some shafts he fletched.

All the wolves were sprawled near Stevee. It was normal to find the wolves clumped together, but normally they gravitated to Dayvee. Stevee sat his arrows down. He ran his hands over several of the wolves, and he was meeting their eyes. To look in a wolf's eyes was to challenge them, and Calupi didn't fondle the wolves. They treated them with the same respect as any human friend. Codee needed to explain wolf protocols to Stevee.

No, Wilee sent. *We don't want Stevee told them.*

Why?

We want him to become comfortable with us and not worry about doing the wrong thing.

All right.

Nolte reached over the wolves to hand a flask of the Kwin wine to Stevee. Codee whispered to him. "You want to be careful with how much you drink of that."

"I learned that lesson already." Stevee passed it to Codee without drinking. "Adrifts can't afford to be careless."

What would it take for Stevee to accept he was Calupi now?

Him trusting it will last, Wilee sent.

Some pretty Kwin girls came over to Stevee. "Come on, Lil Kwin and dance with us."

Stevee shook his head. "No, thanks."

They giggled. "You need to learn to dance the Kwin way." They reached for him and pulled him up among them. The Kwin women seemed as bold as their men.

Reko chuckled. "Kwin women know they're too beautiful for men to really mean it when they say no."

The Kwin women soon had Stevee swaying and moving like them as they taught him their dance. Some young Calupi women approached him. They were from Red Butte Pack. Cackles. Did Foley ask them to convince Stevee to join their pack? Then Elayni went up and spoke to Stevee. Soon they were dancing together. Hmmm. He should tell him that Elayni was in love with Dayvee, or he could get hurt.

While Stevee and Elayni danced, Dayvee sheathed his knife then leaned over to examine the arrows Stevee had been working on. There were four more arrowheads that needed attached. Dayvee picked up one and began to secure it to a shaft. Brando came over and picked up another, then Chaya and Tayro grabbed the last ones. Besides their fierce loyalty to each other, the thing Codee admired most about Dayvee's subpack was how they cared for one another. Without ever asking, aid was given. Geno's legacy.

Lulay, Stevee's stunning sister walked up to Dayvee. She tossed her head, making her long black tresses swing as her large brown eyes locked with his. "I'm Lulay, Nolte's daughter."

"Nice to meet you, Lulay." Dayvee stopped winding leather strips to clasp her forearm in the clan handshake.

She held his arm longer than necessary. "I'm thrilled to meet you." She batted her long eyelashes at him. "And I'd like to get to know you better."

Codee almost chuckled at Dayvee's blushing. Reko went over to her. "Will you dance with me, Lulay?"

"I already talked to you, Reko, since you protected my family, but I'm talking to the Kayndo now." She sat next to Dayvee, crossing her long legs, and said haughtily, "You haven't gained enough status for me to dance with you."

"Okay, Lulay. But you should ask yourself if anyone else you consider will appreciate you as much as I do."

Reko moved off to dance with another Kwin woman. His laughter drifted back to them. Foley's daughter asked Stevee to dance with her, so Elayni came back to glare at Lulay, who had taken her spot.

When the drummers took a break, Stevee escaped the dancing and walked away with Graydee trailing after him. Five other Calupi stood and followed after him. Calupi used a group of five, a Quincee, in a planned confrontation. Did they want to fight Stevee? He only had Graydee with him.

Wilee, where's Stevee's going?

To see Smokee, and take him a treat.

Codee stood and walked after them. *Tell Dayvee that Stevee's got a Quincee shadowing him, and I'm going after them.*

Dayvee says wait for Brando. He will join you.

Codee stopped. It wasn't long before Brando joined him, but Codee was out of patience. "We need to hurry. If Frudo hurts Stevee, I'm not going to be gentle."

"Why do you think I asked Dayvee to let just the two of us go? No one expects us to fight nice if we're outnumbered."

14

Unstoppable

"The past can't be changed, but the future isn't set." ~ Kwutee

Stevee

Stevee gave one more pat to Smokee at the edge of the encampment in the meadow. As he moved back toward the tents, his neck prickled in warning. A rustling sounded. Was someone hiding in the shadows?

Graydee sent, *It's Frudo and his packmates.*

Oh no. Five Calupi jumped out to surround him. Caspian's advice ran through his head. When sharks are circling, they intend to bite. Stevee pulled his slingshot. Graydee's ruff rose, and he growled at them. The White River Pack wolves growled back at Graydee. Stevee's heart sank. Graydee was outnumbered too.

"You could get in trouble for pulling a weapon on another Calupi," Frudo said.

Codee had told Stevee clan members prohibited the use of weapons on each other, and fights between them were settled unarmed in the ring. "Then I'd suggest you stop jumping out at me so I don't mistake you for an enemy." Stevee put his slingshot away. "What do you want?"

"I told you, you shouldn't accept the Kayndo's offer to join his sub-pack, and you shouldn't talk to Elayni. But you didn't listen."

"Elayni should be the one to decide who she wants to talk to, and Brando said I proved I can defend the Kayndo."

Packs here, Graydee sent. Evee, Cato, Topay, and Jaycee raced up to join Graydee, showing their teeth and raising their ruffs. At least Graydee had help.

Frudo ignored the wolves. "You didn't prove anything. You could lose your weapons during a battle, so you need to know how to fight. The first thing you should learn is blocking."

They rushed Stevee throwing punches as the wolves charged each other in a flurry of teeth. Stevee danced back, but a punch connected with his gut. The pain to his injured ribs stole his breath. He gasped and clutched his ribs. Another Calupi knocked his feet from him, and he fell forward scraping his knees. Stevee scrambled up.

The White River Calupi stopped punching, and their companions sank to the ground to show submission as footsteps rushed toward them. Stevee twisted to see Brando and Codee coming with Wilee and Bruno.

"Frudo," Codee bellowed. "You should know better than to fight with a Calupi outside the ring and bring companions into it."

Frudo put his hands up palm out. "We were just helping Stevee. He's not capable of defending Dayvee until he learns to fight."

Brando smirked. "One of the reasons Wolf Mountain is rated higher than White River is our fighting skills. Maybe we should teach you."

A half smile lit Codee's face as they moved in front of Stevee. "I think it's only right we help them learn."

Frudo dropped his hands. "We're not questioning your place beside Dayvee, only his."

"The Kayndo himself invited Stevee to join us, so you're implying he doesn't know what he's doing." Brando's eyes narrowed. "That's an insult I don't take lightly."

Frudo puffed out his chest. "We outnumber you. You could get hurt too."

Stevee moved up beside Brando and Codee. "Frudo only wants to fight me. There's no reason for anyone else to be hurt."

"We aren't adrifts. We fight together." Brando howled.

Codee howled too.

Give them your howl, Graydee sent. Stevee tried, but it sounded sick. *We need to work on your howl.*

Not just his howl. What did he know about fighting unarmed? Clint said it wasn't any different than fighting with a sword. To use his arms to meet their punches and his fists to make strikes.

Codee and Brando lunged forward. Stevee leaped after them. He had to try and help them. Brando jumped in the air and kicked a foot into Frudo's stomach. He staggered back. Brando landed on his feet, then drove the back of his elbow into Frudo's face. When Frudo fell, Brando kicked the legs out from another Calupi.

Codee punched another one in the face. He swayed and crashed back. Then Codee ducked under another guy's fist and drove his own up under his chin. That guy collapsed to land on the ground. It only left one foe standing, but he charged Stevee.

Stevee twirled to dodge out of the way and ended up a little behind his foe. He swung his fist as if it were a sword into the back of his opponent's neck. His fingers stung, but the man crashed to the ground. Hey, it worked.

Codee slapped Stevee's shoulder. "Well met. Now touch his neck to end the fight."

Stevee bent over quickly to touch his neck before the guy could regain his feet.

Brando knelt beside Frudo. "I teach our sub-pack fighting skills, not you. I'm letting you off lightly because Dayvee wants us to save the fighting for the invaders. Don't make me regret it." Brando wrapped his hand around the front of Frudo's neck, then took his hand away. "Now get up. Help your packmates and rejoin your pack."

When they stumbled off, Brando turned back to Stevee. "You should have told us they were threatening you."

"When I let the adrifts help me, some died, so I learned to fight my battles alone."

"Our sub-pack is like a body. Dayvee's the head, but we're his limbs. If anyone hurts a limb, it harms the entire body, so they're no longer your battles but ours."

Was that why Graydee felt bereft without his pack? Did he think of them as one body?

Graydee nudged him. *Yes.*

"But I'm just a temporary member," Stevee exclaimed.

"Do you think Dayvee would have had Gaylo tattoo your hand if he planned on it being temporary?" Brando asked. "We want you in both our sub-pack and our family. But family's for life, so you have to trust enough to commit to it." Brando waved a hand toward their camp. "We need to hurry back. I don't want to miss the show." Brando took off jogging with Codee right behind him.

Stevee ran after them. "What show?"

"When Elayni tears into Frudo," Brando replied. "No one messes with what's Elayni's."

"I'm not Elayni's." The running already had Stevee wheezing.

"You're one of us, Lil Wolf, even if you don't recognize it yet," Brando claimed. "And Elayni's livid about Frudo telling you not to talk to her."

Stevee didn't want to be responsible for destroying friendships. He panted out, "We have to stop her."

"You can't stop a tornado or Elayni when she's really mad."

Codee chuckled. "I'm glad I'm not on the receiving end this time."

#

Dayvee

Dayvee and his friends left the Kwin fire and walked toward where they had set up their tent. A circle of shadows, the Pericards came with them.

It was a beautiful night. The heat of the day had cooled and a light breeze caressed Dayvee's skin. There must be millions of stars twinkling above them. Between them and the moon it wasn't that dark. They moved past White River's fire and their small earth-toned tents to the large gray tent the Pericards had given the Kayndo. Maybe it had been a mistake to camp so close to the other Calupi packs. Jaycee sent, *Codee, Brando, and Stevee are returning.*

Dayvee didn't enter the tent but turned to wait. He reached out for Graydee. *How's Stevee?*

A few more bruises but nothing serious. Relief flooded Dayvee that his newest member hadn't been harmed more in the fight.

Frudo and his packmates came into sight. As they trudged past moving toward the White River tents, the scowl he wore gave Dayvee pause. Did Frudo still plan to cause problems? As an alpha's son, it wouldn't be easy for Frudo to accept defeat.

Oh no. Elayni was charging up to Frudo to confront him. "What right do you have, Frudo, to decide who gets to talk to me? Do you think you own me?"

Frudo and his packmates stopped. "I was trying to protect you."

Stevee, Codee, and Brando jogged toward them. Elayni's face flushed red. "From what?" She flung a hand toward Stevee. "He belongs to my sub-pack. When you attacked him, you attacked me."

Frudo gave Stevee a glare. "I should be in your sub-pack, not him. His dung stinks."

No way would Dayvee let someone as arrogant as Frudo join them.

"He's not dung. He's Renolee's son," Elayni screeched.

"He's a thief and an adrift." Frudo's tone was condescending. "That's like the city people's omega. You shouldn't talk to him."

Elayni threw her hands in the air. "Ughhh."

"Elayni," Stevee called out. "I don't care what Frudo says about me. He's not worth your anger."

She released a heavy breath. "You're right. I have no interest in talking to Frudo." To Dayvee's surprise, she turned away from him.

Frudo grabbed her arm. "I can't believe you'd side with dung against me."

"Let go of my arm." She kicked him between the legs, and he crumpled, bending over. "You'd be my last choice in a life-mate now. Don't touch me. Don't even look at me." Elayni stomped off.

Dayvee had to fight back a smile. There was the passionate Elayni he loved.

Frudo gasped out, "You better watch your back, dung."

Dayvee slashed his hand. "That's enough, Frudo. It was cowardly to attack my trainee with a Quincee and call it fight training. I'm ordering you to leave Stevee alone."

Frudo's eyes narrowed at him. "Your authority won't last forever. How long before you're just a crippled Calupi, and I'm an alpha? You won't be able to protect dung then." He and his packmates stumbled away toward the White River tents.

Dayvee might not like admitting it, but Frudo had a point. "He's right."

"No, he's not." Brando's deep blue eyes flashed. "You'll never be just a crippled Calupi, and I'll teach Stevee to fight."

Nolte and Denee ran up to them carrying torches. "My son was attacked by five Calupi?" Nolte asked.

Great. Although Dayvee appreciated Elayni's passion for protecting her pack, her shouting must have alerted a lot of the camp to what happened, and he didn't need the fight spreading. They had a bigger battle to wage, and he needed everyone able to fight. "Nolte, it's handled. Brando and Codee helped Stevee, and I ordered Frudo to leave him alone."

"Show me any injuries you received from them, Stevee," Nolte ordered.

Stevee shuffled his feet. "It's okay, Nolte."

"It's Father to you, and no, it's not okay." His tone was curt. "Show me."

Stevee hesitated. Would he refuse? Sympathy flooded Dayvee. The memory came unbidden of his own father making him reveal the injuries Nero inflicted on him. Maybe he should stop it, but Stevee's father had the right to see.

After a long few seconds, Stevee removed his shirt. "The bruise on my shoulder, the newest bruise on my ribs." He grabbed his pant leg and pulled it up. "And the scrape on my knees."

Nolte held his torch over Stevee, lighting his body as he examined his injuries. "They will wear the same."

Dayvee blew out his breath. "I don't need fights between clans or even between packs."

"Understood, but they don't get to mark my son without being marked."

"What's on your neck, Stevee?" Tayro asked.

Stevee itched his neck. "I don't know."

"It looks like a poison ivy rash," Codee exclaimed. "You must not have washed it off your neck."

Stevee's face turned a deep red. Tayro took a flask out of his rucksack. "It's jewelweed. Put some on."

Clint came running up. "Are you okay Stevee?"

Stevee applied the jewelweed to his neck. "I'm fine."

Clint turned to Blake. "I've decided to do what you asked. I'll help the Pericards as long as I get to watch out for Stevee too."

"I'm fine with that, and even agree with it," Blake said. "Stevee can't use his weapons against our enemies if he gets clobbered by our allies."

Brando chuckled. "Stevee can't claim he has no one who cares about him anymore. Not when all these people are so concerned."

Stevee slid his shirt back on. "You're right. I can't." Dayvee barely caught the last whispered word, "*Today*."

15

New Skills

"When we're outnumbered by foes, be smarter than them." ~ Caspian

Stevee

It wasn't quite sunrise yet, but people all around them were rushing to dismantle their camps. Stevee put his rucksack on his back. All the rest of the sub-pack carelessly tossed their belongings in a pile while they took down the tent. People walked by their stuff. Stevee should warn the Calupi. "You make it too easy for someone to steal your things."

"Theft isn't a concern between clanspeople." Codee took down the tent's center pole. "Even hyena clan follows the rules of hospitality, so if anyone is truly in need of something, it will be provided. Who'd go to the trouble to steal something they can ask for and receive?"

Brando pulled out another tent stake. "That's why Hoke asked if you had another shirt before letting you bet it. Otherwise he'd be obligated to help a clansman in need and return it if he won it."

When they finished tearing down the tent, they packed it on a mule. Then Stevee and Codee rode over to join the Kwin. Nolte and his herd were already mounted since they were patrolling the first half of the lines today. As they rode through the camp, the sound of yelling rose sharply over the din. Nolte broke into a trot toward the commotion. The other Kwin shot forward on Nolte's heels, so Stevee urged Smokee after them. They came to where White River Pack had camped and were now preparing to leave. Frudo and his friends were being kicked and bucked off their horses. All the Kwin cracked up laughing.

"Why are the horses doing that?" Stevee asked.

Denee's lips twitched as if he were keeping back more laughter. "No horse will allow those that ganged up on Lil Kwin to ride. They wear your injuries now, and they'll have to walk."

Stevee couldn't help his own smile. Frudo leveled glares at Stevee as he rode beyond him with his Kwin family.

No other alarms broke their day. When the sun had almost set, Stevee's stomach wouldn't stop growling. Maybe it was getting used to more food. He and Codee were back with the sub-pack and riding behind Dayvee. Why did the sub-pack keep glancing at him? Could they hear his stomach? He reached into his rucksack for some jerky. A tree frog leaped out. Huh? Maybe it went in earlier and was trapped when he closed it. The sub-pack had all twisted on their horses to watch him. Hmmm.

Elayni dropped back to ride beside him. "Do you know Brando likes to pull pranks?"

So the frog was a prank? "He said he did at Three Hills. Is he mad at me?"

"No, when he pulls pranks on us, it's just to give everyone a laugh when we jump or scream. Didn't adrifts pull pranks on each other?"

So that's why they had all been watching Stevee, to see his reaction. "No. We had other reasons to jump or scream, and no one thought it was funny."

"Yeah. I guess pranks must seem pretty stupid to you."

Stevee wasn't about to claim that. "I can appreciate Brando trying to make everyone happy."

"It's driving him crazy he can't get a reaction from you."

Huh. "Has there been more than one?"

"Yes, the sand in your shoes, and the snake wrapped around Graydee's water bowl. I just didn't want you to think we're being mean to you. It's Brando's way of saying you're one of us."

"I've had people be mean, and this doesn't compare. I'd like to be considered one of you, but frogs aren't one of the things that scare me. Should I pretend?"

"What does scare you?" Codee asked.

"Don't answer that," Brando hollered. "Elayni take my place." She trotted up as Brando rode back to them. "Codee and Leeto made Dayvee face his fears, so you shouldn't tell him yours."

Codee sighed. "Do you really think I'd to do that to him?"

"I think you'd tell Leeto if he asks, and he'd do it." He shifted his gaze to Stevee. "I don't want you to pretend to react. Even if I can't pull pranks on you, you're one of us."

Dayvee glanced back. "Yes. With or without pranks you're one of us."

But wouldn't they get tired of the strange guy that didn't act like them?

"He'll have pranks." Brando grinned. "I'll just have to teach him how to pull them."

Codee groaned. "Please tell me you won't practice on me."

Brando laughed. "Who better?"

A gurgle sounded behind the hum of insects and the song of birds. Water must be somewhere close. Good, Stevee's water bag was almost empty, and his throat was dry.

Dayvee led them off the road toward it. "Beaver and Otter Clan want to aid us. Hardy River Bend Colony is offering us a good camp spot."

"Whose colony is it, Beaver Clan or Otter?" Stevee asked.

"Both," Codee replied. "Beaver and Otter Clan form colonies together because they both benefit. Beaver Clan builds their homes and harvests plants while Otter Clan makes their boats and harvests the fish."

The trees stopped as they came to a broad silty area that fronted a wide river as it curved easterly. An island in the middle of the river had several rounded huts on it, seemingly made from sticks. A couple of clansmen rowed a long canoe toward them from the island, pulling another canoe behind them. Both men wore sleeveless shirts and short pants.

A scraping announced the boat hitting the beach, and the two men jumped out and pulled the canoes further up. The shorter of the two addressed Dayvee. "Hello Kayndo. I'm Gentu, leader of Beaver Clan." He flung his hand toward the other man. "And this is Fujee, the leader of Otter Clan. We welcome you to our territory and invite you to set your tents up here."

"Fujee, the taller man from Otter Clan, pointed at the other canoe. We just harvested one of our mollusk beds, and that entire canoe's full of them. We know you didn't want to accept hospitality, but these are best fresh, so we don't store them for winter. If you'll agree to it, we'll cook them and add them to everyone's provisions tonight."

"Thank you. I'm sure they'll enjoy them." Dayvee held up his hand, spread his fingers, and then flung it forward. Those behind them flocked forward onto the beach to set up their camp. Stevee jumped off Smokee. He wiped the horse's sweat down, then turned him loose to join the herd of horses that the Kwin were caring for.

The sub-pack also released their horses, except Dayvee, who stayed mounted on Ghostee while he spoke to Jentu and Fujee. Fujee gestured toward the river. "Hardy River flows east from here all the way to the ocean, and the road never wanders that far from it. Some of us plan to join you in the fight, but we'll travel in our canoes and keep pace. My otter companion, Glido, knows all the areas by the river well. He can inform you of good campsites."

"Great. That will help." Dayvee glanced at the sub-pack. "Brando, when the tent is set up, you can start teaching Stevee to fight. He needs to learn that before pranks."

Fujee and Gentu started a fire to cook the mollusks while the sub-pack set up the large tent. Brando pulled the tent flap back. "Inside Stevee. I don't teach my methods to everyone." Brando waved at Dayvee. "How about some help? You can sit to demonstrate and throw while I retrieve."

Dayvee took up his crutches and dismounted. "All right." He glanced at Elayni. "The rest of you should do what you can to help Fujee and Gentu fix the mollusks and prepare whatever else you want to go with."

The day's heat hadn't cooled much, and the tent seemed stifling when Stevee went in. Sweat trickled down his back. Dayvee hobbled in and sat down. Brando took five rawhide balls out of his rucksack, then poured some water over them with his water bag. "First, we'll teach you to block. If they can't hit you, you can't get hurt. Watch while I throw these balls at Dayvee."

He flung the balls at Dayvee's face, one after another. Dayvee moved his head, just enough to get out of their way, and deflected a couple of them with his arms. Not one hit his face.

Brando picked up the balls and handed them to Dayvee. "Now your turn, Stevee."

The balls came fast and furious. Stevee tried to block or dodge them, but several hit him. At least they didn't hurt. After several rounds of dodging balls, sweat plastered his shirt to him.

Brando rewet the balls. "You're getting better, but it's also important to block the things you won't see coming." He pulled a black hood out of his rucksack and gave it to Dayvee.

Dayvee slid the hood over his face, then Brando chucked the balls at him. "One after another Dayvee moved his head enough to let them sail by. Not one made contact.

Stevee's jaw hung open. "That's amazing."

Dayvee tossed the hood to Brando. "Watch Brando."

Brando slid the hood on. Dayvee lobbed the balls at Brando. He dodged each one until the last two. Dayvee used one hand to throw a ball at his face while with his other hand he flung one at his legs.

Brando blocked the ball heading toward his face with one arm. He deflected the second ball with his other arm, but it hit his foot. He took off the hood and grinned. "We have to throw multiple balls to hit one another now."

Brando held out the hood to Stevee. "Try it." Stevee ran his fingers over the sleek fur. "It's mink."

Stevee slid it on. No light shone through. "I can't see anything."

"Good," Brando said. "Your body warns you if something's about to hit you if you learn to pay attention. And if you listen hard enough, you can hear the balls moving through the air."

Stevee strained to hear. His body did warn him with a prickly sensation, and he'd dodge or throw up an arm but too late. Finally, after several rounds, he deflected one.

"Well met," Brando said. "We'll work on it more tomorrow, but you can take that off now."

Stevee removed the hood. "Don't I need to know how to hit too?"

Brando chuckled. "We'll get to that, but now we need to join the others."

When they left the tent, there were lots of clanspeople and several city people crowded around the fire enjoying the steamed mussels that Fujee and Gentu provided. Tayro put some shells in Stevee's bowl to try. They were garnished with wild onion, garlic, and sprigs of rosemary.

Stevee lifted a shell to his lips. When he slid the small morsel in, the flavors burst on his tongue. Yum. "This is my new favorite food. It's the most delicious thing I've eaten."

The sub-pack all laughed. It wasn't funny to Stevee. Going without food made him appreciate it. Hopefully, they'd never learn what it was like to have their stomachs gnaw at them.

#

Dayvee

A loud splat woke Dayvee.

Stevee screeched, "That was nothing, Bigham. I deserve more."

Stevee must be dreaming again. He was thrashing around. Another splat sounded. Did he just hit himself?

Stevee cackled. "That didn't even hurt." A crack sounded.

Whoa. He just punched his own chin.

Brando and Codee leaped up and grabbed his arms. "Stevee, wake up."

"Ouch." Stevee's eyes snapped open. He rolled, trying to get free. "Why are you hurting me?"

"We're not," Codee said as he and Brando let go of him. "You were hitting yourself in your sleep."

Stevee stood and pulled on his pants over his shorts. "I'm sorry for bothering you. Go back to sleep."

Brando grabbed his arm. "I'm not teaching you to fight so you can beat on yourself." Stevee shook his arm, and Brando released him.

"You need to talk to a keeper about why you believe you need to be hit."

Stevee buckled his belt. "I'm not talking to Gaylo. He doesn't even like me."

"I don't think Gaylo dislikes you," Dayvee explained. "It's a keeper's job to warn us, even if it might seem harsh."

"I'll talk to you, Stevee." Elayni rose.

"No." He put his weapon sheath on. "I can't share it with you."

Dayvee would have to insist. "You need to talk to one of us. It's an order."

"I'm a good listener," Codee sounded wistful.

"I don't think any of you will understand, but Dayvee might come closest, only I'm not talking where everyone can hear."

"All right. We'll go outside." Dayvee pulled his clothes on. "Brando, don't say it. We won't go far, and you can watch from the tent."

Elayni chewed on her bottom lip, then handed Stevee a hide. "The ground's probably wet, so take this to sit on." She glanced at Dayvee. "Can't this talk wait until later?"

"No." Brando shook his head. "Stevee's fists will hurt him more than damp pants, so stop mothering, Elayni."

Stevee gave her a smile. "Thank you, Elayni. I think mothers are great."

Dayvee moved to the tent flap on his crutches with Jaycee. Stevee and Graydee followed them out into the cool night air. The Pericard guards moved to come with them. "Stay here," Dayvee ordered.

Crickets chirped, frogs croaked, and an owl hooted. The night was full of rustling. Stevee's head swiveled at every noise. Dayvee's newest Calupi was obviously worried. Did he have reason to be? Dayvee sent to all the animals around them. *Is there any danger?*

16

Complicated

"Go with your instincts. Overthinking a problem only gives you a headache." ~ Jaycee

Stevee

Stevee's skin crawled.

"It's just some animals that are nocturnal. They're not going to bother us," Dayvee said.

It wasn't the night or the animal sounds that had Stevee on edge.

They walked about twenty paces from the tent when Dayvee stopped. "This good?"

Stevee glanced back at the tents. The light of the moon let him pick out the shadows of the closest and the Calupi watching at the door of theirs, but he didn't think anyone could hear them. "Yes." He spread out the hide.

Dayvee also glanced back at their tent then sat down. "You like Elayni, don't you?"

Was Dayvee upset about it? Stevee sure wasn't admitting how much. "What's not to like?" He plopped down on the hide, and a pebble jabbed his butt. Not real smart to plop. So close to the river, there were probably lots of pebbles around. Jaycee and Graydee sprawled next to him.

Dayvee sighed. "Did you know that until you finish your training, you're not considered a Calupi adult, and you can't ask anyone to life-mate?"

Figured. Stevee ran his hands through the silt in front of him. There were several pebbles. "That must be why Brando keeps calling me kid."

Dayvee chortled. "He used to call me kid, too, and he's only a month older than me."

Stevee found a smooth pebble, perfect for his slingshot, and put it inside his pouch. "How long will it take to finish the training?"

"Depends on how long it takes for you to learn the skills." Dayvee felt the ground too. "We'll all work with you, but it will probably be several months." He held out a stone. "Here."

Stevee turned around to check the area behind him. "I don't have much chance of her waiting, do I?"

Dayvee moved to the back of the hide too. "Probably not."

"Didn't really figure I had any chance anyway. Did you know Lulay's interested in you?"

"I could tell." Was Dayvee blushing? "Your sister's gorgeous, but I'm not interested."

Stevee put another stone in his pouch. "Codee said that Elayni loves you. Do you love her back?"

"Yes."

"Then why haven't you asked her?"

Dayvee handed him another stone. "It's complicated."

"So was being an adrift, but you keep saying I need to share."

"Our capabilities determine a Calupi's status. If I survive, my status will fall to practically nothing because whatever duty the pack assigns me, another could do better."

"So what does that have to do with life mating?"

Dayvee stopped patting the ground. "Elayni is high status. She deserves someone with status to match, who can protect her. Plus it wouldn't be right to take a mate when Kayndos never live long."

"You beat me in the competition on the nail throw, so you could protect her." Stevee put a few more stones in his pouch. "I could share why Caspian would say your other reasons are stupid if you want to hear an adrift's opinion."

Dayvee twisted to check the ground on the other side of him. "I'd like to know what the all-wise Caspian would have said."

"He'd tell you not to worry about tomorrow. Find joy today because tomorrow isn't promised. And you should never wait to show you care. Then he'd say adrifts don't get status, but we don't need it because we have each other. And if we love each other well, that's more than enough."

"Hmmm. Now I see why you believe he was so smart. I'll think about it."

"He'd say don't be stupid and think very long. Find joy today." Stevee put a couple of more stones in his pouch Dayvee handed him. "Thanks. My pouch is full now."

"You're welcome. In your dream you were taunting Bigham, telling him to hit you harder. You said you deserved it. Did you really do that?"

"Yes. I'd rather get beat than go in the box. If he bruised me enough, sometimes he was satisfied, and there were times I did deserve it."

Dayvee moved back around to face the tent. "I hated Nero when he hurt me. I came close to hating Varian. I'm still upset at Kun for not preventing my injury or Geno's death. I don't think anyone deserves beat like that. So why do you believe you do?"

"Neither Bigham or Kun chose my path. I could have waited for nightfall and climbed the wall instead of trying to go out the gate. I put myself there, and I failed to keep others from being harmed."

"You tried."

"No, not always. Sometimes when I came out of the box I'd avoid everyone, and keep my eyes on the ground so I wouldn't have to step forward and try to prevent Bigham from hurting anyone. I didn't want to go back in the box, but I'd see their bruises later. Those images haunt my dreams because I could have prevented them, and I can't always lock away my shame, especially when I sleep."

"Sometimes I see Geno in my dreams and all the others who died because of my choices. I share your pain."

"It's not the same. Geno chose to jump in front of you. None of the adrifts chose to have a lead that didn't protect them."

"You did protect them. Maybe not every time, but they knew you helped them. If it weren't for you, we wouldn't have even gone there. If you chose your path, so did they. You need to quit blaming yourself."

Elayni moved out of the tent with Evee at her side. They came partially across to them, then stopped and waited.

Stevee sighed. "You said you don't keep secrets from each other. Are you going to tell everyone what I did?"

"No, but you should. Don't you feel better now that you shared?"

Stevee did feel lighter. "Yes."

"They want to help you too. And neither she nor Brando has much patience, so he'll be coming next."

"I'll tell them later."

"Okay. I need to talk to Elayni. Can you go back?"

"Sure." Stevee stood, and Graydee jumped up too. "I'll even try to keep Brando busy. I'll ask him to teach me how to hit myself better."

Dayvee laughed. "That should do it."

#

Dayvee

"Elayni, can we talk?" Dayvee called to her as Stevee moved toward the tent.

"Yes." Elayni's answer was hesitant, but she and Evee came over. Evee plopped next to Jaycee as Elayni sat facing him. Her golden locks caught the moonlight as she chewed her bottom lip.

Those lips captivated him. Dayvee wanted to kiss them and erase her concern. He pulled his gaze up to her eyes. That was a mistake. He could get lost in those shimmering light blue pools. Unfortunately, there wasn't a single thing about her that he didn't love.

Regardless of what Stevee said, the right thing had to be to let Elayni go. If his heart would just stop screaming to reach out and pull her close, it would be a lot easier. Dayvee drew a breath and fought for control.

Jaycee nudged him, *You're miserable listening to your mind. Wolves follow our hearts.*

Dayvee's decision had never been about what was best for him.

She's miserable too. Look at the dark shadows under her eyes.

The stress of going to battle the invaders was probably causing those shadows. But what if Dayvee had? She'd cried when he told her he wouldn't life-mate, but he thought she'd get over him quickly.

Jaycee sent, *Have you been able to get over her?*

Did she feel as deeply about Dayvee as he did about her? "Elayni, could you be happy with one of the others who are interested in you?"

She crossed her arms and rubbed her hands up and down them. Was she cold? The longing to warm her had him reaching toward her, but he pulled his hand back.

Elayni finally answered. "No one else could make me as happy as you." Tears pooled in her eyes. Her lips trembled, and she choked out, "Do you like Lulay?"

What? How could she think it? "No. There's no one more beautiful than you or anyone who could compare. You own every beat of my heart, every breath I take. When you smile, my heart leaps. When you cry, I can't breathe. I don't even know if I can live without you."

She sniffed. "You sure haven't been acting like that."

"Because I love you so much that when it came between choosing what I thought was best for you or for me, I chose you. I don't want you to settle for less than you deserve." He waved his hand toward his feet. "I won't have any status like this."

"Anyone else would be settling." A tear ran down her cheek. "I don't *care* if you're omega." Her voice cracked. "I want you."

Elayni was strong. But Dayvee had broken her. He hated that tear, and everything in him cried out to stop more from falling. Finally, his mind and heart agreed. Jaycee and Stevee were right. She wasn't getting over him, and he couldn't get over her.

Dayvee reached for her hand. When his fingers entwined with hers, it felt like coming home after a long time away. "Stevee and Jaycee's advice was I should give us both joy." He squeezed her hand. "I think they're right, but I don't want to life-mate until after the battle. If we survive it, I'll ask Gaylo to hold a life-mate ceremony for us if you still want to."

"Yes, I want to." She flung herself closer and brushed her lips against his. The scent and taste that was unmistakably Elayni washed over him, as sweet as the first strawberry after a hard winter. He needed more. Dayvee took the kiss over and crashed his lips down on hers. As if lightning struck nearby, the world sizzled. Headiness overwhelmed him. He howled inside.

Stevee's exhausted. Graydee's mind voice demanded his attention. *Can you rescue him from Brando?*

Dayvee pulled back and broke the kiss, leaving them both gasping for breath. "I'd rather kiss you more, but Graydee says Stevee needs me."

"Okay, but if you want to keep kissing like that, we should hold the ceremony today."

Dayvee groaned. "Are you going to tempt me?"

She winked. "Every chance I get."

#

Stevee

Brando had lit a lamp, and it made Stevee's shadow prominent on the tent wall. Dayvee and Elayni better hurry up. Stevee couldn't keep this up forever. He snapped another punch at his shadow and glanced over at his critiquers.

Codee shook his head. "You didn't stay on the balls of your feet."

Petite little Chayla took a step and punched. "You need to step into it like that so you can get your weight behind it."

Tayro shaped a fist and held it up. "Your thumb has to stay on the outside of your fist, or you're going to break it."

"It wasn't fast enough either. Try it again," Brando commanded.

Stevee swung. The tent flap pulled back, and Dayvee and Elayni came in. Finally.

"Brando," Elayni yelled. "Are you teaching Stevee to hit himself harder?"

Brando sputtered, "It was his idea."

Dayvee laughed. "Good job distracting, Stevee." He sat down on his bedroll and put his crutches beside him. Elayni sat next to him, and he took her hand in his.

"So she said yes?" Stevee asked.

Elayni's smile beamed. "I said yes."

Brando's face broke into a wide grin. "Yes to what?"

"I asked Elayni to life-mate," Dayvee replied.

"Woohoo." Brando ran over to Dayvee and thumped him on the back. "About time."

Codee, Chayla, and Tayro went over to congratulate them.

"Come on over, Stevee," Elayni called. "You should share our joy since you gave Dayvee such good advice."

He shook his head. "Not me, Caspian."

"You passed it on," Dayvee said. "So come here."

He went to them, and Elayni gave him a warm hug. "Thank you."

"Yes, thanks." Dayvee clasped his arm.

"When are you going to hold the ceremony?" Chayla asked.

"First, we'll fight the invaders." Dayvee released Stevee's arm. "We'll life-mate when it's over."

Brando laughed. "Sounds like we could end up doing Rashee at the same time."

"What's that?" Stevee asked.

"Newly mated couples go off alone with their companions for several weeks until their souls entwine," Dayvee explained. "And Brando, you better not come looking for us. We don't need help."

Brando chuckled. "Dayvee, I promise that's one thing I'll let you do alone. I'm just really glad you're both happy."

Elayni glanced at Stevee. "Dayvee said you'd share why you were hitting yourself."

"I'll share it with you, but not tonight. I don't want to spoil your joy, and you need to sleep."

"Stevee's right," Dayvee said. "We have only a few hours before we need to get up."

They laid back down on their bedrolls. "Stevee"—Brando's head popped up—"you should sleep on your fists."

Stevee smiled to himself. "According to you, I'm terrible at punching, so I doubt I'll hurt myself."

"Yeah, but you might get lucky."

...

Guilt pricked Stevee when Tayro yawned. All of the sub-pack kept yawning. Stevee wasn't used to sleeping much, but they were. Tayro added raspberries and honey to the grain gruel in the pan cooking over the fire. The scents wafted to Stevee over the wood smoke and set his mouth to salivating.

"Come eat." Tayro dished out a bowl of gruel for him and handed him a cup of chamomile tea.

Stevee sat down on a hide and blew on his tea and gruel to cool it. Fires flickered all along the river as everyone else prepared for departure too. The sun hadn't peeked out yet, but a pre-dawn gray had already replaced the blackness of the night.

Elayni carried her breakfast and sat beside Stevee. "Now you can finish sharing why you think you should be beat."

Stevee swallowed a mouthful of gruel. Elayni wasn't going to let this go. "I told you I wasn't a good person."

Elayni put her bowl down and stuck a finger in his chest. "Don't ever say that. You are a good person. If you can't believe it yourself, then believe us. Brando's right. We'd be lucky to have you join our family."

"No." He couldn't meet her gaze. "You protect each other, but I ignored the adrifts' pain to save myself because I didn't want to go back in the box."

"Cackles, Stevee. How many times did you go in that box?" Brando demanded as he and Dayvee sat by them.

"At least once a week, sometimes more."

"For how many years?" Codee came over too.

"Four."

Brando shook his head. "That's over two hundred times you protected an adrift. There's not any way I could have done it that many times."

Chayla dropped beside them. "I don't know if I could have done it once, certainly not twice."

"I agree." Dayvee stuck a spoonful of gruel in his mouth.

"Clanspeople hate confinement." Codee took a sip of his tea. "There's not one of us who could have done it all the times you did."

"Maybe Caspian tried to avoid it too." Brando's nose wrinkled. "I would have. Be proud of yourself. The adrifts were."

"But I made mistakes, some that got adrifts killed."

"Not intentionally." Codee took another swallow of tea. "Everyone makes mistakes. All we can do is learn from them and try not to repeat them. Mistakes don't mean you're a bad person, and we don't deserve beat because we make one."

"So now will you join our family?" Brando put his empty bowl down.

The yearning bubbled up inside and refused to be buried again. Like every adrift, Stevee wanted family to claim. But he needed to be careful and guard his heart. "I'm a lot of trouble. You already lost another night of sleep."

"You'll cost us more if you don't agree," Elayni said. "Because we'll use every night to convince you."

Stevee had to remember this might be temporary. "If you're really sure you want me?"

"We are," Brando said. "Our family requires a promise to do the best you can to care for one another. Forever. And we also agreed not to keep secrets from each other. Are you willing to do that?"

Stevee hesitated. "My secrets are painful even for Graydee. Some could be dangerous for you to know, and there are too many to tell at once."

Dayvee put down his cup. "You could start with one a day. And we'll keep your confidences like we expect you to keep ours."

They already knew some of his secrets. They hadn't rejected him. Maybe it would be okay. "All right. I promise I'll do the best I can to care for our family and I'll share my secrets."

"Good, you're now family," Brando said. "What happens to you, happens to us, and what happens to us, happens to you."

They surrounded him to give him a group hug. "Welcome to the family."

The pain in Stevee's heart since he left the adrifts lightened. After losing his parents, he'd never take family for granted again.

"Okay, we need to help our family member," Dayvee said. "Frudo's trying to get other clanspeople to treat Stevee as omega, and the city people are still treating him as an adrift. How are we going to change it?"

"I don't care what others think about me," Stevee said.

Graydee sent, *Yes, you do.*

Graydee was right. It hurt to be looked at as if he were nothing. He just got used to denying it, even to himself.

"We do." Chayla grabbed paper. "I'm going to write a story about you and share it tonight."

Tayro crossed his arms. "I'll make a proclamation to the city people that as king I refuse to accept adrifts being treated terribly anymore."

"I'll see if I can get Frudo into the ring for a friendly competition." Brando chuckled. "After I win, I'll remind him I'm teaching you my fighting skills."

Elayni gave Stevee a wink. "I'll talk to the young Calupi women. Probably half already are interested in you, and more will be. They'll side with us."

"Great." Dayvee rubbed his chin. "I can think of one more thing to help the resentment. All of you should share your stories about how difficult it is to guard me when I don't cooperate."

Brando laughed. "We can do that."

Gratitude filled Stevee for what they were trying to do. But if he made them angry, wouldn't they kick him out of their family? Probably. But that didn't mean he couldn't enjoy the support while it lasted.

"Stevee, you should let Nolte know you joined our family, but try not to alienate the Kwin." Dayvee ran a hand through his hair. "Let Nolte know he's still important to you."

"I'll try, but he's not going to be happy." Stevee gave them a smile. Nolte might not be, but he was.

17

Shocked

"What shocks us may be perfectly normal to another." ~ Leeto

Logan

Logan's head ached as he marched alongside his brother at the head of the columns of their soldiers. He'd managed to get Roger assigned to him as a guard so at least he had someone he semi-trusted beside him. Garth should have taken a few of the cannons, but he had deemed them unnecessary since these people didn't even have guns. There was no pretense of Logan being in charge now. Garth was giving all the orders. When Logan tried, the officers just looked to Garth for a counter or approval.

One of their scouts came running up to them. "There's a city up ahead."

Probably Portia. So far the map their so-called allies had given them seemed to be correct.

"How many people?" Garth demanded.

"I'm guessing a couple of thousand, but only a few seem to be soldiers."

"We'll go in shooting. I want only a few survivors to escape to spread the tale."

"Are you planning on killing everyone on this continent?" Logan snarled. "Who will pay Father's taxes then?"

Garth *tskkd*. "After we decimate a few cities and their army, the rest of the population will be too terrified to resist. And I'll stop setting examples when they do exactly as I tell them."

Logan was sickened. "But you're not even giving them a chance to comply."

"First they need to be shocked," Garth said. "Then I'll let the rest have a choice—submit or die."

#

Dayvee

Dayvee kept searching the sky. No seabirds yet. It was already evening, but still no word had come from the coast. Not hearing anything was as bad as hearing bad news. Why hadn't one of the seabirds come? Had they all been killed? This slow speed was killing him. They'd need to camp in a few hours before the sun completely left the sky. Reko had warned him of ruins here. He'd like to get beyond them first. He reached out to Fujee's otter companion.

Glido, do you know of a good campsite on the other side of the ruins.

Yes, Kayndo, not too far from the ruins the woods edge the grasslands.

Good. Dayvee urged Ghostee up the hill. When he topped it, the view opened to include the ugly piles of rubble on the horizon. His sub-pack sucked in their breaths as they too beheld the sight. Another of the ancient's cities scarred the landscape. He'd expected it, but it didn't make it any less ghastly.

The unnatural piles cast dark shadows in the otherwise bright day. Dayvee's neck prickled in warning. He wouldn't risk their souls to get close to that. They needed to detour around it. He descended the hill and guided Ghostee over to Hardy River. They needed to water their horses and fill their water bags. Skyto's voice cried out in his mind. *I think you've got enemies headed your way.*

Can I use your eyes? Dizziness assaulted Dayvee as the disorientation came. When it cleared, he looked through the eagle's eyes to see a crowd of city people below. The grime-encrusted bodies, ragged clothing, and unkempt hair revealed them to be from the bottoms. They split into smaller groups of about a dozen people each and walked into the woods, out of Skyto's sight. How far are they from us? With a few beats of his wings, Skyto soared above the tree line to where the road crossed it. Coyote clan trotted down the road with fox clan behind them. The big willow growing nearby was one Dayvee had passed not long ago.

Thanks. Dayvee returned to his body and dizziness assailed him again. He sent to all the companions. Be watchful. Enemies are headed our way, and they've split into several groups so they could attack us in several places at once.

Reko and Denee came over to where the sub-pack was watering their horses and filling waterskins. Reko waved a hand toward the ruins. "The caravan road winds through the edge of the ruins along with the river. I know you didn't want to get close, Dayvee, but it will be hard to get through these woods or cross Hardy River with the wagons."

"How come you know this area outside Harthome so well when you belong to Grassy Knoll herd?" Chayla returned her water bag to her belt.

Good question. Dayvee had wondered the same. Reko gave them a sheepish smile. "I used to belong to Black River Herd. I did a lot of the short term leases, but I switched herds last year."

"Why?" Chayla asked.

Reko shrugged. "I didn't think Black River Herd appreciated me, so I decided to share my charm."

Denee snorted. "Reko couldn't handle being near Lulay when he didn't have the status for her to consider."

Dayvee rubbed his temple as voices of companions assaulted his head. *We're fighting.*

Worry assuaged him. Brando put his horse closer. "Let me take some of the Calupi and go after them. They're like these gnats that keep bothering us. They need to be swatted."

Codee shook his head. "We don't let gnats distract us or keep us from our goal. They really haven't done much damage. If anything, it's keeping us sharp."

One of the Kwin's horses spoke in Dayvee's head. *All of our enemies are fleeing.*

Did anyone die?

No, but we have some injured. And they stole one of our supply wagons.

Dayvee sighed. "Those wagons make too good of a target, and they're slowing us down. I'm going to have everyone unload the wagons. We can pack the mules, and most of us should be able to carry a few more supplies. If we need to leave the tents, we'll sleep under the stars."

As people began to unload wagons, Elayni asked, "How do our enemies seem to know the weak areas to hit? Are those that join us still giving the vow?"

"Everyone knows not to let anyone join without giving it," Blake answered.

Dayvee scanned the woods. "Our enemies are probably scouting us. The eagles can't tell with so many coming to join us which are enemies, so they look for groups and ask me. I didn't have them alert me for individuals because I didn't believe them a risk."

Reko pointed to the north where the woods seemed less dense. "That's the best way to go if you want to leave the road here to go around the ruins."

"I do." Dayvee glanced back. With so many helping, the wagons had been unloaded already. He turned Ghostee off the road. The others scrambled to follow suit.

Dayvee. The mind-voice sounded distant, but it was unmistakably his father's wolf companion. Could he be so close?

Luko, is it really you?

Yes.

Who's with you?

Your father and several others from the pack. We should reach you in a few hours.

His stomach flipped. He was Kayndo now. Why did facing his father still set his stomach to churning? Even with his nerves, he missed the familiar faces of his pack. Then relief surged through him. Leeto always knew how to get things accomplished. He'd be able to fix this. He might even keep Dayvee from making so many mistakes. He'd better inform the others. "Luko just reached out to me. Leeto and the others from Wolf Mountain are a few hours out."

Codee smiled. Brando groaned. Stevee asked, "Is that bad?"

"No," Codee said. "We'll be able to give you a pack home now."

Brando snorted. "Don't be in any hurry to join. Leeto's not known for being kind."

"Show respect for our leader, Brando," Codee snipped.

Brando swung his horse around a log in the path. "My leader's Dayvee, and I do respect him."

Hold on, Ghostee sent.

Dayvee clasped his legs tighter on Ghostee as he jumped the log. "I'm glad he's coming, Brando. I need Leeto."

"No, you don't, and neither does Stevee or any of us." Anger infused Brando's tone. Could anyone blame him after Leeto sent a Quincee against him? Those penetrating blue eyes locked onto Dayvee. "You should break away from Wolf Mountain and give us our own pack."

"Don't be ridiculous. I can't be an alpha. I can't even fight a challenge."

"None of us would challenge you." Brando caught one of the flies bothering them in his fist. "If anyone did, they'd have to get through me first." He tightened his fist, squashed the fly, then let it fall from his hand.

"I'm willing to leave Wolf Mountain if you're unhappy there, but I won't be alpha, so you'd have to lead. Although you might want to wait to see if any of us survive first."

Jaycee stumbled beside Ghostee. Even though his wolf companion shared the pain of Dayvee's foot injuries, it wasn't like him to stumble like that.

Are you okay?

Yes. Just distracted. I've been relating to Luko everything that's happened so he can tell your father.

Great. There were some things he'd rather Leeto not know.

I didn't tell them you considered killing yourself after you learned how badly your feet were injured.

Thanks. But how much of what happened would Leeto criticize?

Hopefully, he would use some tact and not tear into him in front of everyone. Dayvee should offer hospitality, and it would be nice if they had fresh meat. He hadn't sent anyone out to hunt with Bigham's men around.

Jaycee sent, *We wolves can investigate and make sure the area is safe.*

"Codee, the wolves are going to scout. How about if you take Stevee for a hunting lesson?"

"Great idea, Dayvee." Codee looked at Reko. "I prefer to hunt on foot, so can you have the horses stay with you?"

"Sure," Reko answered as Codee and Stevee dismounted. They trotted into the woods with Graydee and Wilee while other wolves glided into the trees all around them.

A hawk called out to Dayvee. *Kayndo, I have news of the invaders.*

Dayvee searched the sky to see a red-tailed hawk being chased by three sparrows. *Leave that hawk alone. He's bringing me a message.*

The sparrows broke off. *What's your news?* Dayvee asked the red tail.

This morning the invaders attacked Portia and slaughtered their men, women, and children. Only half a dozen survived.

Oh no. Tears that Dayvee refused to spill burned his eyes. What evil people these invaders were. Somehow he had to stop them.

\#

Stevee

Stevee followed Codee into the forest. Whoever said a forest was quiet? Birds squawked, squirrels chittered, insects hummed. All of them assaulted his ears. Graydee's head cocked and the wolf sniffed at the air and then the ground. Codee's head and eyes constantly turned as if scanning for something.

It put Stevee on edge. Were Bigham's men close? He grabbed his slingshot. "Is there danger?"

Codee stopped walking and turned to him. "There is always danger, like that mountain lion that dropped on you. One of the most important things you need to learn is to always be aware of what's around you. That isn't just for hunting but a Calupi's life. We must listen, look, and smell for not only those things that can aid us but harm us because if we relax our guard, we die."

Stevee nodded. "Adrifts have to stay alert, too, but I don't know everything dangerous here."

"Graydee can help with that. If you can't identify a sound, scent, or sight, ask him. Now do you see any tracks or animals here?"

Stevee closely examined the ground. He saw some scratches that kind of looked like a short arrow. He pointed. "These?"

"Yes, those belong to a pheasant. Anything else?"

Stevee studied the ground again. "No."

There are seven animals within a few feet of you, Graydee sent. *But Wilee says we should let you find them.*

Seven, seriously? Stevee couldn't find one animal.

"City people don't look up much," Codee said.

Stevee scanned the trees. "Ah. There's a squirrel up there, and I think that's a raccoon in that other tree."

"Yes. You got two. Only five left, and those aren't in the trees."

"Then why aren't they fleeing from us?"

"They're relying on their camouflage to hide them. Don't look for colors but shapes that are different than the grass or brush."

He looked again and found something pear shaped, then three more among the grass. "There are four birds."

"Yes, those are the pheasants. Now just one more."

Some grass trembled. A rabbit crouched among the stalks with only its breathing marking it as living. "I found the rabbit."

"Good. As soon as one of the pheasants gets hit, the rest are going to explode into the air. So we'll strike together."

Stevee reached for his slingshot then grabbed a stone.

"Why don't you try your new bow?" Codee asked.

"I'm sure I'll get one with my slingshot."

"This is just extra. We'll need more than this to feed our packmates. We'll be hunting the deer next. You missed those tracks."

Okay, he'd give his bow a try. Stevee took the bow off his back and lined up two arrows in it. It had been a while since he tried to shoot two arrows. It meant less force and accuracy, but it might get them two birds. He drew back the string.

Codee had his nails already out. "Now."

He let the arrows fly. Wings exploded as a bird took to the air. He switched the bow to his left hand, and with his right hand drew his cumback to throw it at the bird in the sky. The pheasant plummeted to the ground. He caught his returning cumback.

Codee walked over to where the birds had been hiding. A broad smile lit his face as he picked up the three birds. "Well met."

The joy of accomplishment welled up in Stevee as he retrieved the final bird. Graydee and Wilee loped off. "Where are they going?"

"To flush those deer and chase them back to us, so get ready."

18

Accomplishments

"My best accomplishments were being chosen, life-mating, and having a family." ~ Nolte

Dayvee

Dayvee wiped sweat from his forehead. Maybe it hadn't been a good thing the pack mules had managed to carry the tent. The late evening's warmth made the inside of the tent miserable, and, of course, Brando insisted they hide inside while they taught Stevee to fight at their camp. Dayvee threw yet another ball. Stevee got his arm up in time to block it.

"Good, now do it again," Brando ordered.

Stevee panted with the exertion as he resumed his fighting stance. "You remind me of Caspian when he was teaching me to steal. He didn't believe in breaks either."

Brando laughed. Dayvee smiled to himself. If Stevee was comparing Brando to Caspian, then Brando must have gained Stevee's trust.

Jaycee nosed Dayvee before he could throw another ball. *Our packmates are only a few minutes away now.*

Elayni, Chayla, and Tayro ducked inside the tent. Elayni held a spoon. "We prepared plenty to feed everyone."

"Then we had better go greet them." Dayvee grabbed his crutches and hobbled toward the entrance. He sent to Graydee. *We need horses.*

"Are you going to make them give you a vow of loyalty?" Chayla asked as the sub-pack followed him outside. Pericards fell in around them as he weaved through the city of tents his army of supporters had pitched on the grasslands area they were camping at.

Leeto might not like it, but Dayvee had already promised Blake he wouldn't make any exceptions besides his sub-pack. "I sent Ursans out to meet them and get their vows."

Brando chuckled. "Maybe we'll be in time to see Leeto argue with a bear."

The horses trotted up. Dayvee pulled himself up by Ghostee's mane as the others mounted their horses. The sun was close to setting, and the horizon lit in brilliant shades of orange as the sun sank lower. Out in the grasslands, Dayvee picked out the Ursans moving away from a Calupi pack. It would be impossible to mistake the pack as any other than Wolf Mountain when they trotted forward in complete sync with each other. Leeto could be exacting, but to watch them sent pride flooding through Dayvee.

As they drew closer, Dayvee scanned the faces. Wow. Leeto brought almost every Calupi of fighting age. Then he saw Geno's father, and his heart fell. Would Mozee blame Dayvee for Geno's death? Dayvee's breath caught. What would happen to their pack if Dayvee got all of their warriors killed, and none of these Calupi returned?

Dayvee pushed the worrisome thoughts down as he motioned for the Pericards to move aside. He reined Ghostee to a stop in front of the man that he looked so much like. "Greetings Father." He reached down his arm, and Leeto grasped his forearm in the clan handshake. "I'm honored so many from Wolf Mountain came."

After the arm clasp, Dayvee lifted his arm and spread his fingers out. Leeto did the same. Those they led could break formation. Elayni, Tayro, and Chayla jumped off their horses and ran over to hug their parents. Jaycee left Dayvee's side to nose and greet the pack's companions.

Even though Jonesee was among them, Brando didn't leave Dayvee's side to greet him. He still claimed he had no father. Geno should be hugging his father too.

Dayvee met Mozee's gaze. "I want to tell you how sorry I am about Geno's death."

Mozee choked out, "Thank you."

"Geno died with such honor his story will never fade," Leeto proclaimed. "He *will* be remembered."

Dayvee could never forget Geno. Leeto tilted his head toward Stevee. He wanted an introduction. Dayvee obliged him. "This is Graydee's new chosen, Stevee, and I made him a temporary sub-pack member. Stevee, this is Leeto, alpha of our Pack."

"Greetings, Stevee." Leeto moved toward him. "I admired Renolee not just for his skill but his willingness to share his knowledge with us." He extended his hand. "So I'm glad to meet and welcome his son as Calupi."

Stevee glanced at Brando, who frowned, but gave him a nod. Stevee leaned down on Smokee and clasped Leeto's forearm. "Greetings, Leeto."

There were other things Dayvee wanted to discuss with Leeto, but they could wait until their needs were met. "If you could eat, we have food and drink ready at camp."

A corner of Leeto's mouth turned up. His smile. "We could eat."

"Then follow us." Dayvee turned Ghostee back toward the tent city that stretched along the edge of the woods.

. . .

Dayvee chuckled to himself as Brando shook the hide out and made a big production of spreading it near the fire, the place with the most honor. Brando wanted to remind Leeto the Kayndo was in charge. When Dayvee sat down, four Pericards took up positions at his back.

Jaycee sprawled beside Dayvee, then the other wolves. He didn't need more guards. "It's not necessary for my entire sub-pack to sit with me. Go visit with your families."

None of his friends even hesitated before spreading out more hides to sit around him. They kept scanning the area for threats. Should Dayvee order them to relax? Why bother when they wouldn't listen? Leeto should be pleased. When he appointed Dayvee's friends as guards, he took most of the fun from their lives.

Hard to believe Leeto hadn't started criticizing him yet. Dayvee waved his hand toward the pots of food sitting near the fire. "As our guests, we ask Wolf Mountain Pack to go first and help yourselves to the food provided." Brando probably wouldn't like it, but Dayvee needed to consult Leeto and Codee. "I'd invite my father and uncle to sit with us."

After filling their bowls, all of Wolf Mountain separated into small groups to sit with their sub-packs to visit and eat.

Leeto swallowed a bite of food. "This is good. What is it?"

"That's venison medallions and wild rice, with some of my seasonings," Tayro answered. "You should try the pheasant in mushroom sauce too."

Elayni returned with two bowls of food. She handed Dayvee one as she sat next to him. The aroma teased him and sent his mouth to salivating. "King Tayro's still our best cook."

"I can't take all the credit," Tayro said. "Codee and Stevee hunted with Wilee and Graydee's help."

Leeto's gaze met Tayro's. "Kwutee didn't want to lose you as his apprentice, but he's proud of you like I am. We'll do whatever we can to support you as King."

"Thanks."

Leeto turned to Brando and Chayla. "Our pack is pleased that you life-mated."

"Good because I don't intend to do it again." Brando grinned. "Calupi women bite too hard."

Chayla's face reddened as they laughed. Even Leeto chuckled. "We're also pleased about Dayvee and Elayni's decision to life-mate soon."

Dayvee smiled at Elayni. "I'm happy she said yes."

A waterskin of the Calupi fermented drink, Razi, was going around, and Elayni passed it to Dayvee. He handed the Razi on to Leeto without drinking. "Can I ask your advice about something else?"

Leeto took a drink. "Go ahead."

"How can I get everyone moving faster so we can stop the invaders from killing our people?"

"When you first rode a horse, did you get sore?" Leeto asked.

Did Dayvee ever. "Yes."

"That's because you weren't Kwin and hadn't done it before.

Some of these people have never ridden. And most of the ones on foot aren't used to jogging all day loaded with a rucksack like Calupi. If you push them much more, they'll be too exhausted to fight when we arrive."

Dayvee blew out his breath. "Thanks, I'll take that into consideration."

Leeto set his bowl down. "There is something I think you're handling wrong if you want my opinion."

"Don't even start criticizing again," Brando snapped. "Or I'll challenge you."

Dayvee slashed his hand. "Enough, Brando. I want to know." Dayvee took a drink of tea. "But this is the first time you've asked before telling me what I was doing wrong."

"Kun appointed you for a reason. And you've been doing a great job. If you want my advice I'll give it, but I'm not going to force it on you now."

Was that a compliment from Leeto? Dayvee let his gaze go to Mozee. "Thanks, but I think Geno's parents might disagree about me doing a great job."

"Take one look at the ruins to see how deadly the ancients' weapons are. Your choices kept us from losing more people, but I think it's a mistake to ignore the attacks on our lines. I'd eliminate the threat before the problem grows."

"For once you and Brando agree. I'll consider it."

#

Codee

Leeto signaled to Codee with a touch of his lip. He wanted to speak to him alone.

Jaycee stiffened. Dayvee's head went up. They must have caught the signal. In a soft voice that resonated with authority, Dayvee said, "I told Codee he needs to put me first now."

A reminder Dayvee hadn't forgotten that Leeto and Codee had worked together to manipulate him before and hurt him in the process. The rest of the sub-pack and their companions stiffened. Brando shot them a glare.

Codee was proud of Dayvee for calling Leeto out. Leeto would be too.

Leeto lowered his head to Dayvee. "I wouldn't expect differently. Even my second needs to put the Kayndo first now."

Dayvee flicked his finger. "Then go ahead."

Brando smirked. His disdain of Leeto was going to cause problems. Codee rose and followed Leeto away from the light of the fires and into the night. Leeto probably wanted to talk about Dayvee's injured feet. Would he blame Codee?

Leeto stopped and turned to face him. "I thought you should hear the news about Jolay privately."

Codee's heart lurched. "Is she okay?"

"She's fine. Mad at me because I refused to let her come. She's carrying your child." He clapped Codee's arm. "You're going to be a father again."

Mist filled his eyes as the euphoria hit him. He and his beautiful life-mate were going to have a baby. "Thanks for not letting her come."

"I might not always show it, but we're family. I wouldn't risk your baby."

Guilt flooded him. "I'm sorry I failed to prevent Dayvee's injury."

"I'm the one who separated you. And if you were there, I'd just have two harmed. Do you still want to adopt Stevee?"

"Absolutely, but I can't get Nolte to approve."

"I approve. I'd like a nephew, and I want him in our pack as well."

"Lots of packs want him, along with the Kwin. Everyone knows he'll win weapon competitions. He's going to be an amazing hunter too. He killed three pheasants today in the amount of time I took to kill one."

A corner of Leeto's lip turned up. "I don't care if they want him as long as we get him."

"Then you need to fix your differences with Brando, or we may lose the entire sub-pack. Brando wants Dayvee to separate from Wolf Mountain."

Leeto sighed. "I want to speak to Stevee alone to ask him to join us, then I'll see if I can get Brando and Nolte to change their minds."

Codee moved back with Leeto toward the sub-pack. "Those things aren't going to be easy."

"Since when do we get easy?" Leeto asked.

When Codee and Leeto drew close, Dayvee was standing on his crutches talking to someone, and a crowd had formed around him and his sub-pack.

"Why is the sub-pack letting so many get close to Dayvee?" Leeto demanded.

"Dayvee insists on it. Most nights he tries to speak to anyone that wants to meet the Kayndo."

"The Kayndo can't talk to everyone at once," Brando roared. "Form a line and quit pushing."

Was that man in the crowd holding a weapon? Dayvee must be in danger. Codee grabbed for his nails, but there were too many people between them.

19

Threats

"No one can cope with danger that lasts forever, so be careful about imagining more." ~ Kwutee

Codee

Codee shoved his way forward to get through the crowd. Could he reach the man with the weapon in time to stop him? Brando jumped in front of Dayvee with his nails in his hand. "Drop that weapon now, or you'll die."

All of the sub-pack reached for weapons. The crowd moved in front of the man with the weapon, cutting him off from Dayvee. The Pericards tackled the man to the ground, pinning his arms. The weapon fell to the ground.

"Let him up." Dayvee pointed to a falcon flying above. "I've spoken to his companion. Dulee doesn't want to harm me. Give him back his weapon."

The Pericards released Dulee. They handed him his weapon.

"I apologize, Dulee," Dayvee said. "My guards are good, but sometimes they get a little too enthusiastic." Dayvee beckoned. "I remember us speaking about your weapon. Come here and show me."

"Cackles." Leeto slid his nails back in his pouch.

Brando shot Dulee a threatening glare, but he stepped aside to let him join Dayvee.

Dulee put the weapon in Dayvee's hand. Two blades crossed in an X. Every end was sharpened. The center of the X was wrapped with rawhide where Dayvee gripped it. "This is interesting, Dulee, I've never seen anything like it."

Leeto said softly to Codee, "I'm surprised the entire crowd moved to protect him."

"Most people that get to know Dayvee love him and want to protect him. There's only one other person I know with that ability, and that's Stevee."

Leeto frowned. "Not everyone loves them."

"No, but they don't know them. They resent their accomplishments."

"Hmmm. I won't be able to handle our differences by sending Brando back to the pack. I want him with Dayvee if he's that good at defending him."

Codee shrugged. "I doubt he'd go anyway. The only pack he cares about is that one."

"You think he'd defy a direct order from his alpha?"

"I don't think even Dayvee could order him away from his family."

When they made it through the crowd to join the sub-pack, Leeto gave Brando a chin lift and mouthed, "Well met."

Most Calupi would be overjoyed their alpha commended them, but Brando's expression never changed, and he went back to watching for more threats.

Why wasn't Stevee with the sub-pack? "Where's Stevee?" Codee asked.

"He's with the Kwin." Chayla's face creased in concern. "Tayro's treating our injured people, so Stevee went with Reko to help with the wounded horses."

"Is Stevee a healer?" Leeto asked.

"He knew how to splint and bandage." Codee adjusted his rucksack. "But he wanted to learn more, so Tayro's been teaching him the medicinal plants as well as the edible ones."

"Good. Kwutee needs another apprentice."

Codee chuckled. "You're counting on meat before the hunt."

#

Stevee

Smokee nudged Stevee's back and propelled him forward two steps. Stevee turned and Smokee blew in his face. Stevee and Nolte laughed at his antics, but Graydee growled. *He could hurt you.*

He didn't, Stevee sent back. *He's just having fun.* Stevee patted the horse. "You should return to your friends. I'll ride you tomorrow."

Smokee trotted off, weaving through the different sized tents and around all the fires of the various groups, which lit up the camp. Stevee and Nolte continued toward his sub-pack's campsite with Graydee at his side. After the confrontation with Frudo, Nolte and Dayvee made sure someone accompanied Stevee when he walked through camp. When they approached White River's tents, several Calupi had gathered around the fire there. Tayro and White River's keeper, Gaylo, stood among them, so they must be done treating the people who were injured.

Tayro looked up and called, "Did you have any problem with the horses?"

"No." Nolte stopped walking. "Stevee was a big help."

Frudo was glaring at Stevee, so he slipped his Kwin headband off and put on his Calupi. He shouldn't antagonize the bully, but he couldn't help himself. Frudo couldn't do much with everyone there.

Frudo's eyes narrowed. "I told you you're no Calupi."

"Do your eyes need fixed?" Stevee smirked. "I have a wolf companion and headband that say I am."

Frudo's chin jutted out. "A wolf sickened by grief would choose anyone to fill the void, even a lowly adrift, who's not good enough to be Calupi."

He's wrong, Graydee sent. *I chose the best.*

"Enough," snapped White River's Keeper, Gaylo. "No good can come of you two arguing."

Frudo's teeth clenched, but he stalked away, trailed by some of his packmates.

Gaylo's face was glum as he turned to Stevee. "You should tread softly and try to help Dayvee, not cause problems between packs."

What had Stevee done? Was he trying to cause more trouble so the sub-pack would desert him like Clint did?

Tayro's mouth pursed. "What do you expect Stevee to do? Deny that Graydee chose correctly?"

Nolte crossed his arms. "Frudo's in the wrong, and we all know it."

Stevee took in the rest of the White River Calupi. Their faces revealed nothing. Did they agree with Nolte?

They're not going to say they think a packmate's wrong in front of us, Graydee sent. *Even if they believe it.*

"It doesn't matter who's right," Gaylo huffed, "unless Stevee wants to fight. Frudo sure does."

Tayro's face hardened. "Stevee doesn't fight alone."

Nolte drew himself up. "No, he doesn't."

"I know that." Gaylo put up his hands palms out. "I don't want more trouble." He leveled a hard look at Stevee. "Adrifts keep to the shadows. Why can't you?"

Caspian's words came to Stevee's mind. "Be proud of what we accomplished, and who we are." He raised his head. "Not adrift leaders. We don't hide from bullies. We confront them."

Tayro gave Stevee a smile. "Sounds like Calupi to me." He turned to Gaylo. "Your alpha put you in charge. You can always send Frudo home."

"He'll be our alpha one day. He needs to learn."

Was Gaylo just afraid to cross Frudo?

"I don't think that's going to happen," Tayro said. "If I were you, I'd be considering joining a different pack." He glanced to Stevee. "Codee wants you to meet him at Dayvee's tent."

"Okay." Stevee didn't want to stay there anyway. He and Nolte left the White River tents and walked to the center of camp where Dayvee's and the Pericards' tents were set up.

A crowd stood around Dayvee's tent and the fire burning in front of it. Leeto and Codee moved from it toward them. The alpha of Wolf Mountain had a commanding presence and reminded him of Bigham. The authoritative stance demanded others pay attention.

"Stevee, I need to talk to you. Alone," Leeto commanded.

What? Stevee's neck tingled in alarm. Was he in trouble for what he just did? When Bigham wanted him alone, it meant a beating. Chayla had said Leeto was responsible for Brando being jumped and beat up. Leeto worried him way more than Frudo. Stevee looked for Dayvee. He was busy speaking with people.

Leeto followed his gaze to Dayvee. "The Kayndo gave me permission to speak to you."

Stevee's feet didn't want to hold still. He inched backward and searched for an escape route.

"Leeto's my brother," Codee said. "He's not going to hurt you."

Blake claimed Bigham wouldn't hurt him too. Nolte clasped Stevee's shoulder, making him jump. Nolte's face turned hard. "Leeto, you can say whatever you need to in front of me."

"No, I can't. I don't want Stevee to tell me what he thinks you want him to say. Dayvee gave me permission to speak to him alone, so I'm going to."

Nolte narrowed his eyes. "You just want to drag him off to pressure him into joining your pack. Stevee doesn't want to go with you, and you don't want to be my enemy."

Leeto's neck reddened. "Don't threaten me, Nolte. Unlike citypeople, Calupi aren't dependent on the Kwin for horses to haul supplies."

Stevee didn't want to cause more problems between clans. Who could help? He locked eyes with Brando, silently pleading for him to do something.

Brando motioned to Elayni to keep Dayvee shielded then strode toward them. Bruno's growl pierced the air as the wolf marched stiff legged beside him. Luko's ruff raised, and he met Bruno's growl with one of his own.

Leeto snapped, "Brando, for Bruno to forget his place and growl at an alpha wolf is asking for teeth."

Brando flashed his crooked mischievous grin. "Bruno knows who we are, even if you don't. When you made your vow you should have known if Dayvee's busy, you'll deal with his second. We have more authority than any alpha."

Leeto frowned, but Luko quit growling.

Brando glanced at Stevee. "Dayvee gave his permission for Leeto to speak to you, but I won't let you be hurt." He pointed at Leeto. "Don't even criticize him, or I'll take it personally."

Stevee's forehead broke out in a sweat. He didn't believe Leeto cared about what Brando took personally. The red hadn't left Leeto's neck, and his lips were drawn tight. Stevee didn't want to go somewhere Leeto could take his anger out on him. Everything in him urged him to flee.

Blake and some of the Pericards moved toward them, blocking his escape route. Blake rested a hand on his sword. "We Pericards told Stevee we wouldn't repeat our mistakes. I'm not going to allow someone I don't know very well to take him off alone."

Relief shot through Stevee. Hard to believe Blake would rescue him, but he'd take it.

The red in Leeto's neck moved to his face. Surely he wouldn't cross the Pericards.

"Allow?" Leeto snapped. "I don't need your permission. I have Dayvee's."

He was right. Blake wouldn't go against Dayvee. And Leeto was beyond angry. Did Stevee want to catch the brunt of it? He backed a few steps to run the other way.

Graydee sent, *Don't run. Dayvee's coming.*

Stevee's heart raced, but he waited.

"Sorry, but that's it for tonight," Dayvee announced to the crowd. The crowd moved away as Dayvee hobbled to Stevee's side. "I should have consulted you before agreeing to Leeto's request to talk to you alone."

Did that mean he would change it? Stevee wanted to ask, but he couldn't make his voice work.

Dayvee faced Leeto again. "Jaycee says the wolves have first claim on Stevee since Stevee isn't only Graydee's chosen but their pup. I was wrong to agree without consulting them."

"I don't understand."

"Luko says it's like with me. They called me Clay's pup because I was. I wouldn't have survived without Clay nursing me. When a wolf saves a pup, it becomes theirs. Stevee was in a fight for his life. He wouldn't have won it without Graydee's and the other wolves' intervention. They protected him until we showed up. Stevee is theirs."

Really?

Yes. You're ours.

Wouldn't the wolves get tired of the trouble Stevee brought?

You can't get rid of me. Our bond lasts until one of dies.

"Are the wolves trying to take my son from me?" Nolte asked.

"Jaycee says they're willing to share Stevee, but you need to as well. You can be his Kwin father and teach him Kwin things. Codee can be his Calupi father and help him with Calupi stuff. The wolves will teach him wolf things, but the wolves will have the final say on everything because Stevee's their pup."

"I don't understand." Codee eyebrows shot up. "I've never heard of anything like this."

"They say we don't need to understand," Dayvee said. "All they ask is that we listen to them when it comes to Stevee. Now Nolte, will you agree to share your son with Codee and the wolves?"

"My companion says I should, so yes, I'll agree."

"Good." Dayvee gave him a nod. "We'll work out the details later."

Leeto crossed his arms. "Regardless of who claims Stevee, he's still going to need a home. I was going to ask for a vote today if he agreed to make it Wolf Mountain."

"Graydee says he and Stevee aren't ready to make a decision yet. And Graydee will let you know when they are, so leave Stevee alone."

Relief shot through Stevee. At least he wouldn't need to face Leeto's anger.

Brando clapped him on the shoulder and laughed. "I think I'd have liked to be adopted by the wolves. I had to settle for Dayvee and Elayni."

Elayni shook her head. "Wolves don't like snakes. Who would you have pranked?"

"There is that. Stevee, it's time for your fighting lesson. And

Bruno agrees you need it."

"Go ahead, I'll fill in everyone on what we discussed," Dayvee ordered.

"I'll see you in the morning, Stevee," Nolte called as Stevee and Graydee moved to trail Brando and Bruno to their tent.

Stevee looked back and gave Nolte a wave. "What is Dayvee discussing with them?"

"A bird just updated him on the invaders' progress. If they continue at the same speed, we'll be fighting them day after tomorrow. To prevent Bigham and his men from attacking us at the same time, we're going after them in the morning."

"All of us?"

"No, we can't risk Dayvee. I'm taking Wolf Mountain and some of the other Calupi packs." Brando ducked inside the tent, and Stevee followed. "I was going to let you come too. I need someone to target Bigham since he's the leader, and you're the one who knows him."

Apprehension rose in Stevee. "Clint knows him too."

"Yeah, but after what Bigham put you through, I think you deserve to be the one, unless you'd rather not."

What if Stevee failed, and he ended up in Bigham's clutches again? His mouth dried. Hadn't he just told Gaylo adrift leaders didn't hide from bullies? Stevee's embarrassment rose. He had wanted to run from Leeto, and he wasn't even sure if he was a threat.

He'd reacted like that only because Leeto reminded him of Bigham. Bigham *was* dangerous. But was Stevee going to let him terrify him forever? Did he want to hide from him when he could end the threat he posed? But could he do it?

20

Pack

"Pack means comfort, food, and a shoulder to lean against if you're injured." ~ Graydee

Stevee

Stevee took a deep breath to calm his nerves. His tongue unstuck. "I'll do it. I'll target Bigham." Thank Kun, his voice didn't shake.

"Good." Brando motioned to Stevee's shadow on the hide wall of the tent. "Punch your shadow again."

Stevee rose on his balls of his feet, stepped into it, and swung. Then followed up with another jab, and another.

"Bruno says Nolte asked Dayvee if Denee and Reko could go with us to help you."

Did he really need babysitters? This workout already forced him to pant, but he got out, "There's no reason to risk them."

"I agree with Nolte. I'm going to be busy. During a fight, it would be easy for Frudo to kill you and blame it on our enemies."

Stevee stopped punching to look at Brando. "Frudo, would do that?"

"I don't know if he'd do it." Brando frowned. "He acts like a hyena, and they would. You should always look for enemies, even where you don't expect them. It's great if you have someone to help you do that." Brando pointed to the wall again. "I showed you how to do more than jab, so mix it up."

Good thing the break allowed him to catch his breath. Stevee swung a left hook at his shadow.

"White River is the only pack that hasn't accepted you. Everyone else seems to be happy about having Renolee's son as Calupi."

"They don't even know me." Stevee flung an undercut. "They're just judging me by my father."

"It could be worse. Your father could be a tiger like mine. That isn't considered good for a Calupi, and most everyone judged me by him until recently."

"I'm sorry that happened to you." Stevee stopped to wipe the sweat from his forehead.

"I'm not." Brando grinned. "It motivated me to learn to fight better so I could prove them wrong. And now you're benefitting."

"Is that what you call this?"

"Yes. Take a punch at me now." Stevee stepped into it and threw a right cross at him. Brando caught his fist. "You're quick, you've got good balance, but you don't have endurance or much strength."

Stevee gasped to draw in air again. No kidding.

You'll get more soon. Graydee lifted his head from where he and Brando's wolf companion, Bruno, sprawled near the tent entrance.

"Until you gain those, you're going to have to take your opponent out fast." Brando returned to his fighting stance.

"How do I do that?" Stevee asked.

"Your first strikes need to count. Aim for vulnerable spots, do it quickly and put everything you have into it. If you want to kill them, go for the throat and crush a windpipe. If you only want to take them down, kick their feet out from under them. If that doesn't work, go for the gut, face, or groin. Try it again."

Stevee kicked at Brando's leg. Brando jumped back and caught his follow through jab to his gut. "Better."

Stevee's sweat soaked his clothes as he sucked in more air.

"We've been short on laughs lately." Brando's crooked grin appeared. "You should do your first prank and put something in our sub-pack's boots tonight."

"Does it have to be sand?" Stevee threw an uppercut at Brando's chin.

Brando caught his fist. "Whatever you want. They're used to my pranks, so they'll probably check their boots, but they'll still laugh."

"Okay. I'll do it."

Both Graydee and Bruno jumped up at the crunch of footsteps outside. Brando let go of his fist. "We'll stop now. Bruno says Caylo needs to speak to you."

Even as large as the tent was, when Gaylo, Codee, and Leeto came inside with the sub-pack and their companions, they crowded it. Gaylo's probing gaze turned on Stevee. "Nolte agreed to share you with Codee so we can finish your adoption with a couple of vows."

Stevee would have given anything to have family come to his rescue when his father died. But did he really need another father now? It wasn't like he could back out. He'd already agreed. "All right."

Gaylo turned to Codee. "Codee, do you agree to embrace Stevee as a son, to care for him, and teach him our ways?"

"I do."

"Stevee, do you agree to embrace Codee as your Calupi father, to respect him, and listen to the wisdom he imparts?"

"I do."

"Then Codee is now your Calupi father, and you are his son."

Codee clapped him on the shoulder. "Welcome to the family."

Leeto slapped his back. "Welcome, nephew."

#

Dayvee

Leeto strode over to Dayvee and lowered his head.

Dayvee didn't let his smile show. It probably wasn't easy for Leeto. An alpha didn't show submission often.

Leeto gestured to Brando. "I'd like to talk to your second if he's not afraid of me too."

A sigh escaped Dayvee. Leeto was already on Brando's list of people he wanted to challenge. Fights between packmates weren't needed. He had bigger problems. They would face the invaders in battle all too soon.

Brando smirked. "It would take a lot more than you to scare me. Should I look for a Quincee?"

A corner of Leeto's mouth lifted in his smile. "I don't intend to fight, just talk."

Brando's blue eyes lit with a gleam. "That might be interesting."

Their face-off would happen sooner or later. If it occurred now, maybe Dayvee could keep it from getting out of hand. "Okay, but I need you both uninjured, so *only* talk."

They both gave Dayvee a nod in agreement. But if Leeto pushed Brando hard, his passionate friend would have a hard time keeping his anger in check. *Bruno, can you tell Brando I'm going to be body hopping?* Leeto didn't deserve prior knowledge. Not after he insisted Codee betray Dayvee's confidences for years.

Bruno cocked his ear in a wolf laugh. *Brando just finished saying that he would bet that you were going to body hop. I didn't take the bet.*

Brando had to be the only Calupi who'd try to get his own companion to make a bet. Dayvee smiled to himself and searched through the whispers in his mind. With it dark now, he'd need something nocturnal. He found an owl. *Can I use your eyes and hearing?*

Yes, Kayndo.

Dayvee got dizzy as he oriented to the new perspective of seeing through the owl's eyes. What amazing details. The fires were so bright, and they held more colors. With the owl's hearing, he could easily hear the footsteps of Brando and Leeto as they left the tent and strode toward Hardy River.

Can you follow them?

The owl flew over them until they got beyond all the tents of different sizes and shapes and over to the river bank. Maybe Leeto thought the river would hide their voices.

Leeto stopped and suddenly pivoted to stand toe to toe with Brando. One of Leeto's tests to check someone's mettle. Dayvee sighed to himself.

Brando didn't retreat. He met Leeto's steel gaze and returned one of his own. After a second, Brando grinned. "If you want a fight, I'd love that if you can get Dayvee to agree."

The owl landed on the limb of an oak tree next to the two Calupi.

Leeto snorted. "Do you think I don't know you've won every fighting competition here? What you don't realize is that I'm proud of your performance and the role I played in making you the Calupi you are."

"My skills have nothing to do with you. Dayvee and I put in the effort to learn what worked."

"For something to be valued, it has to be hard to gain." Leeto crossed his arms. "You and Dayvee share strong bonds and superior fighting skills because I made sure they were tested. I molded both of you."

The owl ruffled its feathers. Clay molded Dayvee, not Leeto.

Brando's eyes narrowed. "You might be able to delude yourself into thinking you sent a Quincee after me to help me, but I know better." His tone dripped contempt. "We became who we are in spite of you, not because of you."

Leeto blew out a heavy breath. "We both want what's best for our pack. Can't we set aside our differences and work together to protect them?"

"I could probably overlook what you did to me, but I can't forget things like Dayvee pounding his own head in the wall after you told him he wasn't good enough." Brando's voice lowered to a growl. "You intentionally hurt my family repeatedly, and I won't forgive that."

"You're the one deluding yourself. I'm not the one who harmed Dayvee by leaving him in a dungeon. But you aren't mad at me for Dayvee's sake. You've been angry at me since your father left."

Brando's face turned beet red, and his fists clenched. "Are you going to try to claim you let Jonesee stay away because it would make me strong to grow up without parents?"

"No. I didn't order Jonesee home because he said he'd walk off a cliff like your mother if he had to face the memories."

Brando's shoulders fell. "We could discuss the past all night, and it wouldn't change my feelings about you."

Dayvee had tried before to defend Leeto. If he couldn't change Brando's mind, Leeto sure couldn't. Leeto's jaw set. "I can live with that. But don't hurt our pack. If you come home, you have my word I'll step aside for Dayvee. And if you can't stand being near me, I'll leave and help Jonesee."

A splash sounded in the river. The owl's head swiveled toward it. Through the owl's eyes, Dayvee picked out Glido's sleek body swimming in the water. It looked refreshing. Dayvee sent to the otter, *How long does it take you to reach the bottom there?*

Longer than it takes me to eat a fish.

Thanks. Dayvee sent to the owl. *Can you focus back on the Calupi?* The owls gaze turned.

Brando shook his head. "Dayvee says he can't be alpha."

Exactly. Maybe Leeto didn't understand how badly Dayvee's feet were crushed.

"If he can be Kayndo, he can be alpha. But either way, he still needs to come home. Clay made sure Dayvee loves every spot on Wolf Mountain. And Chayla and Elayni will also be happier there with their families."

Dayvee *did* love Wolf Mountain. He missed the brilliant colors as the sun rose over the summit, the stars reflected in the pool, the beauty of the stalactites sparkling in the cave. The images in his mind made the ache sharper in his heart. But he'd known when he left, he might never return. That ache of homesickness was all too familiar by now, so it held a scab and could be easily ignored as long as it wasn't picked by dwelling on it.

"They already said they didn't want to return if I'd be miserable there. When one of us bleeds, we all do." Brando's mouth set. "I'm not sure if I can be happy there with all the bad memories, but I'll tell them your offer. Dayvee already knows."

Dayvee never had told Leeto about his body-hopping ability. *Can you go down there?* The owl glided to the ground.

Leeto grabbed his nails while Brando jumped to shield the owl. "Don't hurt it. Dayvee's body hopping with it."

"What?"

"Dayvee can share an animal's body. He can see, hear, and feel what they can when he wants to know about things beyond where he is."

Leeto's mouth gaped open. "That's a handy trick."

Yes, it was. *Bruno, tell Brando we should have some fun before we seek our bedrolls. That tree on the bank has branches that hang over the water. We could tie a rope to one of them.*

He says that's a great idea. He'll tie the rope while you bring the sub-pack.

Brando dug into his rucksack and pulled out his rope. "I'm done talking. Dayvee wants some fun."

Dayvee returned to his own body.

#

Stevee

Stevee sat with Codee and the rest of the sub-pack around the fire, waiting for Brando and Leeto to return. Elayni kept chewing her lip. Chayla's finger was in her mouth, and Codee poked at the fire with a stick. Were they that concerned? Dayvee's attitude was the strangest of all. He was slumped over, and his eyes appeared glazed and unfocused.

"Is Dayvee okay?" Stevee whispered to Elayni.

Elayni glanced over at Dayvee. "He's okay, just body hopping."

Huh? Before Stevee could ask more, Dayvee's head shot up. The gaze Dayvee leveled at the sub-pack was alert again. "Brando's done talking, and we agree it's a good night for some family fun."

Elayni smiled. "A fun night?"

"Not the entire night but an hour or two." Dayvee grabbed his crutches and rose. "Who's in?"

Tayro, Elayni, and Chayla scrambled to their feet. "I am."

Elayni grabbed Stevee's hand and tugged at it. "You won't want to miss it."

These Calupi considered things fun that Stevee didn't, but did he want to exclude himself? He ignored the twinge of worry and let Elayni pull him up. "I am."

Codee rose to his feet too. Dayvee shook his head. "Sorry, Codee, family fun nights are for our sub-pack family."

Codee sat back down as Dayvee led them away from the light of the fires. With the moon and stars, it wasn't completely dark. Behind the hum of insects and frogs croaking, the sound of water lapping against the shore got stronger as they approached the river. Dayvee stopped under a large grizzled oak tree.

Brando slid down the trunk. "About time." He held out one end of a rope that was tied to a branch above. "Can I have the honor of going first, Dayvee?"

"Since this is Stevee's first time, I think we should give him the honor."

"What?" Stevee sputtered. "But I don't know what to do."

Brando laughed. "Nothing to it. Grab on to this rope, run off the bank of the river, and when it's safe, let go."

Some honor? Were they trying to kill Stevee?

Graydee sent, *Calupi do consider it a great honor to confront danger first.*

"It's dark." Stevee's voice cracked. "How am I supposed to know where it's deep enough, or if there are rocks down there?"

"Trust me," Dayvee said.

Stevee's heart pounded. Everyone looked at him expectantly. Sheesh. Could it be worse than the box? He grabbed the rope and ran. His feet left the bank, and he was swinging through the air.

"Let go!" Dayvee yelled.

Stevee drew a deep breath, held it, then let go. He plummeted down. His heart pounded like crazy. Please don't let there be rocks. With a big splash, he hit the water and jetted deeper into its chilly depths. When he stopped moving, he kicked for the surface. His head burst out, and he sucked in air greedily. He was alive!

Brando called. "How's the water?"

A little cool but after the heat of the day, he wasn't complaining. "Perfect!" Stevee shook out his hair and swam for the shore. When he clambered up the bank, Dayvee wasn't there. "Where's Dayvee?"

Elayni pointed up. A dark shadow scooted down a limb that hung out over the water. Dayvee fell from the limb. He somersaulted then straightened. He hit the water with barely a splash. When his head emerged, he whooped, "Yes."

So he had meant to do that? Crazy Calupi. Brando was already climbing the trunk. Apparently to do the same.

"Go ahead, girls," Brando shouted from above. Chayla and Elayni ran together holding onto the rope and launched themselves off the bank. They let go of the rope, screamed, and hit the water together. Their laughter rang out as soon as they surfaced.

Then Tayro raced off the bank and swung out to join them. Brando dived off a branch, twisted his body to spin, then plunged in. When he bobbed up, they all called to Stevee to swing out again. He'd survived it once, so he grabbed the rope and flung himself off the bank. When he broke the surface, more water swooped over him as his sub-pack splashed him, so he retaliated.

A snap of a stick, then the crunch of leaves sounded somewhere close. Stevee stopped splashing. Was something out there? *It's Codee and Leeto,* Graydee sent.

Should we tell Dayvee?

He knows. It's not the first time they've watched. But he lets them think he's oblivious.

"Let's do one more dive before we seek our bedrolls," Dayvee called. "Whoever gets to shore first goes first. On the count of three. One."

Elayni grabbed his hand and tugged Stevee forward to the line they formed. "All Calupi love to compete, so you have to race with us."

With Dayvee's feet crushed, surely Stevee would beat at least him.

Dayvee glanced over at them lined up on both sides of him. "Two."

Would the others let Dayvee win? Maybe Stevee should?

"Three," Dayvee shouted.

Stevee put his head down and raced for the shore. He turned his face to catch a breath and look for the others. Yikes. Everyone was in front of him. Dayvee's feet might be crushed, but he rocketed through the water. How could that not hurt him? It must. Stevee forced his arms and legs to move even faster. He drew beside Chayla and finished in a tie with her for last place.

They clambered up the bank. Dayvee grasped the rope and climbed up to straddle a branch above. Brando and Tayro followed after him but chose even higher branches.

Elayni rolled her eyes. "They want to jump from the highest branch so they can do more flips before hitting the water. Typical of the guys to turn this into a competition too."

Didn't Stevee want to fit in? He went and grabbed the rope.

"Not you too?" Elayni said.

Stevee smiled at her. "Believe it or not, I'm a guy." He began to climb. He stopped at the crook of the trunk and branch that Dayvee sat on. He passed the rope back to Dayvee. "How do I do those flips?"

"Tuck tight and reach for your knees or ankles." Dayvee smiled. "You'll get the hang of it."

Stevee looked down at the moonlight reflecting on the river. It sure was a long way to the water. He should have plenty of time to figure it out, if only he survived.

21

Discoveries

"Never pass an opportunity to learn something new." ~ Kwutee

Logan

Logan waited impatiently as the soldiers finished setting up his tent in the wheat field. What did it matter if they damaged the new shoots? Who would harvest them? Surprisingly enough, Garth had agreed with Logan that they should camp outside of the city. Had he been sickened by the carnage, too, or just in a hurry to burn Portia down?

Garth had given the order to set the fires as soon as the soldiers finished ransacking the homes for the few valuables they found. The smoke hung heavy in the air even though the fires inside the city had run out of fuel. The acrid taste choked Logan, and the thick smog blurred the brilliant colors of the sunset.

His brother sat at their campfire with his henchman. Logan didn't want to join Garth. He wouldn't be welcome. The aroma of the beans cooking turned his stomach, but he needed to keep up his strength. Assassins couldn't have poisoned the food with so many eating from the same pot.

Logan went over, ladled a couple of spoonfuls into his bowl, and retreated to his tent. After this day of gore, he had no appetite. To get the beans down wasn't easy, but he managed. Crickets chirped, an owl hooted, and the mournful howls of wolves sounded in the distance. The howling sent a shiver up Logan's spine. There wasn't much wildlife left on their continent, so he wasn't used to hearing those noises.

A shadow played across the sides of his tent. Was it another assassin? Logan pulled his gun. A whisper sounded. "Can you open the flap?" It was Roger's voice.

"Yes." Logan unlaced the tent.

The light of Logan's lamp highlighted the consternation in Roger's olive toned face and brown eyes. The clansman said softly, "I came back so you could come with me."

"Where?" Logan asked.

"I'm going to sleep in the wilderness. I want to breathe in the scent of trees, not the stink of soldiers or Portia's burnt bodies."

Logan closed his gaping mouth. It shouldn't shock him. Roger had lived in the one forest that still existed on their continent due to its impassable terrain. "We could run into our enemies or dangerous animals out there."

Roger's mouth set in a determined line. "I'm going back. I'm Calupi and those wolves are singing to my soul. Besides, it's more dangerous here. I don't want you to deal with an assassin alone."

Unease prickled in Logan. "What makes you think an assassin won't follow us?"

"They can't if they don't know where we went. Grab your pack and bedroll and let's get out of here."

A bloodcurdling scream came from somewhere out there. Logan's heart raced. Did he want to face that? He hesitated.

"I won't let you get hurt. Don't you trust me?" Roger asked.

If the clansmen wanted to kill him, those woods would be a good place to do it. But Roger could have killed Logan the first night they met. "More than I trust anyone else here." Logan holstered his gun, grabbed his pack, and stuffed his bedroll in. He blew out the lamp and moved to follow Roger.

Logan almost bumped into Roger as the clansmen stopped to whisper. "Try to do as I do." Roger kept in the shadow the tent cast as they crept around to the back of it, then into the tree line without alerting the soldiers around the fire or the sentries.

Very little light filtered through the trees. It was almost as dark as if the sun had set. Logan stumbled repeatedly as he followed after the clansman. Roger stopped and drew a huge breath. "Smell it?"

Logan breathed in deep. The air smelled moist and laden with the heavy scent of trees and decaying leaves. "What am I supposed to be smelling?"

"Kun's creation." Roger strode off again.

Water trickled somewhere near. Maybe a creek? A cliff loomed to the side of them. Roger turned to follow it. The face of the cliff lacked trees, so the rays of the setting sun spilled through to light their way. Logan tripped over another branch. Drat. He had better keep his eyes peeled, or he might end up breaking a leg.

A light flickered ahead in the growing darkness that made the cliff glow. "What's that?" Logan asked.

"It's my fire inside the cave where we're going to sleep."

"Bearw."

Logan jumped at the loud bellow.

It sounded again. *"Bearw. Bearw."*

Roger chuckled. "That's a better dinner than beans. Follow me." Roger picked up a couple of branches off the ground, pulled his knife, and sharpened one end of each. He handed one to Logan. "Take this and do what I do."

The sound of water came closer. Roger crept forward to the edge of a brook. The water played over rocks and formed a pool.

Eyes of something broke the surface. *"Bearw."*

Logan's heart raced. Roger plunged the sharpened branch between those eyes. Logan thrust his and hit another. The thing on the end of his branch flopped, the water churned, and the other eyes in the pool disappeared. His rough spear quit moving. He pulled it out to find a huge frog impaled on it. Pride filled him. He'd never hunted anything before.

Roger held up his stick to show another large frog. "Good, now we skin and cook them along with some of these." Roger pulled some cattails out of the water and washed them off. He picked some bulbs off another plant. "Wild garlic will season it nicely." Then he led the way to the cave. The sun's final rays sank behind the cliff as Logan ducked to follow Roger into a hole in the cliff.

The mouth of the cave opened up into a long room with sandy-colored walls. A fire crackled near the mouth. Roger moved around it. "It's just one chamber, but we should be safe here. Animals don't like fire. You can go ahead and spread your bedroll out."

While Logan did that, Roger made short work of skinning the frogs, then peeling the garlic and shoots from the roots of the cattails and cutting them up. With his spear, he scooted some coals from the fire into a depression in the stone floor. He sat a flat rock down in it and put the meat, cattail corms, and garlic on top. Then he put a bigger stone slab over the depression. "It won't take long now."

The aroma of the cooking meat and garlic wafted, and Logan's stomach growled.

"I'd like to hear why your brother and father want you dead," Roger said.

"Do you know who my mother was before marrying father?" Logan asked.

"Queen of Sheffia."

"Yes. Their political marriage aligned our two largest kingdoms without bloodshed, but they weren't in love and kept separate residences. As firstborn I spent time at both. Father and Mother both gave me lessons in ruling. Garth wasn't included in those lessons, and apparently he felt left out. Do you know the rumors about Garth?"

"That he's not your father's."

"Yes. I resemble Father while he looks like Mother. Garth blamed Mother for the rumors. He thinks she started them to make Father jealous. Three years ago Garth told Father our mother was a religious zealot, who was plotting with the Sheffians to overthrow him. Father's paranoid, so it took little to convince him. Since I didn't back Garth's story, Father believes I was in on this supposed conspiracy."

Roger put on gloves, lifted the slab from over the meat, and dished the dinner into bowls. He handed one of the bowls to Logan.

Logan took a bite of the frog. Yum. It was delicious. "Since then, Garth has lived with Father while I lived with Mother. Most of that time he's been on missions with Father's soldiers. Then earlier this year, Father had me lead one to the mountains. You know what happened. I'm still not sure why Father assigned me to lead this one. Garth has to be wondering if Father is going to favor me again. I suspect Father chose me because he knew Garth would react by trying to kill me."

"If the king wants you dead, why doesn't he kill you himself?"

"Probably afraid it might incite the Sheffians to rise against him. There was already an uprising when he threw Mother in the dungeon. The peace is tenuous at best. Father wants Garth to succeed him, but Garth doesn't have the support I do, except with the soldiers. Too many believe the rumors he's illegitimate. But if I'm dead, they'll have no choice. Sheffians will accept one Sheffian prince killing another far quicker than they will Father killing me."

Roger set his bowl down. "I don't agree with slaughtering these people and their animals, and I don't want these trees cut down. When we get close, I plan to leave and join the Kayndo."

Logan swallowed another bite. "I thought you might say that."

"Will you leave with me?"

Logan didn't agree either, but even if the Kayndo won, it wouldn't be long before Father launched another invasion. And if Logan betrayed Father, Mother would pay the price. Besides, the soldiers here were citizens of his kingdom. They didn't get a choice about whether to be here or not. As a prince, didn't he have a duty to them? How could he discard that? "No. I won't go."

"But you hate your father."

"Yes, I'd have no problem killing him after the things he's done to Mother and our people."

"Then you should fight against him."

"These soldiers aren't my father."

"They have the innocent blood of children on their hands. You shouldn't let your hands become drenched in it."

"I haven't."

"If we are there and do nothing, then it makes us guilty too."

Yes, but what else could Logan do?

22

Burdened

"If the burden you shoulder today is heavy, it will strengthen you tomorrow." ~ Leeto

Stevee

Stevee's nerves were stretched taught over facing Bigham tomorrow. The sub-pack slept around him, but all he could do was toss. He got up and crept out of the tent with Graydee following him.

The Pericards nodded to Stevee as he came out. They must be getting used to seeing him wander at night. He moved to the back of the tent because he didn't really want to talk to the Pericards. He sank to the ground and lay back, resting his head on his hands. The earthy scent of damp soil filled his nostrils. Graydee plopped beside him.

Thousands of stars twinkled above, and the moon was three-quarters full. Their beauty filled him with awe. Kun's majesty lit the night. Stevee heard a soft rustle.

Pack's here, Graydee sent.

Yup. All the sub-pack's wolves sprawled around him and Graydee.

Graydee propped his head on Stevee's chest. *We told you, we wolves would teach you the important stuff. You should know how to find your way by the stars.*

Stevee hadn't really had time to process the wolves' claiming him. It still baffled him. But he loved Graydee and trusted him. *So how do I find my way by the stars?*

Graydee's head lifted, and his nose pointed to the sky. His chest vibrated with the deep rumble of a repressed howl. *First you find the star that doesn't move. It's in the North. Follow my muzzle to it.*

Do you mean the bright one at the top of that line? Stevee asked.

Yes. Graydee's head turned. *Now follow Evee's muzzle to the three packmates. They travel in a short line together, rising in the east and setting in the west.*

I see them.

Good. You can use those four stars to figure direction at night.

Stevee stifled a yawn. A group of stars Bruno appeared to be watching in the South looked like a wolf.

Yes, Graydee sent. *Kun put us in the stars. We'll teach you more later. You need to sleep.*

Stevee cut off another yawn. *I don't want to go in.*

Graydee's moist nose nuzzled him. *Then sleep here.*

I don't have my bedroll.

The wolves all pressed closer to him. *You won't need it.*

With the wolves' warm bodies and thick, soft fur pressed against him, Stevee wasn't chilled. But the sub-pack would still hear if he shouted in his sleep.

You won't have any of those nightmares tonight. I'll chase them away.

Could Graydee do that?

Trust me.

Stevee closed his eyes. He snapped awake when the wolves' heads lifted at the sound of soft footsteps. Elayni came around the tent and walked toward them.

"Evee says they're teaching you the stars." She sat next to Stevee and held out a cord with some of the beads he had won. "Chayla and I made these for our sub-pack. We'll be wearing them instead of Wolf Mountain's. This one's for you."

Stevee shook his head. "I wanted you to use the beads I won to replace the ones the sub-pack shared with me. Your ceremony clothes should look nice when you life-mate."

"We have plenty for that." The sudden lilt in her voice reflected her joy over life mating. "It didn't take that many to make these armbands to show our rank, and people need the reminder, especially with you."

Stevee fingered the beads. There were six and one had a red K painted on it. "I don't understand. I thought trainees don't have rank."

"Normally, that's true, but you're also in the Kayndo's sub-pack. He's everyone's leader, and those in his sub-pack have the authority to act on his behalf. You're sixth in his sub-pack, so trainee or not, they shouldn't overlook that. If Dayvee asks you to do something, you can order Leeto, Frudo, or anyone else but the five of us above you."

Stevee put the circlet on his arm over his bicep and tightened it. Then turned it to show the beads like Elayni wore hers. "No wonder Frudo hated the idea of me in Dayvee's sub-pack. But even if they'd listen to me, I don't think I'd be comfortable doing it."

"Dayvee will mostly speak to Bruno and Brando, but this will remind people if Dayvee or Brando asks you to do something, you have the Kayndo's authority to do it."

"All right. Thanks."

She stood. "Will you come in with us now?"

He still needed to do a prank.

Graydee sent, *I'll go in with you and chase away your nightmares.*

Gratitude swelled in Stevee. He couldn't ask for a better friend than Graydee. "I'm coming." Stevee followed her into the tent.

#

Dayvee

Dayvee woke and opened his eyes. The tent had shrunk. Elayni peered down at him. She'd aged as if she were in her thirties. How did one get older overnight? She met his eyes. "Juno's come. He wants to be your companion."

"Huh? I have Jaycee and Juno has Drako."

"Jaycee was four companions ago, and Drako's dead."

What? Could Drako really be dead? Dayvee's heart ached at the thought. He grabbed his crutches and rose. An older companion, who limped from an injury, came into the tent. He recognized the black patch around his eye. It was Juno. "He's injured."

"I know, but you need a wolf companion, and he's the only one offering. The companions know to be at the Kayndo's side is to die, just like all the others. Juno's trying to show the younger pups what they should be doing and his commitment to the Vita."

"Where's Brando?"

"Dead. Don't you remember?"

No. *Pain stabbed Dayvee's gut as if he'd been punched. His heart sank to his toes, and a dark gloom overwhelmed him. He choked out,* "What about Tayro? Is he still king?"

"Except for you and I, everyone who answered your call from our pack died. If you counted all the dead, you'd have as many as a clan meeting. What do you remember?"

The lump in Dayvee's throat and the pain shooting through him stole his breath. He finally gasped out. "The last thing I remember is riding from Harthome to the shore to fight the invaders."

Elayni chewed her bottom lip. "Which time?"

"The only time."

She sighed. "We repelled the invaders five times. Their armies grew, and they brought more boats until we finally stole some of their ships and came here. We've fought them for twenty years, but we're winning and slowly we're restoring this continent. "Come here." *She beckoned him, and he joined her at the tent flap.* "Look," *she pointed.*

An ugly, blackened landscape lay in front of him. No trees, no grass, no plants, or blooms. The scent of ash choked the air, and the scorched land seared his soul.

"They destroyed it all with their constant wars. Now look behind us." Plants, crops, grass, small trees even. He turned his head to see the burnt landscape in front and then the green landscape behind them.

"As we win battles, we not only free the people from tyranny, we teach them the Vita and life is coming back. They've never known peace. This was a desolate place when we came here, but we're changing it."

Dayvee swallowed hard past the lump in his throat. "At what cost?"

"I agree it's been high. Your companion didn't need to give his life. I would have taken the bullet."

"No." Dayvee shook his head. "I won't allow you to give your life for mine."

"You're the Kayndo. I'd give my life willingly."

Dayvee woke up soaked in sweat and shouting, "No, you can't die, Elayni. I need you."

Elayni peered down at him. "I think you're dreaming." She was young again. Brando, Stevee, Codee, Chayla, and Tayro stared at him with concern in their eyes.

"First Stevee, now Dayvee." Brando blew out his breath heavily. "Is there something in this tent that causes nightmares?"

"I doubt it's the tent," Codee replied. "Stress can cause nightmares, and probably half the camp is having them."

Dayvee grabbed his outer clothing. Thank Kun. It was only a dream. The gray around the edge of the tent flap meant sunrise couldn't be far off. He slid on his pants.

Jaycee sprang up with Stevee's bedroll in his mouth. Stevee grabbed it, and they were playing tug of war. Graydee knocked him over, and Stevee rolled around on the ground wrestling with the wolves. Strange how the wolves were often found clumped around Stevee now. For as long as Dayvee could remember, some wolves had clumped around him at home. Probably because Clay had claimed him as her pup, and they felt it their duty to watch over him. It felt weird not to have them around him.

Stevee needs to get comfortable with us, Jaycee sent.

Dayvee laughed inwardly at himself. It wasn't like they were far away. And Stevee did need to be comfortable around the wolves. If he was rolling around roughhousing with them, it was working. Elayni said something he didn't catch. She looked at him expectantly. "What?"

"I asked if your dream was really bad." Elayni and rest of his sub-pack were dressing too.

"Awful. We'd been fighting the invaders for twenty years." Dayvee pulled on his belt and made sure his weapon's pouches were secure. "We were winning and restoring the Vita slowly on their continent, but all of our friends were dead. Maybe it's a warning from Kun to do something differently."

Tayro slid his shirt on. "The dream could be a message from the deceiver. Maybe he's trying to prevent you from protecting the Vita by scaring you."

"I guess..." Dayvee grabbed for his tooth as Chayla and Elayni's screams pierced the air.

"Ewww Brando!" The girls peeled their boots back off. "What is this?" Elayni waved to her feet. Globs of a rusty colored cream coated them.

Brando cracked up laughing. "Ask Stevee."

Stevee's stricken face made Dayvee laugh too. Tayro, Elayni, and Chayla joined in the laughter.

Brando snickered. "What is it?"

"It's what the Kwin use for the horses' cracked hooves. I used it for blisters on my feet, and it made them feel better."

"Do you know what's in it?" Tayro asked.

"Purslane, marigold, purple coneflower, and ground corn in buffalo tallow."

"That should make their feet feel good."

"At least your pranks are thoughtful." Elayni rubbed the cream into her feet. "Unlike Brando's."

"Hey. My pranks are thoughtful. They teach you to check your boots." Brando turned his boot upside down and smacked it. "Like me." He pulled one of his boots on and made a face. Then doubled over laughing. Everyone joined in, even Stevee. "Okay, Stevee, you pranked the master. How did you do it?"

"I put a little pine sap in the toe to keep the bag of cream from falling out."

Brando shook his head. "I can't believe you got by me when I was watching."

Stevee smiled. "I wouldn't be a good thief if I let people catch me."

Dayvee retrieved the bowl from his rucksack and put meat in Jaycee's. He grabbed some dried fruit for his breakfast. Everyone else did the same. Shadows of his nightmare haunted him.

"That dream still bothering you?" Elayni asked.

A sigh escaped him. "What if it *was* Kun showing me the future?"

Codee swallowed a bite. "You were defeating our enemies and restoring the Vita. Except for losing friends and loved ones, it would be a good future."

Dayvee stowed his belongings in his rucksack and put it on. "I couldn't bear all my loved ones dying. Maybe you should leave."

"Haven't you learned you can't get rid of us?" Brando quipped. "I don't think you should worry so much about the future. Just look to do your best each day."

Codee slid into his rucksack. "You can't send everyone home that could help you, or the deceiver wins."

Tayro rolled up his bedroll. "If it takes my death for you to restore the Vita, so be it. We all vowed to protect the Vita."

"Without Kun and the Vita, hope's lost," Codee said. "We'd willingly give our lives to prevent that future for our pack's children."

Dayvee's friends nodded. "But how do you expect me to live with that guilt?"

"It's not yours to carry." Codee checked his weapons. "We chose to fight for the Vita just like Geno. People are going to die in this war. If you take each personally, you won't be able to make any decisions for fear of causing another death."

The burden of responsibility on Dayvee felt lighter after sharing the dream, but he could never accept that amount of casualties without feeling guilty. He had to defeat the invaders without losing all the people he loved.

Brando moved to the tent entrance with Codee and Stevee trailing him. Trepidation flooded Dayvee over Brando, Codee, and Stevee going after enemies. "Be careful."

Brando glanced back. "Always."

"May Kun go with you." Tayro called.

"And with you." Brando ducked out of their tent.

#

Stevee

Smokee stamped in impatience at their slow pace through the camp. He broke into a trot, and Stevee sat back to slow him before he bumped into Brando and Codee's horses.

Reko and Denee's horse companions trotted a few steps to catch up with them and stay at Stevee's side. Smokee snorted. Maybe Smokee didn't like being penned in any more than Stevee did.

The sun rose over the horizon. Orange, yellow, pink, purple, and blue bands announced the coming day. The magnificence brought a lump to Stevee's throat. Only a few days ago he had felt sure he'd never see another.

A bunch of Calupi waited in front of White River's tents for them. None of them were mounted.

Reko winked at Stevee and raised his voice. "Nice armband, Stevee. It goes well with your Calupi headband."

Frudo looked over at them and scowled. But many of the other White River Calupi lowered their heads in deference to him. Wow. What a difference an armband made. "Are the horses still refusing to let Frudo and his friend's ride?" Stevee asked softly.

"Yes." Reko laughed. "All of White River Pack agreed not to ride since then. It's not like we care."

"Most Calupi prefer to go on foot. That's what we're used to," Codee said as the White River Calupi fell in behind them. "Nothing against horses." Codee patted his horse's neck. "But they can't climb. A Calupi moving at a fast trot can cover the same ground. It may take us longer, but we can do it. We'll probably be the only ones mounted today."

They came to Wolf Mountain tents, and the only one on a horse was Leeto. He rode up beside Codee as his pack joined those trailing them.

"Have you ever tracked, Stevee?" Brando asked.

"My father taught me tracks by drawing them, and Codee showed me some, but I've never actually done it."

"Codee is the best tracker in our pack, probably the clan."

"Leeto's good, too, and our companions are better than us."

Codee pointed to Wilee. "They taught us most of what we know."

Brando chuckled. "Okay, I guess the wolves are the best." He glanced at Stevee. "Leeto and Codee are going to track Bigham's group from where an eagle sighted them in brush. Since you, Reko, and Denee are mounted, you can go with them and learn more. But when the prints get fresh, all of you will stop and wait for us."

Graydee's excitement surged into Stevee. *This is going to be fun*

Stevee leaned forward and put Smokee into a canter behind Codee's and Leeto's horses. Misgivings needled him. Nothing that involved Bigham had ever been fun for Stevee, only terrifying.

23

Fleeing problems

"A Calupi's first response to danger is fight, not flight." ~ Leeto

Codee

Wilee had difficulty following the scent, and Codee found very few prints with the trail winding through such dense brush. Good thing their enemies had trampled the foliage. They entered a marshy area, and the prints became clear in the soft soil. Then the ground dipped, and they came back to the river. It spread out wider here like a lake. The smell of decay clung heavy in the air, and the water appeared brackish and unmoving. There had to be a channel somewhere since Otter Clan claimed the river flowed to the ocean.

Denee looked at him. "Should we cross here or find another place?"

Codee studied the prints. "They went in the water, and there's a trampled area where they came out on the other side. It must not be too bad."

"Wait here while Luko and I check it," Leeto ordered.

The wolf waded in, and Leeto urged his horse after him. The water got deeper, and Luko began to swim without much trouble. The water rose to Leeto's thighs, but his horse must have solid footing because he kept walking.

"The footing's mucky," Leeto reported. "But not soft enough to get stuck." When they climbed up the far bank, Leeto yelled, "You can come."

Codee rode in and Stevee trailed him. A gasp sounded behind him, then Stevee cried out, "Oh, Kun. No."

Codee twisted to see. The whites of Smokee's eyes were showing. The horse kicked the water up into a spray with his front legs.

Codee sent to Wilee. *Do you know what's wrong with Smokee?*

No, but Graydee says something scared Stevee then Smokee.

Smokee crow hopped twice, knifed around, and bolted up the bank. Stevee could get hurt. Graydee chased them.

Codee turned his horse and shouted, "Yup!"

Leeto's horse splashed back into the river to follow them. Reko and Denee were in front of them racing after Stevee too.

Reko pulled alongside Smokee and hollered, "Sit back and try to get him to slow."

Stevee leaned back. Smokee slowed, and Stevee vaulted off to crumple on the ground.

Smokee kept going, and Reko and Denee went after him. Codee pulled his horse to a stop and ran to Stevee. Graydee and Wilee already were there. Stevee clawed at his legs.

Leeto rode up. "What's wrong?"

Stevee shouted, "I have to get them off."

Codee kneeled beside him. Spots of crimson painted Stevee's legs. "Why are your legs bleeding?"

Stevee shuddered. "Lift your pant leg. You probably have them too."

Codee pulled up his pant leg. A couple of leeches sucked on his skin. It wasn't the first time he encountered them. He reached down and removed them. "Leeches won't hurt you. We can't even feel them, and they fall off when they're full. Healers even use them to treat infections."

"You're wrong." Stevee shook his head. "I could feel them burrowing in my skin just like when Bigham dumped them on me. But he tied my hands so I couldn't remove them." He stripped his shirt off. "Do you see anymore?"

Leeto crossed his arms. "If you could feel them, you wouldn't be asking." His tone was contemptuous. "If you let your mind play tricks on you, it will."

Codee blew out a breath. Leeto might be right, but it wasn't helping Stevee. His eyes were wide with fear. "There aren't anymore."

Stevee stood and slid his shirt back on. Graydee was pressed against Stevee as Reko and Denee came back with Smokee. The horse nuzzled him, and Stevee stroked him. "I'm sorry for scaring you, Smokee." He glanced up at them. "You guys go ahead. Graydee says he knows a place to cross that isn't full of leeches downriver. We'll catch up to you."

Leeto shook his head. "You have to face this fear, or you'll never get over it."

Stevee snorted. "I faced it more than once. I just choose not to have it happen again."

"If we run from a fear, it weakens us. If we confront it, we grow stronger. Calupi need to be strong, and you're weak." Leeto leveled a hard gaze at Codee. "You're his father. You know what to do."

Stevee had sworn vows to listen to his father, and in the pack that meant following his orders, but Codee wasn't testing that vow already. "Stevee *is* my son, and I'm not forcing him." He locked eyes with Stevee. "The water never went over my horse's back. If you pull up your feet, the leeches won't get on you."

Denee reined his companion closer to Stevee. "Smokee will panic if you do. I'll go with you and Graydee to a better crossing."

Codee didn't like that idea. "There are enemies around here, so it would be safer together, and we don't have the time to make a detour. I'll ride right next to you, Stevee."

Stevee shuddered. "As long as those bloodsuckers aren't touching me, I can cross."

"This coddling of Stevee will only make it worse." Leeto fumed. "The problem needs to be fixed."

"What would you do?" Codee couldn't keep the disdain from his voice. "Throw Stevee in a box and dump more leeches on him? I'll challenge anyone that tries."

Leeto snapped. "There are too many leeches in the world to be able to avoid them forever."

"How about we deal with today and not worry about tomorrow." Codee grabbed his horse's mane and jumped on. "That's Stevee's motto."

"Sure is." Stevee mounted Smokee and raised his feet. "I'm

going." He urged Smokee into the water, and Codee rode right beside him with Wilee and Graydee. Stevee gave him a weak smile. "It's hard to find joy right now. Can you share something that makes you happy?"

"Sure. I just learned my life-mate, Jolay, is going to have a baby, so you're going to have another brother or sister."

"A baby. That's great news. You won't let anything bad happen to my brother or sister, will you?"

"I don't intend to let anything bad happen to you or your sibling if I can prevent it." They reached the bank and climbed up it.

"Thanks. Having a Calupi father isn't so bad."

#

Stevee

Graydee's exhilaration flowed through their bond into Stevee, making it hard to be patient while he and the wolf hid behind thick brush and trees with Reko, Denee, and their horses. Just beyond them, the trees opened up into grasslands. Codee and Leeto had snuck forward to spy on their enemies while they waited for Brando and the rest of the Calupi to join them. The rustle of brush and crack of a twig must be Codee and Leeto returning. Stevee could have moved quieter than that, but they hadn't accepted his suggestion that he should go.

When they got close, Codee said softly, "Our enemies met up with some other people, and they were unloading bundles out of a wagon. One of them was yelling to get it done so they could return to camp."

They couldn't get a wagon through the marsh and dense brush they came through. "Does Brando know?" Stevee asked.

"Wilee informed Bruno. They're almost here."

More rustling and crackling announced their arrival. Brando rode toward them with the Calupi following. "How high was the grass, Codee?"

"Mostly knee high, but there were some places waist tall."

"So if we attack before they get to the tree line, they won't have much cover. Everyone fan out," Brando ordered. "Wait for my signal."

He turned to Reko and Denee. "You can go with Stevee after Bigham."

Denee smiled. "Father will enjoy giving us the reward for Bigham."

They waited as Bigham's men crested the rise and came down toward them. There must have been a couple hundred of them. Many Stevee recognized from the tavern. They were carrying wrapped bundles. In the center, Bigham and Mort marched together. Stevee grabbed his slingshot and some rocks. Brando howled.

Calupi all around them howled, too, and raced out of the trees toward their enemies. Stevee leaned forward, and Smokee sprang out of the woods. Graydee stayed beside him. Reko and Denee rode on his heels. Stevee shifted to send Smokee around some Calupi and over toward Bigham.

"Shoot them!" Bigham and his men grabbed guns out of those bundles.

Calupi loosed their nails, and the guns fired. Explosions rent the air. Stevee's ears rang. The pungent smell of gunfire choked Stevee. Calupi fell.

If Stevee could hit Bigham, would they stop firing? He wasn't that far from him. He slowed Smokee and loaded his slingshot, pulling it back to fire. Frudo ran in between them, messing up his shot. Stevee flung himself back on Smokee, sending him into a sliding stop to prevent them crashing into Frudo. Denee and Reko stopped too. What was Frudo doing?

"He must want the reward or the glory," Denee said.

Frudo had his nails out. Bigham, Mort, and those with them were shooting. Gunfire erupted around them. Bullets screamed by.

Frudo spun as one hit him. He crashed to the ground with a hole in his shoulder.

Denee rode toward him.

Concentrate on the enemy, or more will get hurt, Graydee sent.

Stevee tore his eyes away from Frudo and Denee. He couldn't see Bigham. Was he hiding? Mort pointed his gun toward Denee. The crack of the gun firing rent the air. A bullet whistled by. Stevee flung his rock, and hit Mort in the forehead. He pitched over to land in the grass. Denee held a hand over his side, and blood soaked it. Stevee rode toward him.

"Help, Frudo." Denee choked out.

Graydee sent, *Brando says to fall back to the woods. They're slaughtering us.*

Stevee looked for Reko. Blood poured down his leg. He must have been hit too. "I'll help Frudo. Get out of here, Denee and Reko. Go."

#

Dayvee

Dayvee sighed as he rode down the road on Ghostee. He'd rather be with Brando. Chayla constantly scanned the sky, too, as they waited for news. His eagle scout, Spiro, mind called Dayvee. *Your enemies have guns and are shooting at Brando and those with him.*

"Cackles."

"What?" Chayla asked.

"They're shooting at them with guns."

"Kun help us," Tayro said.

Yeah, right. Dayvee would like to believe that, but Kun either wouldn't or couldn't help him. Dayvee reached out for Brando's companion. *Bruno. Bruno, are you there?* He didn't respond. *Graydee, answer me.* Nothing. *Wilee, Luko?* No voice invaded his mind. *Spiro, can you hear me?* There wasn't one single whisper in his head. What was going on? For months, the animals invaded his mind, but now when he really needed them, they weren't responding. And he felt so empty, like something vital was missing. A black void as deep as when Clay and Geno died.

Oh no. Could it be? Had he lost the Kayndo gifts? A thousand times, he'd regretted the voices crowding his mind, but what he wouldn't give to hear a voice now. *Anyone?*

I'm still here, Jaycee sent.

Yes! At least he could speak to his companion. But he didn't have the Kayndo gifts. A lump rose in his throat. Kun had taken them away.

Oh, Kun, why? Maybe Kun had decided to appoint a new Kayndo, one who wasn't crippled. If so, Dayvee needed to learn who it was.

Jaycee sent, *There isn't another Kayndo, at least not yet.*

What? How could Dayvee help Brando? What could he do without being able to mind-speak the animals? He better figure out something.

Dayvee sent to Jaycee. *Can you mind reach anyone?*

Jaycee's ears cocked. *Yes. Our packmates.*

Ask Bruno what's going on.

He says several Calupi have been shot. We've got injured and dead. They're retreating to the woods so they'll have better cover.

Dayvee's heart sank. This plan had already cost them heavily. They needed to do something different. Brando wasn't going to like Dayvee's order.

Have Bruno tell Brando not to worry about fighting them now. Bring his injured back to the healers before we lose more.

Would Brando follow it?

24

Devastation

"To avoid the devastation of our past, we cannot travel the same path." ~ Kwutee

Logan

Logan clenched his teeth. He had to stop another bloodbath. The scouts came running back from Marshton.

"What did you find out?" Garth asked.

"It's not much of a town, more like a stockade. Probably wouldn't fit five hundred people inside their walls," one replied. "But they know we're coming. They've got a white flag flying, and the gates are wide open. Apparently, they want to surrender."

Somehow Logan had to get through to the brother he used to know. "Accept the surrender, Garth. If they're dead, they can't continue to give us the things Father wants."

Garth gave him a hard look. "It seems awfully quick for surrenders. We only decimated one city."

"Varian said these people aren't used to fighting wars," Logan reasoned. "What's the harm in giving them a chance?"

"All right, we don't go in shooting, but be ready just in case," Garth ordered.

As they approached the town, the walls came into view. If you could call them walls. More like earthen berms. The only thing wooden was the gates consisting of thin logs lashed together, and they stood open. It was too quiet. No sounds of people. Only birdsong and the constant drone of insects filled the air.

Garth and Logan walked through the gates at the head of the column. Their guards marched next to them, Roger with Logan and Garth's two henchmen with him. There were no stately homes in this town, just earthen cottages with one or two rooms. Logan spied movement and lifted his gun. An older man hobbled toward them.

"Come on in. You can take anything you want."

"Where is everyone?" Garth demanded.

The man shook his head. "They left when they heard you were coming. Just a few of us, who are too old to be of much use, remain."

Garth waved his gun in one of those flashy gestured he and Father loved. "I don't see any reason you'd be of use to me either."

The man gave Garth a toothless smile. "I'm not. He lunged toward Garth with a knife. Logan shot the man. Volleys of arrows rained down on them. Soldiers' screams filled the air.

"They're on the roofs." Roger pointed to a cottage. "We need to get under that porch for cover." Garth grabbed Logan and ran under the porch with Roger and his brother's guards on his heels.

The soldiers returned fire, spraying the roofs with bullets. The arrows quit raining, and the soldiers spread out to secure the town.

Garth pointed his finger in Logan's chest. "This is your fault. See what happens when I listen to you and give people a chance."

"Logan saved you, and you're blaming him?" Roger spat out.

It had been an idiotic move on his part. Logan shouldn't have saved Garth.

Garth gave Roger a look of disdain. "He didn't save me. I would have shot that man if Logan hadn't. He got me into this mess."

The sergeant came running up to them. "The men on the roofs are dead. It doesn't appear as if anyone else is here. We found tracks going into the marsh. They're smaller prints so probably women and kids."

"Track them down," Garth ordered. "Make every one of them scream a long time before you kill them. They'll learn what happens when you try to trick us."

Logan's stomach churned. Now he really regretted saving Garth. He had grown into a man as despicable as Father. And Garth would leave the same wave of devastation behind him. He shook his head. "You'd have tried the same thing in their shoes, and you sure shouldn't be punishing kids."

"I don't want to hear it," Garth snapped. "We tried your way. Now we'll do it mine."

"Don't you mean Father's way?" Logan demanded.

"That's better than Mother's way," Garth spat out. "Don't forget which of them is in power."

"Father rules with fear, Mother with love. The only reason he's in power is Mother didn't want Sheffians to die." Logan let out an exasperated snort. "Do you think anyone would rebel if Father ended up in the dungeon?"

Garth waved a hand at his soldiers. "All the adults should suffer, but let half of the kids die quickly. Release the rest of the kids after they witness what happened to the others. It might help to have them spread the word." As the soldiers filed in the woods he turned to Logan. "Satisfied?"

Not by a long shot. Logan hadn't done those kids any favors. The deaths would haunt them forever, but Logan couldn't change it.

#

Stevee

Calupi were fading back into the woods, taking their injured as Bigham's men advanced. Stevee needed to get Denee and Frudo out of here.

"I'm not leaving you." Reko slid off his companion next to them. "Keep our enemies busy while I help them."

Could Reko do it with an injured leg? Maybe, but he couldn't if Stevee didn't keep their enemies away. Stevee loaded stones into his slingshot and cast them out as fast as he could toward their enemies. He hit several, but others replaced them. There were too many. Frudo's and Denee's shirt turned red with blood, but they were conscious. Reko helped Denee on his companion and got Frudo mounted behind himself. "Let's go," Reko shouted.

Stevee grabbed Smokee's mane and vaulted on. They raced away with bullets flinging up dirt around them. Graydee flitted through the grass in a crouched position to stay hidden. Where the grass grew tall, Stevee couldn't see him. *Are you keeping up?*

Yes.

When they reached the trees, Graydee appeared again. *Follow me.*

Smokee weaved between the trees after Graydee. In a small clearing, some Calupi treated the injured. Codee was there tying off a leg bandage on Leeto. When they dismounted, a couple of Frudo's packmates ran from the trees toward them. They helped bandage Frudo's arm while Stevee wrapped one around Denee's side and Codee wrapped Reko's leg.

Brando rode toward them with a Calupi wearing a leg bandage sitting behind him on his horse. "We're going to cut away north and back to the road. I need those on horses to double up and take wounded. Reko, do you and Denee have those folding travois?"

"Yes."

"Good, can you put the two seriously injured in them?"

"Sure."

"Okay, Leeto's and Codee's horses are wounded, so Stevee can take Leeto."

Codee tied off a bandage on Leeto's leg. Leeto stood. "I can walk."

"You'll ride. That's an order." Brando glanced at Reko. "Get our injured out of here. The rest of us are going to cover you in case they try to follow." As Brando moved back into the trees, Codee and those Calupi that weren't seriously hurt trailed him. Frudo and his two packmates left with them.

Stevee helped Reko with the travois that consisted of hides with a frame of bones on the bottom and ropes that ran along the sides. They put the harness around Reko's and Denee's companions and attached the ropes for the travois. After he helped carry two badly wounded over to lay them on the travois, Stevee assisted two more in mounting behind Reko and Denee. The Kwin began to ride away as Leeto limped to Stevee. When Stevee extended his hand to Leeto to help him on, Smokee swung his rear away. "It's alright, Smokee." Smokee kept sidestepping away without any signal from Stevee. "I don't know why he's doing that."

Reko glanced back and stopped. "He thinks like a companion, even though he's not. Our companions don't normally allow another rider, but they've agreed to help with the wounded. Shilo's talking to Smokee. You can't feel uneasy about taking Leeto because he'll pick up on it."

Easier said than done, but Leeto was injured. Smokee snorted as Stevee extended his hand to Leeto again to pull him on. As soon as Leeto sat astride Smokee, he bucked.

If Leeto fell off, he could get hurt worse. Stevee pleaded with him. "Smokee, please don't do that." Smokee stopped bucking. At Stevee's nudge, Smokee walked calmly toward Reko. Graydee and Luko fell in beside him. Stevee patted his neck. "Thank you, Smokee."

"Brando should have let me use my own feet," Leeto said.

"I'm sorry."

"Not your fault," Leeto replied. "Animals have their own minds."

"So are you afraid of riding?"

Leeto snorted. "I fear only one thing. It's not riding."

"So you haven't conquered your fear either." Stevee hadn't meant to sound so harsh, but Leeto had called him weak.

"No, but I face it every day and do everything I can to prevent it."

Stevee's curiosity demanded he ask. "What is it?"

"That my pack won't have a future."

"I quit fearing the future. I know most adrifts don't have one. We live for the moment. And regardless of what you believe, I faced my fears one moment after another."

"You were forced. That's different than choosing to face them." Leeto spoke matter of factly. "If you want them to lose their hold on you, you have to make yourself defeat them like Calupi do, or they'll keep visiting your dreams."

Brando rode out of the woods. Codee and the other Calupi trailed him. Some of them sported bandages but apparently their injuries weren't so serious they couldn't walk. Brando's shoulders sagged and he wore a heavy frown.

Calupi don't normally retreat, Graydee sent. *For Calupi to die, when they accomplished nothing is devastating to Brando. He'd keep fighting until his last breath if Dayvee hadn't ordered him back.*

Stevee spoke softly to Leeto. "I think there are bigger problems to worry about than my nightmares."

"True. With the ancients' weapons, this Bigham poses a much greater threat."

Brando rode over closer. "You know Bigham. If you have any ideas on how to defeat him, you should share."

Stevee had an idea, but he wasn't sharing it.

#

Codee

When Codee and the other Calupi caught up. Tayro called a halt. "Everyone can take a lunch break so the healers can treat the injured."

"How come you're giving orders? Where's Dayvee?" Brando demanded.

Tayro was grabbing flasks from his rucksack. "Chayla, take them and explain."

Both her and Elayni's face were tear-streaked. Something was going on. "Follow me." Chayla directed her horse away at a walk. Codee, Brando, Stevee, and Leeto trailed her into the woods. She stopped after they got far enough away they couldn't hear the others, but she still spoke softly. "Dayvee lost the Kayndo gifts. He spoke to Gaylo and said since he's not Kayndo anymore he was leaving. Since Tayro's king, he's in charge. Then he rode off on Ghostee."

"Cackles," Brando exclaimed.

"Gaylo said not to reveal it yet. He didn't want people to lose hope, so everyone else thinks Dayvee went to take care of something."

"If no one knows, then he's still a target," Brando fumed. "We need to tell them."

"No," Leeto commanded. "Not yet and that's an order. If Dayvee's not Kayndo, you're not his second, and you need to follow your alpha's orders."

Do you know where he is, Wilee? Codee asked.

Jaycee won't reveal it. Dayvee believes he'd be a burden now and says everyone should concentrate on aiding Tayro.

Tell him even if he's not Kayndo, he's a Calupi. He can't run off without permission from his leaders. If he won't come back, I'll track him down.

He says fine but only you.

Tell him Leeto's not that seriously injured that I can stop him.

Then decide which of you will come. He'll only meet with one of you.

Codee filled the others in. "Dayvee's agreed to meet with me or Leeto."

Brando leapt off his horse. "You can ride my horse."

"Codee, go ahead," Leeto ordered. "If it takes binding him, bring him back. I have to speak to Tayro about what we discussed."

Codee rode hard in a northerly direction for close to an hour. Wilee sent, *Luko says to tell you Tayro approved, so they're on the way.*

Thanks. Ahead, the trees and brush thinned. Codee spotted a waving sea of grass through them, the grasslands.

He reined the horse to a walk so it could cool down. When Codee came to the edge of the tree line, a huge herd of buffalo appeared roaming slowly north through the grass while smaller herds of elk and deer grazed on their sides. Was that Ghostee grazing among them? Yes, he was, but Dayvee wasn't on him.

Codee followed cautiously as Wilee wound his way through the grass to a little winding creek. The sandy bottom was easy to detect in the few feet of clear water. When he turned to follow Wilee downstream along the low bank, Codee picked out Dayvee sitting on the other side with his feet dangling in the water under the shade of one of the few scraggly trees. Jaycee sprawled next to Dayvee, but the wolf jumped up at their approach and splashed through the creek to touch noses with Wilee.

Dayvee flashed a smile. It appeared genuine. His posture was more relaxed than Codee had seen it in a long time. What he'd like to do is send Elayni to join Dayvee and tell them both to leave. Hadn't Dayvee already paid a high enough price for his devotion to his pack? But Codee also loved several others in the pack, including his life-mate, his brother, and his companion. He couldn't risk all of them and everyone in all the packs for one individual's happiness, no matter how much he loved Dayvee.

Protect the Pack was ingrained into every Calupi. Leeto and Codee always faced the danger first to spare their packmates. Like Stevee had protected the adrifts. Codee would find it easier to sacrifice his own happiness than ask Dayvee to sacrifice his, but Codee wasn't who Kun chose for Kayndo.

He steeled himself to do what he had to.

25

Consequences

"Think before acting. Rash decisions lead to harsh consequences."
~ Codee

Elayni

Elayni fumed as they waited for the healers to finish treating the injured. How could Dayvee just leave her after asking her to life-mate? What Calupi broke their word? Codee was going to bring Dayvee back, but she didn't even want to see him. They were never going to life-mate. She needed to accept it and move on. Dayvee would always have another excuse to break her heart and make her miserable.

Leeto was talking to Tayro. He was going to attack the invaders ships, and he was taking the best swimmers. She should go with. Then she wouldn't have to see Dayvee. "I'll go, Leeto." She waved a hand at the Pericards. "I'm not really needed here."

Leeto coolly appraised her. "We might not return."

"I understand."

He gave her a chin lift. His agreement for her to come. Branco shook his head. "Dayvee wouldn't want you to go."

"He doesn't have a say after he abandoned us. You know how good of a swimmer I am. There are times I beat you."

Brando crossed his arms. "I don't want you to go either, not alone." Brando rocked a little on his feet. He only did that when he was really stressed. "I won't be able to watch your back this time."

Brando wouldn't want to leave Chayla, and he couldn't stand to be around Leeto. She set her jaw. "I'm going. Look out for our family."

Brando's blue eyes misted. "May Kun protect you."

\#

Dayvee

Relief filled Dayvee at the sight of Codee. His uncle was much easier to deal with than his father. Dayvee had no intention of really leaving. He and Jaycee would go to the coast, but they'd make their own way. He'd be there to help in the battle against the invaders, only he'd have to fight away from his family. Codee crossed the creek, then reached the bank and dismounted.

A couple of robins, who were pecking the ground near Dayvee, flew up in the tree above him. The squirrel that had been scampering around him stopped to look at Codee, then chittered at him as if warning him to keep his distance. A squirrel guard. Weird. Dayvee smiled to himself.

"You might want to tie your horse." Dayvee pointed to Ghostee grazing. "I think Ghostee will come, but it isn't really important since I don't plan to return with you."

Codee led his horse to another tree. "Then why did you take a horse?"

"Reko said Ghostee wanted to stay with me, so I paid for a lease with some of the money Sharmayn gave me."

"Were you planning to go to Sharmayn?"

Dayvee chuckled at the memory of the fiery woman that tried to adopt him. "I do owe her a visit, but I haven't really planned much yet." What could he tell Codee that was truthful and might satisfy him? "I'm just going to relax a while longer. I haven't had a free day since Clay died."

"Calupi have responsibilities, and we don't get to shed them when things get tough." Codee finished tying the horse to a low branch. "Do you really want to turn tail on the pack and make Jaycee miserable? Are you going to break your word to Elayni too?"

The holes in his heart made it ache. He wanted Elayni and the rest of his family with him. The pain that seized his heart from the void felt all too real. But he wouldn't put any of them in more danger. "I said if we survived the battle. The Kayndo didn't."

"You're no turtle. How can you hide knowing it might take all of us to win?"

"If I go back and fight with my friends, they will try to protect me. It won't matter that I'm not Kayndo now. They'll still do it because they see me as helpless. That would put them at more risk and take their focus from protecting Tayro. I'm keeping my vows by doing what's best for my pack."

"That's not going to help us. When everyone learns the Kayndo left, they're going to lose hope. We can't win if you take their hope before we fight."

Dayvee had never wanted the burden of being the Kayndo. And he'd failed miserably. "Look." He pointed at the buffalo. "There's no way to hide that the herds are leaving. What do you expect me to do? Tell them I have the ability to bring them back when I can't?"

"Wilee says your face is the one Kun still shows them if they think about the Kayndo. Whether you have the gifts or not, you're still the Kayndo."

"That's crazy. There's no way I can do it without the animals. Tayro can lead better."

"How can you say that? I gave Tayro a few lessons on leading. You received hundreds to prepare you."

"I'm the one who keeps messing up. If I had attacked Bigham sooner, they wouldn't have had guns, and we wouldn't have lost all those Calupi today. Leeto knew I was wrong to wait. So did Brando."

"I advised you to wait. I like to think before acting. Brando and Leeto tend to leap first, look later. Both approaches sometimes fail. But there's a reason Kun chose you, not Tayro, not Leeto, not me. Leeto has ordered you to return, and if you refuse, I'm to bind you."

Dayvee chuckled. "Even if you did bind me, you won't be able to keep me there. I always find a way to escape."

We have to return with him, Jaycee sent.

What? Why?

Because Wilee's right. If I think of the Kayndo, I see your face. The other animals know it too. Look how that squirrel and the birds are watching you. Are they behaving normally for animals? You're still the Kayndo.

Then why are the herds leaving?

You're not giving them directions so they're following their instincts to find grazing and head north where it's cooler.

But I can't direct them. Kun took the gifts away.

I don't think Kun took them from you. You did.

What do you mean?

What did JoKayndo say you needed to do?

Believe.

Yes. You don't believe Kun will help you anymore, so he can't.

So what do I do?

What you always do. Try your hardest to be a good Kayndo regardless. But it wouldn't hurt to pray and try to restore your belief.

What if I can't?

Then you'll do your best without the gifts, but you are the Kayndo. You can't turn tail.

The heavy mantle of responsibility came to rest on Dayvee's shoulders again, weighing them down. He couldn't keep a sigh from escaping him. "All right, Codee. I'll go back with you. But I'm telling everyone the truth so they can decide whether to stay and fight or not. I'd appreciate if you and Leeto support that."

"I will, but Leeto's gone. Tayro approved his plan."

"What plan? Where is he?"

"He took twenty clansmen with Otter Clan to canoe down the river to the ocean. They'll attack our enemies' ships tonight, so no matter what happens tomorrow, our enemies won't be able to get more supplies, soldiers, or weapons."

Twenty clansmen didn't seem like much. "Those ships have guns on them that destroyed the sea clans."

"If anyone can accomplish it, Leeto will."

Codee was right. His father's abilities shouldn't be taken lightly. Since Dayvee was still Kayndo, would he need to go to the other continent? He shuddered as the images surfaced in his mind from his dream.

"If we need to fight them on that continent, I'll need one ship left intact."

"Wilee's passing on your request, but how will one help you?" Codee asked. "That won't take an army."

Codee didn't need to know everything, so Dayvee chose his words carefully. "If we have one, we can always use it to learn how to build more."

. . .

When Dayvee and Codee rode up to join his sub-pack on the road, they swung their horses out and around him so Dayvee would be back inside their defensive ring, but one of the Pericards, Chase, was riding in Elayni's place.

"Where is Elayni?" Dayvee asked.

Brando dropped back to ride beside him. "She volunteered to go with Leeto."

Worry slammed into Dayvee like a hammer in his chest. That would be dangerous for her. He'd order her back. *Can you mind reach Evee, Jaycee?*

Not anymore. They're too far away.

His apprehension put a snap in his voice. "How could you let her go, Brando?"

"Leeto's her alpha. He agreed, so there wasn't anything I could do after you abandoned us."

Dayvee sighed. "I thought you'd be better off without me."

"Does it look like we're better off?"

Every face in his sub-pack was downcast. Dayvee hated to see his friends' pain. He met Brando's soulful gaze. "I messed up again, didn't I?"

Brando blew out his breath. "When you try to escape us, it makes her believe you don't want to life-mate. Just like I have to believe you don't want to be in our family. Now I have to wonder how long before you hurt us again, and if I should let you keep doing it."

Would Brando expel Dayvee from his family like he had his father, Jonesee? Could Dayvee bear his own heartache if he lost them? His life would be so empty. But wouldn't that be the best for them?

"I don't care how many times you run from other people, but you have to stop running from us. It hurts too much." Brando drew a ragged breath. "Will you give me your word not to do this to us again?"

If his sub-pack fought away from him tomorrow, wouldn't they'd be safer? The Kayndo was always targeted by their enemies in battle. But Dayvee wouldn't be able to see how they fared, and that would drive him crazy. "I won't promise not to do it again. I know you deserve better, so I'm not going to ask you to continue to guard me. I'll have Codee replace you."

"Codee can't replace what we share. You and Elayni are in almost every good memory I have." Brando's deep blue eyes misted. "I can't forget that, no matter how much I might want to. I'm not leaving you, and I don't think anyone else in the family will leave you either."

The sub-pack was all shaking their heads no. But Elayni had left Dayvee to go on a risky mission. Dayvee wanted to rush off to find her. But if she was here, would she be any safer?

He had to put it out of his mind, or he'd go after her, and he couldn't. Not when he had his own battle to wage against the invaders. Better concentrate on it. The sun would be setting soon. They should find a place to camp.

Should he tell all those who followed them how he lost the Kayndo gifts? Yes. He had to admit he'd let everyone down—his family, his pack, all clanspeople, even city people. They were going to be so disappointed in him. And they should be. Couldn't he put off telling them until morning? Maybe he'd regain the gifts by then. But if he didn't, how many of those who supported him, would leave? If he was fighting with only his sub-pack, they wouldn't have any chance. But he owed everyone the truth.

26

Choices

"The right path often has slippery footing and several obstacles to overcome." ~ Kwutee

Logan

Logan sighed. It was fully dark now. Roger must not be coming. Maybe the clansman had left for good now. Logan had waited on dinner, hoping for something better. He left the tent and went to the fire.

"Decide to join us, Your Highness?" The derogatory tone Garth used on his title showed what he thought of it.

"Just getting dinner." Logan grabbed a piece of the hard bread, ladled some of the beans into his tin plate, then took a bite. Yuck.

"I haven't seen your guard around tonight." A smirk crossed Garth's face. "Where is he?"

Did Garth know Roger had been leaving camp at night? If he did, he'd probably think the clansman was a traitor or deserter. Roger could be shot, and if he suspected Logan had accompanied him, he could be shot too. "He's around."

"Neither of you were in your tent last night."

Logan went on the offensive. "Did you think I'd make it easy for the people you hire to kill me?" Several of the soldiers squirmed. Garth's eyes widened. Fearful.

Why had Logan protected Garth for so long? He guessed Garth had weeded out those who supported Logan, but with this many ears, that declaration was sure to reach some of them sooner or later. It was why Garth had been hiring others to do his dirty work. So he could claim innocence. He wouldn't want to give Logan's supporters good reason to refuse to accept him once Logan was gone. Logan gave Garth a cold glare. "I'm not letting an assassin know where I'm sleeping, but the sentries should know we didn't leave camp."

Garth scanned the soldiers' faces, probably trying to guess who might be sharing a tent with Logan.

"Were you needing me?" Roger came out of the dark and walked up to the fire.

Relief poured into Logan. "Yes. Come with me."

He ducked inside the tent assigned to him, and Roger followed. Logan whispered. "Garth suspects us."

Roger shrugged. "I heard. You handled it well. Get your pack and bedroll, and we'll leave."

"Do we dare risk it?"

"As long as the sentries don't see us, Garth can't prove we left, and what you said is true. You shouldn't make it easy for an assassin."

Logan grabbed his belongings, blew out the lamp, and followed the clansman into the night. They sidled around the tent. The moon and stars lit the night some, but it was still dark under the shadow of the tent.

Roger stopped, and Logan bumped into him. "Wait," Roger whispered. A sentry marched past. "Now."

He followed Roger as he glided into the tree line. The night turned entirely black under the trees with very few places the light of the moon penetrated. Fireflies flew around them. Logan was grateful for even the small light they cast. He stumbled and ran into things repeatedly.

"So why did you save Garth today from getting stabbed?" Roger asked.

"I didn't think and separate who Garth is now from the boy he was. I just shot the guy threatening my brother. If I'd have thought about it, I don't think I'd have done it. Is that why it took you so long to come tonight, Roger?"

"I'd prefer you call me by my clan name now, Rogee. And I was just getting things ready. We need to hurry back if you don't want dinner to disappear."

Logan's stomach growled at the aroma of meat wafting. "I can smell it from here. What is it?"

"Wild Boar."

At a gap in the trees, the stars drew Logan's attention winking above them. There were so many. He heard the gentle refrain of water lapping. "There's no way we can eat an entire boar."

The woods opened up onto a beach by a river. A fire was lit, and a spit hung over it with chunks of meat.

"No," Rogee said. "But I invited company."

What? A whole bunch of people dressed in buckskin stepped out of the shadows into the light of the fire. Some wolves were with them. They must've been local clanspeople. Logan pulled his gun. Rogee had betrayed him to their enemies. There were too many against him. He wouldn't be able to kill them all, but he'd start with Rogee.

#

Stevee

Stevee crept out of the tent with Graydee. He could do this. Stevee made his way to the edge of the field where all the horses were. There was a Kwin guard. He whistled softly. Smokee responded and came trotting up to the tree line where he and Graydee hid. He grabbed onto Smokee's mane and mounted. He leaned down low so he wasn't spotted and shifted to guide Smokee deeper into the woods. Graydee padded beside him.

Graydee, do you think you can track Bigham from where we were?

Yes.

It was too dark to tell much about the terrain. Smokee seemed to know to follow Graydee, so he let the horse decide where to put his feet and hoped he wouldn't fall in any holes.

I have good night vision, Graydee sent. *If he keeps following me, he won't hit any.*

Good.

After cantering for a while, Stevee sat back so Smokee slowed to a walk and could cool down. A sudden rustle in the woods alerted him to shadows moving toward them. He grabbed for his slingshot. *It's friends,* Graydee sent.

All the sub-pack's wolves bounded up to him. *What are they doing here, Graydee?*

They came to help us.

But I don't want to risk them too. Tell them to go back.

They think we might need help, so they're not going to go back.

Great. I hope they can stay quiet then.

Wolves can move without a sound.

He could only hope. He put Smokee back into a canter. Graydee stopped. *We're getting close now. You might want to let Smokee wait here and walk in.*

There was no way he'd tie Smokee since that would make him easy prey for any predator that came along. He dismounted and led Smokee to some grass. "Can you stay here, Smokee, and wait for me? I shouldn't be too long." Would Smokee understand?

Graydee led him to the camp. Only one guard sat on a rock near the fire looking out at the forest. He looked half asleep. But Stevee needed to make sure of it. He took his slingshot out and a rock. Then let it fly. The stone hit him in the forehead, and the guard slumped down, out cold.

He slid on Geno's gloves. Hopefully, it would be enough. *Kun, please protect me from contamination of the ancients' things.* He grabbed the guard's gun, then turned to the sleeping men. Each one had a gun lying close to them. He crept nearer. One by one he removed their guns. When his hands could hold no more, he moved back to the edge of the camp and laid them down in the tree line.

We'll bury them, Graydee sent.

Thanks.

He moved back into the camp and did it again. At times, one of them would turn over in their sleep, and Stevee would stop, not even daring to breathe until their snores resumed. He almost had all the guns now.

One last one, Bigham's, and his hand rested on the barrel as he slept. Stevee carefully pulled the gun inch by inch out from Bigham's grasp. Almost got it. Bigham opened his eyes. Yikes. Stevee slid back deeper into the shadows and froze. Bigham blinked then rubbed his eyes. He looked over at where Stevee had been. He must have seen him. Would he start shooting?

#

Logan

Logan cocked his gun and took aim. "You'll die first for your betrayal, Rogee."

"Put your gun down. If I wanted you dead, I'd have killed you long before now. We're not your enemy."

"Then what's the meaning of this?"

"Just a conversation. That's all. I have their vow they won't harm you tonight."

"Then why didn't you tell me?"

"Because you wouldn't have come, and you need to hear what we have to say."

"All right, start talking.'

"First I'll feed our guests. Then we will talk. And please, lower your gun. Their vow won't be broken. You have nothing to fear."

If they wanted to kill him, he had no doubt those wolves could tear him apart before he could get off many shots. Logan holstered his gun. Rogee sliced the meat. The clanspeople filled their bowls and sat on hides around the fire. Rogee brought him a bowl of meat and joined him on a log to eat.

Logan swallowed a mouthful. The meat melted in his mouth. So much better than those beans. He tried not to stare in his study of these clanspeople. They all wore buckskin pants, short-sleeve shirts, and decorative arm and headbands. The more delicate features of a woman drew his attention. Her tanned face and arms, longs legs, light-blue eyes, high cheekbones, and a crown of golden hair combined to make her stunning. He tore his gaze from her to the men around her with their sculpted bodies and chiseled faces.

These people would fulfill an artist's search for perfection. They were undoubtedly the most attractive people he'd ever seen.

The few clanspeople left on their continent didn't really look like these. Like Rogee's, their faces were rounder, their features less defined, and they weren't nearly as tall.

"My name is Leeto." One of the clanspeople said as he sat his bowl down. "I'm alpha of Wolf Mountain Pack. Rogee has shared with us about your continent and your situation with your father and brother so we agreed to wait and speak to you."

Rogee didn't even look abashed as Logan scowled at him. "I wouldn't have revealed so much if I knew you'd be sharing it."

Rogee just shrugged. Leeto continued, "This is what we want you to know." He waved his hand to the trees. "Your continent could look the same as ours if you'd nurture it. But if your people manage to destroy all the resources on both continents, there won't be anything left. We will fight until the last breath to keep that from happening. But if you turn away from this course, many among us would be willing to help you restore your continent. Our council might even be willing to share some of our bounty with you."

"That's a generous offer, but I don't make the decisions. My father does. And he doesn't share, he takes."

"Rogee thought if we eliminated your brother and made the agreement with you, your father might honor it."

"I wish I could tell you that were true. Father doesn't care about restoring our continent. And he isn't worried about what will happen in several years. His concern is if his coffers are empty today so he'd send another to invade you."

"Hmmm. Rogee says you don't agree with him."

"No, but that doesn't mean I can do anything about it. I don't have the ability to change anything. All I can do is try to stay alive so I can change things in the future. That's what you should do. We have guns, so you don't have a chance of winning. The longer you fight it, the worse the slaughter will be. Surrender now and save lives."

"Surviving isn't enough if we have to give up how we live. We'd rather die."

Rogee put down his bowl. "I'm going with them. I'd happily kill Garth, but I don't want to kill you. And I won't be there to help foil the next assassin, so you should come with us too."

"I might not agree with Garth or my father, but I'm not a traitor to my people. Those soldiers have no choice but to be here. Besides, I can do more good with them since I'll try to stop Garth's excesses."

"Whales were killed. Innocent children were slaughtered. The only thing your objection did was leave a few alive that will be scarred for life."

Logan hung his head. "I have to keep trying." He hated to admit it, but he needed to. "I don't think I can find the way back without you, Rogee, so will you take me?"

Rogee stood. "Yes."

Leeto rose too. "I admire your loyalty to your people, but a leader can't lead if no one listens. If your soldiers chose not to support you when you objected, they're as guilty as those that gave the orders."

"I can only keep trying. If I can get some to listen, it will help you more than anything else I can do."

Leeto offered him his arm to Logan, and they exchanged the clan arm-clasp. "Next time we meet, it will probably be in battle. I want to win, but I hope it's not my chakram that finds your throat. May Kun go with you."

Logan didn't know if he believed in Kun, but he knew the proper response. "And also with you."

Logan trailed Rogee back. His clothing seemed to catch every thorn bush. His uniform was going to be ruined after tonight's jaunt. Garth's shout filled the night. "You're sure you searched every tent and every inch of ground in this camp for my brother?"

"Yes."

"Then he's a deserter."

Rogee whispered to him. "When we get inside the perimeter, I'll give you a boost up in a tree. Then laugh so they discover you. If they ask about me, tell them I believe I can protect you better if I'm not seen. If you can make them believe it, maybe they'll hesitate before trying to kill you again."

"All right. Thanks for everything. Be careful, Rogee."

"You too."

They slid by the sentries, and Rogee clasped his hands together. Logan put his foot in and let Rogee lift him to where he could grab a branch and haul himself over it into the tree. Rogee slid silently back into the night.

Logan laughed loudly. "Oh, Garth. You are too funny."

Garth's head swung back and forth. "Where are you, Logan?"

"Over here." When Garth stood underneath him, he shimmied down the trunk.

Garth's eyes narrowed. "Hard to believe you were sleeping in a tree."

"Necessity dictates learning to adapt." Logan gave him a smirk. "Good thing I'm not like you, or I could have killed you as you ranted without anyone knowing."

Fear crossed Garth's face. He wiped his forehead. "Where's your guard?"

"Staying hidden. He thinks it's easier to kill those that put me in peril when they don't know where he'll strike from. I agreed with him."

"I'm ordering him to show himself."

"Even though you and these men refuse to recognize it, I'm first born and in command. Thankfully, Roger doesn't share your delusions, and he will follow my order not to reveal himself."

"Fine, sleep in trees," Garth snapped. "I hope you don't fall out and break your neck," he said with more than a hint of sarcasm.

"I guess I can't count on you to catch me." Logan rubbed his wrist. He'd broken it when he once stopped Garth's fall from their roof. He hadn't regretted it when they were boys. Now he did.

Garth shoulder's hunched, and he dropped his head. "No, you can't," he mumbled as he plodded away.

Logan was almost giddy with relief until he considered what might wait. Where could he sleep safely? Not in a tree and not in the tent. He needed sleep, and he wanted to live past this night. There had to be somewhere he could doze without an assassin finding him.

27

Interrupted Sleep

"Plenty of rest is what you get when you're dead." ~ Leeto

Dayvee

Dayvee sat up. Why did he feel anxious? He checked around him and discovered one of his sub-pack missing. "Does anyone know where Stevee is?"

Brando sat up, looking around. "He probably went out for air like he does sometimes after a nightmare."

"The companions are gone, too, except for Jaycee," Tayro said. "They'll keep him safe."

Dayvee reached out for Graydee, but he didn't respond. It still surprised Dayvee that he couldn't use the Kayndo gifts. But the feeling of distress was coming from Jaycee. *Why are you on edge? Is something wrong?*

Stevee is stealing the guns from Bigham and his men. The other companions are helping him.

"Cackles." *Ask Graydee to get him out of there.*

Graydee says that right now isn't a good time to distract Stevee. Bigham just opened his eyes. One wrong move, and they could be shot.

"What's wrong, Dayvee?" Chayla asked.

"Bigham might have just caught Stevee stealing guns from him."

Brando grabbed his weapons pouches. Dayvee shook his head. "We can't get there in time."

Bigham went back to sleep, and Stevee got the last gun. The companions are burying them.

Is Stevee clear?

Not yet. He's putting something in their water bags.

Would Stevee poison them? After almost being poisoned once, Dayvee didn't think he could ever condone that. He could kill their enemies with his weapons to keep them from harming his loved ones, but his opponent had a chance. Poison just seemed wrong.

He's clear of the camp now and coming back. Relief poured into Dayvee. At least Stevee hadn't been caught. "We can go back to sleep. He's safe and coming back."

Dayvee wouldn't be sleeping. Anger flooded him. He was Kayndo, yet one of his own sub-pack members had risked himself and several companions without even consulting him.

His sub-pack moved as one, rising from their bedrolls. Apparently, no one would go back to sleep until Stevee returned.

#

Stevee

Stevee needed to make a detour before heading to camp. As he came to the swamp, his heart raced. He dismounted before coming to the water's edge. "Wait here, Smokee."

The half-full moon did little to light it. He stripped his clothes off and slid one foot into the inky darkness of the slimy water. His mouth dried. Were leeches getting on him? His chest hurt from his heart pounding inside. Could he go farther?

You can do it, Graydee sent.

Was he going to act like a Calupi? Stevee took a calming breath and forced himself to take another step, and another. When the water was up to his chest, he ducked his head in, then turned around and waded back out.

He dressed and rode toward the camp as the leeches burrowed into his skin. He wanted them off, but he didn't stop Smokee. He kept up a running monolog in his head. *I will ignore them. They can't hurt me. They'll fall off soon once they gorge.* He shuddered.

When he reached the camp, he turned Smokee loose to join the other horses. He brushed his hands down his arms. He couldn't see or feel anything. The leeches were probably all gone by now. As he and the companions approached the tent, the light of a lamp flickered inside. *The sub-pack must be up. Will they be angry?*

Graydee sent, *Jaycee says Dayvee is.*

Oh no. Would Dayvee kick Stevee out of his sub-pack?

When he ducked inside, arms enfolded him in a hug, Chayla's. "Don't you ever do that again. We were worried."

Brando came over and slapped his shoulder. "Well met." His lips pursed. "Would you have thought to go into Bigham's camp if we hadn't fought them today?"

Not everyone was angry at Stevee. "No. We didn't even know they had guns before then."

A smile lit up Brando's face. "Thank you. I can tell the families of our slain now that their deaths made a difference." He shot a piercing gaze at Codee, who was sitting beside Dayvee. "Any Calupi who can steal our enemies' weapons and then faces his fear down deserves praise."

Both Codee and Dayvee's arms were crossed, and their faces wore the same hard expression. Everyone said Dayvee resembled Leeto. They had the same hair color, but Dayvee's body and face were leaner like Codee's. And Dayvee and Codee's mannerisms and feelings often matched.

Codee's withering glare made Stevee's heart sink. "The results don't justify you running off without consulting anyone." His tone was curt. "You not only risked your own life but all our companions."

Stevee had to try and explain. "I told the companions to go back, but they wouldn't. If you'd have known, you'd have insisted on going, and we'd have been caught. I'm a thief, you're not."

Codee harrumphed. "I can move quietly."

Stevee always heard them coming before he saw them. "Not like me. I knew I could do it if I went alone."

"Did you poison them?" Dayvee's words were clipped.

When they fought Mort in the bottoms, Brando had told Stevee not to leave an enemy behind alive. "There were lots of times at the adriftage I could have killed Bigham as he slept. But I couldn't do it, so he kept killing us. I knew this time I had to keep him out of the fight tomorrow, but I still couldn't cut his throat. I put some wild Senna pods in their water."

Tayro busted out laughing. As the others looked at Tayro,

perplexed, he said. "It will give them diarrhea."

Brando chuckled and slapped Stevee's shoulder again. "I had no idea teaching you about plants and how to prank would be such a terrible thing for our enemies."

"All right, Stevee." Dayvee uncrossed his arms, and his face softened. "I guess we did underestimate you, but next time you come to me for approval first." He smiled. "Agreed?"

They hadn't rejected him, even though they'd been angry. Maybe Stevee could trust them. He smiled back. "Agreed."

#

Dayvee

Dayvee glanced at his sub-pack curled up in their bedrolls. Would his friends' survive tomorrow? He didn't even have the gifts to help them. Should he pray? Would it help? *Kun, I don't want to do this alone. If you give me back the gifts, I'll do my best not to disappoint you.* No whispers in his mind. Cackles, it hadn't worked. Tomorrow he wouldn't have the gifts. Despair choked him. How could he win without them? He had to try. His eyes grew heavy. It had been a long day. Tomorrow might be longer. He better sleep. He let his eyes close.

Dayvee threw his chakram at another enemy. Elayni was beside him, and she cast her chakram at another. There were so many. Wait, why weren't there any trees? It was the scarred landscape from his dream. Was he dreaming again? He glanced behind him. Small green trees grew. A bird with a cobalt blue head and a tawny body flew from one.

Suddenly, Dayvee was sharing the eyes of the little bird. They flew higher, and he could see the armies below them, but then the bird turned and took them out over the ocean. The bird kept flapping, then it would soar and flap again. Dayvee could sense its exhaustion. They finally reached a shoreline with several boats anchored below.

People were fighting there too. The bird dropped lower, and Dayvee could pick out the clanpeople in buckskin clothing and the animals with them. A Calupi with a wolf pointed, and people surged forward. He was directing them. The Calupi looked up at them. What?

Those amber eyes he'd know anywhere. Although he was older, it was Stevee.

Dayvee's eyes shot open.

Just a dream. Or was it? Had Kun replaced Dayvee? Excitement welled up. If Stevee had the Kayndo gifts, he could call the animals back.

Jaycee, is Stevee the next Kayndo?

Jaycee's head lifted from where he slept curled at Dayvee's feet. *Stevee can't speak to us yet.*

What did that *yet* mean? Could Stevee be a Kayndo in waiting? Maybe Dayvee would die today, and Stevee would take over?

You better not die. Jaycee rested his head on Dayvee's ankles. *Then we'd be one short.*

Of course. They needed two Kayndos, one for each continent.

Yes, Jaycee sent. *But I don't know who will go, and who will stay.*

I think Kun just showed me. We need to let the others know so they protect Stevee, or better yet, I can send him and Graydee away.

No. He's not received the gifts yet, so it's not certain. He doesn't need to shoulder the burden before it's more than a possibility. Nothing should change yet.

Stevee could die.

So could you or I. Jaycee nosed his leg. *Trust Kun's plan.*

Could Kun's plan be that they'd all die because it sure seemed like Dayvee was leading everyone to slaughter.

If it's Kun's will, so be it, Jaycee sent.

Dayvee couldn't accept that. He wouldn't. Not even Kun should plan that. Dayvee just had to find a way to defeat the invaders without the animals.

Stevee cried out in his sleep. Codee put an arm around him and mumbled, "You're okay. I'm here." Stevee quieted. Codee was a good father.

Dayvee let his eyes close again.

#

Elayni

The sound of the waves lapping on the shore added to the hum of the insects buzzing around Elayni. She swatted one as she peered out from behind the boulder that hid her. Thanks to the damage the cannons did to the cliffs, several stones littered the beach. By the light of the moon, she picked out the strange ships with their high masts bobbing off the shore and the soldiers patrolling their decks. Concern filled her.

Some clanspeople crept toward them on the beach, hugging the shadows, picking their way around the beach rubble. Less than ten. All that remained of Orca and Dolphin clan. Their presence did little to relieve Elaine's worry. They had already been decimated once. Now they were risking their lives again. Would any of them survive this night?

From the relative safety of their vantage point on top of a cliff, Owl Clan would probably live to tell the story to Dayvee and the others. She missed Dayvee's comforting presence. Never had she done something so risky without him or Brando at her back. Knots twisted her stomach. She wouldn't let her worry stop her.

"Now," Leeto whispered.

Elayni slid into the water. Shivers raced through her at its coolness. She swam out, careful not to splash. Something nudged her leg. A dolphin. She found its fin, grabbed on, and let it tow her through the water.

When they reached one of the ships, she let go of the dolphin's fin to tread water, taking the flint ax out of her belt. She fumbled and dropped the ax. Oh no. She frantically grabbed for the ax and caught it. Whew. If it had gone to the bottom of the ocean, it wouldn't do her any good. She pressed her fingers against the ship to find the seam of two planks below the waterline like Rogee had instructed, then waited.

She heard the beat of wings, then the shadow of the owls above them. Thuds and crackles sounded as the owls dropped the clay pots, and they broke on the decks of the ships.

Foreign shouts from above filled the night.

Now, Evee sent.

Elayni hit the boat with the ax. The water slowed down her strike. As gun shots came from above, she struck the ship again and again. Little chips flew out, but she couldn't get the ax to go completely through. At this rate, she could be here a long time.

A commanding voice shouted foreign orders between the bang of the guns.

As bullets ripped into the water around her, Elayni pounded the ship with the ax again.

The foreign voice barked something, and the bullets turned away from her. Thunks sounded as they hit wood and then came the crack of it splintering.

Thank Kun, the distraction was working. Otter Clan would lose their canoes, but no one was in them.

The night sky was lightening to the gray of morning.

More shouts and then a big splash and wave as a ship keeled over.

At least someone had succeeded in sinking a ship.

Evee sent, *Everyone's supposed to stop now and go to the rendezvous point.*

Cackles. She didn't want to leave the job undone. She hit the ship with the ax again frantically.

An orca whale surfaced beside her, and his wake pushed Elayni back. He slammed into the ship where she'd been hitting it. The wood splintered. Water gushed in. Shouts pierced the air.

The gunfire stopped, and dinghies were being lowered over the ship sides.

They would see her. Elayni grabbed the orca's fin and drew a deep breath. The orca took her under, and they streaked away.

When the orca turned, she knew she was close to shore. She let go and bobbed to the surface.

"Toovo! Toovo!" That must be their word for enemy since the invaders in one of their small boats were pointing at her.

Their dinghies filled the area between the ships and shore, but they were veering farther south of where she was. Would they come after her? She put her head down and swam as fast as she could. Her legs touched bottom, and she crawled onto the beach. Evee greeted her, nuzzling her face.

Sand blew up next to them as a cannon ball screamed down the beach. That must be why the boats had veered south. So they could get out of the way of the cannon fire. Elayni staggered to her feet, and she and Evee ran.

The cliff wall loomed in front of them. The cannons barked again, and one of the balls slammed into the cliff somewhere above. Rocks showered them, and boulders slid down the cliff toward them. Cackles.

A dark shadow marked the face of the cliff. Must be a cave. Could they make it? They cived toward the entrance.

28

Inadequate

"There is no harsher judge than my own self." ~ Dayvee

Dayvee

Butterflies racked Dayvee's stomach as he looked out over the huge crowd gathered in front of him. Even mounted on a horse, he had never felt so small. Not even Leeto's disappointment had made him feel so inadequate. The people were quiet, waiting for what he had to tell them. He drew a breath and prepared himself to deal with the scorn that might come. "I asked you here so I could inform you that I have lost the Kayndo gifts."

Gasps rose from the crowd. Murmurs filled the air. Dayvee lifted his hand. They quieted. At least they were still listening to him.

"My companion informs me I'm still the Kayndo. I just don't have the gifts. I am sorry about whatever I did that caused this, and I know it's going to make it even harder to win the fight we face. I wouldn't blame anyone who thinks the risk is too great and decides to leave."

More murmurs broke out and then shouts. "What will you do?"

"How will you direct us?"

"Can you get the gifts back?"

Dayvee lifted his hand again. "I don't think the gifts will come back, but this battle still needs to be fought. I'm not giving up, and I *will* do my best to win. Before I go into the plans, I'd like those who want to leave to go."

No one left. Dayvee should be happy, but his heart felt heavy. There would be more to die when they faced these brutal invaders.

"Choose one person from each of your clans to ride with us so I can give them directions. Their companions can pass them on to yours." More horses had joined them, so they should have enough. "The Accipi have eagles scouting, and they say we should meet the invaders in an hour's ride. Varian shared a lot with Tibalt about how his people fight. Tibalt's going to tell us what to expect."

Tibalt came forward. Dirt streaked the former prince's face. His clothes appeared wrinkled, but his voice was strong as he faced the crowd. "Once they fire their guns, it takes time to reload. That is the best time to hit them. Besides their guns, they keep weapons like daggers hidden in their sleeves and pant legs. And they often apply poison to them. Varian said if they act as if they're going to surrender, it's to get you closer. So don't trust them."

"Thanks, Tibalt." Dayvee waved to the Keeper. "Gaylo, is there anything you want to say?"

Gaylo gave Dayvee a hard look. "I'd just ask everyone to pray that Kun will deliver us. With Him all things are possible."

Possible maybe, but not always done. Dayvee knew better than to count on Kun's help. Look what happened when he relied on his gifts. "We leave in fifteen minutes. Prepare for the battle to come and have your delegates join me before we leave."

Dayvee slid off Ghostee onto his crutches and glanced at his sub-pack. "We should put on our war paint."

Codee pulled hides out of his rucksack. "Leeto gave me these for the sub-pack. He said he regretted not sending them with you earlier, but no one was sure there'd be a battle when you left home."

Stevee frowned. "Those aren't wolf hides, are they?"

"Yes," Codee answered. "These are our war capes. They're very special to us since they're made from the hides of companions that died protecting our pack." He touched Wilee's head. "They insist we use their hides and bones after their death so they can continue to fight for us. None would want to be left out today." He handed one to Stevee. "This was Zago's hide. His bones are in the weapons you carry. Wear it with pride. Zago was a fierce wolf. He will shelter you and strike terror in your enemies." Codee held one out to Dayvee. "Milay sent Clay's for you. She'd want to keep her pup from harm."

Dayvee took it reverently and put it on. Clay's muzzle lay over his head, and her hide draped around his shoulders. Only Dayvee's face lay uncovered. Codee continued distributing the war capes to everyone in the sub-pack. "With the capes and war paint, our enemies' legs will quake."

Dayvee elected to have his face painted with stripes of gray for Jaycee and Clay.

"Give me two colors," Stevee instructed Chayla. "Because I'm fighting for the clanspeople and the adrifts." She painted half of Stevee's face white and the other half red.

Tayro distributed cups of a tea, green in color. "Drink this. It's got Salad Burnet to slow bleeding from wounds along with Stinging Nettle and honey to give us energy."

Brando's eyes roamed over the sub-pack. "Don't forget our first priority is to keep Dayvee safe."

"Not just me," Dayvee said. "All of us. Try your hardest to protect our entire family."

Their faces set in lines of grim determination. Dayvee drained his cup and mounted Ghostee again.

…

Shouts in some foreign language pierced the air. They must be close. Any second now the battle would come. Dayvee's heart sped up. Shuto, the Accipi leader, moved from the group of delegates around his sub-pack to ride over to Dayvee. "My companion just informed me the invaders have turned around and are fleeing back to the coast."

A cheer went up from those who overheard.

I'm in mind reach with Luko now, Jaycee sent. *Leeto attacked their ships last night and was able to destroy half of them. There's not much hope they'll be able to destroy the rest. They have several dead and injured.*

What about Elayni?

Jaycee's sorrow surged through their bond. *She and Evee are trapped in a cave, cut off from the rest.*

Cackles. Leeto wouldn't help her. He'd follow the rule to protect the pack over an individual.

Luko says Leeto would go back for her if he could, but they're pinned down and outnumbered. Jaycee whimpered. *Luko says they'll fight to their last breath.*

Dayvee sent, *Tell them we're coming.*

Leeto says don't. It isn't a good place to wage a battle.

Dayvee couldn't just do nothing. He turned to the others. He didn't enjoy being the bearer of bad news, but they needed to know. "The invaders must have learned about the attack on their ships. They're not running from us but toward Leeto. He's already pinned down, and Elayni's trapped in a cave."

Those around him collectively gasped.

With all the horses that had joined them in the last few days, Dayvee probably had a thousand people mounted now and another two thousand on foot. "We'll split up," he ordered. Those on horseback can go with me to swing around the invaders to help our packmates. Those on foot will continue to advance so we can fight the invaders from both sides."

He urged Ghostee to a gallop. All those mounted followed him as they raced in a large circle around the invaders. The smell of smoke burnt Dayvee's nostrils.

"They set Marshton on fire before leaving," Shuto yelled.

The smoke thinned and was replaced by the scent of salt so thickly laced in the damp air Dayvee could taste it. They came to a line of cliffs.

Reko stopped. "We'll have to leave the horses here and climb."

Dayvee grabbed his crutches off Ghostee and slid down. Somehow he'd make it if he had to crawl.

Jaycee nudged him. *We'll investigate to find the easiest path through.* He and the other wolves spread out and clambered up the cliffs.

It couldn't have been five minutes before the wolves reappeared. *Follow us,* Jaycee sent.

In places, the cliffs were steep. Dayvee scraped his hands and knees climbing the hard stones, but thanks to the wolves, it wasn't as bad as he feared. Most of the time, he was able to hobble up the slopes on his crutches even though the rocks were damp. He topped another rise to find the cliff descended sharply to an area of sand dunes in the South. And beyond the hills of sand, farther south another of the ancients' ruins scarred the landscape. The road wound along the edge of the ruins. He checked the road further west. There, that huge blob had to be the invaders marching this way. To the east, the cliffs dropped in a sheer line straight to a jagged shoreline. Out in the ocean bobbed the invader's ships in a line across the bay.

Don't get too close to the coastal side, Jaycee sent. *The invaders cannons chewed up the cliffs, and it doesn't feel stable. Wouldn't take much to start another landslide.*

Dayvee scanned the eastern drop. The cliffs were scarred, and waves crashed against piles of boulders and rubble. Dark shadows announced more than one cave in the cliff. Only one harbored Elayni and Evee. His heart screamed at him to go get Elayni, but they'd have to go around.

He turned his gaze to the steep southern drop and the dunes below. Holes in the sand marked the extent of where the cannons could reach. They'd need to make their stand beyond those marks. Only a few scattered trees grew, and they were stumpy with thin canopies that looked as if moss hung from them. They wouldn't provide much cover.

The grass and brush grew thick, but it wouldn't hide them very well. They could use the sand dunes for cover, but there weren't enough for all of them. Leeto was right. It wasn't the best place to fight. And they would be hemmed in between the ruins, the ocean, and the cliffs. Couldn't be helped. He couldn't ignore that Elayni and the others needed aid.

Small boats were pulled up on the northern part of the beach, and silhouettes of men moved around the dunes. A longer shadow of a wolf emerged from behind one of the small hills of sand. The crack of gunfire sounded, and the wolf leapt back. That must be where the Calupi were pinned down.

They needed to get down there. They could descend the south face with ropes, but what about the wolves and other animals?

Jaycee's muzzle turned to the South. *Don't worry about the animals. We'll be able to make our way down.*

As clanspeople fixed ropes, Dayvee turned to the delegates. "Do any of you have any ideas to stop or slow the invaders?"

Hoke of Fox Clan grabbed a thin rope out of his rucksack. "We can hide some of these lines in the sand and pull them up to trip them."

"Everyone in otter clan has nets we use for fishing." Fujee held one up. "They're small, but they can net at least one."

Reko gestured toward the ground. "We could use some snares to catch unwary feet."

"Those are great ideas, but we haven't much time." Dayvee rushed to impart his orders. "Otter Clan and Fox Clan will go west and set traps by the road to stop or slow the invaders that are coming. Badger Clan and Prairie Dog Clan will dig some trenches for more cover while the rest of you will go with me east to fight the ones already down there."

Dayvee slipped his crutches into his rucksack straps, then grabbed one of the ropes and slid down.

#

Stevee

Stevee hugged the shadow of the cliff as more of Dayvee's army slid down the ropes. The invaders moved around the beach as if oblivious to them.

Codee whispered, "It's a good thing city people don't look up."

Dayvee didn't wait for everyone to get down. He signaled by opening his hand and cupping it. They spread out to advance, creeping along the cliff wall and through the brush. The only tell against the sand was a flash of color here and there from an animal hide. If their enemies spotted anything, they'd just think it was an animal.

Stevee's heart pounded. It wasn't like this was the first time he faced enemies. The difference was he wasn't doing it alone. Then it hit Stevee. His breath caught as he glanced at his sub-pack as they moved stealthily forward. He not only trusted them, he really cared about them. But they weren't adrifts.

No, they were a family. And that was better because families were forever. Adrifts knew to appreciate those they cared about since their time together was usually short. It ripped his heart every time one died. But not caring or having anyone that cared was much worse. This time it was different. He had weapons now. And he wasn't about to let these invaders take his family from him. He would protect them.

Graydee's excitement surged through their bond. Stevee grabbed his slingshot and opened his pouch full of rocks.

Now, Graydee sent. *Howl.*

Stevee howled with the Calupi, and war cries sounded from the other clans. Dayvee loosed his nails. Stevee threw a stone at their enemies. Ursans threw their spears, Kwin their bolas, Accipi their talon, the Pericards their arrows. A myriad of weapons bore down on their enemies. Many of them fell. The others scattered and, using the dunes for cover, fled past the holes that marked the cannon's reach.

Dayvee had told everyone not to go past it. They halted their pursuit.

Stevee caught a flash of gray of wolves. Leeto and his group ran toward them. Less than ten Calupi were with Leeto. Not even half of those he had taken. They all sported bandages, and some carried others.

The invaders peeked out from behind the dunes long enough to fire a couple shots, but they were wild and went high. None of them hit Leeto's group as he raced to them.

When Leeto's group reached them, Dayvee shouted to Tayro, "Find somewhere that will be safe to treat them. The Pericards can go with you."

"I'm fine," Leeto claimed. "The rest can go with Tayro, but I don't need treatment."

"I'd rather half the Pericards stay with you," Blake said.

Stevee smiled to himself. Knowing Blake, he'd find an excuse to send some back with messages if Dayvee didn't allow it. Dayvee nodded his consent.

Tayro moved off with the injured and half the Pericards. Leeto put a hand on the shoulder of a man dressed in strange clothing that remained with him. "This is Rogee, a Calupi from their continent. He's been a big help in giving us advice about them."

Dayvee grasped Rogee's arm in the clan arm clasp. "Then I owe you my gratitude."

Rogee returned the clasp. "They killed my pack and companion, so I want to help you defeat them."

In the distance, a muted sound like rolls of thunder could be heard. Marching feet.

Cheers erupted from the foreigners hiding behind the dunes.

Rogee grimaced. "The ones coming now aren't crewmembers but soldiers, and they are much harder to kill."

#

Elayni
Pain shot through Elayni's calf as she pushed again with all her strength against the boulder pinning her leg to the floor of the cave. It didn't budge. She fought down her rising panic over being trapped. This wasn't going to work, and she was just hurting herself more. Evee whimpered. Their shared bond meant she felt the pain too.

She regretted her impulsive decision to go with Leeto now. She hated the feeling of being alone, cut off from her pack. She missed Dayvee and the others. Her family.

Light filtered in through the cracks in the rocks so she wasn't completely in the dark. But there wasn't much to see. This cave was really just a depression at the foot of the rocky cliff. Green lichen coated the sides, and it only went back a short distance, maybe six feet. She and Evee took up most of it.

Evee, do you know what happened to the rest on the mission?

We lost quite a few to the cannons. And those that aren't dead are injured from fighting the invaders in the row boats. Leeto won't be able to help us.

Wasn't like Elayni figured Leeto would come anyway. She knew the rules. Protect the Pack over individuals.

Cold seeped into her. The damp earthy smell of soil, rocks, and lichen mixed with the salt scent from the ocean. Was the ground wet where she sat? Yes. A puddle was forming. She ran her hands over the rocks blocking the depression. Water trickled in through them. The tide must be rising.

There wasn't much hope of freeing herself, but she had to get Evee out, or she'd drown too. She scooted closer and grabbed a rock as high as she could reach and pulled. It came loose with a shower of others. Stones fell on her, battering her flesh. She didn't care as long as she freed Evee. She tugged at another large rock. She'd see Kun soon. Her only regret was leaving on such a harsh note. *Evee, are you in mind range of any wolves?*

Yes. I can reach Jaycee.

Surprising. She had known Codee would get Dayvee to come back, but they must have really pushed hard to be close enough for Evee to be able to mind reach them.

Can you ask Jaycee to tell Dayvee I'm sorry? I shouldn't have left. Tell him that he and the rest of our family will always have my love. And I'll see them when they join Kun.

Dayvee says to not give up. They'll come.

The water had deepened in the cave and now covered her leg as she sat pinned. She doubted they could get here in time to save her, and she didn't want her family members to lose their lives to those cannons. She wouldn't ask that, not even for Evee. *Tell him not to.*

But Dayvee was right. She shouldn't give up. Dayvee hadn't even after his feet were crushed. She had to keep trying.

Elayni pulled another rock free.

29

Rescue

"To be trusted sometimes is a heavy burden." ~ Codee

Dayvee

Dayvee needed to do something to get Elayni out. He locked gazes with Brando. "The water's rising where Elayni's trapped, so she doesn't have much time. I need you to rescue her."

Brando's face blanched white. "I can't. I told Elayni I had to stay with you. My duty is to keep the Kayndo safe."

Dayvee blew out his breath. "Then I'll go."

Brando shook his head. "You can't. You're the Kayndo and needed here."

Dayvee gritted his teeth to hold in his frustration. "She's our pack, our family. Do you expect me to ask another to risk their life if we won't? And who else can I trust to get to her in time?"

Leeto shook his head. "She's Calupi. She wouldn't want to put anyone else at risk."

Dayvee shot him a glare. "Don't tell me to forget her."

"You said I'm family." Stevee's scrunched face revealed his earnestness. "So I can do it if you trust me."

Codee gave him a short nod. "I'll go with Stevee."

Dayvee's heart screamed at him to race to Elayni. A groan escaped him as he resigned himself to let others go. He could just send Codee. He shouldn't risk Stevee.

No, Jaycee sent. *If you don't return Stevee's trust, his won't last. Besides, everywhere is dangerous.*

"I do trust you, Stevee. Thank you, both."

The drumming sound of footsteps grew louder. Dayvee glanced at the Accipi leader, Shuto. "How long before they arrive?"

"Maybe five minutes."

"I don't want to leave these guys at our backs. Surely if we strike their crewmen, the ships won't fire the cannons with them down there."

Rogee waved his hand in the air. "Don't be fooled. They'll throw lives away if it's convenient."

"How long does it take their ships to fire those cannons?" Dayvee asked.

The foreign clansmen's brow furrowed. "It takes about thirty seconds for the fuse to burn to the charge if they're loaded. Otherwise a couple of minutes."

Dayvee straightened his shoulders. "Okay, we'll charge past the cannon line, strike them fast, and run back. Our companions can go over the top of the dunes and drop down on them while the people go around their sides. Stevee and Codee will keep going to get Elayni while we have them distracted." Dayvee took a breath. "Now."

They charged.

#

Stevee

Stevee ran down the beach with his nails in hand. He looked over at his sub-pack. Dayvee was pulling away from him. Surprising how fast he could run swinging between crutches. Some of the enemies stepped from behind dunes to fire at them. At the dune closest to them, one pointed his gun at Dayvee. Brando loosed his nails and hit him. Another aimed for Brando.

Stevee threw his nails and hit him in the throat. The man dropped. Blood pooled around his neck. The overpowering smell of acrid gunpowder mixing with the sharp tang of fresh blood choked Stevee. He was going to be sick.

"Well met, Stevee. Thanks for protecting me." Brando's words rang in his ears.

Stevee couldn't be sick. He had to protect his family.

Their companions reached the dune and launched themselves over it. The sounds of growls rang out. The sub-pack ran around the side. They loosed their weapons at the few left standing. Codee knelt down and grabbed Stevee's nails from the man he killed and handed them back. "Let's go."

Stevee followed Codee to race toward the ocean while the sub-pack changed directions and ran back. Their companions, Graydee and Wilee, caught up and then loped in front of them. Waves lapped against the east side of the cliff. The wolves plunged into the water next to the cliff line. Stevee followed them. Cool water soaked him as he splashed up the thigh high water while he ran.

The thief in Stevee rebelled. This was making it easy to spot them. Shouldn't they be swimming?

The water almost covered Graydee's back as he hopped through the waves. *Evee says the water's up to Elayni's neck, so no, unless you can swim faster than run.*

Suddenly, Graydee stopped. *We're here.*

A pile of rocks poked out above the water. There was probably a six-inch gap at the top where he could see a hole beyond it. "We're coming, Elayni."

"Stevee?"

"Yes, and Codee too." Stevee worked frantically with Codee to grab rocks and pull them out to enlarge the gap. Within a few minutes, the gap grew to a be a couple of feet.

"You can probably squeeze through now," Codee panted out. "Go help her while I keep clearing."

Maybe it wasn't so bad being small. Stevee stuck his face in first. The water had risen to right below Elayni's mouth. He wriggled his body in, splashing down in the water beside her. Evee leapt on him. "Good to see you, too, Evee."

"Thanks for coming." Elayni's face appeared pale. "I'm really glad Evee will be able to get out."

Stevee blew out his breath. Since meeting her, he'd been impressed by Elayni's fighting spirit. Why was she giving up? "I plan to get both of you out. Are you hurt?"

"There's a boulder pinning my foot, and I can't get it to move. I doubt you or Codee could either."

Would he have to do the unthinkable? "I hope you're wrong because Dayvee's trusting me to bring you back, and I don't want to cut your foot off."

Elayni's face turned red, and she sputtered. "You're not cutting my foot off."

There was the Elayni he knew. "Then let's try to move it together."

She plunged her hands into the water. "All right. I'm ready."

Stevee bent over beside her and followed her arms to the boulder. It was big, but all they needed to do was roll it a little to the side. He splayed his hands over it and leaned his legs against it too. Please Kun, let us succeed. "Now." He strained with all his strength.

Elayni screamed.

#

Dayvee
Dayvee peered out from behind a clump of tall grass as the columns of soldiers came closer. The enemy took high steps as they marched, strutting like turkeys. With one arm, they held their guns, but the other arm swung back and forth. And they were dressed kind of like the Pericards with padded clothing that covered them from their necks down. Helmets rested on their heads.

Dayvee let them come until they came to their trip lines. He whispered to Hoke, "Now. "

Fox clan pulled their ropes up, and several of the soldiers tripped over them and fell.

Dayvee howled, and war cries sounded from the other clans as they cast their weapons at the invaders. Very few harmed their enemies. Their helmets and clothing protected them.

Their enemies barked orders in their foreign tongue. They broke into smaller squads to charge and shoot at them. Once they fired their guns, they'd reload as another squad took over. Those that fell when they became ensnared in traps or as weapons found them were ignored as the others went around them.

The smoke and foul scent of gunpowder choked Dayvee as one of their squads bore down on where they hid. He loosed his nails on one to hit him across the nose. Another raised his gun to take aim at Dayvee, but Brando's tooth found his eye.

Chayla flung her nails at one aiming at Brando. It hit the soldier in the face, and he fell. The Pericards rained arrows down on them, finishing them. As Dayvee pulled on the rope to bring his weapon back, he scanned the area. Several clansmen were down. His stomach twisted. He'd never get used to the gory sights in a battle. And there were too many getting hit due to the lack of cover.

"Everyone fall back to the trenches with our injured," Dayvee bellowed.

As they ran toward the ditches, he caught some movement at the shore. Several of the invader's dinghies were being pulled up on it, and probably thirty men disembarked from them. They weren't dressed like their soldiers, so why had they come? Maybe they were going to transport their wounded or something? But they were carrying guns. How were Stevee and Codee to bring Elayni through?

Stevee and Codee's heads bobbed up behind the boats. Dayvee's heart skipped. Where was Elayni? There. Golden tresses peeked out from behind Codee. Relief poured into Dayvee. But was Codee carrying her on his back? At least she was alive, but he needed to keep her that way.

Dayvee pointed toward the shore. "Clint, take the Pericards and go help Stevee." Then he jumped into the trench and forced himself to turn away to focus on killing more of the invaders.

#

Stevee
When they rounded the cliff, Stevee's heart sank at the sight of so many invaders between them and Tayro. Elayni's ankle was swollen, and he was pretty sure it was broken. He could probably sneak past alone, but he didn't think Codee and Elayni could.

Wilee, Evee, and I can, Graydee sent. *They won't spot us, but we'll be there if you need help.*

Good. Codee wouldn't be able to do much fighting carrying

Elayni on his back. It would be up to Stevee and their companions.

The wolves slunk to the shore in the shadows of the cliff.

Codee whispered, "We need to get closer to those boats so you can stab the bottoms with your tooth. They need to be stopped from going back and forth."

"Good idea, Codee," Elayni said softly.

Stevee whispered back, "Sure, and while I'm at it, maybe I should kill the men disembarking from them too?"

Codee's eyes twinkled. "If you'd like."

Stevee pulled his tooth and let himself sink deeper into the water, only keeping his head above while he sidled toward the boats.

Luckily, the invaders appeared to be focused on the battle. Stevee grabbed the stern of the first dinghy and plunged his tooth under the water line and into the wood. One down, five more to go.

At the last one, Codee whispered, "Better hurry, looks like the Pericards are going to beat you to killing them."

Sure enough, Clint and several Pericards ran toward the shoreline. Stevee struck the boat, then slammed his knife into his sheath. He pulled out his slingshot and a handful of stones as the invaders jabbered in their foreign language and lifted their guns toward the Pericards.

"Let me go, Codee. I can hop." Elayni's whisper sounded awful loud.

A few of the invaders turned and caught sight of them. They yelled. Stevee slung stones as fast as he could. A splash sounded as Codee released Elayni and drew his weapons.

The Pericards shot arrows. The invaders fired their guns. Some of the Pericards fell, but so did invaders. Graydee, Evee, and Wilee each sprang forward to tackle one.

Clint ran forward and stabbed one with his sword as he tried to reload. "What are you waiting for, Stevee?"

Stevee ran on shore, slinging stones as he went. Codee followed, holding on to Elayni's hand as she hopped on one foot.

"You can't leave enemies alive behind us." Codee stopped to

draw his tooth through the throat of one Stevee stunned with a stone.

Bile rose in Stevee's throat. One of the invaders raised his hands and dropped his gun. Codee let go of Elayni to walk toward him. Chilly fingers of dread wrapped around Stevee's heart. Tibalt said they used surrender as a ploy.

"Careful," Stevee shrieked.

Codee looked over at Stevee as the invader grabbed a knife from his sleeve and threw it.

Codee fell to his knees.

"No." Stevee threw his nails and hit the invader in the face. He ran to his father. "Don't die."

Codee drew a ragged breath. "I'm not dead."

The knife stuck out of Codee's chest, over his heart.

A whine sounded and then a crash as a cannonball slammed into the beach. The percussion threw Stevee back. He stumbled to his feet.

"Everyone run!" Clint scooped up Codee. Stevee helped Elayni, and they ran. Clint crashed to the ground. Blood poured from his leg. Cackles. Stevee couldn't carry them all.

A scream sounded. Smokee. How did he get here? Did it matter? Clint somehow made it to his feet and helped Stevee put Codee on the horse. "Elayni, climb up behind him. You too, Clint. Smokee can carry three."

When they got on, Stevee ran with the wolves beside Smokee as the horse carried them past the line where the cannon could reach.

Some of the trenches were being overrun. Squads of enemies seemed to be everywhere.

Stevee swept a path in front of them but more kept coming. When he was out of rocks, he drew his bow and fired arrows. Never hesitating. He couldn't stop. They'd hurt his father. They wanted to kill Graydee, Clint, his sub-pack, and Nolte. If his family died, he'd be alone again. No, he wouldn't let that happen. *Please Kun, let Codee be okay.*

Bullets screamed around him. He used his last two arrows. Could they get through? They had to. He pulled his nails.

Keep low to the ground to stay under their fire, Graydee sent.

Even wounded, Clint's sword plunged into an enemy. Smokee's scream filled the air as he charged through a gap. Stevee grabbed onto Smokee's mane and ran with him. The wolves stayed at his side. When they came to the trench the sub-pack was in, Ghostee's muscles bunched as he slid to a halt.

Stevee shouted, "I have injured."

Dayvee pointed north. "Get them to where Tayro and the Keepers are treating them."

Stevee followed Dayvee's finger to see a group of people in the distance, near the South slope of the cliff. It must be at least a couple of hundred feet away, and Codee's breaths were already ragged.

"Hold on, Codee." Stevee tugged at Smokee's mane to get him to trot toward them.

Long rows of injured people lay on the ground. The Keepers were keeping busy.

Elayni slid down and used Smokee to support herself. Clint and Codee were both slumped forward. Elayni and he grabbed them to keep them from falling.

Blake and Reko ran over to him. "You need help?"

"Yes."

Between them, they got Codee and Clint off to lay them down. Tayro and Gaylo rushed to them. Gaylo bent over Clint to apply pressure to stop his bleeding.

Tayro knelt beside Codee.

"He's been stabbed in the chest," Stevee explained. "Tibalt said they used poison on their knives."

"I'll do what I can for him." Tayro cut Codee's shirt off then glanced up. "You've got blood all over you. Are you injured too?"

"Must be Clint's, but I think Elayni's ankle is broken."

"I'll get to you next, Elayni. Go ahead and sit down."

She lowered herself to the ground as Reko grabbed Stevee's arm. "Dayvee has the Kwin bringing the injured here. We could use your help since you're the only one mounted."

"My sub-pack needs me to fight with them, but you can ride Smokee. Thanks for sending him to me. "

Reko swung up on Smokee. "I didn't send him. He must have gone over or around the cliffs on his own. He even managed to get through the invaders."

Dizziness swamped Stevee. His legs crumpled beneath him and he crashed to the ground on his back. Why did he fall? Great poofy clouds lined the sky. Kun had sure blessed them with a beautiful sky today.

30

Surrender

"To surrender our own will isn't easy but often necessary." ~ Leeto

Logan

Logan kept his eyes peeled all around him. During the heat of the battle would be a good time for another of Garth's assassins to strike and blame the enemy for Logan's death.

This was turning into another massacre for the people of this continent. Their weapons couldn't compete with guns. "Advance and finish cleaning out those trenches," Garth ordered.

Logan must try to halt the bloodshed. "Garth, call a halt to the firing and let me see if they'll surrender."

"No. They began this fight. We'll finish it. I want every one of them dead, but they shouldn't die easily. Aim for the gut. They should hear their friends scream."

Logan's stomach turned. How could Garth be so cruel? "They fought honorably. Let them die with honor."

"According to Father, there is no honor for those who lose."

"Acting honorably isn't reserved for victors. To have honor, you must give it."

Garth groaned. He turned back to the soldiers. "I don't care where you aim, as long as they die. Go." The men charged, but one of Garth's henchmen pulled a knife and leapt toward Logan.

Logan jumped back and put Garth between them. Some of the enemies' arrows came flying toward them. One hit Garth's henchman, and he fell toward Garth with his knife. Logan threw Garth to the side, but the henchman toppled into Logan.

Logan stumbled and fell back, landing with the man on top of him. A fire spread through his chest.

Garth rolled his henchman off him, exposing the hilt of the knife sunk in Logan's chest. Garth fell to his knees beside Logan. "I don't…understand. Why did you do it?"

Logan gasped out. "Because you're my brother, and I love you."

Garth ran his hands through his hair. "I'm sorry, Logan, for everything."

"It's all right, Garth." Logan coughed. So hard to draw breath. "I could never regret giving my life for a king that our country can be proud of. Be that king, Garth." A giant white wolf walked toward him. "I see JoKayndo, Garth. The stories are real."

"You're sure?"

"Yes." JoKayndo glided a few steps away and turned back to him. Did the wolf want Logan to follow?

Garth grabbed his hand. "Please don't die, Logan. I was wrong. I need you."

"I want to follow JoKayndo." Suddenly, Logan was looking down at his brother holding his limp body in his arms.

"I'll be a king *you* can be proud of," Garth shouted. "I promise."

JoKayndo yipped. Logan walked after him toward the light.

#

Dayvee

More kept falling. Elayni, Codee, Clint, Stevee, and so many more hurt and they kept coming. Dayvee had to do something. Jaycee sent, *Topay says Tayro is doing everything he can. Clint's gone to Kun. Stevee will probably join him. Codee might survive.*

The invaders ran toward the trenches shooting everyone in them. Screams pierced the air as the invaders ran to the next. Why did they leave them alive suffering?

People were being maimed all around them. He'd seen so many people and animals shot. The ancient's weapons were making a blood bath.

What should he do? How could he defeat them and keep more safe? He'd tried everything they thought of. None of it worked.

The feeling of being inadequate for the task overwhelmed him. He had failed. Everyone would die. It would be all his fault.

Was there anything he could do to turn it around? Kwutee always said when things looked hopeless to pray. He'd try. *Kun, I'm desperate. We're losing. If you just stop these invaders, I'll do whatever you want. Please send JoKayndo. Don't punish all these people for my inadequacies!*

A giant white wolf walked toward him. Oh, thank Kun it was JoKayndo.

JoKayndo stopped a few feet from him. *Why do you always bargain and try to tell Kun what to do? Why did you listen when Leeto told you not to contact the hyenas that were trespassing at Wolf Mountain?*

Dayvee could never forget that day. *Because Leeto was alpha, and I thought he knew better than me.*

Doesn't Kun know better than you? JoKayndo's voice rang out in his head. *When the hyena bit you, did you blame Leeto?*

No. It wasn't his fault I got wounded.

Yet you blamed Kun for your injuries and your friend's death.

Dayvee lowered his head. *I was wrong.*

Yes, you were. There is only one Kun, and it is not you. But you refused to accept Kun's will or take Kun's path. You turned away to follow your own.

I'll accept Kun's will, Dayvee cried. *I won't turn away again. But please tell me His will. Tell me what to do.*

Surrender.

Surrender? We don't want to surrender the Vita.

Kun gave you the Vita, it's not yours. Have everyone surrender and sing Kun's praises.

I can't tell everyone. I don't have the gifts.

You never lost the gifts, just your belief. Do you believe Kun can help you?

Yes. The whispers of animal voices slammed into Dayvee's mind. *Thank you.* Dayvee sent the message to every companion he could mind reach and shouted it aloud. "We're surrendering. Sing Kun's praises."

Several companions sent, *My chosen doesn't want to surrender.*

Remind them they took a vow.

Rogee yelled over, "If you surrender, they'll still kill everyone that fought them. They always do."

Dayvee sucked in his breath. He had known they'd kill him. But kill them all? *Must I be responsible?*

JoKayndo's eyes met his. *Kun decides who is fortunate enough to meet him early.*

Had Dayvee been looking at it all wrong? Had Geno been fortunate to go early? He hadn't seen this bloodbath. If Stevee and Codee died, should Dayvee be grateful? Who would suffer? Not them. Him. But Geno's loss wasn't permanent and neither would theirs be. Geno had gone ahead.

Dayvee dropped his weapons and called out. "This is the Kayndo. We are surrendering." He lifted his hands palms out and started singing. His sub-pack let their weapons fall and joined him in singing praises to Kun. More voices joined theirs to raise the song while the invaders moved forward. They'd all die.

JoKayndo sent, *Follow me.*

Dayvee crawled from the ditch and got his crutches underneath him.

Brando and Chayla moved at his side.

JoKayndo's words filled him. *Alone.*

"Stay here. I go alone."

Brando shook his head. "No, Dayvee."

"Yes. I'm ordering it. JoKayndo wants me to follow him."

"But Dayvee I don't see JoKayndo." Brando's brow furrowed, and he whispered, "There's no one there."

"Trust me. I'm not alone."

Dayvee hobbled forward. The invaders brought their weapons to bear on him. He sang louder. "I'll sing my praise to Kun now and forever more..." Even in the midst of the chaos, a sense of peace and security fell over him.

Fall to your knees, JoKayndo sent.

Dayvee fell. Bullets kicked up the dust all around him, but none hit him. JoKayndo stood in front of him. The white wolf's body jerked as it became riddled with holes, the blood pouring from him. JoKayndo howled in pain.

I don't want you to suffer for me.

JoKayndo's voice filled his mind. *That's what Kayndo's do. We follow the path of the one who wasn't just a master of animals but men. Didn't you ask to take your loved one's pain? Your willingness to sacrifice for them was why you were chosen. But you didn't have to hide your pain. Let it out. And thank Kun for it. Scream with me, Dayvee.*

As JoKayndo howled, Dayvee screamed and gave voice to all his suffering. The pain from his crushed feet he'd been holding in. All the agony he felt as those around him were injured and killed. All his despair from feeling inadequate to the task. Tears ran down his face.

Now praise Kun for allowing you to take the pain rather than those you love. Sing with me, Dayvee.

Dayvee lifted his praises to Kun. JoKayndo sang with him. The voices behind him did too. The sounds of praise swelled and merged with a new sound, a roaring that filled the air. As he sang, a maelstrom formed in the clear sky. A black funnel of wind sprang in front of him to suck at his clothes. Sand stung his eyes. The stunted trees swayed, the moss that hung from them rose, and blobs of green flew through the air. The wind covered his voice, but he kept singing.

The swirling cloud descended on the invaders. Chaos followed. Some ran, but it sucked in the invaders and threw them out. "We worship you, Kun. We thank you. We praise you," Dayvee sang.

The funnel rose back into the heavens. *Thank you, Kun.* Dayvee struggled back to his feet.

The shouts of joy and praises to Kun still rose from every corner. JoKayndo sent, *There are a few left alive to aid you. Those that repented and cried out to Kun. And one ship is undamaged.*

JoKayndo fell over, and his pain-filled howl echoed in Dayvee's head. Then JoKayndo disappeared.

The few invaders that were left alive struggled to their feet. Not even a dozen total. Their faces drained of color, and their mouths hung open as they took in the twisted, broken bodies of those around them.

No one hurts them, Dayvee sent. He barked, "Can any of you speak our language?"

"I can," answered one. He had a heavy accent, but Dayvee could understand him.

"Then translate what I say to the others. Tell them I want them to throw their weapons down. All of you just saw Kun's power. He left those who repented alive to aid me—I mean—Him. His doing not mine." The man spoke in his language, and the group cast their weapons aside. "The hidden weapons too."

After he translated, they took weapons out of their boots, their sleeves, sewn in their clothes, taped on their chests and backs, even tucked into their hair. They joined the pile.

When Dayvee looked down the cliff, all the boats but one lay twisted and broken. He shouted to his supporters, "Everyone should thank Kun."

Every human bent a knee, and all the animals joined them in lowering their heads. Could there be a more heartfelt prayer than theirs?

With the help of his crutches, Dayvee stood. The bodies of his fallen supporters littered the ground and trenches. "Our costs today have been high, but they are the fortunate ones. Kun let them meet him early."

Rogee ran up to the prisoner who had been translating. "Garth, where's Logan?"

Garth hung his head. "I killed him."

As Dayvee hobbled over to them, Rogee turned to him. "He's the one responsible for the slaughter. He even killed his brother. Let me challenge him and have the first throw when you sentence him to the ring of death."

Dayvee shook his head. "JoKayndo said they showed remorse, and Kun left him alive for a reason. Death's not an option."

Rogee spit on Garth. "He doesn't know what remorse is."

Garth wiped his sleeve across his face, clearing Rogee's spit. "I am sorry. I promised my brother I'd change. JoKayndo said Kun forgave me, and I should aid the people I harmed the most."

He spoke truth, Jaycee sent.

Dayvee put a hand on Rogee's shoulder. "Jaycee judged him as speaking truth, but if he reverts back, I'll sentence him to the ring of pain. And you'll go first."

Rogee's fists clenched. "That shouldn't take long."

The prisoners were getting a lot of scowls from more than Rogee. The hurt and pain of their losses were too fresh and raw to leave these prisoners where anyone could reach them.

Dayvee turned back to Garth. "Can all of you swim?"

When Garth translated, they nodded.

"Good." Dayvee pointed to an island. "Tell them to swim out there. The dolphins will help you, and there's fresh water there. The animals will bring you food, but don't harm them or swim back. Sharks will eat anyone that leaves or comes to that island without my permission."

#

Stevee

Stevee's head was hurting, and so was his chest. Bigham must be beating him again. He tried to roll in a ball but couldn't. Did Bigham have him tied down on the cot? His heart raced. He needed to get free. He opened his eyes.

A wolf stared back at him, and everything rushed back. Graydee licked his face.

Hi, Graydee.

Graydee's love poured through their bond. *Hi, sleepyhead.*

The battle. They need me. I've got to get up. Stevee moved his feet, but he couldn't rise.

It's over, Graydee sent. *Kun helped us win.*

Stevee sighed. Tayro came up beside Graydee.

"How's my father?"

Codee's voice answered. "Moving around better than you."

Stevee turned his head to see Codee on his other side. "You're okay. The knife wasn't poiscned?"

Codee's eyes sparkled. "If it was, the things Tayro poured in my wound kept it from harming me."

Mist filled Stevee's eyes as he choked out, "I didn't want to be alone again. And my sibling's going to need you too."

"Even if something were to happen to me, you wouldn't be alone. So many love you they'd be falling over each other to assist you."

"It looked like the knife hit your heart."

"No, my breastbone. My heart's thumping like mad with worry for you."

"I must have forgotten to eat again and passed out."

Brando and Dayvee moved up beside Tayro. "You took two bullets and lost a lot of blood." Brando grinned at him. "Didn't you know you were hurt, Lil Wclf?"

"I didn't feel anything."

"*I felt it when we were running with Smokee,* Graydee sent. *I didn't know it was bad.*"

"Well, it can't be that bad. It doesn't even hurt. I just need to eat."

Elayni kissed his cheek. "You almost met Kun twice. Tayro had to breathe for you both times."

"I feel fine now." His panic rose again as he felt a pressure against his chest. "Can you get these ties off my chest so I can get up? Graydee's hungry. I need to feed him."

Codee grabbed his arm. "There's nothing on your chest except for bandages and a hole from where a bullet went through. I wouldn't have allowed anyone to bind you."

Stevee released a heavy breath. "Thank you."

Codee took meat out of his pack and put it in a bowl. "Graydee wouldn't eat for the past three days. You scared us all."

Had he been unconscious that long?

Yes. Graydee buried his muzzle in the bowl of meat.

Tayro put his arm behind Stevee's neck and lifted his head a few inches. Ouch, that hurt. Everything spun. When his head stopped spinning, he noticed the large buffalo hide that formed the wall beside him. He must be inside one of the bigger tents. Several other pallets stood empty nearby. One other held an occupant, and he could see the man was much smaller than Clint.

Tayro lifted a flask to Stevee's lips. "This is broth with medicine. Drink it."

Stevee opened his mouth while Tayro poured some in. Stevee swallowed. "Where's Clint and the rest of our injured?"

"Some recovered." Tayro's face fell. "Some went home to Kun."

Which was Clint?

"So our Lil hero's finally awake." Leeto moved up by Codee.

"Why are you calling me that?" Stevee asked.

"Graydee told us you killed over twenty invaders. Twice as many as anyone else except Kun."

A lump came up in Stevee's throat. He'd killed that many? He drew in great gasping breaths but couldn't get air. "I'm going to be sick." He started retching. Tayro put a bowl under him and held him up as he threw up the broth.

"Can't you stop hurting people, Leeto?" Brando snarled.

"I didn't know he'd take it like that."

Graydee lay his muzzle on Stevee.

"Put it out of your mind," Codee ordered.

Stevee would try, but their faces haunted him. "How many did we lose?"

No one answered.

Tayro wiped his brow. "In your condition, you don't need stress."

"It's more stressful not to know."

Tayro frowned. "We lost several."

"Any of my friends?"

Dayvee answered, "We don't know all of your friends, or even how you managed to make so many."

Codee squeezed his arm. "Everyone you talked to seems to think they're your best friend and have been demanding to come in and see you." He chuckled. "Even your horse forced his way in once."

"Not Frudo."

Brando laughed. "Want to bet?"

"Don't." Elayni glared at Brando. "Frudo's been here every day. He says he wants to apologize." But Elayni wasn't meeting Stevee's eyes. They were hiding something from him.

Stevee raised his chin and locked gazes with Leeto. "You say Calupi shouldn't be coddled. Tell me what they won't."

Leeto gave him a short nod. "Clint and Juvee both died."

A moan escaped Stevee. No. Clint died trying to aid him. It was his fault. Stevee tried to rise and managed to lift his shoulders a little. "I want to tell his story at the funeral."

"The funeral's over." Codee pressed Stevee's shoulders back down. "Tayro says you could tear those wounds open again if you move much. You need to mend first."

"For how long?"

"Until Tayro releases you."

"And how long will that be?"

"A while." Tayro smiled. "I'd rather not breathe for you again."

A creaking came from the other cot as the man in it turned.

"Who is it over there?" Stevee asked softly. All he could make out was a thin, pale face.

The sub-pack glanced over, but no one spoke. Finally, Brando answered, "The man I used to claim as my father."

"Is he going to be okay?"

"Maybe," Tayro said. "A lot depends now on his will to fight."

Stevee sucked in his breath. Memories flooded him of another pale face. "My father lost the will to live. He said I'd be better off without him. I told him if he didn't care enough to live for me, I didn't care either." Stevee choked as the lump rose in his throat. "I really regret those last words to him. Brando, please don't make my mistake. Go talk to him."

Dayvee glanced over at Jonesee. "Stevee's right, Brando. Go talk to your father."

Brando's blue eyes flashed at Dayvee. "Are you going to order me?"

"No, but Kwutee always said it takes a bigger man to forgive than hold a grudge. I believe you're a big man."

Brando drew a deep breath then walked over to his father. The two spoke quietly.

Dayvee turned back to Stevee. "Novu says that Nolte and your Kwin family want to see you." Dayvee signaled, and Chayla and Elayni moved toward the tent flap, but Codee stayed at Stevee's side. Dayvee swung on his crutches toward the door. "We'll come back later."

"You got your gifts back?"

"Yes." Dayvee glanced back and smiled. "But better yet, I got back my belief that Kun could help me, and He did.

31

Waiting

"It is far harder to wait for news than make it." ~ Brando

Stevee

Stevee was looking forward to getting up. Tayro said he might let him walk a little today. He was so tired of lying in bed. Jonesee had recovered enough to leave yesterday, so Stevee was the last one there. And even though he'd had a steady stream of visitors, he was past ready to go outside. He wanted to ride Smokee and run with Graydee.

When Tayro, Codee, and the rest of the sub-pack arrived, all their eyes were bloodshot, and Dayvee wasn't with them. Something was wrong.

"What's going on? Did we lose another? And where's Dayvee?"

Codee's eyes were red-rimmed too. Dread sent his heart sinking. Codee clasped his forearm and squeezed to reassure him, then took his hand away when Brando handed a note to Stevee. "Dayvee left this for you, Lil Wolf."

Stevee's hands shook as he opened the folded piece of paper and read.

Tibalt and I have set sail with Garth and the others to go to their continent. I will try to prevent the invaders from coming here again. It may take some time, and some may still get through. Jaycee said I can tell you now. Kun has shown me your face, and Jaycee confirmed it, you are a Kayndo-in-waiting. If needed, you will become Kayndo, and it will be up to you to get the animals to help you stop them.

I'm sorry, Stevee, but one of us had to go, and one had to stay. I have left my sub-pack with you and Codee. They will help you do whatever is needed. You know you can rely on them as I did. I love you, cousin. I hope to see again one day, but it's not likely. Take care of our family.

Tears threatened, but Stevee forced them back. He couldn't be a

Kayndo. "Does everyone know what this says?"

"He left one for each of us," Brando said. "We all know he was shown your face as a Kayndo-in-waiting, and he left us to help you."

"He'll need you worse than me. You should go after him."

"We already tried, but he's in the ocean. Otter clan's canoes are wrecked, and the Orcas refused to carry us there."

Elayni's pleading eyes locked on him. "Maybe they'll listen to you. The animals helped Dayvee when he was a Kayndo-in-waiting. Will you try, Stevee?"

"Of course, I will."

Brando gave him a chin lift. "Thanks, Lil Wolf."

Stevee concentrated and reached out, *Are there any Orcas that will speak to me.*

Hello, Kayndo came a whisper in his head.

Can you take my friends to the ship with the other Kayndo in it? He will need them.

He doesn't want them.

Maybe not, but he needs them, or he won't be able to succeed.

Then we will take them.

Thank you.

You're welcome, Lil Kayndo.

"They're going to take you to Dayvee."

Elayni hugged him. "I will miss you."

"I'll miss you too."

Brando's face furrowed. "I'd like to be your second, but I think Dayvee needs me more."

Codee's eyes twinkled. "Stevee will have his second."

"Leeto's not going to like losing his."

"Leeto will understand. The Kayndo comes first. He'll appoint another."

Brando ruffled Stevee's hair. "I trust Codee to put your interests first."

"And you'd be right. I have two really good fathers, but Dayvee has only Tibalt and Rogee. What if Garth turns on him? Tibalt said they can't be trusted If I didn't have to stay, I'd go with you."

Tayro ran a hand through his own hair. "If I didn't have to be king here, I'd go, too, so I know how you feel."

Chayla hugged him. "I started the story of Lil Wolf, the sixth Kayndo. I left it in the tent, but I hope one day to return and finish it."

"These are for you to remember us by." Brando handed Stevee two carvings. One was of Graydee and the other of Smokee. "You are the only one I have ever gifted two carvings."

"They're beautiful and I love them, but I could never forget you. I have nothing to give you to remember me by."

"You already gave me something, and I don't think I'll forget."

"What?"

"My life. You protected me, and Elayni too."

"I just did what Dayvee said—try our hardest to keep our family safe."

"And you did a great job, but just like him, you forgot that you're part of the family and need to keep yourself safe too."

Stevee choked back his tears again. "Thank you for everything you did for me."

"It was my pleasure. I'm not always as strong as you, but I don't think there's anyone here that's going to enjoy seeing my pain." A tear rolled down Brando's cheek. "Do you know about my list?"

"Yes, but please don't ask me to fight those on it."

"No." Brando smiled at Stevee. "The reckoning is my job. I just want you to keep one. Anyone that hurts you goes on it. You keep that for me until I come back. If I die, I'll ask Dayvee to send word through the Orcas, and you can give it to Codee. But otherwise, those that hurt my family have to answer to me."

They clasped arms. "Goodbye, Brando."

"Goodbye, Stevee. Keep up your fight training and don't trust Leeto. His love isn't kind. We may not meet again until we see Kun, but I hope we'll win the battle on both continents and can come back."

"I hope so too. I love all of you, and I'll miss you."

To lose so much of his newly gained family was breaking

Stevee's heart. He wrapped his hands in Graydee's fur. Brando, Chayla, and Elayni walked toward the door, Tayro followed them out. "I'll be back, Stevee, after I see them off."

Stevee called out, "May Kun go with you."

They glanced over their shoulders at him. "And also with you."

#

Codee

Codee had barely left Stevee's side for the six days since he'd been shot. He'd return soon, but Nolte was with him, and Codee needed to feed Wilee and change clothes. He walked into the tent.

Leeto came in behind him. "Codee, I just heard Dayvee left. Is it true?"

"Yes. Do you want to read his note?"

"I'd like that. He didn't leave one for me." Codee handed Dayvee's note to Leeto. Codee knew it by heart.

Codee, this time I feel almost certain I'll be meeting Kun. I'm willing, but I need to know someone will take care of my loved ones, so I'm asking you to do that for me. Stevee is very lucky. You're a great father. I'd have loved to have you as mine, but at least I had you for an uncle. Thanks for everything. I love you.

Dayvee.

Leeto read it. "That sounds like he knows. Did you tell him?"

"Are you releasing me from my vow to speak of it?"

"Yes."

"Then you should know I haven't discussed it since that night I gave you my word not to reveal it or interfere in his raising."

"I'm sorry." Leeto groaned. "You probably hate me for extracting that promise."

Codee shrugged. "He'd be dead had it not been for you and Clay. I abandoned him."

"You were grieving."

Codee shook his head. "But I should have been able to see beyond that he took his mother's life. I told you I didn't want him, and I gave you my vow. Only the five of us who were there know it was your child that died. And I'm sure the others kept their vows too."

Leeto chuckled. "I know you regretted the vow not to interfere."

Codee grimaced. "I did, but I didn't have the right to speak except as an uncle would."

"Once he replaced our own dead baby, I couldn't let you decide to change your mind and take him from us. I would have treated my own the same."

"I know. My baby died out of my own failings. My nephew lived. Did Milay even love him?"

"At first she was too distraught. She didn't only lose her baby but her best friend. You weren't the only one a mess. We all were. And I was trying to do everything that the four of us did before. Then Milay's milk dried up, and I think she was afraid he'd die. If Clay hadn't stepped in, he would have. But I think she grew to love him."

"I never saw any love, and neither did he."

"That's my fault since I wouldn't release her from her promise not to interfere either. Kwutee said she'd never bear another child. I didn't know if you'd have another. And I wanted to ensure our fathers—that all our—sacrifices wouldn't be for nothing."

"I know why you did it. And I meant it when I told you I wouldn't come back. But after I dreamed of her, I had to. And then I learned Dayvee had her eyes, her compassion, even her talents like reading the wolves. Once I realized she still lived in him, there was no way I could leave again. I'm sorry, Leeto."

"There's nothing to apologize for. I couldn't do it all, and I'm glad you returned. I was going to tell Dayvee when he left for Harthome, but I was afraid he'd think I treated him harshy because he wasn't my son. If he makes it back, we'll tell him."

"Do you think you'd have loved him more if Milay had given him birth?"

"No. I don't think it's possible to love a child more. That day he was so sick with fever and we almost lost him, I almost told him how I felt, but the tiger kept me from it."

Codee laughed. "I remember that day. I'm going to miss the tiger too. But what about Bunjee?"

"Dayvee will always have a special place as first, but I love Bunjee, too, only Milay said that this time we weren't raising an alpha but a son."

Codee laughed. "She's right."

Leeto chuckled. "Yeah, but don't tell her that."

"The truth is Dayvee's my nephew, so don't ever tell him differently."

Leeto's mouth gaped open. He shut it. "I thought to stand aside was really hard for you."

"It was the most difficult thing I've ever had to do, but it's done now and I understand better after Stevee. Blood is not what matters but the heart. Stevee's my son—Dayvee's yours. And if he comes back, remind him he has your love so you get the letters."

"Thanks. I'm sorry I wasn't a better father to him, but I told you if he survived I'd be content. He's still alive." Leeto left the tent.

Codee reached in his rucksack to grab Graydee's bowl and almost yelled when a frog jumped out. He laughed so hard tears ran down his face. Brando had struck. He found the note wrapped around something. When he undid it, he found a wooden carving of Wilee. He read Brando's note.

If you find this, it means I went after Dayvee. I am sorry I wasn't able to see your face when you found my little surprise. I'm guessing you laughed long and hard. I'll take care of Dayvee for you, and you need to take care of Stevee for me. Stevee is very lucky to have you for a father. I would have loved to have you. Don't let Leeto hurt him. I love you, Codee. I'll miss you.

Tears ran down Codee's face. *I would have loved to have you for a son, Brando. I love you, too, and I'll miss you.*

He put it in his rucksack with Dayvee's note. He'd keep them both. And he was certain now he was right about how to raise a son. He should have told Brando and Dayvee how much he loved them before they left. He could only hope they knew.

#

Stevee

Tayro finally let Stevee leave. He was still sore, but he dared not show it as he walked out of the tent for the injured. He was Calupi now.

Graydee nudged him. *About time you realized that.*

It hit Stevee. Graydee was right. He was no longer an adrift. Adrifts didn't have families, and he had a large one. Only he and Graydee didn't have a pack yet. *Do you want to join a pack, Graydee?*

It's not necessary. Since you are a Kayndo-in-waiting, we will be welcomed in every pack whether we join or not. I don't think we should join except as temporary members.

But I thought you wanted a pack.

We have a pack. And my loyalty will always belong to Dayvee's and Jaycee's pack first.

Stevee's loyalty would, too, and his pack—his family—could count on him. Bigham and his men were still a threat, but they didn't worry Stevee anymore. And if the invaders came again, Stevee wasn't about to let them get by him. He was Calupi, and he'd take up the role of the Kayndo if needed. He'd defend the Vita and protect the clans, every one of them. Dayvee and the others would return. Stevee was certain.

And when they did, they'd find Stevee hadn't failed them. A Calupi would be waiting to greet his family with Graydee at his side.

###
THE END

Glossary

Accipi – The people who have eagle companions. Members of Eagle Clan.

Adrift – A child, without any family or relatives, who lives at the adriftage.

Andee – Wolf Mountain Pack Calupi

Animal Master – Kayndo

Bigham – Criminal leader who runs the adriftage in the bottoms of Harthome.

Blake – Pericard Captain of Taluma

Bola – Kwin weapon (rope with balls)

Brando – Dayvee's friend, Calupi of Wolf Mountain Pack

Bruno – Brando's wolf companion

Bunjee – Dayvee's adopted younger brother

Calupi – People who have wolves for companions. Members of Wolf Clan.

Caspian – Former adrift leader, Stevee's best friend (deceased)

Cato – Chayla's wolf companion

Chancee – Former Calupi of Wolf Mountain Pack, now exiled

Chase – Pericard

Chayla – Calupi of Wolf Mountain Pack in Dayvee's sub-pack

Clint – Master Weapon's Maker who Stevee apprenticed with

Clay – Milay's former companion

Codee – Dayvee's uncle

Convocation – Group of Accipi with eagle companions that work and live together

Cumback stick – Kwin weapon (boomerang)

Cujo – Kwin weapon (long stick with sharp blades)

Dayvee – Leeto's son and Calupi of Wolf Mountain pack

Deenee – Stevee's Kwin brother, Nolte's son

Derrick – Adrift ten-year-old boy, Tanner's second

Drako – Calupi messenger of Wolf Mountain Pack

Elayni – Dayvee's friend, Calupi of Wolf Mountain Pack

Evee – Elayni's wolf companion

Franko – Elayni's father, beta Calupi of Wolf Mountain Pack (trader)

Frudo – Son of the alpha of White River Pack

Fujee – Leader of Otter Colony on Hardy River

Garth – Prince of Sheffia and Lucenda. King Nolan's second born son, who's invading Taluma.

Gaylo – Keeper of the Vita, Calupi of White River Pack

Geno – Calupi of Wolf Mountain Pack in Dayvee's sub-pack (deceased)

Gentu – Leader of Beaver Colony on Hardy River

Ghostee – Dayvee's horse

Glido – Fujee's otter companion

Gojo – Gaylo's wolf companion

Graydee –Stevee's wolf companion (formerly Geno's)

Harthome – Capital city of Taluma, western continent

Herd – Group of horses (Group of Kwin that live and work together)

Herrick – 1st alpha of Wolf Mountain pack

Hoke – Vulape Leader at Three Hills Skulk of Fox Clan

Hubert – Kagard Captain Varian appointed

Jaycee – Dayvee's wolf companion

Jerrod – Pericard

JoKayndo – 1st Kayndo (animal master)

Jolay – Codee's life-mate, Calupi of Wolf Mountain Pack

Jonesee – Brando's father, Calupi of Wolf Mountain Pack

Juno – Drako's wolf companion

Juvee – Stevee's Kwin brother, Nolte's son

Kagard – Kingdom of Taluma's soldiers

Kayndo – Animal Master

Keeli – Brando's mother, former Calupi of Wolf Mountain Pack

Kwutee – Keeper of theVita, Calupi healer of Wolf Mountain Pack

Kun – Creator of Universe, Master, and Maker of all things (God)

Law of the Pack – Protect the Pack, Defend the Vita

Layton – King of Taluma (late king)

Leeto – Dayvee's father, alpha leader of Wolf Mountain Pack

Logan – Prince of Lucendo and Sheffia who's invading Taluma. King Nolan's first born son.

Luko – Leeto's wolf companion

Lulay – Stevee's Kwin sister, Nolte's daughter

Marcello – King of Taluma, former (nicknamed the false king)

Miko – Calupi of Wolf Mountain Pack, Former alpha leader

Milay – Dayvee's mother, Calupi of Wolf Mountain Pack

Misty – Little adrift girl

Mort – Criminal leader in the bottoms of Harthome, tavern owner

Nails – Calupi weapon (chakram with several blades)

Nayti – Calupi woman of White River Pack

Neeshi – Nero's wolf companion

Nero – Calupi of Wolf Mountain Pack Calupi, former training leader

Nolan – King of the Kingdom Lucendo on the Eastern Continent

Nolte – Kwin leader of Black River Herd

Novu – Nolte's horse companion

Pack – Group of Wolves (Group of Calupi with wolf companions that live and work together)

Pako – Calupi of Wolf Mountain Pack

Petee – former Calupi of Wolf Mountain Pack, now exiled

Pericard – Kagard detachment that protect the king of Taluma

Portia – Port city

Razi – Alcoholic beverage

Reed – Botanee Clan member

Reko – Kwin from Grassy Knoll herd

Renay – Calupi of Wolf Mountain Pack

Renolee/Ren – Stevee's father (went be Ren in Harthome)

Rodnee – Calupi of Wolf Mountain Pack, beta leader

Rogee /Roger– Calupi clansmen from the other continent. (Goes by Roger to disguise he's a clansmen)

Rudee – Calupi of Wolf Mountain Pack

Santo – Bunjee's uncle, Ursan

Shakree – Santo's bear companion

Seemo – King Layton's eagle companion

Serano – Kwin leader of Grassy Knoll herd

Shilo – Reko's horse

Shuto – Accipi leader of White Oak Convocation

Skyto – Eagle companion to Shuto, the Accipi Leader of White Oak Convocation

Spiro – Dayvee's eagle scout

Stevee/Steven – Calupi of Dayvee's sub-pack who is Graydee's new companion (Steven is his city name)

Smokee – Stevee's horse

Taluma – The Western Continent Kingdom – (King Layton rules)

Tanner – Adrift 2nd, who became leader when Stevee joined the Calupi

Tayro – Calupi of Wolf Mountain pack (Kwutee's apprentice)

Terra – Planet, soil

Theron – Pericard

Tibalt – Prince of Taluma, Son of King Layton

Tinay – Elayni's mother, Calupi of Wolf Mountain Pack

Tobee – Wolf Mountain Pack adult with deformed legs

Tooth – Calupi weapon (knife)

Topay – Tayro's wolf companion

Tucker – Pericard

Varian – Eastern Continent Visitor

Vita – Religious rules and beliefs given to Terrans by JoKanydo

Wilee – Codee's wolf companion

-Acknowledgments-

They say it takes a community to raise a child. It certainly takes a community to put out a book. It wouldn't have been possible without the aid of my incredible team so I want to acknowledge and thank them.

First there's the One who gave me the inspiration and words. My Lord and Savior.

Second is my awesome family and amazing friends who always had words of encouragement. Their belief in me has been unfailing.

Third I want to thank my writer groups for their help. Fantasy for Christ, St. Louis Christian Writers, CIA, and AFCA offered me great advice, critiques, beta reads, contacts, and encouragement.

And I can't forget my editor and proofreader, Nadine Brandes, and Stephanie Van Wyk. I shudder to think what my books would look like without their help.

Then there's my cover artist Yvonne Less with Art 4 Artists, cover model Matt Luckey, photographer Katherine Cobert with Cobert Photography, web-site designer Joe Vanderjagt, and my cartographer Ryan Proksch. All of them gave their time and energy to help me.

Last but not least, I want to thank everyone that reads my books and tells others about them. Your support is really appreciated.

www.ingramcontent.com/pod-product-compliance
Lightning Source LLC
Chambersburg PA
CBHW020246180626
46810CB00006B/2391